THE DEADLY HOUSES

An absolutely gripping crime thriller with a massive twist

CHARLIE GALLAGHER

Detective Maddie Ives Book 6

JOFFE
BOOKS

First published in Great Britain 2020
Joffe Books, London
www.joffebooks.com

**Please join our mailing list for fantastic free Kindle
books and all our latest news.**

ISBN 978-1-78931-452-6

CHAPTER 1

The scream from the open first-floor window made PC Ian Hessey quicken his pace. His head snapped upwards as he approached the door. The heavy rain pelted down past the peak of his hat to soak his face. There were three officers in front of him; the sergeant was in the lead with the metal battering ram and first to the front door. He thumped it hard with a fist and bellowed for it to be opened. The team waited in a staggered line behind him. A moment passed and Ian heard nothing, only the falling rain and a gurgling drain. High above them, the sky flashed vivid white. Another scream forced its way out into the storm, the unmistakeable shriek of a terrified woman.

The sergeant set upon the door with the battering ram and the door flexed grudgingly in its surround for the first few strikes. Then came a splintering noise as it started to give. It mingled with the sound of another scream. The rain seemed to lash at them harder; the noise of the guttering and drains seemed louder too, now the line of officers had bunched and Ian was almost beneath the eaves. Another streak of lightning acted like a camera flash, preserving the moment the ram struck the door for the final time. The drops of rain seemed suspended for a moment — and so did the officers, all of them hunched forwards like sprinters waiting for the starting pistol. The door gave way with a loud *crack*! It was the signal they had been waiting for. The shrieking house now had an open mouth. Inside was a wall of darkness. Ian was the last to pile into it.

The house was at the end of a row and the entrance was round the side. The stairs faced him directly and the three officers ahead of him all moved up them. They got halfway up before the shouting stopped them in their tracks.

'GET THE FUCK OUT OF MY HOUSE! WHAT ARE YOU DOING IN HERE? FUCK OFF!'

A solid object bounced down from the first floor and the officers parted in front of Ian. A box hit the bottom step and the lid flew off. Bottles of toiletries spilled out. As everyone took a step backwards, Ian took a moment to take in the ground floor. The room to his right was lit with a weak yellow glow from the streetlight pushing in through tipped blinds. Suddenly it flashed the brightest white — once, twice, three times in quick succession. More photoflashes, this time capturing a small boy sitting on the floor, his back against the wall. He was maybe five or six years old, naked from the waist up and scrawny, his head tilted up towards the sudden invaders in his home. He held a stick in his hand that seemed suspended in mid-air. The room returned to a dulled yellow. Ian could just see the boy as an outline now. He stepped in.

'Hey!' Ian tried to hide the surprise in his greeting.

There was another series of thuds as something else bounced down the stairs. And more shouting too, more promises of violence, more demands for the police to leave. He heard his sergeant raise his voice in response; he was appealing for calm, but his tone had already moved past that. Next, there came a pained shout from one of his colleagues. Something small but solid hit the hallway floor. A shocked moment followed where the only sound was the rain pushing through the open front door. Ian didn't think that calm was coming any time soon.

'Are you okay?' He suddenly remembered the child.

The boy was looking away from him, his attention turned upwards to where the ceiling creaked. Then came a thumping sound as something heavy was dropped above them. A powerful shout came from the landing and was projected downwards. Ian edged close enough to see the expression on the boy's face. His mouth hung open, his wide eyes searching the ceiling. His head dipped down between his shoulders as if he were ducking away from whatever was above him. Finally, those wide eyes moved back to fix on the police officer in his living room.

'I c-came down to p-play my drums,' he stammered.

The boy's legs were crossed in front of a set of toy drums. A keyboard leaned against the wall just behind him. Ian sat down next to him, crossing his own legs as best as his uniform and his dodgy knee would allow.

'Mummy said I should. She says I should make some n-noise when they're talking so I c-can't hear them.'

'Do you play?' Ian lightly tapped the drum kit.

'Yeah!' The boy's expression changed. Even in the dim light, there was a sudden spark in his eye. He readied the stubby drumsticks that had dropped so one end was resting on the floor. He started to beat out a rhythm.

'Do you mind if I join in?' Ian reached out for the keyboard.

The boy beamed in delight when Ian pulled it across his lap and switched it on. There was another loud thump, then an angry male voice.

'*Peter! Peter! PETER? Where are you, son?*' The voice carried easily over the officers, still appealing for calm from the stairs, to sweep into the living room. The little boy stopped his drumming.

'Are you Peter?' Ian said quietly.

The boy nodded.

'Is that your daddy?'

He nodded again. 'Mummy tells me not to go up when they are talking, even if he calls me. Not when he's shouting. He's always shouting. Mummy says that's just how he talks sometimes.'

'My daddy was like that too. Sounds like good advice. How about you give me a beat and I'll see if I can play along? Nice to meet you, Peter. I'm Ian.'

Peter started up again. His little hands were skilled, even on the tiny kit that surrounded him. Ian played the keyboard in time as best he could, a basic tune that was a variation of 'Jingle Bells'. He found himself smiling when Peter's tongue poked out in concentration. Ian's daughter did the same. She was about Peter's age, too — a little older perhaps — and her instrument of choice was the guitar. They carried on playing, even when the noises got louder, when his colleagues' patience finally snapped and he heard them go surging up the stairs in their heavy boots. The shouting and the thuds on the ceiling increased, the unmistakeable sound of a fight breaking out, with a woman screaming as the backdrop. The little boy reacted by hitting the skins harder, his beat faster. Ian did his best to keep up. They played on while his dad was being dragged down the stairs, seemingly crashing off every step, shouting bile the whole way down and reaching out to slap his hands on the door surround. As he did so, he screamed '*PETER!*' into the room. By that time the little boy's hands were a blur. He kept his eyes down, his whole face a picture of focus and concentration. Ian did his best to keep smiling, to suppress his own sadness as he realized that this was far from the first time this little boy had needed to play drums as loud as he could to block out the scary noises.

It was a few minutes later when Ian became aware of someone standing at the door. It was a woman, in her thirties perhaps, but it was difficult to age her while she was in such a state. Her hair was soaking wet and hanging down in a clump. From the look of it, some had been torn out altogether. Her face was puffed red and the sleeves of her dressing gown were rolled up to reveal livid scratches on her forearms. Her smile seemed to break through her puffy eyes and tear tracks to rid her of her sadness in an instant. Peter stopped playing to stand up and run to his mother. She stooped to meet him in a tight hug.

'It's okay, Petey. He's gone now. He can't come back either. Not this time. I promise.'

CHAPTER 2

Eighteen months later. Friday.

His van fell silent but his fingers still gripped the ignition key, as clouds of dust moved forwards to surround him from both sides. It had been disturbed from the loose ground despite him taking it painfully slowly.

He didn't want to be here.

He peered out. His view cleared quickly. The dust thinned out to be swept off by a breeze that had a visible presence as it bent and toyed with wisps of long grass. In front of him was a dilapidated brick building. The windows that weren't boarded up were scarred with holes and cracks where they'd been hit with stones — kids, probably. The same culprits were likely responsible for the illegible graffiti, scorched metal bin and drinks cans that littered the area. The whole scene was covered in a layer of dust, adding to the overall impression of a place abandoned. The cans were half buried in it, the graffiti dimmed by the grime that clung to the walls. It looked like no one had been here for a long time. He knew that wasn't true.

They used to make things here — steel fabrication. Back then, it would have been a hot and busy hub of activity. Now the place was silent, dusty and scarred. Along the building line, determined weeds pushed up through the tarmac, as if nature were fighting to take back the ground that had once belonged to it. The building was squat and functional, perhaps designed with the exposed landscape in mind. The bottom two thirds were solid brick with a row of windows along the top. Despite its size, it was still dwarfed by far larger units visible in the distance.

He finally pulled out the keys and sat up straight. He strained his eyes to glimpse a set of faded red double doors. It was the only feature to break up the brickwork on this side. The left door was mostly covered in sheet metal bolted to the brickwork. But the right one was exposed, its steel covering had been peeled away — as if by some extraordinarily strong beast from a movie.

The place was just as it had been described.

When he stepped out of the van, the air was still warm. It was nearly eight p.m. The light of a bright sun still lingered on the horizon, its edges frayed to a pretty haze by the swirling dust.

He moved away from the van. The sound of his closing door bounced back from the building, and the man's head snapped up in panic. Could someone else be here, rushing out to meet him? No. He knew better than that. He told himself to stop being an idiot but kept his eyes fixed on that door. The last thing he wanted was for anyone else to be here. Anyone alive anyway.

He crossed the loose ground to the door which was slightly ajar. In the shade of the building, he reached up, his hand moving up behind the sheet metal until his fingers bumped against something solid. He gripped it tightly and tugged. It came away — a mobile phone.

It took a moment to turn on fully. The interior of the building suddenly echoed with movement — vermin up in the fire-damaged roof space, most likely. Of course, he knew there'd been a fire here — allegedly started by kids. It had come up as a news story when he had googled the site. It was the reason they had added a layer of steel to the outside.

The phone display lit up to the image of a digital key-pad. He typed in a code — *2580* — all the numbers down the middle, easy to remember. The phone unlocked with a click that made him flinch.

Get a grip! he told himself.

The phone had just a smattering of apps on it — all the standard ones. He swiped to a second screen where there was only one, the one he needed. He pressed it with his thumb and the screen changed instantly. The camera was activated and he had a view of the door in front of him. A red dot pulsed at the top of the screen to show it was recording.

He held the phone up as he opened the door and stepped in. A short foyer area led to a set of wooden doors that hung open, with fresh scars that suggested a quick and violent defeat. He was careful to avoid a large splinter as he stepped through.

The building opened up to a large open-plan space. The light was variable. A big chunk of blue sky was visible through a charred gap in the roof on the left-hand side and the last of the daylight piled through in a vertical beam that contrasted with the dark, unmoving shadows to the right. There was enough light to make out the remnants of what must have once been a bustling interior. The right side was mostly a dumping ground where everything seemed to have been thrown together in an ungainly pile. Tables and chairs lay heaped together, their legs pointing out in all directions. Beyond the pile and looping out from the far wall was a stainless-steel counter, its shine tarnished by ash and time. Behind that was the only internal door he could see. This area had obviously been the seat of the fire; a thick black shadow reached out from the top of this door to stain the walls as a column up to the hole in the roof. The news story had said this was once the main canteen for the site. The vandals had broken in and started a fire in the kitchen area. The smell from the smoke was still strong and grey ash layered just about everything in the room. It hung in the air too, lining his throat and making breathing unpleasant. He tried to keep his breaths short as his attention shifted to the floorspace on the left. But now it was impossible not to take in a deep breath.

She was just where he'd been told she'd be. Seated on a chair away from the pile and in the centre of a cleared area. The chair was positioned directly underneath the widest hole created by the roof's collapse. The sunlight made a tattered square on the floor around her. She was facing away, but the palms of her bound hands were turned up towards him.

He reached out a hand to the splintered door, gripping it tightly to steady himself. He snatched the phone up, checking the screen to make sure he was capturing the image. His instructions were to make sure it was pointing at whatever he was looking at. The display shook as he was suddenly overcome with a fit of coughing. He put his free hand to his mouth and held it there, trying to filter the ash from the air through his fingers. He stepped forwards.

The figure was distorted by the brightness of the light. The white plastic over the head was just a flared blob of white tucked in around silvery shoulders. As he got closer, he could make out more details: slender wrists, a long ponytail that trailed out of the end of the plastic, which he could now see was a carrier bag.

'Hello?' His voice sounded loud and sudden in the empty space.

There was another disturbance in the rafters and his gaze flicked upwards momentarily. There was no reply. He wasn't expecting one. He knew he was far too late for that. He was still a step behind her, using the phone screen as his eyes. It kept losing focus in the changing light but this was still preferable. Through the screen, it was somehow less impacting — like watching a TV drama. He could fool himself that he was detached, watching someone else making discoveries . . . someone else reaching out to touch the dead.

He stepped around the chair. The woman's slender legs were encased in tight leggings that rucked up a little around the thighs. She wore a zip-up top that would have been a bright baby blue when clean on. It was far from clean now. Her shoulders and her lap were filthy, streaked with dust that looked like it had gathered and been part washed by the rain. He couldn't remember a recent rainfall.

He put out a hand that looked almost white on his screen. He was reaching for the plastic bag covering her head. The cool plastic against his fingertips made him flinch. He scrunched it up, gathering as much as he could in his fist without touching anything underneath. He held his breath. The back of his throat still itched with dust and soot. He pulled the bag firmly upwards.

It took him a moment to be sure. Her face was distorted, her features wrapped tight in a plastic film. Her top lip folded back to show her teeth, her nose pushed upwards, one eyelid held open. And there was her pallor, too. She was so white as to be almost indistinguishable from the carrier bag that now fell to the floor. He stepped back. The screen that now displayed the dead woman's face was trembling — along with his shaking hand. He tried to steady it with his other hand.

'It isn't her!' A wave of relief left him as he sobbed. 'Oh, God. It isn't her!'

He took a moment. The phone's camera dipped to point at the floor while he gripped his nose tight, trying to get himself back under control. He peered around, now released from having to focus on the figure in the chair. There was nothing else to see. Nothing else stood out as having been disturbed or moved; the thick ash and dust would have shown that up instantly. He looked back over towards the door, to where his own footprints were marked out in a dark, gritty layer of filth. They were the only sign of anyone having been there. It was as if the woman had been lowered from the fire-ravaged roof by the same beam of light she now sat in. He peered up. The sky presented as a blue slate that was starting to darken as the day transitioned to night. Suddenly he yearned to be standing under it outside.

He lifted the phone again, keen to complete his instructions and then to be anywhere else but here. He ran the camera back over the woman's face then stepped back to take in her whole person — to be sure he had done as asked. Then he hesitated, knowing what he needed to do next. His back spasmed in a violent shiver.

Just get this done and then you can go.

His attention was back on the screen. He watched a hand reach out — his hand. He kept his index finger and his middle finger pressed together, willing them to move towards her neck. He stopped just short, closing his eyes. He couldn't watch this part, even through a screen. He shut his eyes, held his breath and pushed out. The instant chill of her skin made him snatch his hand back and the phone clattered to the floor.

'Shit!'

His cuss bounced around the room to hiss back at him. He squatted to retrieve the phone, keeping his eyes down, away from the figure looming above him. He had to blow a layer of ash and soot from the screen. It was still recording, but his feeling of relief didn't last long.

He stood back up. Two fingers again, reaching out slowly. He had been told he needed a count of ten. He kept his eyes open this time and, despite being better prepared for the sensation, he still bit down hard on his lip as his fingers found her skin. He pushed hard enough to make a dent. His eyes fell back shut and he focused on the count.

One . . . two . . . three . . . four . . . five . . . six . . .

He snatched his hand back. He couldn't hold it any longer. That would have to do. He spun away — almost too quickly — the grime underfoot and his dizziness conspired to topple him to the floor. He managed a few stumbled steps away, stopping at the carrier bag, which was still where it had fallen. He scooped it up and rubbed his clammy hands over it. Then he put it gingerly back over her head. He stretched out his fingers, this time standing behind her, not wanting to see that face again, not wanting to stare into the one eye that hung open as she if were just pretending, trying to catch him sneaking a look.

He retraced his own steps back to the double doors. A bright yellow axe stood on its head against the wall by the door. He hadn't seen it on the way in. It looked out of place. It could almost pass as brand new, save for the smudge of red paint across its blade. He stuffed the phone in his pocket so he could pick up the axe in both hands, as if he were about to wield it. Another count to ten and then he put it back on its head, back in the exact same spot marked out in the dust.

Now he could leave. His walk back to his car was much more urgent. Keys in hand, there was no lingering outside. He gunned the engine, and the wheels spun on the loose tarmac, kicking up a much bigger trail of dust than when he'd arrived. In his mirror, he cast one last glance at the building. The sun had now dropped behind it, but its dying rays still reached around the sides to blur in the dust and light up the van he had driven on the way in.

When he got to the main road and turned hard right to accelerate away, he still felt the need to check his mirror — to make sure he'd left it all behind.

CHAPTER 3

DC Rhiannon Davis sat back from her monitor as if she had been shaken awake. She had finally finished reading through a file returned from CPS. It was important, enough to hold her attention entirely from the moment she had opened it. She was seeking charge permission on an old assault case: a young man glassed in a nightclub after daring to chat to another man's girlfriend in the queue for a drink. To Rhiannon it had seemed like a cut-and-dried job, one of her last on CID before her move over to Major Crime. She had brought the file with her, expecting to be able to finalize it quickly. She should have known better.

CPS were refusing charge at this point and had instead set out an 'action plan'. They wanted her to go through the ID procedure, despite the offender having been pointed out by numerous witnesses on the night. It was ridiculous and would ensure nothing — only that the outcome was now much more of a lottery. The ID procedure would involve showing a series of digital photos to her seven witnesses in the hope that they picked out her offender again — months after they had seen him in a poorly lit nightclub. And that was if they agreed to take part in the first place. Rhiannon would need to call each of them and describe the process. She knew from experience that she stood to lose some or maybe even all of them at this point. Four months after the incident, she'd be giving them a call out of the blue, asking them to attend a police station to help her when the feelings of shock, of outrage at what they had just seen, would be long gone.

She rubbed at her face and glanced across the silent Major Crime floor towards the kitchenette. She checked her watch: 9:55 p.m. Calling them now was a sure-fire way of losing more of them. Better to wait until she was on a day shift. She would visit them; a personal appeal for their help would be far more effective. She could take photos of the victim and his ugly, jagged neck injury with her to help stir up those forgotten emotions.

She stood up to make a coffee. Her shift was only an hour old and already she was feeling tired. It was her second night shift of three in a row. The second was always the worst for fatigue. At least she wouldn't have to make a round of drinks as there was no one else to ask. The late turn finished at ten p.m. but the last of her colleagues had gone at twenty past nine, Rhiannon waving them away when they had asked if she *needed anything doing.* She knew what they really meant — *I'm going home, deal with it!* She could hardly object. She was still very much the new girl on the team and, besides, there was nothing going on tonight.

The urn hissed and dripped in equal measure. She yawned again as her cup filled with murky brown liquid. The key to night shifts was keeping busy. She had held back some admin on purpose for this set, but eight hours of paperwork in a darkened office was already looking like a challenge. She spun round suddenly at the sound of the desk phone.

'Major Crime.' Her voice reverberated around the desolate office.

'Ah good, I caught someone there!' A male voice — cheery — the sound of a busy call centre behind him. She recognized a call from the force control centre before he introduced himself. 'Bit of an odd one really . . .' he began, then paused. Rhiannon was already rolling her eyes. 'We've got

13

someone at the bat phone down there, outside Canterbury nick. You guys are based at Canterbury, aren't you?'

'That's right.' He would know that already just from the number he had dialled. Rhiannon sensed he was building up to asking her to do something shitty. Her desk was against the window that overlooked the entrance to Canterbury police station. The *bat phone*, as they called it, was a phone box painted yellow by the public entrance. Most stations had them. It provided an out-of-hours link to the police for those who preferred to stand in the shadow of a darkened building to report an incident, rather than calling from the comfort of their own home. Even on tiptoes she couldn't quite see the bat phone from where she was.

'Yeah, we've got someone wanting to report something *serious*. That's all the information we've got. I mean, we asked all the questions you would expect but he's insistent that he wants to see a detective.'

Rhiannon tried to direct her sigh away from the mouthpiece. 'Okay, our uniform colleagues would normally chat with him in the first inst—'

'Sorry. Yeah, it's a uniform call. We know that. But they're all out. We called the sergeant direct. They've got a vulnerable misper on the go — a ninety-year-old dementia patient last seen in a dressing gown with a shopping bag on the dual carriageway! They're all tied up. They asked if there might be any resources at the nick to help. I wondered if you might be able to pop down there and just take some details?'

Rhiannon could see her own smile reflecting back at her from the darkened window. The caller made it sound so easy — *just pop down there for a chat*. Police work was rarely anything like that.

'Sure. I'll go and see what he wants.' She couldn't really say no. Her admin could wait. She would take her coffee with her, though.

* * *

14

The man outside told Rhiannon much the same story as he'd already given to the person on the end of the phone. The mouthpiece hanging down next to him, he sucked desperately on a cigarette, as though he believed Rhiannon might snatch it off him and trample it into the ground at any moment. Instead she reached across him to put the phone back in its cradle. He stood in the block of shadow cast by the overhang of the front-counter entrance, shuffling on the spot, from one foot to the other. The automatic doors behind him stuttered at his movements but stayed sealed. The front-counter space behind those doors was in complete darkness, making the one source of light— a CCTV monitor — even more stark as it displayed their images as two blurs of grey.

He said he was there to talk about something serious.

Then he gave his name — Adrian Hughes — and a date of birth that made him thirty-two. Then he asked to sit somewhere and talk.

Rhiannon closed her book as he stared back at her. He'd sucked his cigarette down to the butt and what was left began to make him cough. There was desperation in the way he looked at her and, combined with his shuffling, Rhiannon could already see that this was going to be a question of more than just popping down to take some details.

An interview room backed onto the front counter. Rhiannon could see the entrance through the glass but she still had to walk him all the way around to gain access from the rear. The lights in this room were motion activated and clunked on, forcing them both to squint. Now she had a far better picture of Adrian Hughes. He was in beige chinos and the sort of fleece top that was popular with mountain climbers. He didn't strike her as the mountaineering type. The fleece looked a little too small for him, too. Its right-hand pocket made a tight bulge around the shape of a mobile phone. His hand kept dropping to squeeze it, like he was checking it was still there. He deposited a sports bag, the holdall type, on the floor beside him. His build seemed to match his demeanour — slight and unassuming. He had

15

short, dark hair swept over into a neat side parting. He kept licking his lips and blinking fervently. He struck her as agitated. Even when seated, he continually changed his position from lounging back to leaning forwards. He finally settled with his hands thrust in his trouser pockets like a schoolboy waiting to be scolded.

Rhiannon took her book back out. She underlined where she had already written his name and date of birth.

'So, Mr Hughes. How can I help you?'

Hughes's tongue shot out to wet his lips. He lifted his hands out of his pockets and blinked at his fingernails. They looked to be bitten down to the stub. His hands were small, his fingers slender.

'I killed her,' he said.

Rhiannon looked up from writing the time in the margin next to his name. 'Sorry?'

'I killed her. The woman.'

'You killed a woman?'

'That's what I said, right? I killed her. I came here to tell you — I said it was serious. *Murdered*, that's the word. I murdered a woman!'

He fell silent. Rhiannon did too. Her mind rushed with everything all at once. If this was a straight-out confession then there was a lot to consider. If it was a wind-up or a mental-health episode then it would be entirely different.

'So, you murdered someone . . . When was this?' Her pen was still hovering at the ready. So far, she didn't know what to write.

'A few days back.'

'Who, Adrian? Who did you murder?' Rhiannon had heard similar admissions before. Normally followed by 'the Queen' or 'Donald Trump'.

Hughes's head started shaking as he tried to form words. 'I don't know. I don't know who she is. I just . . . I murdered her.'

'You said that.'

'You don't believe me?'

'That's not what I said, Adrian. It's an unusual thing to pitch up here and admit, is all. And we will need a lot of detail. Where is she now? This woman that you murdered?'

'She's . . . You want me to tell you all this here? Now? Don't you . . . like . . . arrest murderers? Take them to the cells?'

'We do. Of course we do. And I will need to justify that to the custody sergeant downstairs. We don't want anyone down there who might need to be somewhere else.'

'Somewhere else?'

'Do you have a crisis worker?'

'A crisis worker? What the hell is that?'

'They work with people as part of the mental-health team. Are you known to mental-health services, Adrian? Maybe there's someone I can call and talk t—'

'Mental health? You think I'm mental? You think I'm making this up?'

'I need to be sure I'm doing the right thing, that's all.'

'I tied her up. I knew where she would be. I found her on one of those running apps — it's called Joggle, this app. She was sending updates out for just anyone to read. There was a bit of her route where it's just woods. I waited there. I got hold of her and I tied her up and I sat her down. Then I put film round her face. I wrapped it tight, so tight you could see it moving with her breath — in and out. Except she couldn't breathe — not for long. Not like that. You have to cover the mouth and the nose . . .' He looked shocked, as if he was seeing what he was describing right at that moment. Then he jerked straight up in his seat and reached for the mobile phone in his pocket. It clicked as it unlocked. He spun the screen so it was towards Rhiannon.

She leaned in to see a digital image, the background filled with fuzzy shades of darkness. But the foreground was what held her attention: a young woman seated on a chair, her arms pulled around behind her, her face wrapped so tightly in plastic film that it distorted her features.

'I took this when she was dead, then I put a carrier bag on her head. I didn't want to see her anymore!' Hughes's voice cut through Rhiannon's focus. Then he took a deep breath, apparently fighting a breakdown.

'Okay then,' she said. 'I think we had better go and see the custody sergeant.'

CHAPTER 4

Saturday

Detective Sergeant Maddie Ives made straight for Rhiannon's desk. Her jacket was zipped up against the early morning chill, her bag still slung over her shoulder.

'Six twenty-nine!' Rhiannon smiled up at her. 'I had a bet with myself you would be here at half past.'

'You had an interesting night then?' Maddie said. She noticed a cup of coffee on the table in front of her and pointed. 'Mine?'

'As long as you're staying.'

Maddie unzipped her coat. 'I suppose I'll have to. Sounds like there might be a bit to do. Where are we?'

'Adrian Hughes. Thirty-two-year-old male in custody after walking in here last night to tell us he murdered a stranger and showing me a picture of the body. He has no trace on PNC, PND or any local systems. I have forms ready to go in for DWP and other agencies. We still don't even have an address for him.'

'No address?'

'He said he's NFA.'

'Ah,' Maddie moaned. '*No fixed abode* . . . the address of the common criminal.'

'Normally I would agree . . . but there's no sign this fella's a criminal. No sign he's anything at all.'

'Assuming those details are correct.'

'No hits on his custody prints either.'

'So he just upped and murdered someone? From nowhere and for no reason?'

'According to him he did. I woke up the DCI. He wanted me to do an initial interview overnight, just to get details of where this woman is. I guess he's thinking that once we find her, we can go from there.'

'How was he?'

'Pissed off! It was one a.m. by the t—'

'Not the DCI! I coulda guessed what *he* was like. Our man . . . What was *he* like?'

'It's hard to say. There was something odd about his whole account.'

'Odd?'

'Odd. You know, like when you get a prepared statement in an interview and they read it out? Odd like that. Like he was reading from a script. Except he didn't have one.'

'Well practised then?'

'Maybe that was it. He wouldn't deviate from his story either. I was asking questions outside of what he was telling me and getting nothing.'

'Solicitor?'

'Nope. Said he didn't need one. He brought a bag with him. He said it was for prison, but it was like an overnight bag you would take for a city break. He even had a selection of shower gels!'

'I like his optimism. Did you put any calls into the mental h—'

'I called the Crisis Team. One of the first things I did. They're the only out-of-hours service I could think of that would have access to their database. He isn't known to them.

20

Admittedly they can only search the system for this county, so I asked that they share his details with colleagues nationally. I'll chase that up later. We both know that mental-health services can be a bit chaotic.'

'They can. I've never known a more stretched group of people. They'll forget — it won't be their fault. What's your gut say? Is this a mental-health issue?'

'Yes . . .'

'But?'

'I don't know. It was the strangest conversation I think I have ever had! I suppose that's what you get with mental-health issues. He's definitely fantasized about killing, though, no doubt about that. Some parts were really detailed.'

'Which parts?'

Rhiannon had her daybook open on the desk. She dipped her head to read from it. 'He found her on Joggle.'

'The running app?'

'Yes. It logs all your runs and then you can share them on social media. Hughes said that the victim was sharing her route and the times of day she was out. She had a distinct pattern and she was happy to post it up on her Twitter feed for anyone to see. He said he spent some time hanging around in the woods over a period of a few weeks. He would watch her run past. Then around a week ago he made his move. He grabbed her and threatened her with a knife to her throat. He got her into a van and took her to a spot where he tied her to a chair. He suffocated her by wrapping her face in clingfilm then topped her off with a Tesco carrier bag. He was really specific about that. He said it was one of the old ones . . . the blue-and-white type with the thin plastic, not like the ones you get now, he said. He taped it tight. He said the clingfilm was so tight he could see her breathing it in.'

'Suffocation, then. That's a method often linked with sexual assault.'

'I asked him if it was a sexual thing. He said no. And it was like he was offended I had even asked!'

'And there's a photo?'

'On his phone. It wasn't very good quality — bad lighting.'

'But you're still not convinced?'

Rhiannon shrugged. 'Someone walks in and admits to killing a woman, provides a photo of her body and a detailed route map of where to find her, and you would think I would be utterly convinced. But it was all so . . . *odd*. You can search the net for that sort of image and take a screenshot. I know because I tried it myself.'

'Did you find *that* image?'

'No, admittedly I didn't. But others like it. You take a screenshot and it goes straight to your camera roll. You could pass it off as a photo you took yourself.'

'Can I see it?'

'The DCI wanted his phone seized and sealed. He asked that no one else look at the image until it's been through the forensic techies.'

'He wouldn't mean me, though!' Maddie said.

'He said you specifically.'

'He knows me well. At least the techies will be able to tell us if it's a photo or a screenshot.'

'They will. They might even be able to tell us where it was taken and when. They're in at eight this morning. I'll be upstairs hanging by their door when they come in. I know how much they like that!'

'He's certain that she's dead, though?' Maddie felt a sudden pang of urgency at the thought of a young woman out there still fighting for her breath while she and Rhiannon supped their morning coffee. She had seen Hughes's method portrayed in countless movies, but it was actually very difficult to get it right.

'He said he waited with her for hours then "pressed her neck for a pulse."' Rhiannon read the last part verbatim then looked up from her book, anticipating Maddie's reaction.

'It certainly seems like he made sure. Clingfilm *and* a carrier bag?'

'About the carrier bag . . . he said he didn't want to see her struggle. That's odd too, isn't it?'

'It is if we believe he didn't know this woman, that it was a random attack he'd been fantasising about . . . until he plucked up the courage to go through with it. If that was the case, he would surely have wanted to see that moment — it might have even been *all* about that moment.'

'And there were other bits that were odd. He couldn't remember anything about the woman's details on Joggle, nothing that might help us identify her. But he spent a lot of time describing the tape he had tied around the film to secure it to her neck. He said it was bright blue, the sort that hikers use to keep their socks up. Then he got fixated on an axe that he left at the scene. The building where he says he left her is an abandoned canteen up on the old steelworks site towards Ramsgate. He said he used the axe to break in.'

'Did he say when?'

'He was vague about that. He said a week ago but he couldn't remember which day. He said he had meant to come to us straight away but he has been in a bit of a daze.'

'I bet he has. And he's NFA? He must have been living somewhere.'

'He went way over the top describing the tape and the axe, but anything I asked that might give us more of an idea of who he is and where he's from, and he just gave me these vague non-answers. It was so frustrating.'

'Where are we with the search?'

'When I called the DCI last night, I had my coat on, expecting him to tip me out to go find our scene. But he didn't want me anywhere near it. We've got uniform out on the two entrances to that site. It's a big area with a lot of hazards in the dark. He wants a proper search at first light. The DCI did wake up the on-call PolSA who was of the same opinion. He's coming here first thing this morning to be briefed and then he'll take his team out there. He should be here any time now. He's the Tactical Team sergeant and his lot are in for seven anyway.'

'Where's our friend's custody photo?'

Rhiannon clicked around on her computer to bring it up.

23

Maddie inhaled a long breath.

Rhiannon picked up on it. 'What are you thinking?'

'Just that I wouldn't be surprised if we didn't find anything at all out there. This all sounds like a fantasy to me, a wannabe murderer at best. Or maybe a police fantasist.' Maddie had heard of that before — the sad and lonely developing a fascination with the police and their processes. Getting arrested was a more common fantasy than she had realized. For some, it came with the delusion that it made them more interesting. She'd even heard of people boasting about spending time in prison, but as for someone attending a police station with a bag packed and a desire to actually be incarcerated for murder? It was a first as far as Maddie was concerned. She gave a sigh. 'So what are your fast-track actions?'

'Dropping the phone up with the techies and briefing the search team for now,' said Rhiannon. 'I expect the search to give us a lot more — and I want to wait for that before speaking with our prisoner again. I'd like to do that myself but it could be a lot later in the day.'

'It could. And you need to get home and get some rest. The team can cover those actions. You'll need to brief the search team and then drop the phone off on your way out.'

'I don't want to go home!' Rhiannon said.

'I know. This is probably nothing, though — you said it yourself!'

'But what if it's something? I can't let you have all the fun!'

'You're back in for nine tonight. By that time, there'll still be a lot to do. Either that or this is all a load of old crap and I'll be writing out a ticket for wasting police time in a couple of hours and cussing you for being at home in your bed.'

'Can I not just go out with the search team? See for myself?'

'Honestly, Rhiannon? I don't think it's worth it.'

'Are you going?'

'I don't think I will. It doesn't sound like a simple search — it could be hours. I think I'll hover around the techies with that phone. We might have all the answers we need on there. If we're going to waste a lot of police time it might as well be the grunts from the Tactical Team!'

'You're convinced this is fantasy, aren't you?'

'Not at all. I'm just ready for the disappointment.'

'Disappointment? You mean when no one's dead?' Rhiannon giggled.

'Exactly!'

CHAPTER 5

For Linda Morris, opening her eyes to the pitch-black was still unnerving. It still came with a moment of panic. It took a moment to remember where she was, what was going on, why she wasn't at home — what that noise was.

The sound of a door being scraped open to her right. Then came a shriek from opposite her that quickly dwindled to sobbing. It was a woman's cry, a young woman, too. The artificial light flooding through the door was intense and sudden, forcing Linda's eyes shut with just the glimpse of a black outline coming towards her. She was grabbed, a familiar coarse material pulled roughly over her head. She opened her eyes again but it was no use; she could see nothing more than pricks of light bleeding through as tiny squares. The same young woman's voice was now quietly begging. Linda heard the scrape of a metal chain then a sharp slap that elicited an instant whimper from the unseen woman. Her voice fell silent after that. The scraping metallic sounds continued, followed by a set of scuffling feet. A dark shadow moved in front of the light. It lingered for just a few seconds and then it was gone, moving from left to right, to where the door scraped and kicked over the surface. Then it slammed shut. The squares of light were snuffed out as the room returned to darkness.

Linda took longer breaths to keep control of her own panic. This was the first time she had been left with the hood on. She tried to console herself, *You can still breathe ... just relax.* She tried to focus on her situation, on what the new arrival meant. Now they were three — at least by her reckoning. A man had already been here when Linda was first hauled in. She had seen him. He had been chained up already when she was led past. She had been pushed to the floor, maybe two metres to his left. She could still picture his face; he'd looked dishevelled and a little bruised. He had watched as she was pushed back into a solid wall and forced to sit, then looked away quickly and silently, as if he already knew the rules. The chains had been so cold; they'd lifted her top to make sure the metal was pulled tight against her skin. When she reacted, she'd been punched hard enough in her stomach to be left fighting for breath.

Since then, there had been nothing but darkness. Linda was backed up against a solid curve so that a comfortable position was impossible to find. Her hands had been left free to move and feel their way around her new environment, which seemed to be nothing but smooth, cold stone. The darkness was absolute, like nothing she had experienced before. She had asked what was going on, whispered back towards where she thought the man with the bruising was sitting. She had asked him who he was and why they were here, all the while trying to hide the fear in her voice. He had only replied to tell her not to speak, that it was important.

'*Did you not see the state of my face?*' he had hissed. '*I talked too, at first.*'

But Linda had asked more questions, demanded that he speak, that he answer her. But there had been only silence. He hadn't uttered another word since. She had no idea how long ago that had been — how long she had been here.

And now they had added another. The bright light that had accompanied her entrance still lingered as yellow dots in her vision that slipped downwards as she tried to blink them away.

'Where are we?' The young woman had recovered enough from her stifled weeping to speak. There was a sound like she was pulling against her chains too. Fear was thick in her voice. 'What's going on?'

'Shut up!' the man hissed. 'You speak . . . they beat you. That's all I know.'

'What do they want?' The young woman's voice was breaking now. 'They didn't tell me anything. I don't know why I'm here. I want to go home!' Her voice was rising, starting to become a wail.

The door over to her right thumped. Linda waited for the footsteps to come through. They didn't. If this was meant to serve as a warning to stop her from talking, it hadn't worked.

'I want to go home! I don't know what this is about. I don't know what this is all about!' Her voice rose higher still.

'It's okay. You just need to stay quiet for now. You just need to play by the rules. All the while, I've been calm and quiet, and no one's done anything to me. They must want something. They just need to tell us what and we can all go home.' Linda was addressing the woman, but the message was not just for her. She didn't know why they were here either. Nothing had been explained. There'd been no threats, promises or demands. It had just been darkness and silence.

'I just want to go home!' The girl sounded like she was weeping again.

'And you will. What's your name? I'm Linda. Linda—' The door thumped again. This time it opened and the same light accompanied it. Footsteps followed swiftly. Linda turned to her right and just at that moment she felt a blow to her chest. It was a dig, a warning. She cried out in surprise more than pain. Whoever had dealt the blow now stumbled as they turned to exit the room and she felt her leg kicked then trampled. The door scraped shut.

Once more, the darkness and the silence were complete. Before, there had been a constant noise, a rumble, like a car running in the distance, that she could only hear when the room was still. Most of the time it was in the background, the sort of noise she only realized was there when it stopped for a short time. She thought there was a pattern to it but she couldn't be sure. Perhaps her mind was playing tricks and she was imagining sounds penetrating the darkness. She'd been using the noise as something to focus on; it helped keep her calm when the panic snuck up on her, when her mind started running with the worst of the *what-ifs*.

She concentrated now, trying to pick it out, despite the added layer of material covering her ears. At first, she just got the woman opposite trying to get control of her breathing and the man to her right shuffling his position, but then it came. She could just hear it — a dull rumble. Maybe it was a car engine? She imagined it coming from one of those big American cars — a gutsy V8. She pictured a roofless Cadillac in the warm sun, her daughter smiling in the driver's seat. The door opened for Linda to slide onto the cracked leather seat and she knew it had come to take her home. *Where you been, Mum?* her daughter would ask — just like she always did. It was now a standing joke. She was away, travelling the world, living new experiences every day, knowing only too well that her mother was rooted in the same town with the same job.

Where you been, Mum? She would often be calling from some back-alley café, anywhere she could use the free Wi-Fi, her cheery voice and excited tales punctuated by the sound of buzzing scooters and their horns in the background.

This time Linda had no idea, no answer. But she would give anything to hear that question again.

CHAPTER 6

'DS Maddie Ives.' Maddie still had some remnants of a chuckle in her voice from Rhiannon recounting her latest disastrous experience after swiping right on some dating app. The voice on the other end of her desk phone was just as cheery, but his words knocked the smile from her lips.

'Anyone order a dead person?'

Maddie recognized the voice of the police search advisor — PolSA — who had been assigned the Hughes case due to the fact that he was the one on call when Rhiannon had alerted the DCI. Now he was jovial and matter-of-fact at the same time.

'You got us one?' Maddie couldn't hide her surprise.

'Sure have. Waiting for us in the old mess hall for steel-workers, and for power station workers before that. One of the few buildings still standing from the Richborough days. Bit of a shit to get to now. A fine choice for your accomplished murderer, then!'

'So why come in and tell us all about it?' Maddie was thinking out loud. The question was rhetorical at best.

'You got me there, sarge. I just find the results of what they do. I'm happy that's where my bit ends!'

'I'm sure you are. So what have you got?'

'Adult female, I'd say mid-twenties, tied up in a chair with a bag over her head. We had to take the bag off. My first call was to CSI and we're already in trouble for that, but our medic's just off his course to be a real-life nurse so he couldn't wait to tongue a corpse!'

Maddie detected laughter from the background and realized he had an audience. She had seen at first-hand what it was like on a Tactical Team. Everything was a source of amusement. She could only imagine the ribbing their new *nurse* might be getting.

'I assume she hasn't been tongued?'

'Nah. Even a fully trained medic who came top of his course ain't got a kiss of life in him that's gonna do anything for this little lady. She's been here a while I'd say. Week or so? I dunno. CSI are the ones for that. Long enough for some of the wildlife to take an interest, put it that way.'

'Anything standing out at the scene that might help?'

'Not to our untrained, short-sighted eyes. I got the EGT team to do the lead up and entry to the building so you'll be able to see it untouched. EGT got the whole thing. You'll see our initial approach and de-bagging.' There was more laughter behind him. The sergeant seemed to take a moment to pull himself together.

'The carrier bag's present and correct then?'

'Yep, just like your pretty little detective said. By the way, one of my lads would quite like the opportunity to take her out for a steak dinner. I can't promise intelligent conversation, but if she agrees to one of those Beefeater places then at least he'll have something to colour in. They have them on all the tables.' The laughter was stronger now. Maddie realized that serious conversation was going to be a struggle while he had such a willing audience.

'I'll be heading out now. The DI will want to come with me, no doubt.' Maddie ignored the reference to her colleague.

'Just you two? I did say *steak* dinner, didn't I?'

'My colleague was up all night, Sergeant. She'll be heading home to get some rest. She should be there already. It might not be the best time to talk it out anyway. This steak dinner you mention might lose some of its appeal if suggested over a week-old corpse.'

'Good thinking!' His voice lifted to call out away from the mouthpiece. 'She's been up all night, Lazza! Sounds like she might be more than you can handle anyway!'

Maddie cut the call. She was done speaking with the Tactical Team for now. When she looked up from her phone, she met Rhiannon's pleading expression.

'No!' Maddie said instantly. 'You've been stalling long enough. Go home! There's not much we can do other than take a look. And trust me, you don't want to be coming along for that, not unless you're desperate for a trip to a zoo.'

'Zoo?' Rhiannon huffed.

'The Tactical Team. I think it must be close to feeding time.'

Rhiannon's scowl seemed to lift for a moment. 'This is so unfair!'

'I'll try not to do everything before you come in tonight, okay?'

'I'll be on my phone. I can come in early if you need me to!'

'Get some rest. Call me when you're up and I'll tell you everything I know. Unless it's before three p.m. In which case I'll ignore it. I need you rested, Rhiannon. If you call me before then I'll throw you into the Tactical Team's enclosure!'

To Maddie's relief, Rhiannon seemed to accept the advice. There might even have been a wry grin as she scooped up her jacket.

* * *

The sun was strong for May. The last couple of weeks had brought an early taste of summer. Maddie was not one to be fooled by the British weather, however. She realized it was far more likely a hiatus from the particularly chilly spring than the beginning of a long and glorious summer.

'I reckon this is it now! Summer's here!' Charley Mace stepped out of her van in sunglasses and seemed far more convinced of the latter.

Charley was the senior CSI for the county and part of her role was to assign the CSI jobs. This meant her attendance at anything Major Crime related was pretty much inevitable. Maddie was glad of it. Not only was Charley undeniably competent, she was always good fun. She had been Maddie's only ally in upsetting her old boss, Harry Blaker, the previous Major Crime DI. The new DI was much easier to wind up — but not at all in a good way.

'Morning, sir.' Charley nodded towards DI Tristan Stepney as he climbed out of the passenger seat.

He had spent the entire journey on the phone and most of the calls seemed to be about an upcoming golfing holiday. He was short, plump and bitter. His ill-fitting suit flapped in the breeze and he pulled the tails in, straightening his stance as he did so. He had previously been a chief inspector, even courting the rank of superintendent, but his move to Major Crime had involved a demotion of some kind — with only rumours surrounding the reasons why. Most of them involved his wandering hands. Another rumour had it that moving him to Major Crime had been about setting him up to fail in a department with nowhere to hide when the pressure was on — a preamble to him falling on his own sword.

Whatever the truth of it, Maddie was praying he would not be around for long.

'I hardly think sunglasses are suitable attire given the seriousness of this case. We have a young girl who has lost her life, do we not?' DI Tristan Stepney screwed up his face in a sort of smile that was directed at their CSI colleague.

'As I understand, sir. But I need to get started on preserving the evidence around her. I'm sure she will forgive my being comfortable as long as I do that right.'

'This is not about *her* forgiveness, Staff Mace. These standards are all mine.'

Maddie grimaced at the use of the word *staff*. Those who worked for the police but not as warranted officers could technically be referred to in this way, but the term was rarely used outside of training school, where new officers were taught the most rigid of standards. Outside of that environment it could only ever sound demeaning. Charley had her hands on her hips. For a moment she stood a little straighter. She took her time removing her glasses.

'Right then, shall we go and see what we have?' the inspector chirped. He stepped between the two women.

'Shoe covers and gloves as a minimum.' Charley already had them in her hand. 'Standards.' She shrugged.

The inspector held his smile.

'Very well.'

'I never thought I would find myself missing Harry Blaker.' Charley's voice was a wistful whisper. Maddie didn't reply.

'Boss!' The Tactical Team sergeant was brash in person, too. He took in each of the three of them in turn but lingered on Maddie with a poorly concealed smile. 'Sergeant Ives! Shame your colleague couldn't make it out. She did a good job with the briefing this morning. We were all very impressed.'

'Even detectives have to sleep.'

'And they rarely have time for chit chat, Sergeant,' the DI cut in. 'What do you have?'

The sergeant's smile had been growing, but it dropped away now.

'We have a body, sir. We found it nice and easy. Seems the instructions were just about spot on.'

'Instructions?'

'From your man in custody. He was nice enough to give us clear instructions on where to find her. You don't get that every day.'

'What have you moved?' Charley's tone carried an instant warning.

'Well, I did have a little sweep and wipe-up when I heard you were coming. It's what you do when someone important is coming round!'

'Very good.' Charley said, her words laden with sarcasm.

Perhaps it was the DI's icy glare that made the sergeant suddenly snap into seriousness. 'We EGT'd our approach and entry. We had all the gear on. We've not touched anything in there. My medic took the bag off but he didn't even bother with the film underneath. She's dead. Has been a while. We've trampled shoeprints into the floor but a metre or more wide of the marks that were there already. We did a cursory search of the building but there's nothing to report. The roof is fire-damaged. As soon as I saw the extent, I pulled my people out of there. It's not a safe environment — at least, I can't say for sure that it is. We've got hard hats and we're happy to work if you tell us it's okay to do so. I can't make that call unfortunately.'

'We'd better go and take a look, then.'

The sergeant led the way with the DI keeping pace. Charley was a few paces behind and Maddie was further away still. She liked to take her time; that way, it felt like she was taking more in. The building was a dirty, brick square that stood out against the green-tinged mess of levelled rubble behind. The most recent function of this site was as a steelworks, but before that it had formed part of something far bigger — a working power station. The original site spread itself between the villages of Minster and Sandwich, near to the Isle of Thanet. The steelworks had been placed close to the Sandwich side. Rhiannon had done a little research on the site overall, enough to know that it was currently the subject of an ownership dispute — part of which centred on who should be paying for site security now that permission was in for a change of land use. The result, as far as anyone could tell, was that there'd been no security at the site for quite some time.

The way into the building was through two sets of double doors. Both bore the evidence of a forced entry. After this, the building opened up completely. Maddie's gaze lifted up to where light streamed through a gaping hole in the ceiling. Debris from the roof littered the floor, lying mostly where it had fallen. It was messy overall, with catering furniture thrown together in a pile to the right. Maddie could see only one clear area on the left. Here, a single chair stood out in the middle of the clearing. A figure sat on it, facing away and unmoving. A Tesco carrier bag lay on the floor next to it. The Tactical Team would have left it there for CSI to seize. It lifted from one end in a breeze that rushed in through the open door. It was just as Rhiannon had relayed after her interview with the man who had admitted to creating this scene.

Maddie had been wrong. Their suspect might still turn out to be a fantasist, of course. But he'd got much further than most, he had acted his out.

CHAPTER 7

'I understand, yeah.'

Adrian Hughes dug around in the murky brown depths of the machine coffee resting in front of him. He was using one of the stubby wooden stirrers that they only gave to the prisoners who had shown neither the desire nor the ability to wield it as some sort of weapon — or to stuff it down their throat as a method of self-harm. The stirrer didn't look like it could be efficient in either capacity to be fair.

Maddie paused after this — his answer to the last of the required formal questions — and leaned back, taking in Hughes's form in full and doubting that he would pose a threat to her even if he'd been stirring his drink with a hunting knife.

'And the last thing to double-check with you, Adrian . . . You have declined a solicitor for this interview. I have informed you that this is an ongoing right, but can I ask why you do not wish to be represented?'

Adrian still stirred his coffee. In the stillness of the interview room, the relentless scraping of wood on cardboard was maddening, the more so given that Maddie was doing her best to hold herself back, to refrain from launching at him with the many questions she had. She'd never been patient when it came to waiting for answers.

'I don't need a solicitor. Why would I need a solicitor? I've told you already what I did. I don't understand why I need to sit here and tell you again.'

Stir, stir, stir. The stirring was becoming more agitated and there was a flash of emotion in Hughes's voice.

'Okay. Last night you spoke to my colleague. The purpose of that conversation was to understand what you were telling us but also to find the place that you described. That was our first priority. We've done that now. We've had time to look at some other things, too. So now I just need you to help us a little more. Is that okay?'

'I don't know if I can help anymore. I've told you everything.'

Stir, stir, stir. His eyes stayed fixed on the drink and the stirrer.

'It's just a few questions.' Maddie had a drink herself. A coffee from the same machine as Adrian's. To her left, DC Andrew McArthur was already scratching down notes. She didn't like it. Maddie would rather interviews were conducted without anything being written at all. Notes were not necessary for recording purposes. Officers made notes of things they wanted clarified as the interview went on, things to ask when there was a suitable break. But Maddie knew it could be misinterpreted. A good enough interview could almost make the suspect forget about the recording equipment that was capturing them via two different media — sound and vision. But a pen scrabbling away in front of them, scratching out words that they would often lean to try and see — always assuming that each word was part of sealing their fate — was a constant reminder. Maddie was gradually working through her team, trying to find someone compatible with her technique. She had discarded most before realizing that it wasn't just someone who didn't scratch out notes that she was looking for, she was trying to replace the irreplaceable. She was trying to replace DI Harry Blaker.

'Well, go on then. I didn't get much sleep last night. I'm tired.'

'I'm sure you are. Tell me again about the girl.'

'Tell you what? What do you mean by that?'

'Why her?'

'Why her? Why anyone?'

'Okay then, why anyone?'

'What do you mean?'

'Why did you kill her? That's a reasonable question, isn't it? I don't think anyone's actually asked you that, have they? Which is understandable. Our priority after last night was to find her, to see if maybe she wasn't dead, to see if we could help her. But she *was* dead, just like you said. She never stood a chance, either. *Suffocated* in thin plastic. That takes some doing and it would have taken some time. She would have known what you were doing . . . you would have had to get close to her when you did it . . . she would have seen it coming. The whole thing would have been awkward and panicked. I went out there this morning, Adrian, and I can tell you . . . that panic is still on her face. A pretty young woman still in her running shoes, plucked off the street to be killed slowly — in agony. By you. So . . . why?'

Stir, stir, stir.

But his movements had slowed. He was now pushing the coffee around rather than working it up into a swirl. He stopped altogether, holding the stirrer poised in the middle of the cup, gripping it gently between a slender finger and thumb with his lips pursed together. He was using it to delay . . . to think.

Maddie's hand shot out. The coffee cup hit the wall and there was the drumming of liquid on the thin carpet. Adrian's eyes had followed the cup as it flew across the room; now, he turned back to face Maddie, a shocked expression on his face.

'You thought you could just come in here and tell me you killed someone and that would be it? That you'd be off the hook? That no one would force you to talk about why? About what sort of person that makes you?' Maddie leaned into him to keep up the pressure. She had already seen him flinch at the volume of her voice.

The sound of a perforated sheet of paper being ripped from a notebook drew her attention and she glanced over. She had forgotten about DC McArthur. He scrunched up the paper for the bin. The rest of the pad he tipped on its side so the brown liquid could run off and onto the carpet. There were large spots on his white shirt, too. He ripped another sheet out to dab at it. This wasn't the time to apologise. She turned back to Hughes, staring at him to force an answer.

'I . . . I'm not a bad person . . .'

'You did a very bad thing. Who is she?' Maddie's tone now carried intent. The pleading-for-help approach had got her nowhere.

'I don't know.'

'And yet you killed her. What does that make you?'

'Is this why you wanted to talk to me again? So you could torture me?'

'I can't do half of what I would like to do to you. What do you think prison will be like for you? Among people who don't have the same constraints I do?'

'I don't know . . . I don't know what prison will be like . . . I didn't sleep last night. I was just lying there thinking about it. I heard people getting locked up next to me. One of them came in shouting and screaming. Every time someone closes a cell door . . . that sound.'

'Who is she?'

'I don't know!'

'Why come here and tell us what you did? Why are you only thinking about prison now?'

'Who told you that? Maybe I've been thinking about it from the moment I started this whole thing?'

'You brought a bag. You have three types of shower gel in there. There's no way you've been lying in bed for days or weeks thinking about what prison might be like and decided that you'll be allowed a selection of shower gels in there. Why come and tell us? Why not just go free?'

'You sound like you're angry with me for making your job easier!' He snorted.

Maddie fought the urge to lash out again, knowing that this time the end result wouldn't be coffee stains.

'And you have, haven't you? Made it easy, I mean. You told us about the axe you used to break in. You told us exactly where you left it and we pulled your fingerprints from it. Your DNA too.'

'I just told you what I did.'

'You did. And some bits in great detail. The carrier bag, for example. You told us about that — how you handled most things with gloves. But you were sure to tell us you didn't have gloves on when you put the bag over her head so we might find a trace of you on there. Notoriously difficult to get prints from a carrier bag — something about the way it moves, I'm told. There's not enough surface area on the handle. Even if the fingertips were to touch it and you don't put enough pressure on the other parts. But we got your prints, a good set. And DNA traces on her neck, of course, where you told us you made sure she was dead.'

'That's good, isn't it? For you?'

'But not for you. So, again . . . why her?'

'I don't know! I didn't know her . . . she was just an opportunity. I saw her around, she seemed to have a pattern. I followed her. I made plans on how I could do it and then, when the chance came, I took it — almost without thinking. I was obsessed with her!'

'Was it sexual?'

'No!' Hughes looked appalled. 'I never touched her . . . *there.*'

'Where?'

'You know what I mean.'

'This is a police interview, a murder no less. This is where me knowing what you mean isn't relevant. The judge who sentences you, who decides how long you spend in one of those prison hell-holes you know nothing about, who decides if you ever get out at all, he'll need to understand what you mean.'

'Then I'll tell him.'

41

'Tell him what?'

'That I never touched her like that.'

'How did she get in that chair? How did you get her off the street and into your van?'

'I threatened her. I had a knife. It's still in the van. Did you find the van? I told you where it was.'

'You did. Still parked outside the building where you left the body, the knife in the back. Walk home, did you? After you murdered her?'

'No, I . . . I walked some of the way.'

'And the rest of the way?'

'I . . . this is not . . . No comment.'

'No comment! What do you mean "no comment"?'

Maddie was getting angry again. She leaned in further, her watch scraping the surface of the table as she shifted her arm. Hughes flinched again. She couldn't say what was more maddening, the fact that he was lying to her or the fact that he was so pathetic with it. Frightened of prison, frightened of her, frightened of the sound of movement . . . frightened of his own shadow. And she was supposed to believe that he was capable of doing what she had seen that morning.

'I can say that. I don't have to answer these questions. I came in here and told you what I did and how I did it. I didn't have to tell you anything more.'

'What did you do to her phone?'

'What? Nothing! I didn't touch her phone.'

'It was in her pocket. No password protection. Just the standard apps it came with. That's unusual, isn't it?'

'I don't know. I don't know what's usual for a woman to have on her phone. I didn't even look at it.'

'Someone cleaned it up. Took off what they didn't want us to find on there.'

'Well, I didn't—' Hughes cut himself short to sigh loudly. 'I've got nothing to say about her phone.'

'If you didn't then who did, Adrian? Who else should we be talking to about all this?'

'What? No one! I told you what happened. I told you how. You found the axe with my prints, the bag too. Did you find anything that points to anyone else?'

'Not yet.'

'No, you didn't! I don't know why you're making this so difficult for yourselves! Why do you want to make this complicated?'

Maddie sat back. He was being petulant now, like a child throwing a tantrum. She sniffed then sipped at her coffee. It was always foul from the machine but even more so now that she'd let it go cold. She fixed her eyes sternly on Hughes, waiting until he locked eyes with her, waiting until it got awkward and then giving it another few seconds.

'This has caught you out a bit, hasn't it, Mr Hughes? You really thought it'd be as simple as coming in here and telling us all about how you suddenly upped and murdered a woman from nowhere, and we would sit and listen, have no need for explanations, and then put you in prison with your selection of shower gels?'

'I didn't know what to expect.'

'Of course you didn't. You've not been arrested before. You tell us you've never been so much as stopped by the police for driving too fast. No parking tickets, never a witness . . . not someone who's ever had anything to do with us. There's a scale when it comes to violence and offenders tend to work their way up it. You'll get a kid who starts by hurting animals or siblings. Sometimes there's sexual fascination or assaults in there. Then they hurt partners. They can often appear on mental-health records, too, for hurting themselves. After partners, they can move onto their own children or start committing violent acts on random targets. Sexual offences and violent offences are interchangeable, by the way. And it's generally someone who has an obsession with control. So you'll see a history of siblings with bruised arms where they've been grabbed and restrained — pulled hair, as it's the best way to get hold of someone with pain, compliant, if you're weak or untrained. Then it moves onto punching and kicking . . . then maybe strangulation that leads to death when they realize that other people can't actually be controlled. Have you ever hurt anyone? Before all this, I mean?'

'I . . . I . . . well, no. But I've always wanted to.' The second part of his sentence was blurted. It struck Maddie as showing off, like a kid would do.

'Wanted to what?'

'Hurt people.'

'How? How have you always wanted to hurt people?'

'Well . . . by hitting and pulling hair, like you said.'

'That's just repeating back what I said. Who else are you repeating back? Who told you what to say when you came in here?'

'What? No one! Don't be ridiculous! This is all ridiculous. I'm tired. I've told you what I can. I've not been sleeping. I need a break.'

Maddie paused a while. They were getting nowhere. 'Okay, I tell you what . . . my coffee's cold here and yours appears to have been spilt. How about we take that break, and I'll go and make a couple of proper cups of coffee from my own supply upstairs. That sound better?'

Adrian's eyes flicked over to where the coffee stain on the wall had now grown into what looked like a permanent feature. 'Yeah, the coffee here is not great.'

'It's awful, Adrian, is what it is. I'll come back down with some decent stuff. But there are still some things I don't understand — important things, okay?' Maddie was intentionally lighter, laying down the groundwork for a different approach when she did return. Who could tell? It could even prompt a different outcome.

'Be my guest.'

'I'll give you an hour or so to rest. The time is 12.52 p.m. and I am pausing this interview.' Maddie spun to press a button on the recording device behind her. Immediately it started to hum loudly and the screen flashed with *finalising* while it burned the interview to the discs. This could take a while too. This was the part when the room became quiet, when the questions stopped and the recorder was off. It was the part where the suspect might drop his guard.

'I can see you're terrified of prison, Adrian. You should be too.'

'Does that make you happy? The thought of me being terrified?' Adrian's tone carried real anger for the first time.

'I like putting the right people behind bars. I live for it. So if you murdered that woman in cold blood then, yeah, I'm delighted that you're going somewhere horrible. But if you didn't . . .'

'We've done this. I've told you more times than I should need to already.'

'And what are you *not* telling me?'

'*Not* telling you? Why should you be bothered with that? When I'm here giving you my confession.'

'Are you a man of faith, Adrian?'

'I have my beliefs, yes.'

'When you stand up in court and swear on your holy Bible, you will promise to tell the *whole* truth. And you might choose to do so at that point. But it will be too late for you . . . a prison sentence will already, be assured, one way or another. Consider doing the whole-truth thing when I come back. With better coffee.'

The discs had finished and Maddie stood up. Hughes lingered for another few moments then stood up when prompted by DC McArthur. Maddie interjected that she wanted to be the one to walk Adrian Hughes back to his cell. She didn't have anything more to say, she just wanted to slam the cell door extra hard.

Inspector Tristan Stepney was waiting for them. He was in the custody back office where Maddie needed to mark up the record. The inspector didn't take his feet off the table when he saw them enter.

'What the hell happened in there?' The DI sounded almost amused. When Maddie turned to him, he was gesturing at Andrew McArthur and his spotted shirt.

'I spilt my coffee, sir,' McArthur said.

'Actually, I spilt it.' Maddie made brief eye contact with McArthur, who curled his lip slightly. 'Fortunately, it went over my colleague. These are new trousers!'

'The levels of professionalism I have come to expect from this place, even in such a short time . . . I'm not sure what happened while I was away, but I'm sure I remember standards being better than this.'

'I've noticed the same, sir,' Maddie said. 'Even the brand-new officers coming out seem to be a step down from how they used to be . . .'

'I can assure you the standards of new officers has never been higher!' Stepney's feet did now thump to the floor. Maddie had known she would get a reaction to that. Prior to his demotion, the recruitment and training of new officers had been very much Stepney's portfolio. 'Did your man have anything more to say for himself? For all the good it will do him.'

'Not really, sir. He's still sticking to the same story as before. But I've not discussed everything we have with him yet.'

'Oh?'

'I mentioned the victim's phone briefly, but I still want to ask him about the photograph.'

'The *only* photograph, you mean. Just one selfie on the whole damned thing. It is a little odd.'

'The whole thing is odd, sir. It just doesn't ring true with me.'

'Which bit?'

'He's lying to us.'

'About killing her?'

'I don't know which part specifically. Some . . . maybe all of it.'

'We have his prints, his DNA . . . his van — all where he said they would be. He wasn't lying about *that* now, was he?'

'We have everything he wanted to give us. Nothing more. I'm giving him an hour to consider his situation. Then I want to speak to him again.'

'And you think you two sitting him down and spilling coffee all over the desk in front of him is going to get more of a result than the one we already have? Maybe I should go in there myself to speak with him.'

'There's no need for that, sir,' Maddie snapped. She looked over to where the DI was sitting under a bank of monitors — one for each cell. She held his stare. He looked away first, leaning back in his chair to peer up at the streaming images of caged humans. Hughes was in cell eight. One of the monitors had a laminated *8* beneath it. The screen showed movement where Hughes, despite insisting on his tiredness, was on his feet and pacing the small space. She could just make out a lifted arm — was he also ruffling his hair?

'Well, okay then. You can go back and speak to him all you want. Just try to put on a professional front, would you? I'd better get going on this press release.'

'Press release?' Maddie repeated.

'Oh, sorry. Did I not run it past you?' The sarcasm was clear in Stepney's tone as he stood up. 'As the SIO, I will make decisions all on my own at times.'

'I only like to be kept up-to-date in case there's anything I need to discuss in there. And I do understand the way a murder investigation works, *sir.* With the previous SIO we found that keeping an open dialogue often got better results, faster.'

'Yes. I am aware that you and Mr Blaker were close. Too close perhaps? My predecessor may have been happy for the rank structure to be eroded but I intend on putting a stop to some of his practices. I am releasing the picture of the victim found on her phone to the media and I will be appealing for anyone who might know who she is. To be honest, I think that is a far better use of our time, DS Ives. You appear to be dead set on getting our suspect to make the same confession over and over again, but our victim will fill in the gaps far more effectively. We just need to find someone who can confirm she was a keen runner, maybe that she mentioned a weirdo skulking in the woods and that she had no idea who the hell Adrian Hughes was and *boom!* Job done.'

'That photo . . .' Maddie didn't have the rest of the sentence.

'What about it?'

'Her phone . . . I mean, it's strange, isn't it? You said so yourself, sir.'

'Is there a point to this, DS Ives? One that is worth holding me up for?'

'Strange in that her phone has been deliberately cleaned. No social-media apps on there . . . no messages . . . call logs . . . no pictures or videos of her messing about with mates or at family dos. Except one . . . this perfect selfie — just what we need to release to identify her . . .'

'There is a point to all this, I can feel it coming!' Stepney lifted his hands to his hips.

'It's strange.'

'You said that.'

'I can't put it into words. Our offender denies touching her phone. So does that mean someone else cleared the phone, then left it in her pocket? If so, when was that done? And did they do it because they want us to identify her quickly — because they know our next move will be to put the photo out to the media?'

'Let me ask you this, DS Ives . . . I know you're not a career detective. I cannot claim to be one either. But do you always believe what you are told by offenders when they're the prime suspect in a murder case? Is that what we do in Major Crime now? Maybe it's some sort of policy change that I'm not aware of. We have an account from our offender. It has thrown up some questions — parts of his account might not be completely accurate, so we are now going to find out what we can from the victim's side of things. Everything seems odd until it has an answer. This is how we get answers. Understood?'

Maddie held back her first reaction. 'Understood,' was all she could manage. She had finished her entry on the custody record; there was nothing more to keep her there — least of all discussing the case any further with the SIO.

CHAPTER 8

The light was just as sudden but half as strong. It came from a different source, high up on the left wall. A white light from a small, flat panel that dimmed quickly to the point where it was hardly enough to penetrate the shadows. She had known something was about to happen. The door had been flung open and the hood wrenched from her head. A moment later, the screen had flickered into life. Weak as it was, it still hurt Linda's eyes to look at it. The panel flickered back to almost black, leaving just a small spinning wheel in its centre. A few more seconds and pixelated images began to form, moving blocks that cleared to come into focus. It was a television monitor. The moving image was a news broadcast with no sound. She recognized the format as from the BBC's twenty-four-hour news channel. While the newsreader spoke silently on-screen, the bottom scrolled a vibrant yellow with a headline within it: *POLICE PUT OUT APPEAL FOR INFORMATION ON IDENTITY AND LAST MOVEMENTS OF MURDERED FEMALE.*

She snatched her gaze away from the screen to the sound of chains being pulled tightly to her right. The man was reacting to what he was seeing. His breathing was quicker and louder, and his eyes flared vivid white in the light. He was looking across her, his attention fixed on the television monitor. Then his face changed. His mouth fell open. He strained against the steel restraints. Then he bellowed.

'NO!'

Linda looked back at the screen. The newsreader had been replaced. The main image was now a pouting selfie of a young woman with dark, curly hair that framed hazel eyes and freckled skin. In the picture she looked pretty and carefree, a raised cocktail glass in one hand to match her sophisticated style of dress. There was a slender arm draped across her shoulder as if the picture had been cropped from a group shot of young women on a night out. Linda didn't think she had seen the woman before. The man bellowed again.

'WHAT DID YOU DO?'

The chains scraped and tensed. He looked like he was trying to stand, his feet scuffed against the floor.

The room fell back into thick darkness and Linda cursed herself for not taking the opportunity to look around. She had been aware of a woman opposite, her face also lifted to the screen. She had seen the walls as grey and curved, and she was sure the curve continued into the ceiling as if they were in a stone tunnel. But it was tight, barely high enough to stand in. The man to her right looked to be big and long-limbed, with a chiselled jaw. His thick neck had been lined with prominent veins — she'd seen them appear as he strained against his shackles. She had caught a quick glimpse of a door in the wall on the right; it looked wooden and flimsy.

The monitor came back on as a flat panel of white and she had to look away. Movement grabbed Linda's attention; something moved past her from right to left and then the silhouette of a man appeared under the lit monitor. It looked like a man at any rate, from the broad shoulders and the shape of his body. He wore a hood pulled up and the light behind him ensured that inside the hood was just thick shadow. He upturned and dropped a wooden box on the ground and then sat on it. The young woman opposite gasped at his appearance, then tried to push away, her chains scraping against the stone. When her efforts proved futile, she pulled her legs up as far as she could.

'WHAT DID YOU DO?' the man to Linda's right roared again.

His legs were bent under him and he was still trying to get to his feet. His arms seemed to be pulled behind his back, tied perhaps. Certainly he seemed to have less freedom of movement than Linda. The hooded silhouette didn't move. Behind him the monitor changed again. The news was gone. Now there was an image of double doors. The image took up the centre of the screen as if it had been filmed through a camera phone. The left door was mostly covered with new-looking steel; on the right one, the steel had been peeled crudely away. She could see something of the brickwork either side of the entrance. The bricks looked tired and old and covered with a layer of sandblasted dust. She could see some graffiti too that she couldn't make out; there wasn't enough visible and the camera was now moving forwards — through the double doors.

There was still no sound. The interior was in a poor state, surely derelict. The camera panned over a pile of items that she couldn't quite identify. It took a moment for the focus to adjust and the light overall was changeable, the lens struggling to cope. Judging by the amount of debris on the floor she wasn't sure there could be a roof at all. The camera moved to the left and settled on the distant image of a chair. Linda leaned forwards to make it out and the chains pulled against her midriff. It took just a few more steps forwards from the cameraman for the unmistakeable figure of a person to emerge, sitting upright in the chair. The figure faced away. Whoever it was, they were not moving. The head looked like it was covered in white material.

'I TOLD YOU I DON'T KNOW! I *told* you . . .' The man's voice lost its anger, now it was pure desperation.

The black silhouette sitting under the monitor moved as if stung. A blur whisked across her front to deliver a solid

51

strike to the roaring man, whose head snapped back from the blow. He fell back against the wall, his legs now folded out so she could see the soles of his shoes. He howled in pain. The silhouette still lingered. The next blow seemed firmer. The sound was different — *sickening*. The seated man slumped to his side. His eyes still had movement and they fixed on the monitor. His head shook slightly. His lips bumped together as he tried to say something. Then his mouth fell open and he drooled on the floor. He sniffed as if sobbing. When he did find his voice, it was a pitiful murmur. Linda thought he was trying to say a name but couldn't make it out.

The silhouette sat back down under the monitor. She ignored the footage behind him for just a moment, trying to pick out some details of his appearance. It was no use, she couldn't even tell if he was looking at her.

The monitor behind him now showed a dusty floor but it jolted back up so the seated figure filled the screen once more. An up-ended Tesco carrier bag covered the head. A hand reached out for it. Linda wanted to look away but found she couldn't. This had to relate to why she was here — she even found herself leaning forwards. The sudden revelation of the face beneath the bag had her jerking back hard enough for the curve of the wall to dig into her back. The heels of her shoes scuffed on the stone as she tried to push herself back still further. The steel restraints pinched the skin on her side and she had to conceal a yelp.

The camera shook unsteadily but the woman's face was clear. Her whole head was wrapped tightly in clingfilm, her mouth wide open where she must have struggled desperately for breath through the layers of plastic. It was wrapped tightly enough to distort her features, to make her unrecognizable to anyone who didn't know her, but they had just been shown a smiling version of her on the news. And the man to her right reacted as though he knew her well.

'Oh Jesus! Oh Jesus Christ . . . Oh Jesus Christ!'

Linda cast him another glance. He was still on his side but wriggling to get up. A slick trail of blood ran from his right eye and caught the light to take on a silvery glow. The eye was already swollen. The silhouette stood again. As she looked up at him, his right hand dropped close to her face, close enough for her to see the outline of something over the knuckles on his right hand. A knuckle-duster would explain the damage to the man's face she had seen on her way in, and the sound of the second strike just a few moments ago. The silhouette stepped back over to the wounded man.

'No! No, no . . . NO! I told you! Please . . .'

He still wasn't sitting upright as he begged from the floor. This time the silhouette squatted beside him. The chains scraped and clinked then made the sound of being thrown into a heap on the floor. The man was now free of his chains. But he stayed seated, his hands still pulled back behind him. The silhouette gripped under the man's arms to lift him to his feet. The man resisted only until the fist with the knuckle-duster was raised above him.

'OKAY! Okay . . .' The blow didn't come. The man looked shaky as he allowed himself to be hauled up.

The door beyond him scraped and dragged where someone else must have opened it. The silhouette was unmoving. The man stumbled towards the door as if he had been pushed.

'OKAY!' he roared again. 'Okay, I'll tell you! I'll tell you everything!'

More scuffling feet. A large shadow reached in to take hold of the man. When the door scraped shut again, only Linda and the weeping female were left.

On the monitor, the footage still showed movement around the derelict building but it had shifted back towards the door. The camera dropped to take in a brightly coloured axe standing on its head against a filthy wall. Then the monitor switched off. Total darkness fell instantly. Even so, Linda clamped her eyes tightly shut. She found this helped her to focus, to control the panic. She tried to listen for the distant throbbing sound that she had come to rely on to keep her calm while her mind raced with images of the woman in the chair and the reaction of the man who had been beaten, unshackled and forced out of the room. They obviously had plans for him. Plans that Linda could only guess at.

She was suddenly less keen to find out what they wanted from her.

CHAPTER 9

'What is Livestream, Adrian?' Maddie had been true to her word and made good coffee from her own supplies. Expensive stuff, too — as good as instant coffee ever got, at least.

Hughes was back to eyeing his drink. He sat on his hands, his face hanging over the mug Maddie had taken from the communal kitchenette upstairs. It was from a previous publicity promotion and displayed the force crest above the slogan: *One person speaking out can make a whole community safer.* The irony had appealed to her. She had also omitted to bring anything that he might be able to use as a stirrer.

'Livestream?'

'The app on your phone.'

'Oh . . . it's an app for recording things. It works the camera.'

'But the camera works the camera, doesn't it?'

'What?'

'The camera on your phone has its own app. What does Livestream do that the standard app doesn't?'

Adrian shrugged. 'Loads of apps do the same thing as others. Some of them seem better so you put them on there but you never actually use them.'

'Have you used Livestream?'

'I might have.'

'What did you record on it?'

'I can't remember what I've used apps for specifically.'

'What sort of things have you recorded?'

'Nothing, really. I take photos sometimes — just like anyone else.'

'What photos?'

'You know . . . if I'm somewhere I've never been before. Monuments, statues . . . museums, that sort of thing.'

'Did you ever use Livestream in any of these museums?'

'I don't think so. I might have.'

'Other than the photo you showed us, what was the last thing you recorded? Or took a picture of for that matter?'

'I can't remember. I don't use it much.'

'What other apps do you use?'

'The usual.'

'What does that mean? Your usual might be very different to mine for example. Name an app you use every day.'

Adrian floundered. He picked up the coffee mug and pushed it to his lips. Maddie wasn't sure he took any of the liquid in; he was stalling again — more time to think.

'I don't want to talk about my phone.'

'One app. Just to shut me up.'

Adrian shrugged again. 'BBC News, okay? I check the news. Like I said, just like everyone does.'

'That's it? News apps? What about something that isn't so generic? Do you have hobbies that might be supported by an app?'

'Not that I can think of.'

'Running? You have a running app on there. You talked about that before. Did you download that initially because you like running?'

'Err . . . sure, yeah. I like running. But then I realized it gave me an opportunity. The amount of people that put their whole life out on their phones . . .'

'Any other apps?'

'I don't want to talk about my phone, okay? It's point-less. All this is pointless.'

'I do, though, Adrian. I want to talk about where it is.'

'What do you mean?'

Maddie dropped a smartphone on the desk. It was an Apple model, a few generations old, grey-backed and with no case. 'Is this your phone?'

'It looks like the one you took off me.'

'That doesn't answer my question.'

'It's the only answer you're getting. I didn't have to give you that.'

'There's barely anything on this. The standard apps that you can't delete, that Joggle app and then just one other . . . Livestream. So is this your phone?'

Adrian crossed his arms but it was as if he was hugging himself. 'If that's the one you took out of my pocket then it must be my phone.'

'But that isn't true, is it? Someone could have given it to you. Maybe it's someone else's phone. Maybe you stole it.'

'I told you already, I don't want to talk about my phone. And I've never stolen anything in my life.'

Maddie sat back. She took a swig of her own drink. Adrian fidgeted again. He was back to sitting on his hands, the posture tipping him forwards. His speech was getting quieter.

'We have techies here — experts in digital media. Mobile phones and their apps included. They've done a little bit of digging for me. Livestream is just as it sounds, it allows you to stream a live video to a number of places online. I'm not really up on what this all means, so they described it to me using the simplest language possible. Basically, you could be skulking about in some woods, waiting for someone to come past who you have been planning to kidnap and murder. You could jump out and snatch that person, bundle them into a van and take them to a derelict building for some time alone. And you could film the whole thing and stream it direct to your social-media timeline — so straight onto your Facebook feed for all your friends to see. Or you could send it straight to another person as a direct video. Those are just two examples of what Livestream is for. It only streams footage live, only to another source and, significantly, it does it securely. The standard camera app saves anything you record to your phone in the first instance. If you send it, you send a copy. So that's not so secure, is it? You can delete the footage from your phone but that can be retrievable. Most people understand this now — that phones are a good source of working out just what people have been up to. With the right equipment, the right expertise and a little bit of time — all of the things that, say, a police force investigating a murder might have — nothing is *ever* deleted, is it, Adrian? Did you know that?'

'I don't know what you're talking about.'

'But Livestream is different. It basically beams a recording straight out. It doesn't leave a trace. That's what you did, isn't it? You streamed some part of this live — maybe all of it. Or did you just stream the bit where you wrapped plastic round her face? The bit where she was fighting for her life?'

'I don't want to talk about my phone.'

'Who did you stream that to, Adrian? And I think it was a *who*, not a *where*. If you streamed it to a hard drive, a cloud service or a social-media feed, then there's still the risk, isn't there? When we find out who you really are and where you really live, we're going to pull it apart — your house and anything we find in it. If there's a hard drive we will see everything that's on there. But there won't be, will there?'

'I told you: I don't want to talk about my phone.'

'This isn't about your phone. Not anymore. You couldn't have done all that on your own. Look at yourself, Adrian . . . you're not fooling anyone here. You're pathetic, terrified and weak. There's no way you're capable of any of this and there's no way you killed that woman. At most, you were the cameraman. So this isn't about your phone. This is about who put you up to this.'

'I don't know what you're talking about. I don't have any further comment — not now. You just keep asking me questions. I've told you all you need to know.'

'You haven't told me the half of it. My job is to keep us all safe, to make sure this abhorrent treatment of a young woman can't happen again and to bring the perpetrators to justice. All of them. For her.' Maddie had two pictures resting on her lap. The first was the smiling selfie that they had just released to the public via the news outlets. She slid it across the desk. The corner of the paper bumped off Hughes's gut where he was pushed up against the table. He glanced down at it but stayed sitting on his hands.

'A pretty girl. Her whole life ahead of her, Adrian.' The next photo was one Charley had taken. It was a close up of the dead woman's face. The plastic had been removed at this stage but she was still sitting up in the chair. She put this picture down more deliberately, moving his coffee cup so it could be right under where he was hanging his head.

'If you didn't do this alone — if you didn't do this *at all*, Adrian — you can talk to me. Tell me what happened. I can't have people out there who are capable of this. How many other young women could end up looking like this? Please, Adrian . . . please help me. The whole truth. That's all you can do now.'

Adrian pulled himself up straight and swept both photos off the table. 'No COMMENT! Nothing more. I'm done with this. Send me to prison like you said you were going to. I've told you everything you need. You're asking me for help. I came in here to help!'

He sat back, his eyes wide, his breathing shallow. He looked like he was about to cry. Anger didn't suit him. Maddie let the silence intensify, hoping he might bumble on. She decided she'd left it long enough.

'Except you didn't. You've told us exactly what you needed to. Look at it from my angle . . . I've got this man who comes into the police station after dark and confesses to a terrible crime. He gives me a few details of how, a picture of the end result and tells me where to find the victim. And we do find her, just like he said we would. And I'm certain you thought that would be it, that we'd just take that and run with it and ask you no more questions. But there are a lot of questions left for me. Why would you do that? Why come here to *help* but make damned sure you don't have your own phone on you? You talked about using your phone for museums and day trips, but there's just one picture in your whole album and that is the one you showed my colleague to back up your admission. We looked for data tags on this phone. Most apps have some sort of tag. When you make a call or send a message, your phone applies a data tag to that action. That means we can see that a message or a call was made, not always the content, just that that action was taken. If you're not careful with your settings, we can also see where you were in the world when you did that action. Guess what we found on your phone? Two data tags. That's how we know the picture of the body was taken by that device. It's also how we know that you took it from where the body was found.' Maddie stopped and waited now.

Hughes's eyes had dropped back to his coffee. She waited until he looked back up, until he met her stare. Then she started again.

'It's also how we know that the Livestream app was activated at the same location as the body was found. We don't know how long for or in what capacity but, crucially, we do know the date. So, let me give you one more chance to tell me the *whole* truth here and now, before it's too late for you … Who else do we need to be talking to about this disgusting crime?'

'No one! No one else, okay? I did it. I did it all. I got obsessed, I found her on the app, then I saw her on *actual* runs … I was obsessed. I wanted to kill her and I did it. I didn't have the stomach to do it with the axe. That was what I thought I wanted, but I couldn't do it. Her eyes when I lifted it . . .'

Maddie sat back as he spoke. His expression was now that of someone recalling something horrific, something that had left a lasting impression. It was the most genuine she had seen him. *Maybe he was telling the truth . . .*

'When did you kill her?' Maddie said.

'A week ago. I told you that too.'

'The tag on your phone, for the Livestream app, it shows as two hours before you came to the police station. How do you explain that?'

'I went back to see her. She was right where I left her. I went back in my own car. I had left the van there, see? That's how I got away yesterday. I drove back to get a picture of her. I opened the Livestream app by accident. I closed it right away! It looks like the normal camera app.'

'Why?'

'Why what?'

'Why go back a week later to get a photo?'

'Because I knew you wouldn't believe me . . . All my life . . . people have looked at me like you're looking at me now. They make up their minds — *oh, he's not capable . . . he's not someone to be feared or respected.* Well, I am! I'm not to be underestimated. The dead woman — she didn't believe in me at first, either.' Hughes gestured at the photos scattered on the floor. 'Even when I pulled the knife! She just stopped her run and looked at it, then tried to walk round me like I didn't matter. I had to thrust it under her neck to get her to realize. By the end she was taking me very seriously!'

'Is that why you killed her? Because she didn't respect you? Did you want to ask her out? Maybe she dismissed you completely? I can see how that could make you angry.'

'No, that's not it at all.'

'Did you have sex with her?'

'What? No! We've been through this.'

'Did you want to?'

'No. It wasn't about that.'

'Did you kill her there? Where she was sitting?'

'Yes! I told you that!'

'Then you went back a week later to take a photo. Why not take one at the time?'

'It didn't really occur to me to get one. I guess I never expected that a week later I would be trying to convince a police officer that I had murdered her. But this last week . . . It's been hell — you should know that. I know you probably don't care. You probably think I deserve the very worst of days every day — and you might be right — but I couldn't live with it. I went back and took the picture and, let me tell you, it was so much worse the second time round. She looked so different . . . just sitting there. She looked sadder. And she was starting to . . . change.'

'Change?'

'Colour. Smell. I think the rats had had a go, too. Oh God . . .' He suddenly looked like he was going to be sick.

'I'm not sure you have the stomach for murder,' Maddie said.

'So it would seem.' His voice dropped lower than ever. He suddenly looked exhausted, spent perhaps. Empty.

'We were always going to check, though. Surely you would've realized that? You come in here and tell us where a body is, and you think we'll just tell you to go away and come back with some more evidence? Did you really think you would need the photo?'

'I . . . I don't know! I've never done this before. I don't know how you work. How would I know how you work? As it was, the first thing your colleague did was accuse me of being a mental patient. I needed the photo.'

Maddie took a deep breath. Hughes was watching her intently now, sensing that she was building up to something significant.

'So here we are. You say you don't know how all this works so let me tell you what happens next. I will charge you then remand you in prison to await your trial. When that happens, that's your chance gone. But you should know that I'm not just going to charge you and then stop looking for answers. I will find out the truth and when I do, I will make sure that the judge knows only too well that you did nothing to help me put it all together, despite what you claim.

I will petition for the strongest possible sentence and my experience tells me that the judge will be on my side. They don't take kindly to people who walk through these doors to deliberately pervert the course of justice.'

'I have helped you. I told you where to find her. I told you what I did. That's an early plea. A judge will know that. Now do your bit. Any punishment I get will be what I deserve. You were wrong about me — I'm not scared of that part. I'm ready for prison.'

'Early plea? That's a legal term. Where did you hear that?'

Hughes huffed. 'You never heard of Google search? It's a wonderful thing.'

Maddie stood up and swept up his full coffee cup in one movement. It clacked against her own.

'That was it. Your last chance to save yourself and your last chance of a decent coffee. For the rest of your life. You think about that. I'll be writing up your charge sheet.'

CHAPTER 10

Linda Morris was woken roughly by someone forcing something over her head. She inhaled a panicked gulp of air, sucking fabric in through her nostrils and then her mouth. Her
mind flashed instantly with the image of the woman tied to
her chair in that desolate building, one eye open and pressing
against the film, her mouth gaping open to show her teeth
and tongue, her expression ever-frozen in her final gasp for
breath. It was Linda who was gasping for air now. But it
did come, even though her breaths were shallow and panicked. Her wide eyes made sense of the bright light leaking
through the coarse material in squares — squares that were
now familiar.

It wasn't plastic. She could still breathe.

It was the same hood that had been pulled down over
her face several times before. She felt a perverse sense of relief
and was almost grateful for it. She knew she could breathe in
this, she had managed it before. She felt a little calmer and
her breathing became more natural. She could feel someone
squatting over her. Their hands moved down her body until
they grabbed roughly at her lower back and wrenched her
forwards. Her head bumped off something that moved away,
a thigh perhaps or a knee. Her chains rattled and clinked,

64

then slithered against her, pinching her skin as they came away. She gave a yelp that sounded strange to her, half contained under her hood. The rough hands grabbed her wrists. Something was wrapped around them — a solid rope, she thought — and pulled so tight that she yelped again. She felt a slap on her head through the material. She knew what that meant. She bit down on her lip to stop herself from crying out again. She was grabbed roughly under her arms, yanked to her feet and made to walk.

The first few steps were a struggle. The muscles in her legs didn't work as they should; they felt numb and shaky. Nor could she see her surroundings well enough to avoid obstructions. She kicked something. It might have been the young woman's leg, but she didn't hear a reaction. The younger woman must have learned the rules by now.

Linda was pulled to a halt by her shoulder. She was even less steady when left to stand still. The door scraped and kicked the way it had every time it had been opened. She was grabbed again and led forwards, stumbling on a solid lip that she reckoned must mark the threshold of the door. The door was kicked and scraped shut. She heard metallic clangs ahead and a squeal like something being twisted. Then came a blinding flash of light. Even behind the hood she had to squint.

She was pushed again, this time directly towards the light. It was daylight — unmistakable. The sun's warmth wrapped her in an embrace that was enough to lift her mood, despite the circumstances. The feeling of being out in the open after being shut away for so long was so wonderful, she began to hope that she wouldn't be returned to the darkness. A light breeze ran across her exposed ankles and she looked down. She could peer out of the bottom of the hood, enough to see the ground at least. Her shoes were now a filthy black as was the loose ground underfoot.

She was led up a steep slope. It reminded her of the terrain when she had trekked up an ancient volcano on the island of Tenerife. Despite the strong sun, she knew she wasn't so far from home today. She was still being held tightly around her shoulders and under her arms. Her hamstrings were burning by the time the ground levelled out. The terrain didn't change and she continued walking until she was stopped.

'Steps.'

The voice in her ear was low and gruff. A male's voice for sure and the first word she had heard anyone utter other than the snatched conversation she'd had with those chained to the walls around her. She slowed and reached out gingerly with one foot until it came to rest on something solid. Looking down, she could see metal steps with a grey safe-grip surface. She moved up them and the daylight was once again snuffed out.

It wasn't as dark in here, but she was inside again; the fresh air was gone, along with the breeze and the sunlight. But this had the feeling of a room with curtains drawn over windows, rather than one with nowhere for light to enter at all. Her footsteps echoed as if the room was empty and she felt a slight give underfoot. The grip on her shoulder moved to push her downwards. A firm, plastic chair scraped as it slid back an inch under her weight. The coarse hood was pulled swiftly up and away from her face.

'Linda Morris.'

Linda took a moment. She didn't know where the voice had come from. She peered quickly around the interior of a sparse Portakabin, trying to assess any potential threats. The windows were covered by ragged curtains with light leaking around their edges. In front of her was a blue, two-by-two-metre self-standing partition, the sort she had seen in open-plan offices, dividing up workstations and providing sound deadening. The voice had come from behind it. The partition split the room in half, with plenty of room on the other side for the man who had dragged her out here. If that was who the speaker was. She glanced around again. The door to her left had been pulled firmly shut, the handle still lifted at an angle.

'What is going on? Who are you?' Her own voice caught her off guard. She hadn't spoken for so long that it sounded like it belonged to someone else.

'Now you know what we are capable of, what lengths we will go to.' The reply was instant.

Linda reckoned this voice was different to the one that had ordered her up the steps. It was harsher, instantly more confident and projected. It sounded like the voice of an older man — late thirties or early forties — giving her the image of someone strong and self-assured.

'What do you want?'

'Information. The specifics are not a conversation for now. All you need to understand is that you are the second person who has been asked for this information. The first believed she did not need to follow the rules. The video footage you have seen should have made it clear how that ended.'

Linda took a breath and held it as the words sank in. The image of that young woman's face frozen into her last gasp had slipped from Linda's mind. But now it came rushing back in an instant. She had looked so sad and forgotten. The face had been horrific enough, but the lasting impression for Linda came from the final few moments before the screen had gone dark, when the camera had swung back for a last glimpse of the seated woman. It had reinforced the emptiness of a scarred place left to fall in on itself. It was nothing to anyone now, a place to be forgotten. Linda didn't want to die alone in a place like that. She couldn't bear the thought of it.

'What information?' She found her voice at last.

'You will not be told the specifics here.'

'Then why bring me here?'

Linda's initial fear was giving way to anger. She had never been good with vagaries. Her directness had stood her in good stead in her professional life. If someone wanted something from her, she liked to know exactly what, so she could go about exceeding their expectations. She demanded the same from others. She was good at using her voice too. Professionally, she knew she could be stern and intimidating.

But this was not a workplace and these men were not about to relinquish any of their power over her.

A vague shadow flashed by. It appeared from behind the divider and leaped across the space to grab her roughly. The same hood from before was forced over her head and pulled hard from behind, knocking her off-balance and wrapping tight over her nose and mouth. She might have tipped backwards entirely but her head remained in a firm grip. She felt fingers close around her neck, pulling the base of the hood so tight that it began to restrict her breathing. She felt something bump against the back of the chair then a voice hissed in her ear, so close she could feel the heat of his breath through the coarse material.

'The questions are for us to ask. The rules are for you to obey. Do you understand?'

He tightened his grip around her throat now, lifting the chair's front legs off the ground. Linda could still breathe — just — but she couldn't speak. She managed a nod.

'If I tell you what we need now, you'll think this is a conversation . . . that you can argue . . . negotiate. You cannot. Do you understand?'

Linda nodded again.

'Yes!' she got a croak out, trying to relay her discomfort in her voice so he might ease his grip.

'This is not a negotiation. You have seen what can happen. Do as you are asked and the same will not happen to you. Do you understand?'

'Yes!'

The grip around her neck was released. Now she was free to fall backwards. She felt the impact in her restrained arms where the back of the chair banged into them as it hit the floor. She just managed to lift her head to protect it. That was the only movement she could make. A man still stood over her.

'You will be released from here. This does not mean you are free.'

Almost instantly, she was grabbed under her arms. Someone must have moved around behind her. She was yanked upwards. She yelped in pain when cruel fingers pinched the loose skin under her arms. She took her own weight in a squat as the chair was kicked out from under her. She straightened her legs and stumbled backwards — and would have fallen once again had someone not gripped her in a tight hold. She was immediately shoved to start moving. The door opened in front of her in a burst of light. She stumbled down the steps and back across the loose ground. The hood was tighter around her neck and she couldn't see the floor this time. She was still aware of the slope downwards, then the change in light and temperature. And the smell. It was instantly familiar. She was back in the tunnel structure. There was the sound of the door again, kicking and scraping as it was pulled open. She was pushed forwards then down to the floor and heard the sound of metal chains being gathered up.

'What is this? I thought I was being released. You said—'

The blow to her stomach pushed all of her air out in a rush, taking her voice with it. She gasped. Her top was lifted roughly. The freezing cold chains against her skin might have taken her breath away had it not already been knocked out of her. She was pushed back against the solid curve of the tunnel and she felt the hood snag at her ears as it was yanked off her head. Her chains were given one last tug to test them. Then the shadow in front of her stood up straight. His heels crunched as he spun on them. The next sound Linda heard was the young woman opposite crying out. Then the sound of chains being pulled free and discarded onto a solid concrete floor. The young woman's feet scuffed as she was pushed out, her breathing heavy and frightened. She already knew it was her turn.

The door skipped and dragged to a close and the darkness was complete. Linda still fought for her breath to return.

* * *

Maddie fixed Adrian Hughes with a firm stare. His eyes dropped away as he was led towards her at the custody desk, just like she knew they would. Much as she despised liars, she might have had a little more respect for him had he been brave enough to hold her gaze.

He looked smaller with his hands cuffed at the front and his shoulders rolled forwards. This wasn't necessary, not for this part of the process. It was a short walk out of his cell and back again, but Maddie had insisted he be put in handcuffs. She'd told the custody officer she wanted Hughes to have the full prisoner experience. She still stared at him as he rested against the custody desk, which was high enough to brush the top of his chest. His gaze might have been directed downwards, but she was certain he was aware of her stare. The desk sergeant's booming voice cut in from his elevated position on the other side.

'Adrian Hughes, we have a charge authorized by our colleagues at the CPS. You are required to listen to Detective Sergeant Ives who will read these charges. Any response you make will be noted by me and can form part of the evidence. Do you understand?'

Adrian lifted his head to nod. Maddie noticed a redness to his puffy eyes. It was the first real sign of emotion she had seen in him. This part was often emotive, of course; she had seen it many times before. The point of charge was the point where people realized that all the questions were over, that they were looking at nothing other than a long stretch in a succession of prison cells. The sergeant nodded to her and she focused on the words on the charge sheet that she held in her hand. She leaned in to talk directly into the ear that was turned towards her.

'Adrian Hughes . . . You are charged with the offence that, in May 2020, in the County of Lennockshire, you did murder an unknown female, contrary to Common Law. You do not have to say anything, but it may harm your defence if you do not mention *now*, something which you later rely on in court. Anything you do or say may be used in evidence.'

Adrian lifted his head. His eyes finally filled to the point of overflowing. They shifted to Maddie and the movement pushed a thick tear down his cheek.

'You don't understand,' he whispered. 'You couldn't possibly.' He turned his eyes back down to the floor. When he shook his head, it freed another tear.

Maddie was desperate to probe him, to ask what he meant — this was exactly where she had wanted to get him in the interview room. Those were the first spontaneous words he'd uttered since the moment they had met — in what finally felt like a deviation from the script. The sergeant shot her a warning look. He was a former detective himself and would sense her desperation to prompt him. She knew what the sergeant would say if he could, that the interviews were over, the charges read, and that any questions asked at the charge desk could only undermine any future legal proceedings. She and Hughes had both had their chance.

'Okay then . . .' the sergeant's booming voice cut back in. This time it was aimed at the custody officer who had brought the prisoner out and remained in the background. 'Could you put our friend here back in his cell, please? Make him a hot drink if required.'

The soles of Hughes's trainers squeaked as he turned and shuffled away — any opportunity for the whole truth disappearing along with him.

* * *

The next time the door was opened it was yanked rather than dragged, making such a sudden noise in the darkness that Linda jumped hard enough to make her chains rattle. The door let in a little light, just enough for her to see the outline of the young woman as she was pushed across the room to be dumped back on the same patch of ground she'd occupied before. She let out a little whimper as her chains were secured but she made no other sound. Linda reckoned she had been gone about the same amount of time as they had taken with her.

The monitor came on to her left. It flared bright white then settled to a dark grey with a spinning wheel, just as it had done before. Seeing the off-white spinning wheel appear, Linda looked away, fearing what she might see this time. She had seen terrible things as part of her job. But it was different seeing them here, knowing the footage could affect her so directly. She followed the movement of the man who was still pacing about the room. Somewhere over to her right, near to the door, he stopped, his hood up and facing away. He stood still, his feet shoulder width apart, his hands out of sight in front of him.

The screen flickered then the picture started moving. Linda braced herself. She still feared what she might see, but she knew she was supposed to watch it, that maybe they wouldn't let her leave until she had seen it.

When the picture came into focus, she could make out the interior of a car. The car was moving. There were glimpses of scenery and the camera shook as the vehicle moved over bumps. Again, there was no sound. The angle of the footage suggested it was from a camera held at shoulder or chest height. This time it filled the whole screen. She could make out two hands on a steering wheel positioned the way a driving instructor might teach. The left hand wore a wedding band made of a golden-looking metal. The angle was high enough that Linda could see out through the windscreen to where the top of a large gate now slid open from right to left. The word *FORD* was prominent in the middle of the steering wheel. When the gate disappeared entirely, the car moved forwards again. It went through the gateway and seemed to pull up between other parked cars. The camera shook again as it was lifted out of the car. It was then turned back towards the vehicle, so close that she could only make out the white roof and the blue lightbar that ran across it. The camera moved backwards, to show the side of the car in full. The camera stopped, giving Linda time to read the word *POLICE* — she had a sense that the pause was deliberate. The camera then shifted towards a large building. She recognized it instantly, a place she knew well, the enclosed rear yard of Canterbury Police Station. It was where she worked. Access from there was via a set of white, double doors. There was a security panel to the right side, a card had to be swiped for access. A hand reached out to rest a white card against the panel. A small light changed from red to green and the door pushed open.

The monitor froze then flared bright white again. As Linda looked away, her eyes fell on the young woman opposite. She was sitting up straight, her wide eyes staring right across at Linda as if she had been waiting to make eye contact.

'We're a t-team now,' the woman stammered, her voice full of fear. 'That's what they told me. They have ways of watching us — more than we can know. You have something to do, then I have something to do. And we get to watch each other. If you fail, I'll see. And then they'll bring you back . . . and you'll see what they've done to me . . .' Her voice broke. A tear ran down her cheek and she sniffed as she hung her head. It shook from side to side. 'Please . . . Please just do as they ask! Oh Jesus . . . don't let me die . . . not like that!'

Linda turned to where the hooded man was standing. He didn't react. The young woman had fallen silent, still looking at the floor. The light from the monitor reflected from her tear tracks. Linda knew that she had said what she had been asked to say. There would be no more talking.

There was a swift movement to Linda's right. The hood was thrust back over her head. She didn't resist, but it was no less rough. When she stumbled back out into the light, the sun felt a little weaker, as if it were late in the day. She walked further this time, past the running engine that had penetrated her captivity. She didn't think it was a bassy V8 anymore; it sounded more like a tinny lawn mower engine. She then felt the back of her head shoved downwards and her knees met with a spongey material as she was sent sprawling into the back seat of a car. She felt it move off the moment the door shut behind her.

The rocking movement of the car shifted Linda's hood a little. If she wriggled a bit, she might have been able to see some of the car's interior. She didn't try it. She had every intention of following the rules for now. She just wanted this to be over. And these men had been so careful to keep themselves hidden. She could only pray that this meant they intended on cutting her loose once her part in this was done — as long as she did as they asked.

For the first ten minutes or so, the car bounced and shook. It grinded at a couple of points when she felt something solid strike the underside and heard the driver curse. The hood slipped a little anyway, enough for her to stare down into a bland footwell littered with clumps of black rock and dirt. She kept her eyes down, even when the ride got smoother and the driver seemed to take that as his cue to speak.

'You just need to do as they ask.'

It was a male voice, possibly belonging to the same person who had warned her of the steps. She didn't reply — she didn't get the impression that the man was wanting a reply.

'I'm taking you to your car. You will find instructions in it. Just do as they say. Any deviation and . . . I've seen it, okay? These people . . . they don't mess about. If you're not straight down the line they'll just cut you loose and then move onto the next one.'

He stopped talking, maybe even for as long as a few minutes. The only sound was the revving engine and the occasional ticking of an indicator.

'And I think you know what I mean by "cutting you loose",' he said finally. 'You're staying home tonight. What they want from you — your task — will come to your door. Seven o'clock. Be there for it.'

'To my door?' Linda's words fell out of her mouth as a reaction. All she had been focusing on was getting home, closing her front door and regrouping. It was her safe place. Now she was being told that these people knew all about her safe place and that someone was coming there to speak to her. It suddenly didn't feel safe at all.

'Just be there. Just do what they say. I know what you saw, but you should know that people have walked away from all this, too. The people that just did what they were told are now getting on with their lives elsewhere. You can't beat this. You can't beat them.'

The man fell silent. It was some time before the ride turned bumpy again. The change was sudden and this time the terrain was worse, another unmade road or track. The car slowed to a crawl but the dips and bumps still pushed Linda against the harsh interior. She did her best to lock her legs, to stop her head banging against the back of the seat in front. After a couple of minutes, the ride became a little smoother. Then the light in the car dropped considerably.

'Keep the hood on. That hood comes off and everything changes. This is your first opportunity to show you can follow instructions.' The voice was a little different now . . . sterner.

A door opened then thumped closed. There was a moment of silence when Linda felt she'd been left alone. Then the door closest to her head popped open. She was pulled out of the car. The grip and her handling were less rough, as if she were being led rather than pushed. She walked a few paces. She could see out of the bottom of the hood again. The terrain looked to be dried mud on stone, interspersed with clumps of straw. She stopped when she was told and sensed her captor move away. She heard another car door being opened. Then she was led forwards and told to feel her way in. The vehicle was instantly familiar. She clambered up to sit behind the wheel of her own car.

'Hold the steering wheel. Both hands.'

She did as she was told.

'Count to one hundred. Loudly. When you get to one hundred you can let go of the steering wheel and take the hood off. You are being watched. If you remove the hood early, they will know and that will count as a deviation. I don't need to tell you what that means anymore. And not just for you, remember that.'

The door slammed shut before she had any chance to ask questions, to clarify. She gripped the wheel. The engine in the car from which she'd been pulled had been left ticking over. She heard it surge and knew the car was moving off from behind her. She started counting.

CHAPTER 11

'A charge, then, Detective Sergeant Ives — and for murder! Is that your first?'

'No, sir,' Maddie said.

DI Tristan Stepney was sitting at her desk, ensconced in her chair as if he had been there a while, waiting to show her his smug face. If she was curt, he showed no sign of noticing.

'Ah, yes. Quite the seasoned murder detectives down here, aren't we? You and Mr Blaker have a bit of a reputation up at Headquarters. Most of it good.' He grinned as if he had made a joke, but Maddie still wasn't sure.

She managed a flicker of a smile in return. But it was an effort.

'How did he take it?' Stepney went on, oblivious. 'Cry for his mummy, did he?'

'No.' Maddie paused for a moment. 'He told me there was something bigger, something that I didn't understand.'

'Isn't there always?' Stepney's feet thumped to the floor as he stood up. He made a show of dusting his hands. 'Another loser off the streets who can't chat up the opposite sex without a knife held to her neck . . . another case solved for Major Crime. A good day all in all, I would say. Not often you get a murder investigation in the can in just a couple of days. I'll be calling the chief personally about this one, DS Ives. You will be getting a special mention, of course.' He pointed at her with a hand shaped like a gun, winked and made a sound like he was clicking his tongue.

Maddie had expected no less. Even if Stepney hadn't been desperate for good results to get him out of whoever's bad books he was in, she reckoned he was still the sort to *personally* make the chief constable aware of his exploits. They would be his, too; she wasn't actually expecting a special mention, which suited her just fine.

'I appreciate that, sir. I do think the congratulations might be a little premature, however. There is still a lot of work to do.' Maddie said.

'Work? Evidence gathering is ongoing and then it's building a case file for a guilty plea. Nothing too onerous. Not for someone of your experience with murder cases. The sooner we draw a line underneath all of this, the sooner we can get back to the other cases blighting this department. We could do with closing a few more of those with such a positive outcome too, DS Ives. It's all about the figures. The chief looks at them daily, you know.'

'I'm not really happy to draw a line under this one just yet. There's a lot Hughes hasn't told me.'

'Maddie Ives!' Stepney fell back into her chair. He lifted one foot to rest on his knee and steepled his fingers together, the grin fixed on his face as he peered up at her. 'Some of your people out there said you wouldn't be happy. Perhaps you're never happy. Major Crime investigations are rarely neat and tidy — you just don't get answers to all the questions you might have. I've seen it before, with officers who are diligent at their core but also obsessed — not just with the truth but with the *make-up* of the truth. And sometimes there just isn't one. Sometimes a sick weirdo who can't talk to women just ups and murders one while they're out on their daily run. It happens. History has taught us that many times over. Our job then becomes putting them away quickly and effectively and, my goodness, have you done that! Fine work, DS Ives. Like I said, I will be telling the chief as much personally.'

'I'm not sure this is quite so neat and tidy, though, sir. What if there's another offender involved? I think there must be at least one other person who has knowledge of w—'

'There you go! Looking for work where there may not be any for you. It's admirable, really, not something I should criticize, but there is plenty of work out there on those other cases I mentioned.'

'Okay, but there are still lines of enquiry. We still don't know who the victim is—'

'The victim? I seem to remember a conversation in the custody suite earlier today where you were not bothered about the identity of the victim. Didn't think it was a reasonable line of enquiry?'

'That isn't what I—'

'Well, the image we put out made an immediate impact. While you were downstairs flogging your dead horse, we had a good few calls, all mentioning the same woman. I sent two of yours out to speak to the best of them — the victim's brother. He reported her missing a week ago. She was marked by us as low risk on Compact, which may prompt a question or two. I reckon I can head that off, though . . . I just need to find out who made that call to see if I can ruin their day!'

Compact was a separate computer system used for tracking missing-persons cases. The low-, medium- or high-risk moniker was applied by the uniform sergeant responsible for the team who took the report. Most were assigned low risk unless there were some suspicious circumstances or medical factors that made their disappearance more concerning. Experience in policing told Maddie that people often went missing out of choice: relationship breakups, work pressures, kids who were being prevented from seeing their mates or crushes — or sometimes just a desire experienced by a reasonable adult to step off the world for a few days. All were common, entirely understandable and nothing that should prompt a high-risk response. No doubt the sergeant who'd made the decision to class their victim as low risk had seen nothing in her case that they hadn't seen a million times before. There was still a look of glee on Tristan Stepney's face when he had talked of ruining this person's day.

'So we have a confirmed victim?' Maddie said.

'We will. The brother should be on his way to confirm ID as we speak and then we'll have dotted the i's and crossed the t's for your little case file.'

He gestured with a typing movement above her computer keyboard. Not for the first time, Maddie found herself taking a breath and swallowing her initial reaction. She was done with being patronized for now.

'Okay then, seems like this is all coming together,' she heard herself saying. 'Who in my team did you send out to the brother? I would like to check in with them.'

'Of course you would! Barry Carter and a female officer — I forget her name. I tasked Barry with it directly.'

'I'll see how they're getting on.' She spun away, reaching for the phone in her pocket.

'Barry Carter has almost twenty years as a detective of all things Major Crime, DS Ives,' Stepney called out behind her. 'I reckon that's more than the rest of this department put together — including the supervisors in here — don't you?' His tone had moved from patronising to carrying a slight edge.

Maddie turned back to him. 'He's an excellent detective.'

'Then he can be trusted?'

'No doubt about that.'

'When I was a lowly DC, there was nothing that caused me to lose respect for my sergeants or inspectors quicker than being micromanaged. That may be some time ago now, but I'd put a month's wage packet on it being the same today.'

'Thank you for the advice,' Maddie said.

'It's always free with me!' Stepney was grinning again. He stood up and dusted his jacket down. 'And this other offender that you have created in your mind . . . Unless you have real evidence of their existence — more than just a *feeling* from a twenty-minute conversation with a man wriggling on a hook — we shall be referring to him as "sleeping dog". Do you understand?'

'Sleeping dog?' Maddie repeated.

'That's it. And you know what they say about them, right? The guilty-plea case file comes to me to sign off when complete. I think it's reasonable to expect it to be with me by the end of the week — allowing time for CSI *et al.* to endorse it. I'll be reading your evidence summary with interest. I don't expect any mention of *sleeping dogs* in there. A good summary is one with an admission, evidence to confirm that admission and a charge with no loose ends. Am I clear?'

'I think so.'

'Excellent. I speak to your team, too. A lot. I know for a fact there are a lot of very experienced detective sergeants who would give their right arm to be in your position — people who could do a very good job in here, just like you are doing. Some of them have been working long enough to learn the lesson I mentioned about micromanaging. I am always in with your team, Maddie. I listen to what they say. I know the previous DI was a very strong supporter of you and your post in here. I can be the same.'

Can be. His message was not lost on Maddie.

'Best I get back to work then, sir.' Maddie said, meaning it as the strongest possible hint that she wanted to be left alone.

'That's the attitude!'

Maddie waited until he was out of the room to call Barry Carter's mobile. If he was upset about being *micromanaged*, he didn't sound like it at all. He was cheery if anything. He said they would be taking an account from the victim's brother and then they would have to go and see the body by arrangement. He even said there might still be time for Maddie to get there if she wanted to come out for herself. Even as she was taking down the brother's details from Barry, she was already considering going out to meet him for herself. But Barry's suggestion made it his idea, as if maybe he wanted her out there. Her eyes fell to the chair that DI Stepney had just vacated — *her* chair. She would go out. Barry was perfectly capable of taking an ID statement and dealing with everything that came with it, but he didn't know what had been said in her interviews with Hughes. He didn't know that there might be more to this. She could be damned sure that Tristan Stepney wouldn't have mentioned it to him.

Before she left, she was sure to swap her chair for another.

* * *

The pleasant ambience of a falling sun wrapped around Maddie the instant she got out of her car. It took just a few steps to snuff it out. Ashford Hospital loomed large in front of her and the change in temperature was marked. The evenings were still serving as effective reminders that summer had not arrived quite yet. She shrugged on her jacket and zipped it up, knowing that the temperature was about to fall much further. Already she could hear the mechanical whir of the fridges and air-conditioning units of the hospital area assigned as the morgue. It always seemed fitting to her that it was in the basement.

Here, the niceties of hospital interiors, if they could be called that, were entirely missing. The walk to the morgue was down a concrete slope that levelled out where concrete pillars and bare pipes provided the barren grey frame for the wards and treatment rooms enclosed above. She could see double doors some way ahead towards the back of the building. The walkway to get to them was flanked by big black squares made out of a canvas-like material with large zips running up their middle — all of which were tightly shut. Each of them showed white numbers, three down each side, lined up vertically and with their own swirling air-conditioning fan visible on top. The only flashes of colour were the words written in yellow on the face of each square: *OVERFLOW FRIDGE*. Maddie shivered. It wasn't just from the cold.

The double doors were heavy. A solid rubber edge dragged along the floor when she pushed them open. A technician was walking towards the door on his way out.

He looked surprised to see her. His hand jerked up to pull headphones out of his ears.

'Can I help?' he said.

Maddie lifted her warrant card. 'DS Maddie Ives. I understand my colleagues are here with a witness . . . to identify a body . . . Marie Foreshaw?'

'Marie . . . ah yes. The asphyx. Her visitors have been and gone, I'm afraid.' He shrugged and rolled his eyes. 'What can I say, I even offered to put the kettle on!'

'Gone?'

'Yeah, they didn't hang around. You tend to get two types of people for the ID bit. Some you can't get rid of and some you can barely get to sign back out again. He was the latter. You haven't missed them by much.'

Maddie now pulled her phone from her pocket. A text message had somehow snuck its way onto her screen: *We're all done. Meet you in the coffee shop at the entrance?* It was from Barry Carter, five minutes earlier. Maddie thanked the technician who continued on his way while Maddie typed out a quick reply. She had to walk back the way she had come to get to the main entrance. She passed the man she had just spoken to. He was already smoking while scrolling through his phone, his headphones were back to trailing from his ears and his foot was up against an overflow fridge where he was nonchalantly leaning. Maddie shook her head. She didn't think she could ever become so casual around the dead.

Barry Carter stood alone at the bustling entrance. 'We took the brother to a quiet room. The staff here are good. I just popped out to get him a coffee.'

'Are you finished with him?'

'Yeah, we've got a statement to confirm the ID. It's definitely Marie Foreshaw. Seems they were close, too. So we talked about the last few months and everything relevant . . . relationships, anyone she might have upset, any links to the offender — all the stuff you would expect. It took us a while — he's got the hump. I managed to convince him to answer the basics at least. Looks like he gives us nothing.'

'Nothing?'

'No links to the offender . . . no real answers as to why she might have been a target. He did confirm that she's a regular runner and he follows her on the Joggle app. They go out together a bit. He was able to show us what was visible on there, regarding his sister's runs. There's a clear pattern . . . the same route, and mostly the same days and times that she does it. Not a great way to keep yourself safe.'

'I'd like to talk to him.'

'Thought you might.' Barry grinned. 'The coffee's a ploy to stall him but he knows he can go any time. You might not get too much conversation from him.'

Maddie smiled back. She pulled a folded twenty from her pocket. 'The coffees are on me.'

Barry took it without hesitation. 'Well, you do earn the big bucks. He's in that room over there. You can see the door. He knows you're coming. I can't say he was too happy about it.'

Barry took a few steps towards the coffee counter.

'Barry!' Maddie called after him. Her tone must have been sharper than she intended; he spun around as if she had grabbed him. 'You know I trust you — to do the job, I mean. I'm not checking up on you or anything . . .' Maddie stumbled to a stop, feeling a little foolish.

Barry let her off the hook as his grin got wider. 'Tristan Stepney speak to you by any chance?'

'And to you?' Maddie said.

'All of us. Specifically, he said that he'd be willing to listen if anyone was concerned that they might be being "micromanaged" by their supervisors, or if anyone in the supervision team smacked of "lacking experience". We all get the impression that there is someone in Major Crime that he would like to replace. I was gonna mention it to you, Mads. A few of 'em might warn you. I think he would love it if someone went to him with an issue about you.'

'I think you're right.'

'He won't get it from me.'

'That's good to know.'

'Or anyone else, I don't reckon. Bad enough losing the boss, let alone his other half going, too.'

'Other half?'

'You and Blaker. It was a standing joke at one point. He never worked with anyone else — nor did you. It's not so funny now.'

'It's not.'

'He has a reputation — Stepney, I mean. Divide and conquer. He's toxic for whatever department he's working in. We would all rather he fucked off.'

The hospital foyer was busy with people pushing past, some walking right into their conversation. An elderly woman stopped at the profanity and stared at the transgressor.

'Sorry, love. But if you can't swear in one of these places . . .' Barry chuckled and the woman nodded. She continued her walk.

'I've heard the same.' Maddie sighed. 'Not much we can do right now, though, Barry. Keep your head down and do as he says. That's my advice.'

'He tasked us to come out here. Said that there was no need to tell you about it, that he would let you know. He gave us both the impression that he didn't want you coming out here at all. Did he tell you the same?'

'Pretty much.'

'And here you are! That's the reason he won't get any complaints from me. Some supervisors lead by getting the rest of us to do the shit bits, the bits they don't wanna do — like talking to an angry grieving bloke who reported his sister missing long before she turned up dead. But here you are. Don't ever change, Maddie Ives.'

'I might have left you to it if I'd known he was angry!' she called after Barry, who turned his grin towards the queue for the coffee.

She headed for the door he had pointed out. She considered knocking but opted just to bundle through. DC Jane Mayers was on the phone and gestured a *hello* to her sergeant.

A man was seated at the table, his head hanging forwards from his strong shoulders. His posture put Maddie in mind of a drunk at the end of the night. And, in keeping with some drunks she had dealt with, he snatched at her presence with more than a little hostility.

'You must be Colin.' She was keen to get in first.

'And you must be Sergeant Ives — the reason I'm still here.'

'I guess so. Sorry about that.'

'You should be. This might be the last place on earth I want to be right now.'

'I understand that. I am sorry. I want to find out exactly what happened to your sister so the person who did this goes away and stays away. That's all I care about. I'm pretty sure that's all you care about too.'

'Any chance you can put him away in a wooden box? That's pretty permanent.'

'Just off the streets will do me. For now at least.'

'Ha! Like you would. You cops will say anything to get what you want.'

'I'm here to get what we both want.'

'So how am I supposed to help with that? I answered all their questions. I couldn't give them anything of any use. The bloke out there told it to me straight . . . some random weirdo was stalking her. He caught up with her on a run and that was that. He . . . What I just saw in there . . . that's what he did. Did you see her?'

'I saw her picture, Colin. I know this must be diffic—'

'Don't even say it! Don't even tell me how sorry you are, how hard this must be for me and my family! Don't even tell me . . . I reported her missing a whole week ago and do you know what has happened since then?'

'Fuck all,' Maddie finished. His lips had already been forming the *F*; she'd seen it coming and taken it right out of his mouth. It was an escalation word, one that you could put some real energy into, one that could only have made him angrier. He looked surprised momentarily, then a little calmer.

'Exactly that. Not a great day for the police, is it?'

'No. Sums this job up, to be honest. Some days are like that, but the thing about being caught on the back foot is how you respond.'

'The back foot? Is that what you call it when someone dies? It's a little different for me, for my mum and dad. I have to go and see them now. I have to tell them. My dad . . . He doesn't understand so well anymore. We've been struggling with him. I can't tell you what this will do to him. I know he'll forget . . . I know we'll have to tell him again . . . over and over . . .' His eyes glazed over as if he were lost in his thoughts.

'They don't know?'

'My mum does. She watches the news. My dad . . . it can be on when he's in the room but it doesn't register. You have to be direct with him. They've been getting calls from other people too. Aunts and uncles . . . family friends . . . all telling them that the mugshot of the murdered girl on the telly is their daughter. My mum's terrified of answering the phone or the door anymore. She still hasn't sat Dad down and told him. That's gonna be hard. She can't leave him at home. It's why she's not here . . . that and she wasn't sure she'd be able to cope with it all. This is going to knock him, my dad. This could be the final nail.'

'It would knock any family. But we're more resilient than you might appreciate — people, I mean. They still surprise me on a regular basis. Your dad might be stronger than you realize.'

Colin suddenly threw himself back in the chair. He patted the pockets of his jeans like he was checking he had all he needed. His eyes regained their focus, seeking out the door. 'I should get back to them. You got any more questions for me or what?' He stood up.

'My mate out there . . . he told me that you went running with your sister sometimes?' Maddie said quickly.

Colin took a moment. Then he leaned forwards, reaching out to take his weight on his palms, his eyes down to the table.

'You've got him.' His voice was low, so low that Maddie had to lean in to pick out the words. But the vitriol in his tone was still clear.

'Got him?'

'The loser. The piece of shit that did this. Your mate said you've got him. He came in and told you all about it like he was showing off. It was nothing you lot did. He just walked right in and fessed up. So why the hell do I need to be answering more questions on how me and my sister went running? We know what he did, *you* know what he did because he walked in and told you!' The emotion was back now as was the anger. Maddie needed to control it.

'He did. He walked right in and told us he murdered a girl who was a stranger to him. I've been at this a long time, so I know that's not an easy thing to do. Not without anyone else knowing what he was doing — maybe even helping. If someone had even the slightest inkling of what he was planning and they did nothing to stop it, I want to know about it. And I will prosecute them every bit as hard as the man we have in custody.'

'You think there was someone else?'

'He says he was on his own. The easiest thing for me would be to take him at his word, to charge him to court and then write up my paperwork as case solved. Job done. But I owe your sister better than that. I want to be sure.'

'Okay then. I'm listening.' He pushed off the table to stand up straight and cross his arms. He was easy to read. She might have bought a few minutes of his time but everything about his stance was saying, *this had better be good.*

'My mate talked to you about a running route. Did you go on that route with Marie?'

'Yeah, not all the time. She was bang into her running, but I never get the time. Or I make a lot of excuses — that was what she said.'

'Did you do it recently? That run?' Maddie persisted.

'A month ago, maybe. That was the last time. I've only been doing it the last few months, since she split up with her last fella.'

'Did my mate take details of who that was? Her ex, I mean.'

'Yeah. Bit of a nob but, I mean . . . not like this. No way he would want her dead.'

'What happened for them to split?'

'She was upset, actually. Blokes don't bother her too much normally. She always had a bit of an ice queen vibe going on when it came to blokes. You know what I mean? Tough nut to crack. But she liked this one. Friend of a friend, I think. I met him a couple of times when they were out on the town. I could see straight away that he was a bit of a player, I knew it wasn't going to be a long-term thing — but not for me to tell her, right?'

'Player?'

'You know what a player is.'

'I know what I *think* a player is. Never hurts to check.'

'A player. Enjoys the chase but, once that's done, they tend to move on. Chase someone new. Not always before they cast off the last one. I saw them out together when they had been official for, like, two weeks and he was already looking out.'

'Looking out?'

'Yeah, it's a phrase. You know you're in a good relationship because all you're doing is looking in. You can be in a room full of women but you don't even see them. I'm lucky. I've had that a while. But I've got mates who are constantly looking out — outside of what they've got. That was him.'

'So, he ended it?'

'Yeah. But no cheating that we know of. I ain't saying that.'

'But you suspect?'

Colin shrugged. 'How would I know? I barely knew the fella. I know my sister, though . . . she woulda said if he was doing the dirty, and she didn't. She didn't talk about it much, though. Like I said . . . she's normally the one calling the shots with the blokes. I think this was a bit of a new experience for her.' His face contorted. He'd suddenly remembered why they were there. 'Now she doesn't get to find happiness, does she? Marriage, kids . . . family life. I used to take the mickey about how cold she was, but I know she wanted all that. I think we all do deep down.'

'And he was a friend of a friend you said?'

'Yeah. One of her mates at work.'

'Where did your sister work?'

'She's a social worker. Social Services. She works with some real needy families. Families with wife-beaters, kids with issues — little terrors, some of them. Some of the stories she could tell . . . she loved it. But I always said that was why she couldn't settle. She got to see the worst of family life. I had to keep telling her that it ain't all like that.'

'And you don't know of any connection that she might have had with her killer — Adrian Hughes? Any way she could've known him?'

'No. Your mate showed me his mug — don't show it to me again!' He fixed his eyes on her, his stare carrying a warning in case she had missed it in his tone.

'It's okay. There's no need.'

'I don't want anyone to clap eyes on him ever again. I want to know that he's rotting in a dark cell somewhere. That's all.'

'He's got the shock of his life coming — trust me on that. He is not a man suited to life in prison.'

'Good.'

Barry Carter bundled through the door. The thud and his appearance carrying a carefully balanced tray suggested that he had needed to use his foot to open it.

'Sorry! The queue isn't long out there but they're not in any rush!'

He handed out the drinks one by one.

'Thanks, Barry,' Maddie said.

Colin Foreshaw settled back into his seat. His haste to leave seemed to have passed.

He looked at Barry. 'Listen, mate . . . I was pissed off — I mean, I am pissed off — but I was a dick earlier. I know you're doing your job and I didn't mean to take it out on you.' He spun in his seat to where DC Jane Mayers had quietly finished her call and had remained standing. 'You, too, love. I'm not a dick, I'm just a bit . . .'

'Not a problem, Colin,' Jane said. 'I know what it looks like. But there was nothing to suggest she was at ris—'

'I know.' Colin's tone was accepting and a long sigh followed. 'She's an adult. She can take herself away for a while. She doesn't need to pick up the phone to me, to any of us. But when she didn't turn up at work . . . I spoke to some girl there that I tracked down on Facebook. Saw she had liked some stuff my sis put up — most of what she put up. She told me she couldn't get hold of Marie either. She agreed it was out of character. I mean, she can ignore her brother — she's done that before — but not her mates. I knew it was wrong. I get why the cops didn't . . . I couldn't really put it into words myself.'

'The girl you spoke to . . . what's her name? Has Barry got details of her too?'

'Nah, I didn't talk to Barry so much. Like I said, I was a bit of a dick before you got here.' His face offered the flicker of a smile. 'When he said that the sergeant was on the way up, he said it like when I was at school, when they used to say, like, "if you don't behave, we'll go get the headmistress." They said I would talk to you. They built you up like some mega-bitch. I thought you was gonna come in here all guns blazing!'

Both of Maddie's colleagues were doing a poor job of concealing their grins.

'I guess it was lucky for you that you warmed up a little,' Maddie smiled wryly. 'You know, before I had to get angry.'

'I guess so. So, what happens now?'

'It's like I told you . . . I want to be sure that this all starts and ends with the man we have in custody. If anyone else had so much as an inkling, I'll find them and they'll see what a mega-bitch looks like!'

'Ends . . .' Colin's strong frame seemed to slump. His shoulders fell forwards, his arms rested on the table as if he couldn't hold them up anymore. It was as if all of his strength had slipped away in one moment.

'Sorry . . . poor turn of phrase,' Maddie said.

'But it isn't, is it? It's bang on. Just like that . . . it all ends. She has.' His hand reached out to fiddle with the sugar sachet balanced on top of his coffee cup.

'And your parents, Colin . . . they're going to have questions. I can come out with you. We can speak to them together. If nothing else, it gives them someone to be angry at. Someone who isn't you. It tends to go better when it comes from a copper. Maybe it would register better with your dad, too — if it came from someone he doesn't know?'

Colin sat back up to stare at Maddie. He chewed on his bottom lip and his eyes slowly widened as if he was considering it. 'You would do that?'

'Anything I can do to make this easier.'

'I think that it would.' His words dripped with relief. 'What time is it? It's teatime — they'll be settled in for the night . . .' The relief was suddenly gone; he looked agitated again.

'There's never going to be a good time, Colin. I say we go and get this done. If we don't do it now, you're still going to be talking to your mother anyway. I imagine she's waiting by the phone right now. Am I right?'

'She will be, yeah. It's not like it's a normal evening, is it? She knows where I am. She wanted to know if she could come and see Marie tomorrow.'

'Did you ask down at the . . . downstairs?'

'Yeah. They said Marie's booked in at eleven. For a post-mortem. So Mum would need to be there before then. I guess she's better off seeing her before your lot chop her up . . .'

'It's not a nice thing to think about. I get that. It's a respectful process — as much as it can be. But think of it as evidence gathering, because that's exactly what it is. That process could be the last thing we need to throw the book at the man who took her life. I can't tell you how important that is.'

'And you'll tell Mum about that? About the post-mortem . . . about what it means? She's already talked about it. That might even be what she's most upset about. She doesn't want Marie touched, not until she sees her at least.'

'She won't be. She'll be resting until the morning. The timings are strict. It's a slick process. But I will talk to your mum about it. I'll go through it all with her. She can get angry, that's okay. This is an emotional time, but it's better she does that at me than at you. You're going to need each other, Colin.'

'Thank you. I think it will really help. Fuck, I was dreading it.'

'Then that's what happens next. Did you bring your own car up here? I can follow you back or give you a lift?'

Colin's eyes flicked to his watch. 'It's late. Have you been on all day?'

'Major Crime isn't really a job for people who want a nine to five. It's fine. This is important.'

Colin held eye contact with her for the longest period yet. 'Thank you,' he said.

CHAPTER 12

THE MOBILE PHONE STRAPPED TO YOUR DASH IS SENDING A LIVE STREAM DIRECTLY TO US. WE CAN SEE AND HEAR EVERYTHING YOU DO. THIS IS WHERE YOU WILL PUT THE PHONE WHEN YOU ARE DRIVING. AT YOUR HOME, YOU WILL SEE FIXED CAMERAS. THESE ARE NOT TO BE MOVED OR OBSTRUCTED. YOUR OWN PHONE IS ON THE PASSENGER SEAT. WE ARE NOW ABLE TO MONITOR ITS USE.

WE HAVE ACCESSED YOUR HOME, YOUR PHONE AND YOUR CAR. DO NOT ASSUME FOR ONE MOMENT THAT THE DEVICES YOU SEE ARE THE ONLY ONES WE HAVE.

YOU WILL ALSO FIND A BUTTONHOLE CAMERA ATTACHMENT ON THE SEAT WITH INSTRUCTIONS FOR USE. YOU WILL USE THIS AT ALL TIMES WHEN NOT IN YOUR CAR OR AT YOUR HOME.

DO NOT DEVIATE.

Linda looked up from the printed text. She had read it so many times she could almost recite it word for word. No matter how many times she read it, it didn't become any less terrifying.

She had finished her count to one hundred, then repeated it just to be sure before removing the hood. She was in an open-sided barn of some sort. Her car had been parked tight against the wall at the front with the shell of an ancient-looking tractor close behind. It had taken a few minutes of manoeuvring to get it out. She figured the car had been left in such a tricky spot on purpose, removing the option for her to go hurtling after the car that had brought her here, had she decided this was the best course of action. Nothing had been further from her mind. She had stayed far longer than instructed, finding comfort in the knowledge that every passing minute was another minute where they, whoever they were, put distance between them and her. Her own phone was indeed on the seat next to her. It had been snatched from her on her abduction. It was switched off. She turned it back on now.

There was only one track to follow. There were no other buildings in sight, not even a farmhouse or an enclosed barn. There were no signs of animals either and the only suggestion this might still be a working farm came from the machinery she passed, although most of that was in bits and covered with established layers of rust.

The rutted track led finally to a public road, but the scenery remained very rural: tight country lanes with high banks that looked to be struggling to hold back the regular pockets of thick woodland. It took a few miles of driving to get any clue as to where she was and this came in the form of a tattered-looking, white-backed sign announcing the village of Elham. She recognized this as being on the outskirts of her home city. It took another few minutes to find her way to the A260 and from there to the A2 and a direct route to Canterbury.

The whole time, the rear of the phone was facing her from where it had been left in its holder. On a couple of occasions, the cover of the trees caused the light to dip enough that she caught sight of the phone's screen reflected in the windscreen. It was a reminder that she was still being recorded. She remembered the words of her captor: *You will be released from here. This does not mean you are free.*

The presence of the camera in her car had been unnerving. But worse was to come when she finally made it back inside the confines of her own home. She lived in a spacious, second-floor flat close to Canterbury's Marlowe Theatre, with a view of the River Stour as it weaved its way under the medieval cobbles. She loved this area of the city and had adored her flat from the moment she had first walked through its grand, communal entrance. She had bought it outright with a lump sum inherited from her parents. It was the one positive to have come out of an awful situation.

And now she found herself staring at an alien webcam fixed upright on the windowsill in her living room. There was another in her bedroom covering the door and her bed. In the kitchen, she'd found that a panel in her back door had been smashed. The floor was scattered with pieces of glass — left where they had fallen — and some looked to have been crushed smaller by heavy footsteps. Two more webcams covered the kitchen area. It was the largest room in the house, where she had taken down walls and lost a bedroom. She checked the bathroom quickly and was almost thankful that at least she couldn't see one in there.

She fought back tears. This wasn't the time. She needed to tidy up the glass and get something to drink — something strong. The sound of the glass falling from the dustpan into the bin was harsher than she'd anticipated and it made her jump. It also jogged a realization in her and she lifted her eyes to the oversized clock on the wall: it was just a few minutes to seven o'clock. She moved back into the living room. From there, she could see down a short hall to the front door. She consoled herself in the knowledge that the communal door had a camera; they would need to buzz in first.

The window in the living room had a glow about it that came only when a warm day was giving its last hurrah. It was wide open. She was eager to get fresh air circulating after sitting for so long in a still, stale environment.

From here, she could hear the flowing of the river past her window and the calls of birds, any number of which were attracted to its banks. The winter had been one of the wettest on record and the river was fatter and richer than normal. The birds seemed determined to make sure they ended up the same.

Her building contained six flats. All were owned, four were occupied all year round. Prices meant that the occupants needed to be affluent. Security was correspondingly tight. The communal entrance was on the other side of the building. The buzzer had a harsh tone — like an electric shock — and she tensed, listening for it now. She found she was holding her breath and told herself off as a result. She stood up and walked to the window. From there, she could get a glimpse of the cobbled pavement of the high street. At the right time of day, she could wave as tourists were punted past on little boats by students dressed in traditional attire and earning a little extra to fund their time at one of the city's universities. Away from the high street were the good-sized grounds that housed her block.

She thought about Friday morning, the last time she'd been home. Before she left for work, she had watched the groundsman on his ride-on mower. She'd been peacefully eating her breakfast. He had just started a new pattern — it was a different one every two weeks through the spring and summer. The delicious smell of cut grass had mingled with the sounds of the lazy mower and fresh, running water to make her wish she didn't have to go to work at all. She remembered thinking that so clearly. If she had known in that moment what the day had in store for her, she would have done anything to avoid the bad dream ahead — a nightmare of metal chains, cold surfaces, pain and darkness. She looked down at the camera in the middle of the windowsill. It had a red light that seemed to flicker in time with the movement in front of it. This was so much worse than a bad dream. It was real — all of it.

A fist thumped the door.

It was firm, angry almost. Her hand shot to her mouth instinctively, a whimper still escaped her lips. She scolded herself under her breath. She held onto the thought of being watched and used it to make herself determined. She didn't want to show weakness. She considered that her captors would surely be watching now and they might even delight in her fear.

She paced across to the front door. It thumped again. She felt it this time as a vibration through the door handle. She pulled her hand away and steadied herself. The peephole out into the corridor was pitch-black; the communal buzzer had never gone off. She was just going to have to open up.

'Did you have to hit my door quite so hard?' Linda was bullish as she wrenched it open, instantly barking out at the threat, sending a message that she wasn't to be intimidated. She stood down immediately. Then took two slow steps back, her mouth falling open when she tried to utter words. Nothing came.

'Surprise!' The face in the corridor lit up with a beaming smile coupled with arms outstretched. Then the smile started to drop away quickly. 'I tried to think of something a bit more original to say, but you can't beat the classics. You okay, Ma?'

'Okay?' Linda's mind raced. 'H-Hope . . .' She stammered her daughter's name as if it had just come to her. 'You're a-away . . . India . . .'

'I was, but obviously I'm not now.'

'How did you . . . ?'

'What? Get in? I know all your neighbours, Ma. But, as it happened, there was some fella working on the door. He said he was supposed to come up here after anyway so he asked if I would give this to you.' Hope clumsily held out an envelope; the flared sides of her backpack seemed to get in the way. Linda had picked it out when Hope had first announced that she was going travelling. Linda's reaction was typical *mother*. She read far too many *travel-backpack* reviews online, trying to work out which options were best.

Her searches had come up with results for other things, such as, *how to keep safe when travelling as a lone female* along with examples of some genuine horror stories. Linda had done her best to ignore them. It wasn't like she was ever going to talk Hope out of it and, besides, she had no right to. Now the backpack looked and sounded heavy as it dropped to the floor. Hope still held out the envelope. Linda didn't take it. Not straight away.

'I don't think it's a bomb, Ma. Honestly, are you okay?'

'Some fella? What fella?'

'Some maintenance fella. Overalls, chiselled jaw, older but kinda good-looking in that rough and ready sort of way. The sort of bloke I was thinking you might wanna take a can of Diet Coke down to, if you get what I mean.' Hope was back to beaming now. She had such a beautiful smile; it lit her big eyes and, in turn, lit up her whole face. She knew it, too. Linda had seen her consciously use that smile to get what she wanted. She was still holding out the envelope, her smile fading with every moment that passed while her mother kept her hands by her side. 'Everything okay? Do you want me to open it?'

'No!' Linda snatched hold of it now. It was almost an involuntary movement. She instantly played it down. 'It's fine. I just know it's a bill is all. All the residents . . . we all have to pitch in.'

'A bill?'

'For . . . for the door. For fixing it.'

'Do you not pay maintenance here already?'

'Yes, of course. But the management company were dragging their feet and a few of the residents were worried that people could just walk in. It's no issue — it's not much.'

'And you wouldn't want just *anyone* walking in!'

Linda smiled. The initial shock was ebbing away a little and she stepped in to wrap her daughter up in a tight hug. She felt Hope grab her just as tight. Linda inhaled the scent of her daughter's hair and felt a wave of emotion that nearly leaked out as a sob. She held it back, knowing this reaction would be out of character. She was damned sure that Hope had never seen her cry.

'It's so good to have you back,' she said instead. She took Hope by the shoulders to look into her eyes. 'Even if it is two months early? And you feel thin — slim, I mean! Have you been eating well?'

'No! I ate terribly. But always enough, I promise you that. Then I worked it all off on incredible hikes or out on the water . . . I took up climbing, too. It took me twenty-two years to find something I love *and* I'm good at. Climbing is really just a big strategy game that happens to make your shoulders ache.'

'So why leave two months early? Did you run out of money?'

'I ran out of money almost straight away, Ma — it seemed to be the thing to do. Everyone was doing it. But that's not it. I hooked up with a good group and I changed my plans to move round with them and then their journey kind of came to an end. There were a few stragglers left, but they were going in different directions so it was a case of start out on my own again or come home in time for my mum's fiftieth. So I cut it short. It always bothered me that I was going to miss your birthday. We had a big night for my friends' last night and when I woke up in the morning in a beautiful place with a bit of a muzzy head, I suddenly realized that I had no sense of direction. At that point, I decided it was time to come home. I figured I could regroup and plan my next big adventure. Flights back can be a bit hit and miss on a budget — you can't get much direct. I made the decision just over a week ago. I put out on Instagram for a lift back here when the flight was confirmed. I swore everyone to secrecy, but I still can't believe I made it all the way to your front door without anyone telling you! It was a pretty public chat. I half expected you to be the one that picked me up from the airport.'

'I didn't . . . I didn't have a clue . . . So it was on your Instagram page?'

'Me hawking for a lift was, yeah. One thing travelling the world teaches you is that people help people — they want to. It's a wonderful thing to know. When you sit down and put the news on, it's, like, all bad. But that's not how it is. People are inherently good. Some even do things for nothing.'

'Not everyone, though, Hope. Remember that . . . there are bad people too. Not everyone wants to help you.' Linda had taken hold of her daughter by her shoulders again. Her grip was too hard, the intensity in her voice was too much.

'I know that! Jeez, Ma, you're the worst for seeing the bad in people. You need to change your job.'

Linda released her daughter. Perhaps now wasn't the time for a lecture about putting her plans all over social media. The fact that bad people must have been looking at it was all her mother's fault. She had brought this threat into their lives. She still didn't know the reason why. She gripped the envelope tightly.

'So . . . is it okay to stay for a little while — you know . . . back in the old room? Or if you are going to chuck me out, can I at least use your loo? It's been a long journey, see.'

Linda suddenly realized that they were still standing in the doorway and she was pretty much blocking Hope's access. She stepped aside, doing her best to smile.

'Of course! Sorry, love. This has all caught me out a little bit. What a surprise! A lovely surprise! Get yourself a shower maybe or freshen up. Have you eaten?'

'Not since the plane. I thought I would shout you a takeaway if you hadn't? And by *shout*, I mean order one using your credit card! Seriously, you won't have to lift a finger.' The smile-that-could-get-you-anything was back.

Linda nodded then felt a peck on her cheek.

'Oh, and what's going on with the chess? It's your go!' She lifted her phone to waggle it at her mother. They were playing a game on a chess app — a way to feel connected, despite being a world away.

'Yes, I know. It's been a busy couple of days.'

Hope rolled her eyes then moved across the living room. Linda's heart stopped when she saw her daughter cross in front of a digital camera she had missed with her initial sweep. It was concealed against the side of the television and was the same colour. It had been pointed out to cover the hall, perhaps, as well as the rest of the living room. It held Linda's attention and sucked all of the joy out of her. For just a moment she had almost forgotten. The sound of the bathroom door closing snapped her back to grim reality.

She ran the envelope through her hands to find the seal. She tore at it and a single piece of paper pulled free. She checked the envelope. There was nothing else inside. She cast a last glance down the hall, where her daughter had disappeared to. Then the boiler fired up; Hope must have started the shower running.

Linda focused on the piece of paper. It was folded and felt thin, cheap — almost greasy to the touch. She opened it up to find a small block of printed text on one side. The font was the same as the note left in her car. She had to take a breath. Her hands were shaking.

THERE ARE PEOPLE WATCHING YOU. THEIR LIVES DEPEND ON YOUR ACTIONS. THEY WATCH YOUR EVERY MOVE. AND SO DO WE.

YOUR DAUGHTER DEPENDS ON YOU THE SAME.

DO NOT THINK THE CAMERAS YOU CAN SEE ARE THE ONLY METHODS WE HAVE.

DO NOT THINK YOU CAN RUN.

DO NOT THINK YOU CAN DEVIATE.

YOU ARE THE CPS LEAD FOR OP ICICLE.

MONDAY MORNING YOU WILL RETURN TO YOUR PLACE OF WORK AND YOU WILL CAPTURE THE NAMES AND RELOCATION ADDRESSES OF THE THREE LIVE CASES WITH THE EQUIPMENT PROVIDED.

YOU WILL THEN AWAIT FURTHER INSTRUCTION.

DO NOT DEVIATE.

WE HAVE TWO CHAIRS READY IN A PLACE THAT WILL NEVER BE FOUND.

ONE CHAIR FOR YOU. ONE FOR HOPE.

Linda tore her eyes from the letter to face down the webcam on her windowsill. Then her eyes lifted to search the rest of the flat. Suddenly everything looked unfamiliar, like she was standing in someone else's home. Worse still, everything now looked like a camera or a listening device. The smoke alarm, the alarm sensors up in the corner of the room . . . In her line of work, she had even read about a stalking case where the screw of a light switch had been replaced with a tiny camera. It had amazed her then. It terrified her now.

She would never find them all, not for certain. And not when she was pretty sure that any attempt to even look for them would be treated as a clear deviation. *Do not deviate.* She need only do what they asked. She read the note again. One part stood out: *Op Icicle.* This had been lauded as her finest professional achievement. Even she had thought of it that way — right up to this moment. Now she was having to consider just how flawed it might be, that it might not be capable of doing the one and only thing it was set up to do — keep vulnerable families safe.

Op Icicle was around eighteen months old and, like all the best ideas, it had been conceived from a passionate determination to do the right thing. She could clearly remember the morning when she had come in to find a uniform police officer sitting on the wrong side of her desk. He had stationed his chair there and met her with a look conveying he was not to be moved. It was the first time they had met. He was as apologetic as he was determined. She knew she had a reputation among the rank and file police officers: they were scared of her. She secretly liked that. It cut down on time wasted. She knew that anyone who dared approach her with a case file or query would have been everywhere else, tried everything else and genuinely needed her expertise.

That morning, the officer had been PC Ian Hessey. He had been involved in a job overnight: a run-of-the-mill domestic violence case on the surface. A neighbour had called the police to report a disturbance next door. Ian and his response team had needed to force the door. The offender had resisted violently. After he was taken away, Ian had stayed behind to get statements from the victim and their young son. It had taken most of the night. The beaten and bruised woman had seemingly reached the point where she could stand it no longer and had finally reached out for help. She had given Hessey everything from the last four years. The violence and terror of the woman's home life had dripped from the pages of her account.

Straight away, Ian Hessey had been on the offensive, telling Linda that she needed to authorize the charge and remand the man in custody. But he had also splurged his ideas for keeping families safe in instances when offenders were released at the first hearing. It was a single stream of consciousness, as if he had been waiting for her, going over it again and again in his head. Now she was here, he couldn't hold it back anymore. She had listened, picking out what she could, not even bothering to try and stop him mid-flow. It was a diatribe about their approach to domestic violence in general, about how remanding an offender could make the situation worse, about how the police were powerless to actually keep victims *safe* once the legal process was complete. She had waited out this rant from an exhausted, emotionally affected officer, still damp from his night's work, and then watched his face change from rage to sudden self-awareness. He'd realized that he was sounding off at the most senior member of the Crown Prosecution Service in the region. His tone had switched back to apologetic. He seemed to stand down from his offensive posturing to wait for the inevitable, for Linda Morris to dress him down, to question who he thought he was . . . coming in here . . . ranting at her.

But she hadn't. Instead, they had got two strong coffees and talked it out. He had needed to start again, to calm himself and get his thoughts in order. But she had been impressed with him. Ian Hessey's passion was highly contagious, his ideas sensible and, with some development, she knew they could really make a difference.

Op Icicle was the eventual outcome of that conversation. Ian Hessey worked tirelessly, to the point where he was taken off his response job and moved into the CID office where he was given the time and resources to dedicate himself to it entirely. Linda agreed to act as the CPS representative and later it became a truly multi-agency effort when housing, Social Services, education reps, legal services and probation completed a panel of professionals. Their purpose was simple: identify those families most at risk from offenders of domestic violence and get them to safety. The criteria were strict: the offender had to be remanded but with a high possibility of release at the first hearing; there had to be children in the household as well as a firm belief that the offender posed a serious threat to the lives of their family when released. Linda, Ian and the rest would then relocate the family — hide them, with everything in place before that remand hearing. They would also get all of the legal papers and processes completed to ensure that a restraining order was also live. The whole thing had been lauded as a success, closing off an oversight in the process. Theirs had become a pilot area. The scheme had been given the name 'Op Icicle' and was now very likely to be rolled out to other forces.

But it was far from perfect. Of course, offenders had been released from remand prison and immediately gone on the hunt for their families. One had landed himself almost straight back in custody for attacking police officers, his rage tangible and inconsolable. All he could see was that his family had been hidden away while he was in prison, despite the fact that he was never convicted. The police had no right. But his rage was not only directed towards them; towards his own family it was worse — exacerbated by the knowledge that they had to have been complicit. His threats towards both were real.

But Op Icicle was still running. Some of the senior police officials who had offered their support initially had started to back away. One even suggested that the threat of serious harm might actually be increased by the process. Linda had dug her heels in. The observation only served to justify Op Icicle all the more. These men, as they invariably were, could be as full of rage as they wanted, just as long as they never found their families.

'Long letter, is it?' Hope interrupted. Linda didn't know how long she had been standing there, lost in her own thoughts. She stuffed the letter back in its envelope and forced a smile.

'Not really.'

'Expensive then?'

'Expensive?'

'Your door repairs? How much are they stinging you for it?'

'Oh . . . a couple of hundred, nothing major.'

'For a door! Is that each? What are you getting — gold plating?'

'I think it must be something like that.'

Hope collapsed onto the sofa. Her hair was wrapped up in a towel and she had changed into a snug-looking onesie. 'Expensive evening, then. What with a two-hundred-pound door and a hungry daughter with a Just Eat app!' She waggled her finger over her smart phone.

'I'm sure I can cope. I'll just go get my purse.' Linda walked along the back of the sofa to her bedroom. She closed the door behind her, suddenly craving the privacy to break down. She felt like she was about to go over the edge, but then her eye was dragged to the slim camera facing her from her dressing table. There was nowhere left for her, nowhere she could be on her own, nowhere she could get the space she needed to think. She still gripped the letter. She knew what it meant and she knew it left her no choice. Her task was simple enough: she just needed to go to her place of work and point her phone at a computer screen.

But her mind flashed back to that arrest. To that rage, to those threats made to his own family when he found them. She remembered his name now: Malcolm Grant, a shaven-headed beast of a man with a full sleeve tattoo who had fought them all the way. Even his custody mugshot featured the hands of several officers who had been required to restrain him while it was taken. She remembered his reply when he was charged: *I will find them. I will kill them.*

His defence solicitor had managed to pass it off as a heat-of-the-moment remark and the judge had suspended any further sentence. Grant was set free with a warning about his future conduct. The judge had used the fact that his family were in a location unknown to Grant as a large part of his reasoning.

'They are safe,' he had said, as part of his summing up.

Linda knew that their safety now depended entirely on her.

* * *

For Maddie Ives, her final approach to the office, on a shift that had started more than fourteen hours earlier, was in darkness. It was just gone nine p.m. The civilian staff and officers on day shift had long since left for their homes, leaving just the late turn and now the poor bastards coming in to start their night shift. She would often see the end result of a night shift: officers trudging out at seven a.m., blinking at the sun, their eyes sore from a whole shift fighting the natural instinct to sleep when it was dark. It was a regular reminder of how lucky she was not to regularly have to spend all night at work.

Today had been a long one for her, however, and she was every bit as exhausted as her nocturnal co-workers. Today wasn't about the physical demands of such a long shift, it was the emotional impact that had left her feeling flattened. And sad. She had just left the comfortable home of Marie Foreshaw's parents, having confirmed their worst possible fears. She didn't think she would ever get used to such conversations or the nervous tension on the drive to get there, knowing that it didn't matter how she delivered her next words; they were sure to crush a family in an instant. You couldn't sugar-coat the premature death of somebody's only daughter, not when she'd died in terrible panic, alone in a decrepit building. Maddie could offer them no assurances to the contrary. Instead, she had told them everything she knew. She owed that family the truth — all of it, a complete enough version that it wouldn't prolong their agony with unanswered questions.

Colin Foreshaw had warned her that his dad's mental state was in decline, that it might take a few goes to explain. It had been playing on her mind as she entered their home. She'd declined the offer of a hot drink in her eagerness to just say what they needed to hear straight away. 'No delay,' she'd insisted. 'Let's get this done.'

Colin's dad surprised them all. Sharp as a tack, he took in every word, processing what it all meant more quickly than his wife. Maybe the illness played a part in his acceptance. He never once asked if Maddie was sure, insisted that she must be wrong or told her that she was lying. Not like his wife. Helena Foreshaw had searched her son's face as Maddie had said the words, desperate for a chink of hope. And when it hadn't come, when all she had got from Colin was a nod of confirmation that the policewoman was telling the truth, she had fallen into her son's arms, a sobbing mess. She had continued to deny . . . refused to accept. Maddie had said all that she could and then promptly left them to their grief. There were no questions back at her, just a family who had welcomed her in as a strong unit, hopeful but braced for the worst — and she had left them in pieces on the living-room floor when the worst was all she had.

Maddie was delighted to see a familiar grin greeting her from under a desk lamp in the middle of the Major Crime floor.

'Hey, Rhiannon.' Maddie flopped into her chair, spinning it away from her desk.

'You're still on duty then? I tried calling you.'

'I know. I saw you were ringing. I was out at the Foreshaw family home. I could hardly pick up.'

'No, I'll let you off this once, then. How did it go?'

Maddie sighed. 'How does it ever go? I just ruined their lives forever.'

'You didn't, Maddie. Hughes did that.'

Maddie rubbed at her face. 'Not on his own he didn't.'

Rhiannon's chair clattered as she wheeled herself closer. 'This isn't finished then?' There was a glimmer in her eye from the desk lamp that could easily be mistaken for excitement. 'And there was me thinking I had missed all the fun!'

'Plenty more "fun" to be had here, I reckon,' Maddie said. 'Just as long as we're allowed to have it.'

'I called in earlier today. I spoke to the DI . . . asked him if he needed me in earlier for the investigation. He basically told me it was all over. What's changed since then?'

'That's what I mean by not being allowed. We all know Tristan Stepney is a pompous arse. What I didn't know until today, but makes a lot of sense now, is that he's only interested in giving good news about quick results. Hughes affords him a very neat conclusion to a very nasty murder, thank you very much, and Stepney had already told the chief *personally* all about it. So, the last thing he wants to hear is that there are other suspects for us to concern ourselves with.'

'But are there?'

'He hinted as much — Hughes, I mean. And the evidence tells me the same. I can't quite put my finger on it, but there are chunks of the story missing.'

'Missing?'

'The victim. There's no link between the killer and the victim.'

'He said it was random.'

'Nothing's ever random. There has to be a reason at least. His phone was cleaned down to nothing. Hers too. Both were left with one photo each, both of which were key to our investigation. And Hughes denies doing that to either phone. But even if he did, why do that if you were planning to walk in here and tell us all about what you had done?'

'Maybe he was going to try and get away with it to start with. Then he realized he had no idea what he was doing — or the guilt was too much?'

'Get away with it? With murder? A man who has never so much as nicked a choccie bar from a newsagent's goes out and murders a stranger in cold blood. Even if that was the case, why not tell us his home address or *anything* about his personal life?'

'Okay, fair question. So, what now?'

'Now I need to get some sleep. Fourteen hours in this place will do that to you.'

'Are you back in tomorrow?'

'On a Sunday? The Sabbath day? Probably. Not sure what for, though. Just to look back over it all, I imagine. I just made a promise to a family that I wouldn't rest until I had the whole truth.'

'Didn't you also promise the DI that you would draw a line under it immediately?'

'That's probably what he heard. But I know who I won't be letting down — and it isn't Tristan Stepney.'

'Is there anything I can do overnight?'

Maddie rubbed at her face again. An idea forced its way from her tired mind. 'There might be, actually.' The glint seemed to brighten in Rhiannon's eye. How Maddie loved her enthusiasm. 'I spoke with the victim's brother. He reported her missing but he had already checked with one of her work friends first.' Maddie opened her daybook to the last page. 'A Janet Taylor. I got the impression that this Janet was a close friend of the victim. I want to talk to her. She might have more of an idea if a man was giving Marie hassle, hanging around or following her on runs. It's not the sort of thing you'd want to discuss with your brother. I think Colin Foreshaw is the protective type.'

'So you want me to find out what we have on Janet Taylor?'

'If you have the time. Colin thinks she works at the same place and on the same shifts as his sister did, so that's office hours at Sessions House in Maidstone.'

'Sessions House! Sounds grand.'

'It's the main headquarters for the county council. She works for Social Services there. I'm going to head up there first thing Monday, but if you can get a home address overnight, I'll go and see her tomorrow instead.'

'I'm on it.'

Maddie pushed her daybook towards her colleague. She had underlined the few details she had taken about Janet Taylor. It wasn't much to go on, but if anyone was going to make something out of it, she was sure it would be Rhiannon.

'Don't bust a gut on it,' Maddie added. 'I'll be heading up there on Monday either way for a general ask-around. I'll be interested in her social-media presence, though. The usual stuff . . . any links to victim or offender . . . where she goes . . . what she does . . . what they did together. I'm too tired to think of anything else. Go nuts, really.'

'Nuts it is. Hopefully the night will stay q and I'll be able to get stuck in. I'll text you anything interesting.'

'Yeah, do that. And just send me a short summary of what you've done in an email. Just so I don't task anyone else with the same thing. I'll pick it up in the morning.'

'So that's it? Your plans for your one day off in the week are to sit up in bed and read a summary from work, then try and think of a reason to come back in?'

'What are you trying to say?' Maddie giggled.

'That we're as sad as each other. I've swapped my rest days. I got in contact with Duties last night. I'm back in Monday morning now. I thought I'd be coming in to get involved in a murder investigation. Nothing better to do, see? How sad is that?'

'Very. I do have plans for tomorrow, actually. Although admittedly they're still kind of work related.'

'Other plans?'

'Yeah. Something that might just be the most effective thing I can do for this investigation right now. I'm going to go and see Harry Blaker.'

CHAPTER 13

Sunday

PC Ian Hessey kicked off his patrol boots in the hall of his own home and sighed away the end of another night shift. This was always a big part of becoming just Ian Hessey, not a police constable in big, heavy boots — just a man at home with his family. Another big part of this was now rushing towards him in the form of his two daughters, their nighties trailing behind them, their blonde hair bouncing off their backs in crinkled clumps where they had slept on their plaits. The eight-year-old hit him first, the six-year-old a second behind, sending him sprawling back to sitting on the stairs. He got his balance and emerged as a roaring, tickling monster, swearing his revenge and chasing them along the hall, his feet skidding in his socks as he reached the tiled floor of the kitchen. His wife scrunched up her face at the high-pitched shrieks as the girls split up to outwit the monster. Another roar and he set off again, chasing after them.

His wife Claire was still scowling a few moments later when he stumbled back into the kitchen, six-year-old Shannon hanging upside down against his thigh — her face already changing colour, her giggle still unrelenting, her nightie slipping to fold back over her face.

'You're home then?' Claire pulled open the oven and leaned back as it billowed out heat and the aroma of hash browns.

'I know, I like to sneak in. How was your night?'

Claire moved over for a kiss, careful to avoid a kick in the face from their wriggling daughter.

'Living the dream. You?'

'Quiet, actually. The worst sort of night shift.'

'Breakfast's ready. Any chance you could make sure our daughters make it to the table? Preferably the right way up.'

'I can get them there. No promises on which way up.'

He stumbled to the table. Shannon squealed again as he gently bumped her shoulders into a chair.

'DADDY! LET ME DOWN! I can't eat this way up, Daddy!'

He caught Claire grinning as she filled their plates. She was last to sit at the table. When she did, it already had three occupants, all the right way up and all smiling.

'Can we go swimming, Daddy? Like you said. You said in a few days. That was a few days ago, I think!' Shannon said.

'Oh, not right now, honey. I really need to get some sleep first, and then me and Mummy are still unpacking here. There's so much to do.'

'When are you going to paint my room, Daddy? I hate that blue. I'm not a boy, you know.'

Ian had a good measure of bacon and egg balanced on his fork. He halted it mid-air to laugh, fearing he might choke otherwise. 'I know that, honey. Your room will be the first thing I do — for *both* of you.' He was quick to head off Lily, his elder daughter, who was about to remonstrate. She still flopped back in her chair and huffed.

'First, we need to unpack, girls! We moved house a week ago and I've had to work just about every day since.'

'Why don't you stay at home and get your own things done before you go and do things for other people?' Shannon was matter-of-fact. She was always matter-of-fact. For her, the world was such a simple place. Ian only hoped that she never had reason to see it any differently.

'Life's not quite like that. Not when you grow up and go to work. There are things you have to do. You have to go to work when you are told. I couldn't get the time off, girls. A few more days . . . I just have to go on a course and then I'm all yours!'

'So you can paint my room?' Shannon's response was bullish and instant.

'So I can do all the jobs that Mummy has for me. And, yes, one of those will be to paint *both* your rooms.'

'What course, Daddy?'

'A very important course,' Claire said. 'One that cannot possibly wait.'

When Ian met eyes with her, she was smiling, but it was a sore point that wouldn't go away.

'That's right. It's a driving course, girls. Those don't come up very often. I've been waiting to do it for a long time — years. It's terrible timing, but it's just a few days and then it will be out of the way forever.'

'But you can already drive, Daddy.' Shannon wasn't letting him off so easy.

'I can, honey. But this will mean I can drive faster.'

'To the shop? For the paint?' Shannon chanced. Even Claire giggled at this.

'Exactly. With all the lights flashing so everyone knows to get out of my way. "Police coming through! Pink paint emergency!"'

'Would you really do that, Daddy?' Shannon said.

'We'll see, honey.'

'So a few days and then we can go swimming?' Lily joined in, piling on the pressure.

Ian looked over at Claire. She rolled her eyes and shrugged.

'I'm sure I can fit an hour in down the pool while Daddy's away. And maybe he can make a start on some of the painting before he goes off on the course. He still has an evening or two before.'

Ian shot her a look but backed down just as quickly. This was not the time to be pointing out that he needed to get back to sleeping normal hours as soon as possible so he could be fresh for a course that had an early start on Tuesday morning. He didn't think she would care. Both girls were cheering and Ian had to raise his voice to be heard over them.

'AS LONG . . . as long as we are eating all of our meals up. That's fair, isn't it?' He gestured at their plates stacked with hot breakfast. 'And what a wonderful spread your mother has done for us this morning.'

'And not talking with our mouths full,' Claire added.

Ian pointed his fork meaningfully at both girls in turn, his mouth stuffed as full as he could get it.

'Yeah, no talking with your mouth full!' he managed while crumbs tumbled from his lips.

Both girls fell about laughing. Claire shook her head but her face did break into a smile. She looked tired. He knew why; moving house was just about the most exhausting thing they had ever done. Nothing about it had been easy. The date had moved three times and damned near fallen through altogether at the last minute. The stress of that alone could have floored them both. To add into the mix, he'd had a run of nights he couldn't get off on leave. Of course, he'd had the first week booked off but when the move date had shifted, his work couldn't accommodate him. He understood, of course he did. He knew how a response team of police officers worked, but his wife was a lot less understanding — despite working for the police herself. She was part of the civilian staff, based at Headquarters in Maidstone. They had been a lot more flexible and she was into her second week of leave — time that she had mostly spent feeling frustrated at how much she could be doing if her husband was with her.

'It'll all be worth it. Look at this place.' Ian spoke loud enough for the girls to hear but stayed fixed on his wife.

'Of course it will.' Claire sighed. Her smile might have looked tired but it was genuine. She reached out for his hand. 'We're here, that's all that matters. These girls might have blue rooms but they have one each at least. You didn't moan about getting your own rooms, did you?'

'No way! Lily does smelly bum pops!'

The Hessey family breakfast table resonated with laughter.

CHAPTER 14

Maddie trudged up Harry Blaker's drive. She waited until she was within the shade of the house to pause. She had known it would be impossible to approach this place without her mind going back over the last time she had been here, the last time she had approached that door and stared in through his long, front window. It had been cold that night, the darkness stifled while every surface pulsed a vivid blue. Amid the chaos, they had taken a slow walk up the road to this house. Maddie had hung just a few steps behind Harry all the way, all the time considering that she should say something, that she should stop him. But there could be no stopping him. He knew he was walking towards the scene of his daughter's death – a madman had left her there on show for him, presented in the stark lighting of his own living room. Maddie and Harry had both been chasing the killer. They had both been too late.

When the chaos was over and the dust had finally settled, Maddie had replayed the whole investigation over and over, looking for ways they might have been able to make a difference, maybe even got there quicker. It was a futile exercise — such things always were — but it had actually provided some comfort. She was still convinced that there was nothing they could have done differently — not with what they had known, what they had faced. They had been fortunate not to have lost more. That realization had left her able to move past what had happened, or at least to move on from it.

She hadn't been at all sure about Harry.

In the aftermath of it all, he went missing. Shut himself away from the force, from friends and colleagues, refusing visits, doing the bare minimum to make sure no one turned up at his house to check he was still alive. They had all backed away, Maddie included. She knew he would be hurting and was desperate to help, to make everything better. But she knew that was an impossibility. Even attempting to reach out before he was ready would have been nothing but counterproductive. She knew Harry.

Then she had heard that he had returned. DCI Julian Lowe had spoken to her, after swearing her to secrecy. He had told her how he had met Harry in a quiet meeting room at Headquarters so as to minimize the risk of seeing someone he knew, someone who would tell him *how sorry they were*. They had talked through options. Harry was struggling at home with endless time on his hands. Maddie couldn't imagine what it was like to be living here, to walk into that living room, to be constantly confronted by the backdrop of his daughter's untimely death.

In just over two years, he'd be able to walk away with a reasonable pension. Two years and he could retire. Maddie had never had him as the sort to opt for early retirement. Some people just had *copper* written right through them, there was nothing else they could ever be. But people could change, despite what Maddie had believed previously. You just had to destroy them first.

As a result of that meeting, a place had been found for Harry to work at the training school. She didn't know the whole job description, just that he was delivering lectures to brand-new constables around first actions when discovering a major crime scene. It was sold as a swap deal with Tristan

Stepney. Harry would take some responsibility for probationary officers overall and Tristan would take up the vacant role in Major Crime. There had been no discussion within the department and no announcement either, just Tristan Stepney turning up and introducing himself. At the time, Maddie couldn't help but feel hurt that Harry hadn't called ahead to warn her — not even a text message or an email.

He had been back working a few weeks now and it was nearly six months since the last time she'd been here. All that time, she had been looking for a reason to come out and knock on this door, something that he wouldn't see through instantly. Something that might even get him enthused about being a detective again. The strange death of Marie Foreshaw might be just the thing she had been waiting for. She dared to hope it was just the thing they had both been waiting for.

Harry lived in a dormer bungalow, the first-floor addition only visible from the back. The front was dominated by a long window with tipped blinds that shrouded the living room behind. She was desperate to turn her mind's eye away from the image of how this room had looked the last time she'd glimpsed behind those blinds: one of her uniform colleagues urgently pumping Melissa Blaker's chest on the living-room floor while any number of colleagues stared wide-eyed back out, desperate for a miracle that was never coming.

Instead, she focused on the here and now, the lazy buzz of a clumsy honey bee that crossed her vision, the breeze that carried a pleasant warmth with it and the scent of moist, freshly disturbed soil. She had half expected that she would arrive to find that Harry had moved house, but no one else maintained their borders like this; they were sharp, with vibrant colours and not a weed in sight. The parked car, too, was the same neat silver saloon and its position backed up close to the side gate was just as she remembered.

Harry Blaker might have been a creature of habit, but that didn't mean he was predictable. She took a deep breath. She needed to prepare herself for an angry reaction. It was a

Sunday and she was uninvited. She genuinely had no idea of what to expect.

The doorbell was easily loud enough for her to hear from behind the heavily frosted door. There was no response. She pressed it again — twice this time. Nothing. Finally, she moved back to the front window where she had an obstructed view through the blinds. Through an open internal door, she could see just a sliver of the back garden. It flared bright white where the sun was beating down. Just at that moment, something moved past to break the light. It flickered. Maddie stepped away, far enough to take in the whole frontage. There was a thick row of conifers to the left of the front door that turned in an 'L' shape, tracing the footprint of the property and also acting as a barrier to the rear. She walked right up to it and bawled Harry's name into his conifers. It took another couple of presses on the doorbell and more shouting to finally get the front door open.

Harry appeared in a short-sleeved shirt done up with metal poppers and tailored shorts. His shirt was spotted with sweat and his brow was slick with it too. He had gardening gloves on both hands. He looked underweight, angry and expectant all at the same time.

'I saw you through the window,' she said, 'the one in the living room. You can see right through if you contort yourself just right!'

She smiled, more in hope than expectation. Harry didn't reply.

She felt forced to continue. 'I'm glad you answered. Me staring into your window like that . . . someone might have called the police!' She chanced a nervous laugh.

'Have you any idea how little of the back garden you can see through that window?' Harry cleared his throat as he spoke.

'I got lucky.'

'You did.'

'And you didn't?' Maddie said.

'And I didn't.' His voice was a low growl, his stance straight on so his broad shoulders filled the doorway.

'I thought I would come round for a cup of coffee.'

'Did you?'

'I was gonna call ahead and try and sort something out but I haven't had much luck with you and phones — or email. I figured this might be the better option. You know, who can ignore a shouting hedge?'

'What made you think I would ignore you?'

'Because you have been. Calls . . . emails . . . texts. I just wanted to meet up for a coffee, that's all. Not tried recently, though. Even I get the hint eventually!'

'And yet here you are.'

'Yes, here I am. I'm worried about you. We all are. Working a department like Major Crime is a big thing, even bigger when you're basically running the show. You're a legend in there. You leaving was always going to be a big deal. You can't just slink away and expect us all to get on with it, to not ask questions.'

'Maddie Ives and her questions,' Harry said. Maddie had thought he might be livening up a bit, but she was finding him harder than ever to read. She blurted her next words.

'I know it's the weekend, but I spoke to your office. They said you were taking some time off on leave . . . to do some gardening . . .'

Harry put his arms out slightly, as if to communicate that he was most definitely doing as she had said. Either that or he didn't quite see her point. Maddie didn't really have one. She was simply stalling until she could get her thoughts together.

'I don't work Sundays,' he said eventually. 'Not anymore.'

'I'm not here to pry, okay? Or to make you talk about anything or to lecture you on how to leave a job . . . that's not at all why I came here. I've got a work-related issue. What I mean is that I would have come to see you at work rather than here . . . I just wanted to run it past someone who might have a bit of experience in this sort of thing, someone I trust, whose opinion I respect.' She was rambling, but it was all true. There was nothing she wanted more than to be able to run all her issues past Harry Blaker.

His arms dropped and he sighed a little.

She took it as weakening and seized her opportunity. 'And all those people were either busy or not answering me, so I thought I would come here instead.' Maddie even giggled. *Now or never.*

His face flickered with a smile — just a flicker, nothing she could take for granted. But then he stepped back. 'You can make the coffee. And then we talk while I work.'

'Suits me.'

The sunlight and Jock, Harry's dog, hit Maddie at the same time as she stepped out into the rear garden. Jock was light brown and bigger than she thought typical for a King Charles spaniel. His coat caught the light, making him little more than a blur as he threw himself at Maddie's thigh. He bounced off excitedly while she tried not to spill the drinks. Harry told him off and the assault was instantly over.

The bright sun was a little more difficult to call off. Harry's lawn ended where a sharp bank rose up to meet the woods. The area beyond was still part of his garden, with steps that snaked up into the tall trees. But the sun was almost at its highest and, rather than offering any shade, the trees were only effective at blocking any cooling breeze. Harry must have seen her squinting. He was scraping a flower bed with a large fork, something he'd been doing for some moments. Maddie had watched his progress through the window while the kettle was doing its thing.

'Some shade.' He gestured towards a sturdy-looking wooden bench. It looked bespoke — home-made, even. The sides had been carved into elegant round shapes, the knots in the wood polished to stand out. Pretty vines held it in a firm grip and it faced out over a small pond. A water feature in the pond's centre made a pleasant gurgle. Above the bench, a carved wooden bird was perched atop a custom-made platform.

'I see you brought Robin out here!' Maddie grinned but Harry was back to scratching at the soil. He didn't look up.

'Whenever the sun's up.'

'I'll put your coffee down by the bench. You look like you need a rest.'

She could see the sweat patch had spread to cover most of his back now and his shoulders heaved with effort. He wiped his brow with the back of his hand as he looked over at her. He seemed to hesitate. Then he tugged off his gloves to drop them by his fork and took the seat beside her. Jock had slunk off to lie in the shade but now moved to sit under his master's hand for a pat.

'What did you need to talk about?' Harry said. He used the dog as something to focus on.

'Nothing really. I guess I'm just frustrated and I needed a rant. I thought it had been a while since I had ranted at you, so I would come over and show you what you're missing.'

'Nope.'

'You don't miss it then?'

'What specifically?'

'Nothing *specifically*. The whole thing. Major Crime and all that comes with it.'

'No.'

'Well, we miss you.'

'I imagine you do. Mine was a job swap. Seems people are very keen to seek me out when I'm up at the training school and tell me all about the man I swapped with. They don't seem to care that it's none of my damned business. Or theirs.'

'That's interesting. What did you hear about Stepney?'

'It's none of your damned business either, DS Ives.'

'I've missed that!'

'What?'

'The scolding. You only call me "DS Ives" when you're putting me back in my place.'

'Well, since I'm not about anymore, I assume you're getting out of your place a lot more often.'

'No, actually. Tristan Stepney doesn't give me much room to get out of anything.'

'Really? All I hear are people running him down, but I like him already.'

123

'Not in a good way. He's not so different to you in some ways. Things have to be done his way and he likes — *needs* to know what you're doing and why you're doing it at all times. But he just doesn't listen. He has no interest in theories or hunches, or in giving you any freedom to go and *detect* — which is everything this job is about. He has an admin background, hardly any policing. He's a proper shiny arse. He keeps getting moved around because no one can stand to work with him for long. I hear he's still under investigation. We're all hoping it ends with him being moved again. Permanently.'

'That's pretty much what I've been told. And I tell everyone who comes to me what I'll tell you . . . my replacement is none of my business and I have no interest in him whatsoever. They also made the same mistake you are making right now. They tell me all this because they seem to think I have a vested interest in the Major Crime department at Canterbury Police Station. I left that job months ago and I don't make a habit of looking back. It is only ever destructive. I can't help you, Maddie.'

'You could . . .' She noted his body language as he leaned forwards to shake the remnants of his drink onto the lawn and stood up over her. It said that it was time for her to leave. '. . . if you wanted to.'

'Fine, then. I don't want to. I want to get back to my garden. British sunshine is not something you can take for granted. Any gardener will tell you that.'

'What about friendship? Can you take that for granted?'

He made his way back towards his gloves and discarded fork. 'I need my garden.' He bent to retrieve them and started scraping at the soil again with his back to her.

'What if a friend needed you?'

'I left Major Crime because I realized that I didn't care about it anymore.' His digging seemed more vigorous.

'Or anyone left working in it?'

'Don't, Maddie.' His tone was stern as he turned to face her.

'I'll leave you to it,' she said. 'Don't worry about the staying-in-touch thing. I don't want you putting yourself out for someone who means so little to you.'

She stood up. Harry had spun away from her and was on his knees leaning over the bed of plants. She made her way towards the back door to the house, ready to walk through it and out without a backwards glance. She heard his voice call after her.

'Some things aren't about you, Maddie. Maybe you'd get on with your new boss better if you remembered that.'

'I'll bear that in mind.' She glanced back to see his reflection in the glass of the conservatory. He still had his back to her and was back to doing what he wanted to be doing. She thumped her mug down on the kitchen counter on the way out.

* * *

Maddie watched the ice in her drink shift and bump against the glass as she supped from the top. A gin and tonic. The first sip was always the best.

'I have to say, Rhiannon, for someone so young, you have a real talent for mixing up a gin and tonic.'

'It's because I'm young that I have such a talent. It's all the rage these days.'

'I'd heard gin had made a comeback. It was my nan's favourite tipple. I guess that's the image I have of it still.'

'Your nan would be right on-trend now. She wouldn't look out of place in the coolest cocktail bars in town!'

'I remember she used to take her teeth out to drink a gin. She said it was the only way she could make a seal on the glass.'

'Well . . . maybe she'd stand out just a little then!'

Both women laughed. Maddie had been delighted when Rhiannon called, inviting her round. She only lived a short walk away and had been at home, stewing on her conversation in Harry's garden. Rhiannon had called to say she was intent on staying up all day so that she'd be in some fit shape to return to a day shift in the morning. Maddie was supposed to come around and keep her awake until a reasonable time at least. Maddie was aware that all she had done so far was moan about Tristan Stepney and Harry Blaker. She stared out to sea now. The view from Rhiannon's balcony was unobstructed and, as she insisted every time they sat out there, the only reason Maddie pretended to be her friend. It was a lie, of course — Rhiannon was great company, but it was a good source of amusement.

Maddie's phone rang to cut through the sun-drenched tranquillity. There was no caller id, just a row of numbers. Rhiannon announced she was popping to the loo anyway and Maddie took the call.

'Maddie.'

She hesitated for a moment, suddenly unsure of how she felt. 'This isn't a number I have saved for you, Harry. Did you think I wouldn't pick up?'

'No. This is just the phone I'm using now.'

'You changed your number. Another way to rid yourself of your old life? Of your old fr—'

'I called to apologise.'

She didn't answer.

'Maddie?'

'Well, go on then.'

'I am sorry.'

'What for?'

'You know what for.'

'I just want to be sure you do.'

'I was unfair to you earlier. We're friends. That's not something you should undervalue. But I did and I'm sorry. You just . . . you caught me on the hop.'

'On the hop? If we're friends like you say, me turning up on your doorstep after you hid yourself away for six months — *six months*, Harry — shouldn't have come as a surprise at all. You must have been expecting me at some point. And you were scratching the ground with a fork, Harry. I hardly caught you at a sensitive moment.'

'I was stimulating the soil, Maddie, it's a little bit more than just . . . That doesn't matter. I called to say I'm sorry. And to say that I didn't mean that I didn't care. About you, about the job. I do miss it. I made a mistake agreeing to all this.'

'A mistake?' This stopped Maddie in her tracks. She had been practising her rant at Harry from the moment she had pulled away from his home. And there was much more of it left. She swallowed it now.

'The move. It's tedious. I thought I wanted tedious. Turns out it might be the last thing I want — or need.'

'I could have told you that.'

'I bet you could. What have you got anyway? This job at the moment . . . any good?'

'You want to hear about it now?'

'I got the impression you wanted me to hear about it?'

'Dead woman. Rhiannon was minding her own business when the night-duty DC and someone came knocking our door to tell us all about it. Told us what he had done, where to find her, how he had done it. Even showed up with a photo of how he'd left her.'

'Unusual.'

'Very. Even more unusual is that it was all exactly as he had described. He gets nicked and charged, the scene is processed, and we find DNA and fingerprints linking the scene and the victim to the offender — right where he said we should look for it. His van was still parked at the scene and the keys to it were in his pocket when he came to the police station. The whole investigation came with a big bow wrapped around it and now it's tea and medals time.'

'Except it isn't,' Harry said.

'Not for me. But our new DI can't believe his luck. A strong rumour suggests that the need to swap you out from Major Crime was an opportunity too good to miss. Senior management figure that they can put Stepney in somewhere where the pressure's on, where there's nowhere to hide — a sink or swim scenario. I get the impression everyone is expecting him to sink and then comes the formality of adding this latest failure to whatever the hell else has gone wrong in his career, and he's out on his ear. So, I imagine he's delighted to have a murder on his patch all wrapped up and charged to court forty-eight hours from its discovery. Called the chief personally to tell him about his exploits.'

'I bet he did. And you're not convinced we have our murderer?'

'I know how it sounds. Adrian Hughes is his name. Sure, he's involved. Of course he is. He knows too much and his traces were all over the scene. But he was there as part of something. Something bigger. There are other people out there who had something to do with this and I cannot imagine why. Hughes told us what we wanted to hear, all that he thought we would need to know. He's a sad little man with no police record, but the DI is satisfied with his story — that he just upped and murdered a stranger out of nowhere. When I charged him, Hughes told me straight there was more to it. That's the only time he has ever deviated from his story. It was in his eyes, too. There's something else. He wants to tell me but there's something stopping him.'

'Plenty of murderers in the past have been nerdy-looking oddballs. People who struggled to find their place in the world. His victim's a woman, you said. That would go w—'

'This wasn't sexual. There's no evidence of any sexual assault. But whatever the motivation, Hughes is not right. Not for this. I sat opposite him in the interview room. I know what you're saying and I know what you mean. But this Adrian Hughes . . . taking a woman off the street at knifepoint? He's not a fit for that.'

'You have good instincts, Maddie.'

'I'm learning to trust them. If there are more people out there then what's to stop this happening again to someone else? And the family, Harry . . . I had to tell them we found their daughter. They fell apart in front of me. I don't want to have to go through that again.'

'So what's the status? With the investigation, I mean?'

'Officially? It's closed. The only outstanding work is identifying a home address for Hughes. The boss is at least letting me send a search team in there. But if my instincts are right, that won't tell us anything new. I think the boss knows that, too. It's just the last box to tick before he draws a line under it and we all get ordered to move on.'

'Any other leads you would be following up if you could?'

'Not if Tristan Stepney asks.'

'I assume you are ignoring him completely and carrying on regardless?'

'What makes you say that?'

'Funny. Very funny, Maddie.'

'The scene. It isn't too far from you, actually. I was heading out there to have another look when I saw you earlier. Just to be sure we're not missing anything. But after our conversation . . . I lost the motivation.'

'It's been searched, though? CSI, fingertip and then the area PolSA'd by a search team as per SOPs?'

'SOPs? Tristan Stepney doesn't know Major Crime Standard Operating Procedures! All he knows is the direct number for the chief.'

'So it wasn't searched?'

'It was. But it's a big area. The old steelworks, the canteen building—'

'The one that was badly damaged in a fire?'

'That's the one. And it still is, it would appear. It was searched but Stepney set the criteria. The offender told us about an axe he used to get in . . . the van that was left at the scene . . . what he touched and how. The boss wanted those things to be the focus. A site that size and it was done in four hours and most of that time it was Charley left on her own.'

'I see . . .'

'What?'

'Nothing. At least, it's not for me to criticize. I don't know the details.'

'But if you were? To criticize, I mean?'

'I remember a job early in my career. I was just a DC. An uncle came in and confessed to a sexual assault on his niece when she stayed over. He was babysitting. Told us what he had done, where and how. The search team were briefed with his account and their search was tailored to verify everything he had said. He was charged and dealt with. A few years later the victim took her own life. She didn't make it to twenty. She left a note and the case was reopened.'

'It wasn't him?'

'It was her dad. He was able to carry on with the abuse. He had a hold over his wife's brother, a hold strong enough that he took the rap and kept quiet all that time. The mistake we made was briefing the search team with exactly what the uncle said had happened. They entered that flat already knowing what they would find and then stopped the moment they did. Human nature. Had they continued they would have found the evidence that pointed at her dad, the stuff his daughter listed later in her suicide note. We all learned a lesson with that one.'

'Seems it hasn't been passed on too well.'

'It's not Tristan's fault. He's never had a detective role before.'

'So I hear. But that doesn't make it okay.'

'It doesn't.

'The search isn't his only mistake either. This admission . . . Hughes was lying to me *and* telling the truth. The problem I have is that I can't separate them out and I'm not being given any more time to try.'

'Are you still thinking of heading to this scene?'

'It's been stood down. It would just be a walk round an old building. But I do want to see it again.'

'Want some company? I'm done scratching my dirt.'

'Now?'

'Are you busy?'

'Rhiannon's making me gin and tonics in the sunshine.'

'Ah, okay then. Well, if you do fancy—'

'Yes, Harry! Right now is ideal. I've had a sip, that's all. I can't even pretend to be unable to drive.'

'Maybe you could ask Rhiannon to drive.'

'What makes you think I'm going to bring her along?'

'Rhiannon Davis? You know they call her *mini-Maddie*, right? She's basically you but younger. Which means she won't be told otherwise.'

'I'll take that as a compliment. I've just realized my mistake with you. All this time I was asking you out for a coffee, all I needed to do was find a grim murder scene for a catchup!'

Rhiannon reappeared on the balcony with timing that was perfection. She looked puzzled as Maddie turned towards her, a big grin on her face.

'And you're right about Rhiannon. We'll meet you there.'

* * *

The dust shifted forwards to swamp the car and force Harry to turn away. He had changed from his gardening attire into a pair of navy chino trousers and a crisp-looking, short-sleeved white shirt. He was likely regretting his fresh look, coated as he now was in the fine dust from the decomposing rubble. Richborough Power Station had once stood on part of this site. It had been a vast area of bigger buildings and tall chimneys, the majority of which had been demolished in the last decade. Demolition appeared to have been the easy bit; to say the clean-up operation had stalled would be an understatement. The site was fifteen minutes up the road from Harry's house, so neither Maddie nor Rhiannon was surprised to find him leaning on his car when they arrived.

'Afternoon, sir,' Rhiannon chirped.

'Harry's fine,' he said. 'This is just a pleasant walk in the sunshine while we're all off duty, according to DS . . . Maddie.'

Maddie smiled. 'Just a casual walk to look for a dead body or two!'

Rhiannon spun to face Maddie, her eyes wide with excitement. 'You think there might be another one out here?'

'No! I just wanted to have a second look. It was difficult to take much in with Stepney breathing down my neck. Especially as he had already decided that it was a waste of time.'

'Early to be standing a scene of this size down,' Harry mused. He had his hands in his pockets and was facing the old canteen building in front of him. The breeze was stronger here, running freely over the flat and open landscape. The building was the only solid mass until much larger buildings appeared as dark shapes on the horizon. Maddie could see a padlock swinging against the doors it held shut. Harry must have noticed it, too.

'I take it that's an addition by our people, leaving the site secure?' he said.

'It was. One of the keys was handed over to the landowner. The other was booked into Property. I thought I'd borrow it for the weekend . . .' Maddie lifted a key from her pocket.

Harry shook his head. 'And I assume it's been booked out to you, as per policy?'

'I've always said that's your one weakness, Harry. You assume too much!'

He walked towards the building. 'Tomorrow I'm giving a lecture on crime-scene management to probationer officers. I'll be telling them that you can't just go poking around a scene just because it might be exciting. I can hardly quote policy at you.'

'Good thing this isn't a scene. Not anymore.' Maddie removed the padlock and stepped inside. She glanced back at Harry as they moved into where the building opened up around them. She pointed to a cleared area amid the debris. Their victim was missing, of course. The chair was gone too.

'She was left directly under that hole in the roof over there. Facing away from the door. Tied to a chair with plastic wrapped tight round her face. No other obvious injuries. No defence wounds to her hands, wrists or forearms, and still wearing her jogging clothes.'

Harry still had his hands in his pocket — force of habit — ensuring control over what he touched. The place still had the feeling of a crime scene. He looked up towards the sound of movement in the rafters. They'd disturbed a pigeon and its wings whistled as it fluttered across to the other side of the room. Maybe seeking a better view of the intruders.

'Nice place,' he said.

'Not somewhere anyone would choose to spend their last moments,' Maddie replied.

'He killed her here?'

'He said he did and CSI agree.'

Harry looked downwards. Everywhere, the ground was thick with dust and soot. The floor was now littered with prints. Prominent patterns from the steel-toed boots the tactical team wore for their searches.

'We have footsteps . . . no dragging, I can see.'

'No,' Maddie said. 'And the Evidence Gathering Team filmed their initial approach. I've seen the footage. When they first came in here it showed one set of prints in a neat line to and from the victim. CSI have her here a week or so — not long enough for the dust to have covered any other marks completely. The offender admits to coming back to take a picture. He said it was so that we'd believe his story.'

'So the only prints were from him returning?'

'Yes.'

'So none from when he brought her in here initially to kill her?'

'None that we could see.'

'The dust looks thicker over on that side. He might have dragged her in but it's been cleaned up . . . So, what are we saying here? That he did what he did, then swept or — even better — hoovered away his tracks? Then left it a week or so, for another layer of dust to gather . . . then came back to take a photo to bring into the police station and prove to us what he'd done?'

'He didn't mention the hoovering bit.'

'And he got her to a chair out there in the middle of the floor while she was still alive and fighting for her life?'

'Despite being built like Mr Bean. Toxicology isn't back yet. Maybe she was given something that took her fight away . . .'

'Maybe. But dragging a woman against her will, carrying an unconscious woman as a dead weight . . . neither of these things is easy on your own.'

'He said he took her with a knife to her throat. So maybe she walked herself?' Maddie said.

'Maybe . . .' Harry looked back up to the rafters. The sound of his steps bounced around the open space as he walked across the floor to stand in the sunlight. The pigeon fidgeted again. He looked back over to where the two women had remained.

'She was a runner, you said. Athletic? Fit?'

'Yes,' Maddie said. 'Similar build to me I would say.'

'Okay, then. So, imagine I bring you in here after snatching you from the street and bundling you into a van with a knife to your throat. I've probably made verbal threats to your life to back that up, to make you realize I'm serious so you do what you're told. Then I drive you here, to this place. It has an atmosphere, doesn't it? A resonance. It's creepy. So you're driven out to the middle of nowhere and pushed into this creepy building, across the floor to a single chair out on its own — it would look like it was waiting for you, wouldn't it? There's only one possible reason for a set-up like that. What would you do?'

'Fight.'

'I think you would. I think anyone would. The moment you stepped through that door, knife at your neck or not, you would see the place where you were being brought to die. You would know that once you were bound to that chair, your last chance would be gone. Did they find any restraints?'

'Her wrists were tied. But they were tied to the chair.'

'So after he sat her in it.'

'Exactly. Then we think he wiped his phone, apart from the photo he showed Rhiannon here as part of his admission. The victim's phone has also been cleaned up — I'm certain of it. There was nothing but a single selfie on there — which was handy . . . It was just what we needed for the press to put out as an image so we could find out who she is.'

'You think that was intentional?'

'I can't think of any other reason why. His phone, too . . . no pictures, videos or even any apps — apart from one . . . Livestream.'

'Which is?'

'As it sounds. An app that works the camera function but sends video footage elsewhere live — and *without* storing it in the phone's memory.'

'So that's really significant. He must have livestreamed whatever happened in here . . . but to where?'

'To whom.' Rhiannon cut in.

'And Tristan's done with this?' Harry said.

'He thinks we all are.' Maddie said.

Harry shook his head. 'It's not possible with one man. It's barely possible with two. Then suppose it's streaming out to somewhere else . . . three people would be a conservative guess.'

'I agree. Could you talk to the DCI maybe? I don't know what Stepney's told him, but it can't be the whole picture. Mr Lowe's more thorough even than any of us.'

Harry finally lifted his hand out of his pocket to rub over his short-cropped hair. 'Only if I really wanted to upset a lot of people very quickly.'

'This is more important than that. We're going to have to upset some people. And I made a promise to the victim's family.'

'What you're saying is that *I* need to kick up a stink because *you* made a promise,' Harry said.

'Not at all. You can just go back to your day job and forget any of this happened if you want to.'

Harry didn't reply. He walked over to where old furniture was piled up and covered in a thick layer of grey dust and soot. 'This hasn't been disturbed.'

'So?'

'So it hasn't been searched.'

'Searched for what?'

'No idea. That's the idea of a search.' He pulled at a table leg. It was like a domino effect, the whole stack shifted. The sound reverberated around the empty space. It kicked up enough soot and dust that Harry had to turn away from it with his eyes narrowed.

'I don't think we should be smashing the place up.' Maddie laughed.

'The dust. It's thicker on the chairs than the floor.'

'So?'

'So, maybe someone swept up over here, too.'

'Why would they do that?'

Harry didn't answer. He was pulling at chairs, making a racket as he threw them into a clear space behind. He wrenched at a table to lift it onto its side. By the time Maddie got to him he had a clear black smudge across his shirt. She made a comment about it. He ignored her, his attention on the floor. He dropped to his knees, seemingly unconcerned about messing up his trousers as well. Maddie moved in closer.

'What does that look like to you?' he said.

Maddie knelt down next to him. She didn't mind the dirt either. Not now. Whatever Harry was pointing to was still tucked under a mess of interwoven chair legs. But she could see it clearly enough.

'A webcam,' she breathed.

CHAPTER 15

Monday

On the surface, Canterbury Police Station was just like always; the same bustling uniform cops on the ground floor, the same clunking lift, the same heavy door to push through onto the fourth floor where Linda's office was located. But beneath the surface and despite all these familiar components, to Linda at least, everything about this place seemed different. Today she was the enemy. An imposter skulking through the building, sneaking past her colleagues with guilt written all over her face, expecting at any moment to be detained by a stern-faced police officer.

It was ridiculous, of course. But anxiety was its own mistress. It needed no permission; it did not come from a place of logic and that morning it was strong enough to divert her away from her desk to take a moment in the kitchenette. She had got this far, passing through the building with nods and mumbled greetings, but once she entered her office, she would meet the people she worked with every day, people who knew her better, who would ask how her weekend had been, who would ask where she had been on Friday. Maybe they were even following her daughter's Instagram and would know that Hope had returned home. They might even ask why she was moving so stiffly and occasionally snatching at her bruised side. She just needed a moment to gather herself.

The kitchenette was little more than an oversized cupboard that acted as a communal facility. Each floor had one. It was just a few steps in to get to the end, to a window that overlooked the car park below. She was early. It was 7:30 a.m. Most of the office-based staff started at eight a.m. and the flow of cars was steady through the barrier below. She watched three of them park up outside. She pressed her hand to her side, just above her hip where the pain was worst. The pressure seemed to ease it slightly. It had loosened up a little bit since this morning at least. When she had first got out of bed, she had shuffled around her bedroom a few times in an attempt to be walking naturally by the time she stepped out into the living area — just in case her daughter was up. She hadn't been. Linda had taken her a cup of tea. Hope had stirred just enough to roll onto her back, a grin lighting her face as she stated her only plans for Monday morning — to make 'future plans'.

Hope had always had a laid-back, carefree approach to life. Linda had never been more jealous of that than on this morning — or so grateful for it. Hope had announced that she'd be using the flat as 'a bit of a base' for the next few days while she visited friends to share stories of her adventures. She had been out just about all of Sunday. Linda had stayed in, somehow conscious that she was supposed to, trying to act as normal as possible while every moment she was consumed by the knowledge that she was being watched.

Someone stepped into the kitchenette behind her to snatch her mind back to now. She didn't turn to look at them. She didn't want to prompt a conversation. She heard someone else bundle in, too, making the tight space seem smaller than ever. Whoever it was needed to put on the brakes suddenly.

'Ooh . . . nearly!' It was a man's voice. 'Busy in here. Anyone would think we all needed a coffee kickstart.' He gave a polite chuckle.

'It's that time of day.' It was another male voice. Familiar but Linda couldn't place it. Then it came to her all at once and spun her on her heels.

'Blimey! Alright, alright — I want a coffee but I'm not gonna fight you for it. You been in the wars?'

The man who had just entered was speaking to the man who had been chained next to her not two days before — the one who had reacted so vehemently to the video, who had been punched to the ground and dragged out in front of her and who now stood a few feet away in full police uniform, his radio flickering on and off where it was strapped to his chest. He locked eyes with her. An empty cup with the words *#1 DAD* written boldly across it hung from his grip. He was taking too long to answer the man behind. His eye was split and ugly with lurid colours, purple mixing with red, black and green.

'Nah, just a good game of rugby,' he said finally.

The man behind him was carrying a kettle from another part of the building. He seemed to be studying his face intently.

'Who tackled you? Was he driving a train?' He gave another polite chuckle.

'Big bastard. In fact, there were three of them. You should see *their* bruises!' He smiled weakly then turned back to focus on Linda.

'They're not letting you out in public like that, are they?' The man with the kettle stuck to his infuriating habit of chuckling at the end of every sentence.

'No. Hence I'm up here filling up my teacup while the rest of my team are out doing proper police work. I'll be in the station all day. It's not such a bad thing . . . I get to see what goes on back here.'

'Nothing important, I can tell you that! Present company excepted, Linda!' The man gestured towards her with his empty kettle. She tore her gaze away from the bruised man to acknowledge him. She had no idea of his name.

'Nothing important at all!' The words didn't come easy; her throat felt closed up. She was sure her voice sounded different. She turned back to the bruised man. 'Sorry to see you had a bad weekend.' They were still staring at each other as their colleague nipped in to fill his kettle.

'It happens. I'm telling everyone the rugby story but let me just say, when my wife asks you to wash the dishes, you wash the dishes!'

The man at the sink forced another chuckle. 'I know what you mean! I married one of those. Best thing I ever did . . . the learning to do what I'm told bit, I mean! Happy wife, happy life is what they say — works for me! Have a good day, all.' He positively skipped out, still giggling to himself as the kettle sloshed in his grip.

Linda watched him disappear from sight. The officer now turned his back to her, filling his own mug from the urn. She had followed the instructions. The camera attachment to her phone was pushed into the buttonhole of her top pocket. It was live. She had almost been impressed with just how well it blended into her outfit. No one would see it unless they were looking for it. She didn't know what to say.

'Number-one Dad, hey?' she chanced.

He was still filling his cup. He stopped the flow, then added to it a couple of times to make sure the level was just right. It was maddening, the action of someone considering his next words carefully perhaps.

'The mug don't lie. A son. He's all that matters to me and I'll do *anything* for him.'

He snatched the cup from under the nozzle and he was gone. Linda considered calling after him but she didn't know what for. There was nothing they could talk about, nothing he could tell her without risking everything. Uniform had their own kitchen on the ground floor. She had seen someone walk out of it supping at a steaming cup when she was waiting for the lift. This man had come up to the fourth floor for a clear reason, to make sure she knew who he was, that they were linked by their tasks — depending on each other. She wondered what they had asked of him. Whatever it was, just a few words had confirmed that he had every intention of getting it done.

She pulled at her jacket to straighten it out. She could delay no longer. It wasn't so bad. She acknowledged a couple of her colleagues and they greeted her, but there were no awkward questions about her long weekend, no references to her daughter and nobody commented on the way she was walking, as if she had been punched multiple times in the ribs.

She had a separate office in the far corner. The door displayed her job title — *Senior CPS Prosecutor* — and at a height that couldn't be missed. It was a title she had been proud of once, just a few days ago in fact. Now she couldn't bear to look at it. She pushed the door roughly shut behind her. Her computer was already on. She hurriedly typed in one password and then another to access the shared file labelled *OP ICICLE*. This opened to reveal three more folders, each crammed with documents. She only needed three of them. *1068 LOXTON* was the first one she found, labelled with just the number of the form and a surname. It was a report she had written. That was how she knew it had the information her captors needed. It was a summary of the case as a whole, then the rationale as to why the family should qualify for Op Icicle. The new addresses were the last thing she had written. She wasn't sure about the quality she'd get from filming a digital screen with a digital camera. The only way to be sure would be to print the documents first. There would be no issue with filming paper, surely. She highlighted *1068 LOXTON*, then located the other two: *1068 GRANT* and *1068 WATSON*. With all three documents selected, she clicked *PRINT*. She had her own printer; it was on a separate desk to her right. It started with a clunk that made her jump so hard she clutched at her ribs. It sucked in the first sheet.

'Linda, good morning!' Linda flinched as she turned away from the noise. The door opening and the sound of the voice had arrived together.

'Ooh, you okay, love?' Despite her best efforts, Linda must have grimaced. And Helen Newman didn't miss a trick.

'Yes, fine. Thank you, Helen.'

'I'm just doing a round of teas. I know I can always rely on you to get in on a round. Can I grab your mug?'

'Oh, sure.' Linda slid open her drawer. She had to hold her breath as she did so. Twisting and leaning down to her right pulled at her bruised muscles. She put the cup on her desk. It hurt to lift her arm too high so she slid it along for Helen to take the hint. Helen scooped it up to clank against the fistful of mugs she was already carrying.

''Are you feeling better?'

'Much better, thank you.' Linda had been waiting for this question and she was a little too quick to reply. It came across as abrupt. Helen seemed to take it as such and made her way out of the office with no more small talk.

'Thank you, Helen!' Linda called after her. She got a pleasant 'no problem' that just made it through the gap as the door closed.

The office was silent again now. The printer had finished its work. She looked over at it; a stack of papers lay face down in the *out* tray. All she had to do was turn to the last page of each report, to where she knew the relocation details were written, and make sure the camera had picked them up. Then that was it . . . job done. She could get back to her life, maybe order another takeaway with her daughter. She would be able to speak freely and with this colossal weight off her shoulders. Hope had obviously detected that something was wrong, even hinted that maybe her mum was annoyed at her sudden arrival — as if her own daughter could ever be an unwelcome surprise. She would make it up to her. Just as soon as she could. Just as soon as this was done.

She stood over the printer and gripped the stack of papers, lingering on it then lifting it to feel its weight. Her thoughts moved away from Hope and to the families that were face down at her fingertips. She herself could get back to normal, but what about them? What happened next?

'We messed up.'

The words fell from her lips before she could stop them. All that work, all that effort, all those good intentions. They would be undone by just a few lines of text. She took the stack of papers back to her desk to sit in front of it. She focused on Hope, flooding her mind with happy memories of their time together. Hope's dad had left when their daughter was still growing inside her. They had never wanted children. Linda had been able to embrace her pregnancy, looking forwards to the birth of her baby, but he couldn't see it that way. He had acted as if it were Linda's fault, accusing her of trying to trap him, to ruin his life. She was left alone, destitute and more determined than ever to make it work.

Hope is all I've got, she had said to fill the silence after he had slammed the front door shut for the final time. The name had stuck. It had been a fine choice. And the words were still true.

'Hope is all I've got,' she whispered out into the silence of her office.

She turned the first sheet over.

* * *

'Tristan!' DCI Julian Lowe barked out the name then moved into the room that he referred to loudly as 'Harry's office'.

Maddie looked to Tristan for a reaction but glanced away again as the DCI continued, 'You too, DS Ives.'

The DCI was standing in the doorway to the office. She hadn't seen him in the building for some weeks. More and more, he had been managing the department remotely from Force Headquarters while he ran a project that was part of his promotion to the next rank up. His appearance was a surprise, his demand for her presence in their meeting was a bigger one.

She picked up her daybook and hunted for a pen. When she looked back over, Stepney had slunk past the DCI to take a seat on the opposite side of the desk he had been occupying since Harry Blaker had vacated it. He looked every inch the naughty schoolboy.

'You don't need anything,' the DCI snapped over to her.

She was aware of a sudden hush. Everyone else was now trying not to look, keeping their eyes diligently glued to their monitors, and she knew she was the cause. She could feel herself burning up as she crossed the floor.

'Julian—' DI Stepney began, the moment Maddie closed the door.

'*Sir* would be better.' Lowe's retort was instant.

Stepney's mouth twisted in a sort of smile. 'When you showed me around the floor and said this was *my* office . . . I think I may have called you "Julian" the whole time.'

'You did. It annoyed me then too.'

Maddie was sitting almost shoulder to shoulder with Stepney, the same side of the table but a little further back. She shifted in her seat a little, enough for it to creak under her.

'Then I should apologise. I didn't mean any disrespect, of course. I guess I'm still getting used to my current circumstances.'

DCI Lowe turned away from him. His eyes strayed to where the blinds hung, floor to ceiling, across a glass partition between them and the main office. Maddie did the same. They were still being watched by a roomful of detectives feigning disinterest. Julian Lowe was a very emotionally intelligent man. He didn't give anything away unintentionally. Today he would have realized he was going to get a lot of attention from the moment he strode onto the floor, an evidence bag tucked under one arm, a document in hand and a sense of purpose in his step. He hadn't acknowledged anyone, just marched into their DI's office to shut the blinds. But only halfway. Maybe this was all part of a show of strength. Maddie didn't think that boded well.

The DCI now dropped the clear bag on the desk in front of them both. But his stare was fixed on the DI. Maddie bit her lip.

'What's this?' Stepney's tone was guarded. And justifiably so.

The DCI moved his hands to his hips. 'It's what you missed.'

'Missed? Missed where?'

'It's a webcam. It was found out in the derelict building, still pointing at the spot where your murder victim had been propped up in her chair.'

'A web . . . I mean . . . the search team. I sent them. If they missed some—'

'I spoke to the PolSA, to the CSI staff who were deployed. You were very specific. The focus was the body for CSI, and the vehicle and surrounding area for the PolSA. Who did you specifically task with the remainder of the building?'

'I . . . I assumed CSI would cover—'

'Well, they didn't. You tasked Charley Mace with the victim only and, besides, CSI are evidence capture, not a search resource. Now . . . the search documentation that you should have got back from all search resources deployed to a Major Crime scene . . . the stuff you study before you step down from a scene as per Standard Operating Procedures . . . where is it?'

'I didn't . . . I mean, I don't—'

This was the document DCI Lowe had in his other hand. Maddie had seen numerous examples of reports of this kind before. They were standard in any murder search and would often find their way to her late in the investigation to be included as part of the unused material. It was an A4 pad, completed by the PolSA but with input from the CSI resource and anyone else involved in searching any area of a scene. It was designed to ensure the SIO didn't miss anything. It was thick enough to make a satisfying thud on the desk.

'I found this in your tray out in the corridor. The PolSA was going to give it to you personally on Saturday, but you had gone home so he left it in your tray.'

'It was my rest day. I came in to—'

'You came in to do nothing. Not enough anyway. *You* missed that camera — no one else!' He gestured again at the exhibit.

The DCI's anger was rising. Maddie had never seen him like this.

'Okay then . . .' Stepney's words trailed off, ending with a chuckle, which was not very wise. 'No harm done. We'll get it booked into the evidence and we can go from there.'

'Booked into the evidence? You stood the scene down! Removed all police personnel, left the vehicle gate to the scene wide open and *then* this was found. AFTER! Do you understand what that means?'

Stepney wasn't chuckling now. 'But no one . . . It's an empty building. Unused. No one goes there—'

'It's not evidence. Not now. It's just something found in a building where a murder victim was *once* found. A coincidence. The moment you lifted the restrictions on that scene, we lost control of it and it became nothing. Any defence solicitor worth his salt will have this chucked out of court as nothing more than something that was put in that building at any point *after* the scene was processed and stood down. It wouldn't even make it in front of a jury. It would be tossed as part of the legal arguments. That's if we even had the gall to put it up as evidence, allowing a judge to see our incompetence. You have heard of *beyond reasonable doubt*, I assume? Even in your limited time investigating crime.'

'I'm an accredited detective. You know—'

'An exam. You passed an exam and got an accreditation fifteen years ago when there was a bonus in your wage packet for doing so. There's a lot more to being a detective than that.'

Stepney's mouth flapped open. Either he was insulted or he had finally worked out that silence was probably his best option right now. Maddie didn't reckon it was the latter. She was right.

'You talk about a defence solicitor. There won't be a defence solicitor. We have a direct admission — a guilty plea. Maddie here is putting a guilty case file together. The only trial will be for sentencing . . .' Tristan ran out of words. He fixed on the DCI as if he knew he was clutching at straws.

'Fortunately for all of us, DS Ives didn't take your advice to build a guilty case file and move on. Instead she took a trip

146

back out to that building and found this piece of the puzzle, something that might just give us a fighting chance to prevent this whole thing from coming back and biting us firmly on the arse. From biting ME firmly on MY arse!'

Maddie turned to look at the tipped blinds. She was certain they could be heard now as well as seen. When she turned back, Stepney was staring her down, one side of his mouth curled up in disdain. She knew he was furious with her. She didn't care.

'She's a fine detective . . . thorough,' Stepney spat, his attention still on Maddie.

'And maybe you are not.' The DCI's tone came back markedly different. It was quieter for sure but also a little warmer, encouraging almost. He followed it up with a sigh. 'Look, Tristan, we both know this move was born out of something other than your desire to lead a murder investigation. You are out of your comfort zone. You don't have the experience to be here. You've been stitched up to be honest and it's not your fault.' The DCI stopped talking and there was a silence that grew quickly.

'So how do we move forwards? Away from this?' Stepney spoke quietly now.

The DCI straightened up; this was the invitation he had been waiting for. 'We have two choices, the way I see it — actually, *you* have two choices. I need to make a call to the chief. You called him personally, I'm told, to make him aware that you had resolved this matter, so he will now need to know that the case is to be reopened and why. As you know, murder investigations are discussed daily in SMT's morning meeting. He will have questions. I can either tell him how this came about, including DS Ives's extracurricular work, where she felt the need to save this case on her day off, or I can brush over that part entirely. DS Ives here is not concerned with the chief knowing of her excellent work.'

Stepney flashed another glower in Maddie's direction. She had to resist the temptation to smile back at this one.

'Brush over?' Stepney's words were forced out through a locked jaw.

'I tell him that this appears to be a far more complicated investigation than we anticipated and, unrelated to this, you are taking a month's leave to deal with a stress-related matter. Doctor's orders. I'll propose that we bring Harry Blaker back into the fold to lead this one in your absence.'

'Blaker? B—'

'This is not your fault — none of it. This was a forced move. You cannot help what experience you do or do not have, and in what part of the business. I will be sure to tell the chief that, actually, you show potential for this area. However, maybe this has all been a case of too much too soon.'

'And if I refuse?' Stepney had been leaning back in his chair for as long as the DCI had been on the attack. Now he leaned forwards. The chair's mechanism creaked underneath him as he shifted.

'This is my department. That makes it my head on the block when a second girl turns up wrapped in plastic because we didn't investigate the first one properly. I will not have incompetence in my department. Take this option and you get a month off work and then a phased return into a different role that might be a bit more . . . *suitable*. For everyone. Life in Major Crime can be very difficult when the head of department wants you nowhere near it. Clear this desk of any of your things and get yourself home. If you refuse, your only alternative is to make another of your *personal* calls to our chief constable. You can tell him all about the fact that you closed a murder case without investigating the other suspects involved.'

'Other suspects?'

The DCI picked up the bag again. He shook it in Stepney's face. 'This! And still you have no idea what it means! Get out of my sight. Take your things with you and get to your GP today. You'll need a doctor's note.'

There was another silence. Stepney's attention was entirely on the DCI now. His only movement was to lean back as if he were making himself more comfortable. The DCI stood up to lean over him, his fists pressing down on the desk between them.

'This is how you save your career, Stepney. You have fifteen minutes before this office will be needed.'

It took another few moments of silence for Tristan Stepney to assess his options and realize that he didn't have any.

Maddie turned and walked out behind the departing DI without another word. The last thing she wanted was to stay in the office. The floor was hushed, even more so than when they had entered. All heads were down, the typing frenetic. Avoiding eye contact, she slumped back behind her own monitor and set about making herself look busy. Another couple of minutes passed. Still she hadn't looked up.

'DS Ives.' Julian Lowe was at her shoulder. 'Would you mind?' He gestured for her to follow him out into the corridor and then into a waiting lift. The DCI leaned on the button to shut the door but didn't select a floor. He began speaking the moment the corridor disappeared.

'Needless to say, that was a private meeting, DS Ives. What was discussed remains within those four walls.'

'Did you need me in there for that?' Maddie said.

'No. I just wanted you to see the outcome of your actions.' His voice was low.

'Are you angry with me, sir?'

'Never with your endeavour. Sometimes your methods . . . the position you put me in.'

'I . . . I didn't go out there with the intention of finding something to undermine the DI. I just wasn't happy . . . I wanted to be sure and he wouldn't listen.'

'I know that. That's the difference I hinted at in there. That's experience, your instincts . . . you can't teach that. Someone like Tristan Stepney doesn't want to learn it anyway. No chance of him acting on his inner doubts . . . not if they'd got in the way of a phone call to the chief constable to brag about how well he'd done.'

'I get that.'

'That wasn't the only reason I had you in there. He's a slippery character is our Tristan. Having you as a witness was the only way to make sure he didn't point the finger at you.' The DCI finally selected the ground floor. The lift whirred into movement.

'What happens now? Harry's either at Headquarters delivering training right now, or at home scratching around in his garden on a day off. Were you serious about bringing him back? We're right in the middle of this, sir. I know transfers can take time.'

'They can.' The DCI spoke as the lift settled and the doors opened. 'Which is not something we have, not now that we seem to be on the back foot.'

Harry Blaker leaned on a wall opposite. He pushed off to shake Lowe's hand. The DCI turned back to Maddie.

'How do you think I got hold of this?' He still had the webcam exhibit in his hand. He held it out for Maddie to take from him. 'It also came with a suggestion as to how I might use it to deal with Tristan. I assume you two know each other by the way?'

Maddie was aware she was grinning. She knew it might be inappropriate. She couldn't help it. 'We've met.'

'I need to get back to Headquarters. I'll go and see the chief myself. I don't like walking in that office with my tail between my legs because my department has made a mess of a job, but the chief needs to take some responsibility. This move of Stepney's was always going to end in disaster. I think it was meant to and I don't appreciate my department being used like that.'

'Is that what you're going to tell him? That bit about how Stepney has potential as a detective. Are you going to say that?'

'Am I hell! Sometimes an incompetent fool is just an incompetent fool. I'm going to go big on that. I'm also going to go big on the fact that I now have the solution, that I now have the right people in place and he will see quick progress. Don't let me down. The pair of you. Am I clear?'

'Clear,' Maddie said.

'And wipe that damned grin off your face, DS Ives. Anyone would think you liked working with this old bastard.'

'Not for a moment, sir.'

'Since when was I old?' The sound of Harry's growl was utterly joyous.

* * *

Four floors above, the Senior CPS Prosecutor for the region was shut away in her office doing some reading. The horror and the violence that lifted off the paper was unrelenting, even in the form of a summary report and despite these being her own words. Somehow the cold, factual style she'd used — as part of her justification for charge and then the protection of the victim under Op Icicle — made it worse. Linda could remember the full story behind each of these cases — the raw emotion. The top report was for Anna Loxton and her son Peter. This was the case that Ian Hessey had taken so personally, the one that had prompted him to station himself at her desk and wait for her to arrive at work. As part of the research for her report, she had watched the video interview with the victim. She had still been watching when the woman's son was led in. At the time, he'd been just six years old. PC Ian Hessey had brought him. He seemed to be the only person young Peter could feel comfortable with apart from his mother. Linda could still remember his tiny frame and the drumsticks he'd been carrying, held tight across his chest.

The interview had been carried out at a neutral location, a safe house for victims of sexual offences, somewhere that didn't feel like a police station, somewhere they were supposed to feel comfortable. It was featureless: neutral colours, police-themed leaflets and cheap sofas — hardly comfortable. Ian Hessey joined the two DCs who had been speaking with Peter's mother. The officers wore casual clothes — all part of an attempt to make the experience as normal as possible.

But it was far from it.

In those *normal* surroundings, that six-year-old boy had been asked to talk about the times when his daddy had hit his mummy. Specifically when he had beaten her with a length of knotted rope. When he had made the boy join in. When he had told Peter that his mummy was going to die and that he was going to have to watch and how no one would care because she was nothing to him — nothing to anyone. Because she was worthless.

But that would come later. For the first ten minutes Ian Hessey had talked softly with Peter about playing music, about how Ian had two daughters who liked music, too — his youngest especially, who was learning the guitar. The little boy's eyes had lit up, his grip tightening on the drumsticks as his enthusiasm grew and Linda found herself wondering if he ever put them down. His mother quickly referenced the drumsticks, feeling the need to explain that they were like a comfort blanket to him. Ian had waved her away. There was no need for explanations. After what this kid had been through, anything that might help him cope had to be positive. Skilfully, Ian had involved his two plain-clothed detectives more and more in the conversation until they had taken over and the information they needed had started coming. It had been seamless.

Linda had worked for the CPS for nearly twenty-five years. This was a job where the very worst of mankind was presented to you for your consideration and she was beginning to think she had seen it all. But this case stuck with her. It was the first Op Icicle case, the catalyst for all the others.

She flicked the sheet over. Her report came to an end halfway down. It was succinct, to the point, everything important covered and not a word wasted. She had a talent for that, after a lifetime of practice. She knew the next page contained the update, copied over from Social Services. She turned to it. It was longer, wordier. It covered more dry facts, including the change in his schooling that would be necessary and how the difficulties with this would be managed. She turned another two pages. The text went on and on. She scanned to the bottom, to the last sentence on the page.

Family A have now been assigned a new home address as follows:
This was it. She remembered the format. Social Services had referred to Peter and his mother throughout as *Family A*, but she had used real names. She hadn't seen any reason not to on a police document graded *secret*. She had written the new, safe address at the top of the next page, as you would in a letter. It was centred, too; she remembered doing that to make the document look neater, more pleasing to the eye, more professional. This was going to be good for her after all, she'd told herself. It was going to attract a deal of attention from the senior management team of a number of agencies; it could open doors for her. She flushed with guilt at the memory. That had been part of her motivation for this operation. It hadn't been all about protecting vulnerable families. But that's what they'd accomplished. And now all that work was about to be undone with the turning of a sheet of paper.

She flicked it over. The address was set out just as she remembered — and in bold. It would leap right off the page and into the camera lens. She made sure the paper was level with her buttonhole. The documents had come out of the printer one on top of the other. She quickly whisked through. She didn't want to read the other two reports. She remembered them both and didn't feel the need to linger on the details. She held each of them up in turn.

Then she stood up. She gathered up all the papers and forced them into the shredder in the corner of her office. She listened to the mechanism whirr and chew. She forced too many sheets in at first and had to step back to calm herself as the shredder snarled up and stopped. Finally, it was done. She actually felt better, as if the damage might have been minimalized, even reversed. But it hadn't. It was done. She was done. She wondered how she might receive her confirmation that this was all over.

She scooped up her suit jacket and made for the door. A flustered-looking Helen hopped back just as she was coming through.

'Oh! I was just doing another round. We have visitors out there, see? Are you coming back?'

Helen was already stepping past her to head into Linda's office, her head turning left and right as she did. She always was a nosey bitch. She was an admin assistant for the office, not even for Linda directly. Even so, she liked to know what was going on with everyone. That was why she was always so keen to make the tea, giving her frequent opportunities to sneak up behind her colleagues, to glance at their screens or loiter in the background while they spoke on the phone.

'Yes. Just getting some air.'

'Oh . . . you didn't drink the last one. Are you okay today?' Helen walked around her desk to pick up her cup.

'I just forgot it was there. Busy morning.'

'Busy shredding, I hear. Destroying the evidence, are we?' She laughed as her eyes moved to rest on the shredder.

'You got me!' Linda stepped through her door. She had no desire to prolong this conversation. She had to get out. She didn't look back.

CHAPTER 16

Janet Taylor walked up the grey steps that lolled from the entrance to Sessions House like a stone tongue. She hated this building. It was the county council's headquarters. This was the first time she had worked at this main hub, having spent most of her career out at ancillary buildings. It was also the first time she had spent any time in the company of councillors or senior members of the council's management team for that matter. They all seemed very similar types: pompous and self-righteous, in keeping with the pompous, self-righteous building they occupied with rooms humbly called 'great halls', 'chambers' or 'galleries'.

She worked an admin role in Children's Services and felt she was getting nowhere fast, having been overlooked for several promotions in recent years. The department did a lot of important work; she just didn't feel like any of it was done by her. Instead she got to view and organize the reports submitted by social workers who were out doing the work that was really changing lives for the better. She had access to everything they did, everything that was done with a family and what was planned for their future. This had made her important enough to be singled out, to be chained up in a dark, stone tunnel. To have her life threatened.

She kept her head down. Two men came out of the sliding entrance doors, carbon copies of each other in Janet's eyes. They were both old white men, wearing blazers with the council crest stitched onto the breast pocket over mismatched trousers that brushed the tops of their impeccably shiny shoes. They parted to go around her, guffawing at each other, aware of Janet as an obstacle only. She hesitated at the door for just a moment then smiled over at the woman on reception and the security guard leaning next to the front desk with his mug of tea.

Suddenly her mind ran with images of Marie Foreshaw, tied to her chair — the awful images they had shown on the screen. Marie had worked here, too. She would have walked this same route, past these same people, maybe feeling the same apprehension — aware that she just needed to do what she'd been tasked with and then the nightmare would all be over. Except it hadn't been — not for Marie. She had ended up suffocating to death, alone and terrified.

Janet walked up the stairs, away from the buzz that leaked from the canteen door at the foot. She made it to the more sterile corridors of the office area. It was an old building, one that quite literally bumped up against Maidstone Prison — all of the higher windows on one side had a good view down into exercise areas and across to individual cells. Overall, she reckoned this building had a similar feel about it to the prison. Every floor had its own central corridor that curved round in a loop, with offices coming off it on either side. All that was missing was the stereotypical prison guard running his baton down the walls as he patrolled the halls. She stopped at the entrance to her own office. All the answers they needed from her were just the other side of this door. It had a security sensor. She swiped it with the card hanging around her neck and it unlocked instantly.

* * *

If Harry sensed the elephant in the car, he was not going to be the one to address it. Maddie and he had the kind of relationship where they could talk to each other about personal lives, about home, about lost loves and hopes — even if such conversations with Harry would always be brief. Goodness knows, it had taken Maddie long enough to get to that point. Now it was like they were back to square one. Maybe it wasn't an elephant so much as an interior full of eggshells. They were half an hour into their journey and Maddie was tired of treading lightly.

'How have you been, Harry?'

'Half an hour. I thought you would have asked me that way back.'

'You knew it was coming, then. You didn't think of letting me off the hook?'

'I didn't realize I had you on a hook.'

'You know I worry about you.'

'You know you don't have to.'

'Don't I?'

'I've become rather experienced in looking after myself. Practice makes perfect an' all that.'

'You've had more than your share. No one should go through what you have. That must be difficult to process.'

'Only if you try to.'

'You must have, surely?'

'That's what the counselling sessions are for. I did. I started by comparing myself to other people. That can bring you down — you start taking it all personally. Especially with us, where we deal with the worst people. The worst people don't always get the life they deserve.'

'They don't.'

'You can start thinking you've brought it all on yourself. Maybe that's what I did. But I've talked it out. I know that's not how the world works, so I get to be at peace with it all.'

'Shit happens?' Maddie summarised and Harry spun to face her. She looked away from the road for just a moment to make eye contact. 'Sorry.'

He turned back to facing out his window. 'I mean, that's not how my counsellor put it, but I guess it amounts to the same thing.'

'And he's got qualifications? I could have told you that.'

'And I wouldn't have listened. Nothing personal. He has to drag it out of you. People like me don't get told things. They realize them.'

'He said that?'

'He did.'

'People like you?' Maddie turned to grin at the back of Harry's head.

He was still facing away. He still knew exactly what she was doing.

'Smile away, Maddie. I'm sure you have a quip about "people like me" but we all have to own who we are in the end. And maybe we're not so different.'

'I could take that as a compliment.'

'I wouldn't if I were you.'

Maddie pointed her grin over her shoulder as she backed into a parking space. As far as conversations with Harry went these days, this felt like a giant leap forwards.

They fell silent as they approached the building — back to the job in hand.

The receptionist smiled curtly. 'Can I help you?'

Maddie lifted her badge and the man in the security uniform, who had been leaning and flirting in equal measure when they had walked in, now stiffened with enough of a start to slop his drink.

'I was hoping to be able to have a quick chat with one of your employees. Nothing to worry about — she'd just be assisting us with our enquiries.'

'Enquiries? May I ask what enquiries they are?'

'No.' Harry lifted his own warrant card. 'I'm DI Harry Blaker. She won't be expecting us and we'll need a private room. We're not looking to embarrass anyone.'

The receptionist sat forwards, peering over the top of a pair of black-rimmed glasses. Her smile lacked warmth of any kind. 'I see. If you could sign in here, please. And can I at least ask the name of the person you wish to speak to so I can make the necessary arrangements?'

'Certainly. Janet Taylor. I understand she works in Children Services.'

'One moment, please.'

* * *

Everyone carried an aura of guilt with them when summoned unexpectedly by the police. The finest, most upstanding member of the community could fold in front of a person identifying themselves as a police officer — and it never mattered how you did it. Maddie got it out of the way hard and fast. She guessed Janet would already have been told anyway, but she didn't look any less shocked.

'Sorry to appear out of nowhere like this,' Maddie began. 'It's nothing to worry about. Please, take a seat.'

Janet did as she was told. Her attention flicked from Maddie to the already seated Harry, and back again. Maddie had already introduced them both and received nothing but wide eyes in response. Janet had a slight build, made all the slighter by the way she sat. With her crossed arms and her elbows resting on her thighs, she looked as if she was giving herself a hug. Her naturally curly hair hung down over her face in tight ringlets as she leaned forwards, like she might be trying to hide behind them.

'What's this about?' she said.

'A friend of yours . . . Marie Foreshaw . . . Is that right? That you two were friends?'

'We were friends here. Not really outside of work, though. She's my supervisor.'

'Work colleagues can become close, though, can't they? You spend a lot of time with each other for a start. Is that right? Did you sit near each other or . . . ?'

'The next desk. I know what happened. I saw the news. People are talking about it today. Everyone recognized her.

159

My boss called the police — they were asking for people who knew her. He might speak to you when we're done. I think he wants to know what to tell us all today. Everyone wants to know what happened.'

'He can talk to us, sure. We can't tell him much more than what's already been said on the news. We don't know much more. That's why we're here talking to you.'

'How would I know what happened?'

'Knowing what happened can be a long process. Part of that involves speaking to people who knew Marie best. You were friends — tell me what you know about her.'

'Know?'

'Was she in a relationship?'

'No. She was until recently, I think. She was popular with the lads . . . Oh God — *was*! I still can't believe it. I mean, I saw it on the news but it didn't seem real. I'm still waiting for her to come in and sit at her desk. But now you're here . . . it's all true, isn't it?'

'I'm afraid your friend is dead. There's no way I can skirt around that or make this any easier.'

'Murdered!'

'The circumstances support foul play. We're Major Crime det—'

'She was murdered.' Harry cut in. 'You have any idea why?'

Janet's face was a mask of shock. Her wide eyes now settled on the gruff inspector. 'Why? No! I've no idea why anyone would want to hurt Marie. She was such a lovely girl . . . She was just . . . cool — you know the type? It didn't matter what she did, what she wore, she just looked good in it. Never looked out of place. Good at everything. I should have hated her, really.' She managed a weak smile as her head dropped again. She sniffed and wiped a tear from her cheek. 'All the girls should have done.'

'Did anyone? Hate her, I mean.' Harry continued to aim straight to the point. Maddie tried to make eye contact with him. If he was aware, he ignored her.

'No! She was impossible to dislike. I know she got a lot of attention from the lads, even the ones who were seeing other people, but she never did anything about it. She never would have done. I saw her tell a fella off once. He was giving her some attention, turning up at her desk and following her whenever she went out for a break. I think he sent her something through the post. I don't know what. She called him straight away, said the next thing he sent she was diverting to his girlfriend up in HR with a note telling her exactly what had happened. She hates . . . *hated* cheats. This place is rife with all that. That's every office I've ever worked in, though, to be honest. I thought maybe she'd been cheated on before. Like that might explain her hard-line attitude. I didn't ask.'

'Do you know who this fella was?'

'No. That was ages ago too. A year, maybe longer.'

'Did she end up diverting anything to his girlfriend?'

'No. He backed right off. They do, don't they? Men, I mean. If it's not easy — if *we're* not easy.'

'Did you see her outside of work at all?' Maddie cut in before Harry could go again.

'A few drinks from work. We used to go into town to buy lunch a couple of times a week — always on a Friday, for sure. That was it.'

'Did she ever talk about a man she knew? Someone called Adrian? He might have been just a friend or someone who went running with her.'

Janet seemed to ponder for a moment. 'Adrian . . . No, I've never heard her talk about anyone with that name.'

'Would she have talked to you? If someone was hassling her?'

'I don't know, really. Like I said, we weren't best friends or anything. I'm not sure she was the type to complain, though. She would have just dealt with it. Is that who did it? Someone called Adrian?'

'We're looking at a number of theories right now. Did you ever go running with her?'

'No, thank goodness! I'm not much of a runner.'

161

'Did she talk about it? The running, I mean.'

'Not really. I know she liked it. She used to run with a group but she backed away from it. She said she didn't like the fact that there were definitely blokes just going along to look at her arse. She wasn't being arrogant — didn't love herself or anything — but she knew she was attractive and that she looked good in Lycra! Like I said, I should have hated her, really.'

'Is there anything that stands out for you, that you think might be important to a detective looking to find out why someone did this to her?'

'No . . . I really don't know what to say to you.'

'You don't need to say anything more. Let me leave my card. It has my details on it. If you do think of anything important then give me a call any time.'

'Important? I don't really know what that might be.'

'Anything at all. Just let me know and I can decide if it's important or not. Thanks for your time. Do you mind if I take an address and phone number for you? I don't like bothering people at work if I can help it.'

'My address . . .' That look of terror was back. 'What for? I really don't—'

'I'm sure I won't need it. It's just in case I think of something more I want to ask.'

'Then we can leave you alone,' Harry said.

'Okay, right . . . yes.'

Maddie thanked her one last time, then asked if Janet could point them in the direction of her boss's office. Janet showed them through to a separate office where a tall man stood behind a desk. Maddie took in the embossed letters on his nametag: Stephen Harris. Stephen Harris had a Bluetooth device hanging from his ear displaying a bright green light that, combined with his crooked stance and raised finger, made it clear that he was on the phone at that moment. The phone hosting the call was laid flat on the table. Harry stepped to it and pressed the big red button to cut him off.

The light on the device turned red — just as instantly, the man's expression turned furious.

'What the hell?'

'Police. Investigating the murder of one of your employees. You know that already, of course.'

'That was an important call.'

'More important than a murdered member of staff?' Harry dared him.

Harris's expression softened a little. He took his seat, pushing the phone to one side to symbolize that they had his attention.

'Of course not. Marie's not getting any deader, though, is she?'

'Life goes on, eh?' Harry said.

'I'm not insensitive. I said to that lot out there that they need to answer any questions, to tell you whatever you need to know. I assume they've been helping?'

'We spoke to Janet Taylor. We know she was close to Marie. Was she her closest friend here?'

'I don't know, to be honest. Janet was in Marie's team. They sat together. I think they were mates. I don't think it amounted to much outside of this place, though. Marie was a bit . . . aloof. Is that the right word?'

'You tell me. It's the second time we've heard something like it. What does it mean to you?'

'You know . . . nothing really impressed her. Nothing fazed her either. Like one of the cool kids at school that everyone knows and wants to be seen with. You had to work really hard to impress her, I know that much.'

'You were her boss, right?' Maddie said. 'Surely she should have been working hard to impress you?'

'Unless you're not talking about her work.' Harry's growl cut through the room to change the atmosphere once more.

'Hey! I'm a married man, okay? She was a good-looking girl, that one, don't get me wrong. She knew it, though. And, besides, I'm not that kinda guy. Definitely not here, not with someone I work with.'

'You don't wear your ring,' Harry pointed out.

'Neither do a lot of people.'

'For a lot of different reasons.'

'I'm sure you're right,' Harris replied. He eyed Harry, his expression back to being pissed off. He wasn't about to offer any more.

'What do you think happened to Marie, Mr Harris?' Maddie said.

'I saw the news. She was murdered, right? Found dumped at the old steelworks. They didn't say what happened to her. I guess it was a sexual thing.'

'What makes you say that?'

'Isn't it always? I watch a lot of dramas. The killers always go for the pretty young things. They can't get what they want so they take it. Poor girl didn't deserve that.'

'Anyone round here pay her any interest?'

'Everyone with a dick. And some without . . . but with the same *interests*, if you get what I'm saying.'

'Janet out there . . . she seems quite shaken up by the whole thing. Have you spoken to her?'

'Of course. We treat our staff well. I've told her that she doesn't have to be here today. I've got stuff to do with Marie's desk anyway. I need to clear it up and get her job out as a vacancy. I could do with Janet not being here for that, really. Like you said, she's all upset and that would probably set her off again.'

'Life goes on,' Harry said again.

Harris fixed on him. 'Which reminds me . . . I need to make that call you just cut off. This is how life works around here. Marie, this whole thing . . . it's sad but our targets and our work are still very much our primary focus. She had a heavy workload. She'll be missed in more ways than one. No point me standing up in front of our senior management team or as part of our independent reviews and explaining how we missed our targets because I let the team run rudderless out of respect. No one will care then, I can tell you that much.'

Maddie spoke. 'Let me leave you my card. Janet also has one. If she's struggling and needs someone to talk to, remind her that I can be that person, too. Sometimes it helps just to talk to the investigating officer. It can be a comfort to know there's a lot of work going on in the background to get Marie the justice she deserves.'

'Justice? The news said someone came in and fessed up to you lot. What's justice? Whoever he is he wants stringing up by his bollocks. Is that an option?'

'Not yet. We're working on it, though.' Maddie tried a smile, it seemed like a good way to leave it. Stephen Harris was already back to his phone call. Her card was still laid out on the table where he had left it. The light on his device turned green.

'Sorry about that. We got cut off . . .' he started as Maddie turned away to leave. Harry was a few paces behind. She waited until they were clear of the office and back out in the hushed corridor.

'You okay today?' she said.

'Okay?'

'You just seem to be going for the jugular. With anyone we come across.'

'Someone's daughter got plucked off the street and mur-dered. We didn't have time for that man to finish his damned phone call.'

'I agree with you. But we do want him to call us when he realizes something that might be important further down the line. Even if it isn't.'

'We won't get anything from him. The only thing important to Stephen Harris is Stephen Harris.'

'And you know that for a fact, do you?'

'Just as well as you do.'

Maddie didn't reply. She was supposed to have brought Rhiannon along that morning. Rhiannon hadn't minded when she had called and told her there was no need. She'd sounded positively delighted when Maddie had explained why. *Harry Blaker's back!* In all the excitement and with the relief of getting rid of Tristan Stepney — feeling like she could finally get back to working without one hand tied behind her back — Maddie hadn't stopped to consider what version of Harry might be returning. Impatient for results was one thing, but it didn't always get you what you wanted right away. Sometimes patience was the key.

Harry himself had taught her that.

CHAPTER 17

By the time Linda got back to her desk, her mug had been refilled, only to go cold again. Helen might have mentioned it as Linda passed her on the way back in, but Linda had ignored her. She had taken a walk out of Canterbury Police Station and into the city centre. She'd gone there via the underpass, which took her under a traffic-choked roundabout to the top of the high street. She had intended on finding a coffee somewhere, one she could bring back to the office. She reckoned it would create an opportunity for a phone call to confirm that she had done what was expected of her and to explain what happened next. Her phone had stayed silent.

She had walked back slowly, even including a lap of a nearby park then lingering by the entrance to the police station. When she'd finally gone back inside the building, she'd moved quickly, desperate to get back to the privacy of her office. Maybe that was when they would call her — once she was back behind her closed door.

Now she sat staring at her mug of cold tea, her stomach turning over with so much tension that she felt she might be sick at any moment. She hadn't touched her day's work. She realized in that moment that she couldn't be in the building any longer. Not today. She was so anxious that she felt barely able to hold a conversation, should anyone come to knock at her door. People would notice that she wasn't okay; they would ask questions. She needed to get out, to be anywhere but here. She started gathering up her things. She would tell the office that she was working remotely, that she wasn't feeling one hundred percent. She didn't expect anyone to question her. She didn't count on Helen.

'Are you okay?'

'Well, obviously not. That's why I'm heading home.'

'Nothing serious though?' Helen said. She seemed genuinely immune to sarcasm or a short response.

'Let's hope not. Sure it's nothing, but I wouldn't want to be the one that started spreading something around the office. I can be reached on my phone.'

Helen called out behind her with another question. Linda ignored it and kept walking. Her anxiety seemed to increase with every step she took away from her workplace. She would go home. She could appeal to the cameras. She prayed it would prompt the phone to ring.

She opened her car door and collapsed into the driver's seat. But she didn't even get to start the engine before her phone began to ring. She stared at the screen, temporarily dumbstruck. It showed *no caller ID*.

'Hello,' she answered after a moment.

'You are leaving work. You will be sent three words. Copy them over to the red application on the last screen on the phone you were supplied with. They will take you to where you need to go.'

'And then?'

She heard a click that confirmed she was talking to herself.

She dropped the phone into her lap in her haste to work it. 'Red application . . .' she murmured to herself, her thumb shaking as she worked through the screens. A red square occupied its own final screen. She pressed the icon and it changed to a map. Old Dover Road was labelled in front of her. The police station was marked too, as was the Riding Gate Roundabout, which she could see from her place in the yard. The map was criss-crossed with gridlines. A blue dot pulsed in the middle — right where she was sitting in her car. A bold black line came from the dot to label the square surrounding her: *target.wiring.sunset*. The words sat in a white box at the top of the screen. The phone vibrated in her hands and a text message slid down from the top of the screen. It contained another three words: *electrode.compliant.choirs*. She typed them in. The map changed instantly to a block of green sliced up by a couple of white lines. She zoomed out and saw the first place name she recognized: Bladbean. The map told her it was ten miles away. She pressed on a button marked *navigate* and a thick blue line showed the way from the police station. She balanced the phone where she could see it and started out.

* * *

Maddie and Harry joined the traffic trickling towards the M20 at junction seven. Ahead of them they could see brightly pulsing yellow lights and an oversized blue arrow informing traffic to pass the slow-moving vehicle to which it was attached. The irony wasn't lost on Maddie; the very presence of the slow-moving vehicle had bottled the traffic sufficiently to ensure a crawling pace. Her phone sounded over Harry's tutting and mumbling. It was Rhiannon.

'Hey!' Maddie was delighted to launch herself into a conversation where she didn't feel the need to be so guarded about what she said.

'Hey yourself!' Rhiannon sounded just as chirpy.

'How are you getting on?'

Maddie had tried to make up for not taking Rhiannon out to meet Janet by tasking her with digging around for anything on their offender. The key to closing this case, to convincing herself that this was just a random killing by a part-time madman, was to find out where Adrian Hughes lived and worked. And with whom he associated. Maddie was just as open to discovering other victims as she was to ruling him out of any involvement at all. There was definitely more to his story.

'I think we're finally getting somewhere. A man called Adrian Hughes registered with DWP a couple of weeks ago. At that time he claimed to have been unemployed for over thirty days after being laid off from a previous job.'

'A man *called* Adrian Hughes?'

'Yes. It's a different date of birth to the one our man gave, but it's close enough. Same year, so same age. That was how we missed him with the first checks. The search was too specific.'

'Okay.'

'I contacted the Home Office, the team that issues passports. You *have* to be specific with them. When I gave them this new date of birth, they confirmed that they had issued a passport in Hughes's name — it's still current. They sent me through the photo that was provided as part of the application. It is him.'

'So why lie about his date of birth?'

'At least now we can say he has definitely been lying to us. It might be something to go back to him with?'

'But what are we looking to achieve there? We need more and it would need to be relevant to the investigation for it to be worthwhile. Do we have an address for him now?'

'Yep. He gave the same address for his passport application three years ago as he did for his recent benefits claim. The electoral register shows it to be the home address of an Audrey Hughes. There is a much older passport application on file, too, from when he was a child and his mother had to apply for it on his behalf. Can you guess his mother's name?'

'Audrey.'

'Well done, Detective! And she's not far from here. Tankerton area, out on the coast.'

'Whitstable. I know it.'

'We're going to need to head over there. See if the mother has any answers.'

'We are. Are you still at the nick?'

'Yeah, of course.'

'Okay, great. See if you can get a search team together. This is our chance to get some answers. I'll head straight to that address with Harry and we'll see if we can speak with the mother first. There's no way of telling what she knows. Bring the search team to the area but stop a few miles out somewhere until you get a call from us.'

'No problem. I already spoke to the Tactical Team sergeant. They've been and done the woods where Marie Foreshaw's running route took her. Finished much faster than anticipated. They seemed really keen. I even got an invite to sit on the front seat of their bus!' Rhiannon chuckled. 'Tac Team buses are sacred, right? I should be honoured.'

'Excellent. Get them to the area and hang back for my call. And, Rhiannon . . . take your own car.'

Maddie ended the call. Harry had kept his eyes forwards throughout. He looked as expectant as he could from the side.

'Tankerton. Rhiannon's sending me an address. Hughes's mother. Looks like he was living there with her. You and I will go and say hello first. Then I have a search team making their way to the area. We might finally be able to get some answers about our man.'

'We might.' Harry didn't look away from the road. They still moved at a crawling pace. The car fell silent once more.

'We might not,' he added.

* * *

The map on her phone showed *2m to destination*. Linda had been watching the distance tick down, her eye flicking back to it almost every few seconds. She didn't know how to feel now she was getting close. She had done everything they'd asked but the response had been nothing more than further instructions. She dared to assume that getting her to drive all the way out here had been about them needing to meet,

171

so they could take the phone back off her, the camera too. Maybe they were in her flat right now. She knew Hope was out for the day. They could be removing all the cameras, putting her home back to normal. *Oh God*, she hoped that was why she was here.

0.5m

She had almost arrived. She was in the same place she'd been left in her car to count to one hundred. She recognized the dirt track that turned off the tarmac to lead away on her left. The gate had been pushed open, just like last time. Tall, lush grass lay flattened underneath it, looking out of place among the greenery. Clearly the gate was normally shut, and the grass able to grow as nature intended. She turned onto the track. The red pointer on her phone screen showed as though it was in the middle of a green field. She was certain it would actually fall over the open-sided barn she knew to be on the other side of the horizon. Her wheels rode over hunks of scorched soil then dropped down into the ruts the other side. Her car was an SUV. The sales patter had included a boast about its off-road ability and how it had 'quattro four-wheel drive' — whatever the hell that meant. Linda had never had any intention of actually taking the thing off-road but now she was glad of it. It came down heavy on the right corner, and the wheel closest to her shuddered and creaked like it might be too much for it. The sudden crunch forced the air out of her in a moan, along with much of her confidence in the vehicle's off-road ability. She slowed down. She just needed to get there and then away again.

The barn appeared the instant she cleared the brow. It was both familiar and new to her at the same time. The last time she had been here she was only intent on fleeing. Her eyes had been fixed firmly on the track ahead, with only occasional glances in the rear-view mirror, which had bounced and shuddered to blur the image behind.

Her progress was slower and more deliberate this time. She pulled under the cover of the barn until the sun was snuffed out. The sound of the engine through her open window was different, as was the smell. The scent of straw, dried soil and stale animals all drifted under her nose. She could see a stack of straw to her right. It was three bales high, two deep and seemingly pushed against the wall. It was starting to go dark orange at its exposed edges.

She had received further instructions on her phone. They had insisted she drive in front first and to aim directly for a tennis ball hanging from the rafters, stopping only when it was resting against her windscreen. She spotted the ball instantly. It was bright yellow and spun in the breeze. It was quite a way in. Her car had a long bonnet and she wasn't sure she was going to make it without hitting the wall in front. She leaned forwards in her seat to see as far over the bonnet as possible. The car edged forwards, her foot only on the brake as the automatic gearbox wanted to push her forwards. All her concentration was fixed on the swinging ball.

When her door was wrenched open, she never even saw it happen. Her foot jerked off the brake and the car rocked forwards; the thud of her vehicle against the wall was enough to lurch her forwards in her seat. By the time the engine died, she was already subdued under a hood. She yelped in surprise but she knew better than to fight it.

'Okay, OKAY! I did what you said!'

She was let go. The hood was made from the same material as the one she had been left with, the one she had been told to put back on the moment she stopped the car. She had every intention of doing it too. She had played by their rules up to this point, why stop now? She stayed in her seat, expecting more instructions, her arms out like she was egging them on, telling them to get on with it. She heard a back door open. The car shook a little beneath her as someone seemed to take their place in the back seat. Then there was nothing; no noise, no movement — just the sound of birdsong entwined in the warm breeze that pushed in through the window to move the hood and tickle her neck.

'I did what you said! You must have seen it?'

This hood seemed tighter; she felt her own breath bounce back from the material. Then it was gone, whipped upwards. She'd barely had a moment to blink when two hands reached down from above in front of her eyes then split in a blur. Then she felt her face gripped tightly by cool plastic. It wrenched her backwards into the headrest. The plastic film covered her face. Her head was fixed tightly in place. She shifted her eyes and found she could just make out a side window in the barn. The plastic was pulled tighter still and she instinctively tried to lift her head away from the headrest. Pain shot through her neck. She lifted her hands and scraped at the plastic with her fingertips but it didn't seem to make any difference. Her efforts earned her a shove in the lower back through her seat rest, where a knee had surely been placed as a brace. She had been holding her breath to this point, a shocked reaction. Now she gasped for air — but got nothing — just plastic sucking into her mouth and nose. In her mounting panic, she reached for a deeper breath. She felt the plastic again; this time it was slippery with saliva, pushing deeper into her mouth, filling every available space like water. She could now feel her lungs burning in her chest, as if they were being heated from the inside. Her fingers bumped and scratched against the thick layer of plastic. It was clearly multi-layered and pulled so tight that it felt entirely solid. There was no way to get a grip on it.

Her neck flashed again with pain, the muscles on either side stretched beyond their limit. Still she wasn't moving. Her vision was starting to close in. The block of light that was the window on her right was gone already. Now all she could see was a circular smudge of yellow at the top of her window and the dark wall behind it. She gasped again for breath. This time she took the plastic so far in she felt it scratch her throat. Her nose was blocked too. Her neck pain was now constant, she still fought but her struggles grew weaker. The resulting pain was muted and she could feel consciousness slipping away. The darkness in front now turned a bright white. This was it . . . this was how it ended.

Linda's mind flashed with an image of her daughter smiling on the doorstep, home unannounced from her adventures, so delighted to see her mum that it radiated from every part of her. The rays were white light. It came out of her mouth when she opened it to smile, and it came from her eyes. The light was growing and Hope was the source of it. She had brought it with her. She was here to take her. Linda had given up trying to draw breath; she felt calmer somehow. It was over.

Something tugged at the back of her throat and then the white light was gone. Dark shapes appeared once again. Instinctively, Linda gasped for air, taking huge gulps of it now the obstruction was gone. She was grabbed and rolled onto her right side. She could make out her driver's door; it was open. She was pushed in the back and her shin struck something as she was bundled out of the car. Now she could see nothing but the filthy floor. She seemed to hover above it, staring down at dried straw and mottled grey. She was wrenched downwards, her face and head grabbed so that her right shoulder took the brunt of the fall. She was then dragged away from her car and rolled onto her back. Each gulp for air was accompanied by a hoarse croak from her throat.

As the grip on her was eased, her first sensation was that of the cold floor. Then came the breeze against her exposed skin and the farmyard scents it carried. She was aware of someone standing over her, a figure that now dropped to a kneeling position, a head covered in a hood to appear as a block of darkness. A voice fell from the dark.

'Temporary addresses.' The voice was a muffled snarl, barely above a whisper. She didn't know if she had heard it before. 'You had a task. You failed.'

She was pulled to a sitting position directly facing a metal chair that was out on its own in the middle of the barn. Another hooded figure stood next to it holding a broom. She watched as he discarded the broom. It clattered on the concrete, but her attention stayed on the chair. She was now gripped under her arms and pulled to her feet.

175

'No! NO!'

She pulled her legs up at first but then realized she was being carried; despite her efforts, she was still moving towards the chair. Then she locked her legs out in front her, trying to get enough grip to push back, to push away from that chair. It was desperate. It was pointless.

She was bundled onto the cold metal seat. She resisted as someone tried to get hold of her hands, but her resistance was broken quickly with a blow to the chest. Her wrists were bound. The sensation of rope against her skin, the scraping chair, the breaths and grunts of the person behind her — it all came to an end and then everything was silent. She might have been alone in that barn, but she knew that they were standing right behind her. She expected the plastic to reappear at any moment, to be wrapped tight against her face. Her neck still ached; she wasn't going to be able to fight against it this time. It didn't matter. It hadn't mattered when she had been at full strength.

She wasn't going to beg either. She sat as straight as her tied wrists would allow. She faced the open side of the barn, which framed a rural scene of rolling fields of brown and green. A breeze moved white blossom through the sun's orange haze, and the long grass swirled and danced as it too became caught up in the breeze. It was beautiful. Linda felt a calmness that belied her situation. It wasn't the lonely, decrepit building that she had feared so much. She knew what was coming and she'd already sampled what it felt like. It only hurt when she fought it. This time she wouldn't try. This had been all about her so far. Hope had no idea anything was going on. With Linda gone, these men would move on. Hope would be left alone. She would be safe.

There was movement behind her. She sighed deeply. Then came a sound that she wasn't expecting — a metallic clunk. She looked to her right, to where an identical-looking chair was being scraped into position. A mobile phone appeared in front of her, lowered from above in a gloved hand. A glimpse of bare wrist between sleeve and glove gave away white skin and dark body hair. The screen on the phone showed movement. The format was instantly familiar — mobile phone footage of someone walking, captured at around chest height and pointed towards where they were walking. That was something more besides: Linda was looking at her building.

Another phone appeared for her to view, suspended from a different wrist. This time it showed footage from a fixed camera. It was angled downwards, towards a long sofa and a young woman picking at a bag of crisps on her lap while facing the television, her legs propped up, her whole body relaxed. It was Linda's flat. It was Linda's daughter. The image of Hope was snatched away. Now all that was left was footage of the communal door to her building. The door was pushed open, the camera now moving along the corridor towards the grand staircase. From here, Hope was two floors up. It looked like the stairs were being taken two at a time.

'What?' It was all Linda could manage.

Both phones were now gone and her captor kicked the empty metal chair so that it slid out to face her. The serene farmland beyond still fluttered with blossom, but it was now a blur as Linda focused on the chair. She knew who it was for.

'I did what you asked! I did it all!'

'Temporary addresses. They were useless. The families were moved to permanent addresses shortly after. You told us nothing. You knew they were temporary. Now you will both die here. But Hope will die first.'

'Please! I didn't know . . . I can find them! The addresses, that was a document written at the time but the addresses now . . . I can find them! Please!'

Someone appeared next to the empty chair. They moved it closer to Linda, close enough to bump lightly against her knees.

'I'm going to leave this right here. You'll be face to face when your daughter suffocates in front of you. She won't know why. Not ever. She will just know that it was because of you. You'll get to see every moment.'

177

'Please! She's got nothing to do with this!'

'The family NEVER do. But they suffer all the same.' The raised voice had so much power it was like another blow to her chest.

'Please! I'll do whatever you ask! Just leave my daughter alone. Whatever you need, please . . . not Hope. She's just a girl. I thought I had done what you asked! I tried!'

The chair scraped back. A hooded man now sat in it. He held a roll of plastic film stretched between his hands.

'You have failed to complete a simple task. You saw what happened to the last person who did that. She didn't get a second chance. Why should you?'

'I'll do anything! Please . . .'

'We can get to you. And your daughter. Any time we want. You belong to us. Do you understand?'

Linda jerked a nod. 'Yes! I know that. I thought I had got what you needed. I was so careful! I even printed them. I was worried the camera wouldn't wor—'

'Shut UP!'

This time the blow to her chest was tangible, a back-hander. It had shock value, enough to stop her talking.

'You understand that you cannot fail. Not again. The next information you give us cannot be anything other than everything we need.'

She nodded again. 'Anything! Please . . . I did what you asked . . . I didn't know—'

'There is a police officer . . . Hessey. You know this man. He is your friend.'

'Hessey . . . Ian Hessey? Yes, I know him.'

'He lives with his family. You are tasked with finding where this is.'

'His fam— Why do you need that? What has he—'

'His family or yours, Linda Morris.' The man lifted her off the chair. He kicked it away for it to scrape across the stone floor. He leaned in close enough for her to see where the hood was pulled tight over his nose. His words caught on the material, distorting them, but the menace and the bile were easily detectable. 'You need to decide, Linda Morris. I think you know what I mean.' He lifted his left hand out of her view. When it came back, he was holding a mobile phone for her to view. The screen still streamed a video image. It was her front door from chest height. The camera moved as if its holder was agitated — keen to get started.

'He waits for my instruction. Once that door is breached there are no options left. Your daughter will *have* to die.'

'Okay! I'll do it. I'll find out! I don't know him well enough to . . . I'll find out — I can do it.'

'An address on a piece of paper is not enough. You must go there. I want to *see* where he lives, I want the layout, the front door, the windows . . . the security.'

'Security?'

'Do you refuse?'

'No! No, I j—'

'So you choose his family?'

Linda couldn't find a response. There was nothing she could think of to say to that.

'I'll do it,' she said eventually. 'I can do it, okay?'

'His family or yours? SAY IT!' The muffled roar was delivered right up close. The hood backed away enough for the phone screen to push in front of her. '*Say* it . . .'

Linda felt a tear plunge down her cheek, blurring the digital image of her own front door. She filled her lungs with a deep breath. Without the chair, she had been left in a sort of squat and her thighs burned. She moved her eyes away from it all for just a moment, just as a gust of wind brought the blossom, like a ticker-tape parade, across the front of the barn. She felt the tear tickle as it rolled over her lips, as if it were trying to push them apart, to force her to speak.

'His family,' she whispered.

CHAPTER 18

Adrian Hughes's mother leaned around the door, sizing up the police officers who'd come knocking for her. Maddie knew instantly that she was Hughes's mother. Around the eyes, they were identical. The slight build was the same too, as was the nervous twitch of the head and eyes, the way she rolled her top lip back over her teeth as she prepared to speak.

'Can I help you?'

'I'm Detective Sergeant Maddie Ives. This is Detective Inspector Harry Blaker. We need to speak to you about your son.'

'My son? He isn't here.' She half turned away, like she was unsure of what she was saying. 'Is he okay? Did you find him?'

'Find him?'

'I haven't seen him. Not for days, not heard from him. But that's not unusual. Is he okay?' She was back to facing them, her eyes wider and her mind likely running with the worst-case scenario.

'He's fine.'

The woman's relief was clear, even though she was still mostly hidden by the door.

'Can we talk inside perhaps? I don't know if you have nosey neighbours, but I wouldn't want to discuss personal matters out here on the street.' Maddie was damned certain they had an audience. Audrey Hughes lived on a tightly packed housing estate interspersed by a rat run of alleyways. It had the feel of a place where very little could be done in secret.

'Personal?' Her eyes burst wide again.

'We need to talk about your son. Like I said, he's fine, but it's still a conversation that you might rather have in the comfort of your own home.'

'Okay . . . but I'm not really dressed. Can you come back in twenty minutes? Or an hour. I have to eat my meals at the right time or—'

'I'll come in with you. My colleague here can wait outside. He won't mind.' Maddie smiled encouragement then chanced stepping forwards to take hold of the door. Audrey Hughes's wide eyes locked onto her and, for just a moment, she held her ground. Then she stepped back. Maddie nodded at Harry and then worked the catch on the door so it wouldn't shut completely. Audrey was already moving down the hallway. She took the first left and then she was gone in a wisp of white nightie.

'I'm just getting changed.' Audrey's voice had a tremor in it when raised.

Maddie called back to say that was okay, that Audrey should take her time. She resisted the urge to walk through into the house and start poking around.

'Okay . . . I think I'm ready!' The Audrey who reappeared was cheery, her hair unbrushed but pulled back into a tight ponytail that showed off the whiteness of her scalp. She had pulled on a pair of grey leggings but her feet remained bare. Over the top, she wore a loose-fitting jumper, her hands mostly lost in its sleeves. Maddie worked the catch on the door and leaned out to make eye contact with Harry. When he stepped in, Audrey's smile seemed to drop away a little.

'What is this about then?' Audrey said.

'Audrey, your son attended Canterbury Police Station a few nights ago where he spoke to a colleague of mine. He told her that he had murdered a woman.' Maddie paused for just a moment. She wanted to let that sink in. The only response was a sudden flurry of blinks. She remembered a similar reaction from Audrey's son in the interview room when Maddie had increased the pressure. 'He then gave us enough detail for us to confirm that he was telling the truth. Adrian is now in prison. He is charged with that murder.'

Maddie waited for a reaction but the only one came from Harry; he collided with Maddie's elbow as he pushed past her. He was just in time. Audrey's legs seemed to give out all at once. Her head flopped back and the colour drained out of her complexion as if someone had pulled two plugs from out of her feet. Harry swept her up, stumbling forwards as he did so but keeping his footing. He leaned her back until he could pick her up, one hand under her knees and the other across her back. He bumped her hip gently into a door at the end of the hall which led into the living room. The curtains were drawn but there was still enough light for Harry to lay Audrey out gingerly on the floor, lifting her legs and positioning her head as they taught in basic first aid. He left her feet resting on the sofa and then looked over to Maddie.

'That could have gone better,' Maddie said.

Audrey's eyes were shut but her eyelids showed some movement. Suddenly they shot open.

'Are you okay?' Harry's low growl filled the room. Maddie whipped back the curtains closest to her and daylight flooded through a set of glass doors. Audrey turned towards it from the floor.

'Oh! I haven't done that in a while now . . . my blood pressure . . . sometimes it can drop — just like that. I'll be fine. I just need a few moments.'

'I'll get some water,' Maddie said.

'It's okay. Just give me a minute and I'll make some sugary tea. It's the best thing.'

'I'm sure I can work your kettle.'

Maddie found the kitchen. She always hated trying to do anything in someone else's house. Nothing was where it should be. When she took the drink back through, she found Audrey sitting on the sofa that still bore the indents from her feet.

'Feeling better?'

'I'm not sure I would say that. Did you not make yourself a drink?'

'No. I didn't like to. Besides, we've not long had one.'

'You should. You can't work without the right tools. It's like fuel for an engine. I always said that to my . . . to my husband.'

Maddie scanned the room, looking for a pair of discarded men's slippers or glasses folded neatly on top of a newspaper. Any sign of a male presence in the house. There was none. It was a small room. The house in general was small, part of an affordable housing development built in the eighties. All the houses had the same drab grey exterior, though some were weathering better than others. They were arranged in rough squares. The corner plots all had faux wood weather boarding that would have been white when it was installed but was now a washed-out grey. Audrey's place was one of the corner plots. The front door was actually on the side and accessed by an alleyway. Everywhere around here seemed to be accessed by an alleyway.

At least the interior was a bit more welcoming. It was neat and tidy with clean surfaces. The tiny television carried a smear mark from a cloth and sat on a low table opposite an armchair. There was another sofa but it looked like it was just filling a space. It had likely come as part of a set and had been pushed against the only wall long enough to accommodate it. The whole place had the feeling of a home arranged around a single person.

The outdoor space was cheery too. With the curtains open, Maddie could see a small slabbed yard through a set of double doors. It was dotted with numerous pots of different shapes and sizes, each sprouting a brighter display than the next.

'Who else lives here, Audrey?' Maddie said.

'Well . . . it was just me. Adrian, my son, he came back. He had his own place but he gambled the whole damned thing on love and lost. They do that, don't they? Men, I mean. They see a bit of something they like and they're willing to throw just about everything they ever had at it.'

'A girlfriend?'

'Not for long. He never keeps them for long.'

'What was her name?'

'No idea! Adrian doesn't talk to me. I'm only his mother!'

'So how did he lose his place?'

'He was renting. Overspent trying to impress her and then missed a couple of his rent payments. He got a warning and I told him to sort it out. It was a nice place. I even said I'd give him the money but he had other ideas. He said he was moving in with this girlfriend, that his landlord could "take a running jump for it". That's not like him at all. I've never known him not to pay his way. It was her influence — it must have been. He seemed angrier, too, just recently. Then he lost a job he'd had for ages. Said he got laid off, but I'm not so sure. It's a strange thing to be living with your son and feeling like you don't even know him anymore. I assume that's what this is. Did he hurt her?'

'We don't think this was anything to do with a girlfriend. Adrian told us that his victim was a stranger to him, a young woman he was monitoring on a running app.'

'A running app?'

'It's a thing people have on their phones. They post when they've been out for a run. Adrian used it to work out where she was going to be and then he waited for her.'

'Waited for her?' Audrey's eyes seemed to scour the room, looking beyond the two detectives. 'Murder . . .' The word seemed to have finally taken on meaning. Her posture stiffened and her eyes opened wider than ever, but with no focus. She had to steady herself by moving her hand to grip the armrest.

'Adrian killed this young woman. He says it was a random act. That this was something he had wanted to do for a while. I have a team of police officers coming here to search this house. Your house. I want to be sure that he hasn't hurt anyone else.'

'A runner? Oh . . .' Audrey's head was shaking. She suddenly seemed to fix on Harry. Maddie had been doing all the talking; maybe Audrey was looking to him for a different story. 'The news . . . on the radio . . . they said about a girl. They wanted to know who she was. She was picked up and murdered . . . they said she was a runner! They said someone had been arrested . . . Not my Adrian . . .' The plugs in her feet seemed to have been pulled again, the colour drained from her face just as quickly, her breathing turned shallow, her eyes rolled back in her head.

Harry was ready. He steadied her in her seat then pulled her forwards, manoeuvring her feet so they were higher than her head. Maddie took the opportunity to slip out to make some more sweet tea.

She also called Rhiannon, who updated her that she was just around the corner with the Tactical Team. Maddie didn't see the point in waiting any longer. She ducked her head in the living room to find Audrey over her faint and huffing in her seat, and then called Rhiannon and the team forwards.

Her uniform colleagues arrived soon after. Everything about them was heavy, their boots and every step they took in them. Even their search kit was stored in a large toolbox with a handle that retracted with a heavy clunk. One of the officers carried a ladder that folded out from nothing to reach up into lofts and cubby holes. Despite it being neatly folded away, he managed to bounce it off every wall and cabinet in Audrey's compact home. He apologised the first time but didn't bother after that.

'How long does this take?' Audrey breathed. The cup of sweet tea was noticeably shaking in her hand. She was rattled. Maddie could hardly have expected any different, but her shock and despair were turning to anger and stubbornness. Any questions were now met with one-word answers, and not helpful ones.

'I'll go and see how they are getting on.' Maddie nodded at Rhiannon who had been making her best attempts at small talk since unleashing the search team on the house.

Then she headed upstairs. The search was focusing on a room that had been identified as Adrian's. It was small, made smaller by the fact that boxes and overflowing bags lined either side, all covered in a consistent layer of dust that suggested long-term storage rather than daily use. The officers searching the room rolled their eyes as if this was something they'd seen a million times. One of them summed it up without being prompted.

'Boxes of shit, really. A lot of old toys, models and old school books and I don't think his heart was in it really.'

'His heart was in what?'

'His schoolwork. Collected up more than a few *see-me*s, if you get what I mean!'

Maddie stepped in. A dusty box marked *World of Warcraft* clogged the sill of the only window. The sleeping area comprised just a mattress laid out on the floor. All around the mattress, boxes were stacked at jaunty angles, as if they had been pushed to make way for it in a hurry. Next to the pillow was an open laptop with a dark screen, the power light still flashing where it was plugged in. That and some freshly painted figurines were the only signs of recent life. It fitted with the account his mum had given. A man who had lost his girlfriend and his accommodation in one fell swoop, who had needed to move back in with his mum into his old room where his entire childhood was still being stored.

'Anything of interest?'

'Not really. So far, we've seized unopened mail, a note-book with some thoughts scribbled across it and a whole book of bizarre drawings. Did you want to see them?'

'Bizarre?'

'Lovey-dovey crap. What I'd expect my thirteen-year-old daughter to come up with. Two people sat inside a heart, that sort of thing.'

'Any names mentioned anywhere? Any idea who the missus was?'

'No names. Hearts, though, lots of hearts!'

'He's really not making this easy for me. Can you drop all your exhibits into the Major Crime office? I'll book them into special property. I like to have a look at the stuff as it goes in.'

'You sure? Most of it's gonna be shit. We usually have a few of us logging it. Saves time.'

'It's okay. I like to see everything that's come out.'

'No problem.'

In the living room, Audrey's sulk had worsened. Maddie was now sulking herself. She had dared to hope they'd find answers here. Even if the search had been a waste of time, there was always Adrian's mother . . . she should know more.

'Who is Adrian's ex-girlfriend?' Maddie blurted.

'I don't know her. I already told you. I never met her. He said he was going to bring her round but he never did. Always had an excuse not to. I knew he was keen right from day one. It must have been her. She changed him, she did. My little boy would never have hurt a fly. But that woman . . . She got him all het up!'

'But you don't know anything about her?'

'Don't need to. I know my son. She got him spending all his money on her. He's never been in debt in his life. Then she came along and suddenly he's got himself a credit card, suddenly he's got no savings, suddenly he didn't have the money to make his rent. The Adrian I knew would have walked over hot coals to pay his rent on time. He's always been terrified at the thought of owing money. He gets that from his father; he always paid his debts. He was a good man. Adrian's a good boy!'

'Do you know how they met?'

'Work. That's what he said. He worked in IT. He used to go round different places. He installed software or something. Sometimes he would work at one place for a long time — months, even years. I was happy at first. A man his age should be meeting girls. I just wish she'd been the right one.'

'Where was that? Where did he meet this girl?'

'I don't really keep up with what he's doing, you know? I'm not there with him all the time. He goes to work and then he comes home. He was living on his own when he met this girl.'

'How long ago?'

'I don't really know. Six months or so since I first heard about her. But he doesn't talk to me. It could have been a while before that. Not long in the grand scheme of things, but long enough to change him.'

'You must know a first name at least. He must've talked about her.'

'Look, Detective, it sounds like my son is in enough trouble. I don't really want to be answering no questions, not about Adrian. I already told your friend here. I don't know what you're trying to get out of me and I don't like it.'

'So you do. Know a name, I mean.'

'Did you ask him?'

'I'm asking you.'

'All I'm saying is that it's him who needs to be answering your questions. He needs to talk to you. I don't know him anymore.'

'I'm not sure he murdered anyone, Audrey.' Maddie was aware of Harry shooting a look over at her. She ignored him. 'Not as sure as I want to be.'

'What? You come here and tell me my son's a murderer. Now you're telling me you might be wrong? That he might not have killed that woman?'

'I'm just saying that I want to be sure. Adrian couldn't convince me. I need to know that this ex-girlfriend's okay to start with. If Adrian is indeed capable of murder, I need to know that the victim we know about is the only one. No matter what you think of this girl, she has a mother too. And if he isn't capable of murder, if he didn't kill that girl out on her run, then his girlfriend is the best person to fill in all the blanks here. To tell me what's really going on. If you know anything that might help me find her, now's the time to share it. This could really help Adrian.'

Audrey took a moment. She blinked in a flurry. 'I don't know much, even though she was all he ever talked about. It was all, "Jan said this and Jan did that."'

'So, Jan then.'

'I don't know a surname though, okay? He never told me.'

'You said he was going to live with her. Did he mention where?'

'I know they were looking at Maidstone for a while. I think that suited them both for work.'

'Maidstone . . . Did he ever work at the council building up there?'

'He worked for the council off and on, has done for years. His firm have a contract with them — his old firm, at least. He even got himself laid off from there. I don't know where . . . all over. He talked about putting a whole new computer system in for the council. It was a big thing, one of the projects that took a while.'

'So Jan could have worked for the council?'

Audrey shrugged. 'Maybe. I can't be sure. I said that already. How much longer is this going to take? I need to eat regularly — doctor's orders.'

Maddie glanced at her watch. It was well gone five p.m. 'Dammit!' Her response was almost involuntary. Audrey must have heard her.

'You got somewhere to be?'

'Council offices. They'll be shut for today.'

They were interrupted by the officer she had spoken to upstairs. The Tactical Team were done. They would see themselves out. Maddie waited for them to close the front door behind them. She winced as it slammed.

'We'll get out of your way, too, Audrey. I am sorry for the upset. I can't imagine the shock of us turning up — and with what we had to say.' Maddie held out her card. She put it on the arm of the sofa when Audrey didn't reach out to take it. 'Those are my details. You may have some questions, when you've had time to think about everything that's been said here.'

'Here's a question . . . What happens next? Does he just get thrown into jail and forgotten about?'

'Not quite. There will be a trial for sentencing at least.'

'For sentencing? Don't he even get to defend himself? A lawyer, like you see on the TV?'

'He's choosing not to defend himself. He came in and told us he murdered that girl and he's sticking to his story.'

'But you don't believe him?' Maddie felt herself being studied closely.

'I never just believe anyone, not without the facts to back it up. But he's making it very difficult to look anywhere else. He's not giving us much choice right now.'

'Where is he?'

'The Isle of Sheppey at the moment. HMP Elmley. But he's likely to be moved after . . . when it's all sorted.'

'Can I see him?'

'Of course. I'll have someone contact you to set that up.'

'Okay then. I shouldn't need you for anything else. Goodbye.' Audrey didn't get up. Maddie made eyes at Harry. They both hesitated for a brief moment.

'You're not going to be feeling faint again, are you?' Harry said. 'Anyone I could call to come and sit with you?'

'My son! How about that? He's the only one left to look after me. If you can't do that then I suggest you leave me to it.'

Maddie was already at the front door. Harry waited for the front door to shut behind them before he spoke. 'The council offices . . . are we sure they'll be shut?'

'I'm sure *Jan* won't be there anymore.'

'You think she's the same young woman we met earlier?'

'If she is — if she knows Hughes — why wouldn't she tell me? I specifically asked her about the name *Adrian*.'

'You did. Slipped her mind?'

'I can't wait to ask her.'

CHAPTER 19

'Ian? It's Linda . . . Linda Morris. I'm really sorry. HR gave me your number. I hope you don't mind . . .'

'Linda! Of course I don't mind.'

Ian Hessey's voice was cheery, even over the phone — just like it always was. Linda gripped the steering wheel tightly and her stomach knotted. She pulled over suddenly, feeling like she was going to vomit. The car door seemed heavier than normal. Outside, the warm air carried the scent of the countryside. She was just a few miles from the open-sided barn, a place she had convinced herself she was never going to leave. The shock of it still lingered. The scenery here was similar: churned fields and a distant copse of mature trees. She focused on the horizon; she remembered hearing that was good for nausea.

'Linda? Can you hear me okay?'

'Ian . . . sorry! You picked up just as I was getting out of the car.' She had to battle a tightening throat to get the words out. She took some deep breaths away from the mouthpiece of her phone.

'My fault entirely!' The cheeriness was back.

She and Hessey had worked together a lot in the early days setting up Op Icicle. It had been hard, particularly during that first month or so when they'd had to work their way through the senior management team, looking for support. They'd had to repeat their message over and over to make themselves heard, for something to stick. Trying to stay passionate and determined had been exhausting.

When the idea had finally got the endorsement it needed, it had been necessary to brief the rank and file, to interrupt team meetings and send out training packages labelled *mandatory*, forcing their project on busy officers who already had a million things to remember when attending domestic calls. It had been hell at times. She had doubted herself — her ability to stick it out — and wondered countless times what she had got herself into, whether it was even a good idea at all. Ian Hessey had never doubted it for a second. He had been the driving force right from the start, the linchpin holding the whole thing together. And, no matter what, that cheeriness had never left him.

'Sorry to call you out of the blue.' Linda forced a couple of swallows to lubricate her tight throat.

'Always a pleasure. Long time no speak, though, Linda.' Ian's tone darkened a little. 'Is everything okay? Calling HR for the number . . . anything serious?'

'No, no, nothing terrible. Just something I needed to run past you.'

'I see. Well, what can I do for you?'

This was it. She had been able to access the internal police website from her phone. From there, she had checked Ian's shifts. She knew he was off duty today. Tomorrow, he had a cell note that showed *residential course*. This was her only opportunity. It had to be now.

'Actually, I was hoping to come and speak to you in person. Like I said, I'm sorry it's out of the blue. I wouldn't have gone to this effort if it wasn't important. I wanted to run a case file past you. Are you in work?' She tried her utmost to sound casual, despite the pain and the tension that she could feel in every part of her.

'No, unfortunately. I just came off nights and I go on a driving course tomorrow. That takes up the rest of my week.

I'm back next Monday if that's any good? I can pop up then — always happy to. You know I'm off Op Icicle now?' He sounded a little unsure, like he was embarrassed to even ask the question. He had told her personally when he was redeployed, made a point of coming to see her. It was always the plan that he'd return to his team once Op Icicle was set up. That hadn't happened long ago either; Linda couldn't claim to have forgotten.

'Of course. And I'm sure you just want to leave the whole thing behind you. It's just, I'm in need of a fresh set of eyes and there's no one I can think of more experienced with all this. It's okay if it's a problem . . .' She knew Ian Hessey and people like him; they could never say no. Still, she silently prayed he wasn't about to prove her wrong. She needed him to agree . . . but she also needed to keep her request casual. Her desperation threatened to undo her, to make her beg — something so out of character that there would be no coming back from it.

'Well, I'm flattered! I'd be glad to help. Be nice to keep my hand in, I suppose. I start at seven on Monday. I can come in early an—'

'Actually, Ian—' She stopped herself. There was nothing casual about talking over the other person. 'Sorry! It's an urgent one. We have the possibility of a new Icicle case. We need to apply for the court papers today. I was hoping to be able to speak to you before the deadline.'

'I see. Well, like I said, I'm not at work. Not sure I can—'

'Could I pop out and see you? I have a few errands anyway. It'd be two minutes of your time — only I can't talk about it over the phone.'

'Oh.' The surprise was thick in his voice.

Ian had suggested swapping personal numbers before in case they needed to speak to each other out of work. She had been the one to make it clear that work and personal life needed to be separate, that he needed to switch off. She was already behaving out of character, but there was nothing she could do about that. His next words were so important to her she was actually holding her breath.

'Sure . . . I mean, I'm out myself at the moment. We've just moved, see, and I ran out of pink paint! It's a long story. Maybe we can be somewhere at the same time for a quick coffee?'

Linda tried to think fast. 'I'm all over the place myself. What time will you be home? That seems like a more sensible idea. Otherwise the logistics might be a little difficult.'

'Home? Oh . . . Well . . . I've got some bits to get, then I need to drop something off at the solicitors' and some other stuff. It won't be until a little later. Around half six, I think. You'll be off work by then and I'll still have some painting to finish. Sorry about this. This is the worst time for me — you couldn't have known that — but just moving house and all that. Is it something you can make a decision on without my massive expertise?'

There was a chuckle in his voice, but it didn't fool Linda for a second. He was refusing her visit; he just didn't want to say it directly. There shouldn't be the need anyway. Etiquette now demanded that she recognize he was busy, that he was on leave and away from work and had a lot to do.

'Half six is fine. Where do I need to come?' Linda was holding her breath again. She'd backed him into a corner. This was where Ian Hessey could surprise her — tell her that, actually, it really wasn't a good time, that she was easily qualified to assess a case and determine if it merited Op Icicle protection or not.

'Oh . . . okay then, yeah. We're out in Lympne now. I'll text the address. You'll need the postcode for the satnav. I don't actually know it off the top of my head — haven't got used to it yet!' He chuckled again then fell silent.

Linda waited. She heard an announcement over a shop tannoy in the background. '*Half off all kitchen units . . .*' She pictured him with tins of paint in his trolley, old clothes, hair unkempt, ready to start the next chapter in their new family home, his mind anywhere but on his day job. He had talked about moving a few times. They needed a bigger home, he had said. His daughters were sharing a room.

Oh God . . . his daughters . . .

Linda had been so fixed on her own situation she had barely had the chance to consider anyone else's.

'Is that okay?' Ian's voice again.

The silence had been too long and she hadn't replied. His children were young — two girls, both at primary school. Ian had talked about their school, how they didn't want to move them too far.

'Linda?'

She needed to answer. She could tell him to forget about it. She could go back and get Hope, and they could run. She stared back over at her car, suddenly considering going to the police, telling them everything. She knew enough people to be able to raise the alarm without alerting anyone to what she was doing. But then what? Her mind raced with images of the bruised police officer — *#1 Dad* — then the young woman still chained in the darkness, waiting for Linda to complete her task . . . what happened to them if she didn't go through with it? How many other people and their children depended on her doing as she had been told?

'Thank you, Ian,' she managed. She was still staring at her car. It was not going to be a getaway vehicle today; it was going to take her to Ian's new family home.

'No problem. Are you okay over there? Is there still a lot of politics around it all?'

'Yes! Politics . . . always. Thanks again.' She stumbled to a finish and ended the call, aware that her voice was starting to shake.

She checked her watch. Half six was an hour and a half away. The knot in her gut tightened. She dashed for a hedge-row and heaved. Nothing came.

'Get a grip!' she scolded herself. She stood up straight, her focus back on the copse of swaying trees. She tried deep breaths but couldn't shake the remnants of that phone call. *Two daughters.*

She heaved again.

* * *

Maddie stopped the moment she turned into the bare corridor, her hand resting on the cold banister. She was still a little out of breath from the two flights taken up the middle of the large block of flats. She now knew for certain what she had suspected the whole way here. This was not Janet Taylor's address.

The elderly woman who answered was an instant match with the fake flowers that hung either side of the door and the welcome mat with a daffodil stitched into its corner. She told Maddie that she herself had lived there about four months.

'Just enough time to start putting my stamp on the place,' she had chuckled. And no, of course she didn't have a forwarding address for this *Janet* girl they were asking about. She had never even met her; it was all done through a letting agent. She handed their number over willingly and wished Maddie the best of luck with it. The number had rung out. Maddie hadn't expected anything else at this time of the day. She knocked at neighbours' doors. Most were in. Some vaguely remembered a girl living there, but no one had more to say than that.

As Maddie and Harry stepped out of the building the sky seemed to carry a warning. Tinged grey with a hint of purple, it gave the whole evening an angry look, as if it were building up to something spectacular. It matched Maddie's mood.

'So what are we saying?' It was the first thing Harry had said since they had arrived at the building. 'That this Janet is involved? That this wasn't a random killing after all? That Janet was part of the reason Hughes chose Marie Foreshaw?'

'Well, we don't know that, do we? That's why we're here,' Maddie snapped. She hadn't meant to. She continued her walk away from the building, suddenly conscious that her voice might be carrying, that this might not be the best place to discuss it. 'Sorry, Harry. I'm not angry at you — obviously. I am angry, though. I really don't like being lied to.'

'I get that.'

'She can come in . . . conspiracy to murder.' Maddie stopped a little further away from the residence, her voice a little more hushed but no less determined.

'You want to arrest her?'

'You don't? We have reasonable suspicion. She gave me a duff address. I think she's linked — she has to be. Hughes was dating a *Jan*, almost certainly met her at the council and they were house-hunting in Maidstone. This just seals it for me. She lied to me.'

'So you said.' Harry smiled. Maddie did too.

'What?'

'I just realized I might have missed you too,' Harry said.

'Which bit? The excellent detective work or the patience of a toddler?'

'The patience thing.'

Maddie continued walking towards the car. 'Well, she'd better turn up for work tomorrow. She doesn't want to make me go looking for her.'

'Even if she doesn't, we'll find her.'

'I could call a few of the agencies . . . DVLA, the Home Office for passports . . . maybe she updated one of them with a new address. They always have an out-of-hours service.'

'They do. For emergencies. And what are the chances? She'll still be there for us in the morning. For you, I should say. It's a few hours. Nothing's going to change overnight, is it?'

Maddie sniffed. 'Let's hope you're right.'

CHAPTER 20

Linda's satnav made her jump, despite its soft, female voice suggesting that she *take the next right*. She was in the village of Lympne, just passing the back of Port Lympne Zoo. As she slowed ready to make the turn, her eye was dragged left, to where the perimeter of a tall cage came right up to the road. Two large wolves circled behind the bars, their sides brushing against the steel. The knot in her stomach tightened again.

She had now entered a housing estate, filled with pleasant family homes, forty or fifty years old perhaps, constructed back when estates were made up of logical rows of semi-detached houses rather than a warren of turns and traffic-calming measures. It meant she could see all the way along to where the road came to a dead end and the row of houses turned to face her. The pointer on her satnav told her that Ian's was one of the last on the left before the dead end. She rolled the car to a halt, though she was still some distance from Ian's door.

This was it.

Ian had done as he said he would. His door number and postcode had appeared as a message on her phone within seconds of her ending the call. Her feelings had been mixed when they had come through. She had half expected him to send an apology, to say that it wasn't convenient after all. But she had his address now. She had what they needed.

She got out of the car and started walking. The camera in her buttonhole would be capturing the whole street, her whole approach to Ian's door. The houses passed slowly to her left and to her right. Number nineteen was prominent on her left, the estate agent's board skewed at an angle on the edge of the front lawn to confirm she was at the right place.

The gate out front came up to her hip. It squeaked as she pushed her way through. Suddenly, she was struck by the feeling that she was there a trespasser — there to do wrong. Guiltily, she took a moment to look around, to see if anyone was out on the street and taking notice of her. A man was out on the other side of the road wiping his car. She remembered passing an elderly woman who had been down on her knees tending to flowerbeds, her backless gardening shoes peeling away to show the cracked skin of her heels. She didn't reckon either of them had even glanced at her. She didn't look out of place. Why would she? She lived in an area like this — good people with good jobs going about their lives.

She knocked the door. The answer took her breath away.

'Girls! I told you not to answer that door!'

Ian's shout sounded like it came from the back of the house. But it was two children that stood in the doorway. There was no mistaking they were sisters, one a slightly older-looking version of the other. The younger one had slightly darker hair but the blonde tips were just as light as her sister's. Both wore dresses; both smiled in the sunlight that put a twinkle in their eyes. The younger girl took a step back, her smile dropping away quickly, as if she had been expecting someone else. The elder held her ground but with a wary expression.

'Sorry!' Ian was flushed and stumbled on a cardboard box as he rushed to the door to pull his girls gently away from the open door. His feet were bare, and he wore tired-looking shorts and a T-shirt with spots of fresh pink paint on them. Beyond him, Linda could see a lot more boxes. The walls were light grey with darker squares where pictures must have hung until recently. The whole house smacked of changing hands. It had the look and feel of chaos.

'They were expecting their mother. She's bringing them McDonald's. For a treat!' Ian added hastily, as if he was worried she might judge.

She held up her hands. 'The last thing you want to be doing is cooking, I'm sure.'

There was an awkward silence. Ian didn't back away from the door, and Linda realized that she had just acknowledged his situation.

His eyes dropped to her hands. 'Did you bring the file? That's what you wanted to talk about, right?'

'Oh . . . no, I didn't in the end. I don't like taking files out of the station, you know . . . you don't want to be the person to leave something crucial on top of their car roof!' She laughed. No way was she convincing.

'I can put the kettle on. Were you staying for tea, or . . . ?'

'No. Thank you. Just a few minutes of your time.'

Ian's relief was obvious. He finally backed away from the door and called out as he led her down the hallway.

'Mind the boxes! I always used to apologise about the mess when people came round. I don't bother since we moved. People can see we're all over the place!'

'Yes, I know what it's like. Don't worry.'

Ian's house might have been a mess of boxes with faded patches on the walls, but it was already becoming a home. The main bits of furniture had all been put in place; coats and shoes were neatly stacked. When Linda walked into the kitchen, she saw a fridge already dotted with pictures and colourings that she could easily imagine in the clutches of the two girls as they bundled out of school, their faces beaming with pride.

The kitchen was a nice space. It stretched the whole width of the house. The back wall was a lot further back than it had been originally, extending out into the garden to double the size of the room. The view out was through large doors, which folded over to one side to leave a wide gap, allowing the chirps of garden birds to float in from outside. The kids had already thrown themselves down onto bean bags that had been shaped to face a cartoon playing softly on a wall-mounted television.

'This is a lovely room,' Linda said.

'The main reason we bought the house, really. Somewhere we all get to be together. It's so nice.'

Ian surveyed the room, hands resting on his hips, his face a half smile. She could tell he was in love with this place. The knot of anxiety in her stomach came back in a wave, threatening to make her heave again. She had been careful to point her buttonhole at the front door before knocking. Then she had been aware that it would be getting the hall as she walked the length of it. She had deliberately turned her top half towards the door that led into the lounge to show the layout. In the kitchen, she had been sure to face the doors, even taking a sideways step to get a better angle from behind where boxes were stacked, with two dolls propped up against them, on the table. She was in work mode. Going above and beyond, considering how she might be able to get a view of the handles of the bifold doors, just in case that was something that was needed. She had been given a task and she was doing it to the best of her ability. Guilt was quick to mingle with her anxiety. The hooded man hadn't shared their intentions for Ian Hessey. She didn't know why they might want to know the layout of his home, the type of locks, how many occupants . . . but she wasn't naïve. Or stupid.

'Are you okay?'

Linda was still struggling. It must be showing externally. Her mind flashed again with the question they had put to her in the barn, *His family or yours?* She might have struggled to say the word in reply, but she had known the answer instantly: *his family*.

Now she stood in his kitchen, in his new home, somewhere to escape his job and the horrors that went with it. People like Ian Hessey couldn't compartmentalize those so well either. She knew him well enough to be able to label him as a type. He cared about people. He couldn't just see suffering and walk away from it without taking a little bit with him. He needed a family to come home to. A room where they could all be together.

'Sorry,' she said finally. 'It's been a long day. You know what . . . I shouldn't have come here.'

'Really, it—'

'No!' She was forceful. She had what she needed and now she yearned to get out of there. But she couldn't just let it come spilling out. That would be more than she'd be able to explain away as mere tiredness. 'I don't know what I was thinking. Look at how busy you are here. This case . . . I know what I need to do. I was just looking to you to ratify it. I respect you, Ian — you know that, right? You're a good man.'

'I . . . you . . . thank you. And I respect you, too.'

The surprise was all over his face. She thought it was tinged with confusion. She needed to get out of there. She knew she was acting strangely. She started for the door. 'Please accept my apologies. If you do have the time when you're back then maybe you could come up and have a look over what we have . . .'

Ian agreed, said it would be no problem. She spun back to say goodbye. The younger of the two girls appeared beside Ian as he held open the front door, chewing absently on her hair. Her dad put his hand on top of her head and she leaned into his side. She looked as bemused at this flying visit from Linda — a strange woman who'd turned up on their doorstep — as her father must have been. He called out that he would see her on Monday, that it had to be Monday as he was off for the rest of the week. His wave was cheery. He was always cheery. He *was* a good man.

When Linda got back to her car, she quickly opened the message Ian had sent to her phone. She lifted it so that the postcode and door number would be clear on the camera. She held it until her arm ached.

'I did what you wanted! I did it right this time. That's enough now . . . I've done enough. I'll come back like you asked. To give all this SHIT back! But that's IT!'

She scrabbled with her top. The button camera didn't detach immediately. It had a small wire in the back that hooked into a power pack. Pulling at it in a hurry would break it. If she broke it now that would be a deviation, she was certain of that, and then all that she had just done would be for nothing. She settled with just scrunching the camera up into a tight fist. Blocking its view for just a few moments. She needed to think; she needed some space for that.

She took her own phone out and opened a message to her daughter. She watched the cursor blink. Her mind ran with the warnings on the note: *we have accessed your home, your phone and your car . . .*

She didn't know what that meant. It wasn't enough. She had seen stalking cases before, boyfriends hacking phones, installing something in the background so they could see every message sent or phone call made. Linda dropped the message back down to show the home screen. Here she saw the chess game she was playing with her daughter. There was a messaging function in that. *Could they monitor that?* Linda didn't know enough. She was risking her daughter's life just contemplating it. But then she thought of that poor woman, the one she had been shown on the video, sitting alone in an empty building. Dead. Forgotten. Lost.

'Please don't let me die like that . . .' She still had the camera scrunched up in her hand, but her words were barely a murmur anyway. She had to get herself together. One more short drive and this should all be over.

CHAPTER 21

Maddie Ives thought the *THUMP!* was part of her dreams, that it was the last thing her mind had conjured before she was startled awake. But that idea lasted just a moment — another thump was quick to follow. Then the bedroom door slammed open and someone ran out of it. There were heavy footfalls down the stairs. The next sound was of smashing glass. This was further away — from the kitchen, she reckoned.

She threw back the covers and leaped to her feet. The door had swung back to being almost closed; it stood out as a black square against the dark grey. She wrenched it open and made for the stairs. She was halfway down when she heard the shouts. A male voice, very loud. The stairs finished with a kink at the bottom that led towards the kitchen. She picked up the pace, her feet skidding where the carpet ran out and the kitchen's lino started. The door out into the conservatory was open. There were some solar lights along the fence but they were weak, even in the dead of night. The ones at the end flickered as a shadow ran across them. The door out to the garden was open too. She sprinted through it.

'I DIDN'T KNOW!'

The same male voice. Now it was whiney and terrified. By the time Maddie was close enough to pick out any detail, she could see a man lying face down on the decking. Her boyfriend, Vince Arnold, was on top of him, his knee pressing into the intruder's upper back and acting as a focal point for his considerable weight. Vince had the man's right arm yanked upwards in a tight hold, its position the direct opposite to how nature had intended.

'What you reckon, Mads? I could snap his arm and say it happened when I was restraining him. These things do happen. Our word against some little shit burglar? I'm getting away with that all day long!'

Vince changed the angle just slightly; the reaction from the decking was instant. Their 'little shit burglar' was clearly just a boy. Even with half his face mashed into wooden planks slick with dew, she could make out a face hosting a battle between freckles and an invading army of acne. His hair looked like it had been shaved off by the boy himself, with tufts highlighting the bits a professional wouldn't have missed. The thin arm being gripped by Vince sported a poorly constructed tattoo, the bottom half sketched out for more to come. There was another tattoo under his ear: three stars that lifted up from his shoulder, getting bigger as they did. Even without a glimpse of the freckles, acne and panicked eyes that she now knew to be touched with hazel, she would have recognized him from his right arm alone.

'Tommy Wilson,' she said. She stood over him now, her hands on her hips. Wilson's eyes snatched up to peer at her. Suddenly she was aware she was wearing boxer briefs and a vest. She took a step to the right, enough for Vince's bulk to cover most of her lower half.

'Sorry, miss! I didn't know. I didn't know this was his gaff — or yours . . . I didn't know.'

'You think that makes it okay?' Maddie said. She must have told him ten times in her dealings with him not to call her 'miss'. It made her feel a hundred years old. 'What did I tell you would happen if you went out on the rob again, Tommy?'

'You said they'd throw the book at me. You said I wouldn't be no kid anymore — no juvie. You said I'd go to prison with men, that I'd be treated like a man. You said I wouldn't cope with that.'

Maddie dropped to one knee to be closer to him. 'So you remember, then. And just about word for word. You just chose to ignore it, did you?'

'I got myself up the creek, you know — shit creek. I owe money. I just needed to get myself back up to square one. I needed money faster than I can get straight.'

'Drugs?' Maddie said.

'Only a bit of green.'

'How much? Money, I mean.'

'Six hundred.'

'A *bit* of green, you say? So you're dealing now?'

His only response was a silent grimace.

'Now you go quiet on me. Maybe we *should* break his arm.'

Vince twisted the arm another inch. Tommy's grimace leaked a scream instantly.

'Okay, yeah! A couple of brothers. Ollie, that's all I know to call him. Lives over on the coast. He stood me up for some green to get rid of. I got robbed, okay? I turned up to some house. I don't normally go out to houses, but they wanted, like, an ounce. That was a good chunk right there. They came out of nowhere soon as I got there.'

'You're an idiot, Tommy. You know that?'

'Am I breaking this bone or what?' Vince grumbled. 'I could just take his shoulder out of its socket.'

Tommy still stared up at Maddie the best he could. 'Can you get the boss here off me, yeah? I ain't going nowhere.'

Vince looked to Maddie. Maddie didn't know how she had become the decision maker.

'High fences either side, Tommy. You ain't making it out of this garden without PC Arnold getting hold of you again. Then I give him permission to take *both* arms out of their sockets. You understand?'

'I know him. I know he's a gavver! I ain't going nowhere!'

'He's a police officer, Tommy. An angry one. There is literally no house in Deal worse than this place for your sticky fingers to take you.'

'I ain't going to run. Your man here numbed my leg anyway. I can't feel my toes.'

'You ever turn up in my street again and that becomes permanent!' Vince growled right in his face. Tommy cried out again as Vince pressed on his arm one last time.

Maddie gave Vince the nod. He straightened up, letting Tommy go at the same time. Tommy stayed down, careful not to push his luck. He sat at their feet, massaging his arms and legs to try and get the blood back into them.

'You gonna nick me, miss?'

'This is my house, not hers,' Vince cut in. 'So this is down to me. I'm a fair man, though, yeah? You smashed my window down there. You might have something that belongs to me in your pocket. But the worst thing of all? That smell you're chucking out, like piss and vinegar. That's gonna linger on for a good few days. Whenever I go into my kitchen, I'm gonna be reminded of your spotty, pathetic little face. So your options are to either get yourself nicked and I'll get some colleagues out to see if we can't hurry along that vacation in a man's prison . . . or we finish off our little wrestling match. Winner is the one with all his limbs in the right place. You choose.'

Now her eyes had adjusted to the dim lighting, Maddie could make out the finer details a little better — like the widening of Tommy Wilson's eyes as he took just a moment to mull over his options.

'I guess I'm getting nicked, then.'

'You sure? Only, out here is one on one. You get yourself in your man's prison and it could be winner stays on. And a different type of wrestle.'

Tommy's head drooped from his shoulders. He sat with his legs up, his forearms across his knees.

'I'll go and get my phone!' It was all Maddie could do to stifle a chuckle.

The police were quick. Maddie knew how to play the system. Call it in as a detained, compliant burglar sitting in the garden of two off-duty police officers and there would be no need for the night shift to stop the kettle. They would turn out, but only when they were ready. Call it in as a burglary in progress and she knew that the response cars would be racing each other for the glory.

The double-crewed car of PCs Mike Hall and Lucy Hart won the race. They had been just around the corner supping from flasks on the seafront. Maddie commented on how romantic it sounded.

'Not as romantic as you two, though!' Mike quipped instantly.

Even if Maddie hadn't been standing in her dressing gown in Vince's kitchen, giving an account of how she'd woken in his bed, her burning face would have given her up. She and Vince were not common knowledge. There was no real reason for keeping it under wraps; she was a long way from ashamed or even from caring what people thought. She just didn't want to be the subject of station gossip. There was nothing she could do about that now. It was always going to come out at some point. So what if they were seeing each other? It was no scandal, just two single people who had been through a lot together and realized at some point that their connection ran deeper than they'd thought. It had been a few months now and Maddie was enjoying herself, not that she would admit as much to Vince.

Tommy Wilson was carted off. Maddie was updated on the outcome later: a search of his person had come up negative but a quick search of the garden had revealed some Bluetooth headphones, a mobile phone and bank cards in the name of the occupier of the house four doors down. His vacation with a whole host of new wrestling partners looked assured.

Maddie walked out into the garden. It was long and thin with a gentle upward slope that meant the bench at the end had an elevated view of the back of the house. To her left, the dawn was starting to bleed over the night. Soon the sun would emerge over the sea. It would take another hour to peer over the terraced roofs. She liked it here. This spot. With this man. Especially when his hand reached out towards her, clutching a mug of tea.

'Thanks, Vince!'

'You okay?'

'Tommy Wilson?' Maddie laughed. 'That kid's hardly going to give anyone nightmares.'

'Bit of a shock, though. The little shit's been inside my gaff. That'll piss me off for a while. I should have popped his shoulder out. Young lad like that, it woulda popped right back in again. Hurt like hell, though.'

'Bit of a shock, yeah. I was just thinking . . . I just upped and ran after him. If it had been last night . . .'

Vince looked at her like he wasn't sure what she meant. She scrunched her dressing gown so it rode up her thigh a little.

'Oh shit, yeah! The little black set, with the—'

'Yes! The black set.'

'Shit! He mighta thought it was his birthday! I remember thinking it was mine!'

'You want another birthday treat?' She hid her smile behind her cup. 'I'm wide awake now.'

'Me, too,' he grinned. 'Two in two! I mean, I don't blame you. Ain't no one seeing this one night and not wanting another taster the next!'

'One day you'll get over yourself, Vince. And I'm finishing my tea first.'

'Not while I got you round for encouragement.'

They both laughed. There was a natural pause. The birds were starting to wake to fill the silence.

'I need a favour,' Maddie said.

'Never just a shag with you, is it?'

'Ha! It's a nicking.'

'Okay, so now I'm interested.'

'I thought you might be. I was going out first thing to do it myself but, thinking about it, you would be better. I'd like to make a bit of a scene. A couple of loud uniform officers with stern faces and handcuffs could manage that better than just me and Harry.'

'That's what you're thinking about? Right now, I mean.'

'Well, yeah.' She did her best to stay straight-faced.

'You not finished your tea yet? Only now I can only think about one thing.'

'I can't help it. It's too hot.'

Vince stood up from the bench and paced down the path. He was dressed in shorts and a hoody. He pulled both items off as he walked — he had to stumble to a stop to get the shorts off. Both items were thrown down onto the grass. He continued to stride through the second half of the garden. She giggled, her eyes suddenly searching the neighbour's windows which overlooked them at the back.

'You don't know nothing about hot, Maddie Ives!'

He stood naked at the door to the conservatory. He leaned on the door surround like a cheap burlesque dancer on a pole, lifting one leg with his finger to his lips. Then he was gone.

Maddie knew she was supposed to follow. She also knew the message it would send if she followed immediately. She swigged again at her tea. The sky was lighter, the sun was already making a start on the day, but they still had plenty of time before work.

She swilled out the rest of the tea and stood up. She would only be a few seconds behind him but she told herself she had made him wait long enough.

CHAPTER 22

Tuesday

Ian Hessey took a moment to turn and take in his house from the end of the path. It looked even better in the stillness of five a.m. with its windows full of the brand-new sun. He was in love. He and his wife had both been smitten the moment they saw it from the kerb. To Ian, it was more than a house; it was the last piece in the puzzle, the final thing they needed, to be the family he had always pictured. Their previous place had been holding them back. Now they could make decisions on where to settle for work, where to send the children to school, where to enrol them for clubs and where to spend their money to make the place even better. Hopefully that wouldn't include much more pink paint.

He reached out to run his finger over the word *SOLD*. It immediately ran with dew. He took one last look, then checked his watch. His lift was due at 5:15. It would take him a few minutes to walk to the end of the road.

His wife had suggested he take the suitcase with wheels. He had refused. It was huge; he would have felt silly being picked up for a three-day residential course with a case designed for weeks away. And it was spotty. The bag he had chosen as more suitable had to be thrown over his shoulder and had slim straps that dug into his flesh. It only took a few steps away from his house to make him yearn for the big spotty case with the wheels.

Looking ahead, he saw a car pull into his road. At this distance it was just a set of headlights. He lived in a cul-de-sac; it had to be for him. He was due to be picked up from the bus stop on Stone Street. They were obviously running early. He took a few more steps then dropped the bag to the ground. He would be sure to thank them on behalf of his shoulder. A marked police car emerged slowly from the early morning shadow. He had been expecting an unmarked pool car. He was pretty sure you weren't supposed to take marked cars to the site where he'd be training. They ran some of the counter-terrorism courses there, too. The building was supposed to be low-key. No marked cars, no uniform. When the car pulled up, the driver stepped out in full uniform. And it wasn't who he was expecting.

'I assume you're not here for m—' It was all Ian managed.

The pain was instant from a blow to the back of his head. His vision flashed bright white, then he felt cold and damp down his front and a pain in his knee. His fingers scrabbled over a coarse surface — he was on the ground. He heard a scuffing sound close to his ear and rolled towards it. The tip of a black boot came into focus. He mumbled something at it. It moved back in a blur then swung forwards again. This time he felt the blow. All of the air rushed out of his lungs in an instant and he was left gasping for breath. He felt his head being grabbed roughly; his neck shot with pain. Then a coarse material was pulled over his face, and the bright new sun and fresh breeze were replaced with darkness and closeness.

He was yanked to his feet. Shallow moans escaped his chest and throat instead of breaths, but his lungs burned with the effort. He tried to straighten up fully to open them, but his head was pushed back down to bend him double. He bumped off something solid until he felt the softness of a bench seat underneath him. His legs were folded to fit into the gap, and then he heard a car door shut. Another opened near his head, and someone got in to sit next to him. His head knocked against them. He felt someone grab his hands and twist them together behind his back, then the sensation of something being wrapped around his wrists. He fidgeted, the beginnings of resistance. There was another blow to his head. Then it was over. His wrists were released; he wasn't being gripped anywhere else. He was finally able to snatch a small breath that wasn't accompanied by a moan or a wretch. Then came a voice, almost against his ear.

'Now, now, Ian Hessey. Your home, your wife, your kids . . . they're all just a few metres away from here. This is about you. But if you want to play games then I'll gladly wake them up and make it about them too.'

The voice was low but he could feel the bile, even through the material of the hood he was wearing. He stayed still. He couldn't manage a reply anyway; he was still struggling for air, the material around his mouth making it difficult to breathe.

His wrists were grabbed again. He didn't resist. They were already tied behind him. He was on his side, his forehead now resting against the back of the seat. He silently prayed for the car to move — away from his family. He got his wish. The car's engine had been running the whole time. Now the car surged away.

* * *

'Quite a night.' Harry Blaker appeared at Maddie's desk at 6:25 a.m.

She had been in for twenty-five minutes already. She hadn't seen the point of going back to sleep and needed to do a statement for Tommy Wilson's arrest before the early turn came in anyway. They would want a complete handover to read. CID looked likely to take this case on. When Maddie had met Wilson previously, it had been part of assisting CID.

At that time, the area had been experiencing a slew of burglaries and people in the community were starting to ask what the police were doing about it. Maddie didn't suppose for a moment it had all been the work of Tommy Wilson. He was a petty thief, a terrible burglar whose method was to smash a window then hide in the garden to see if anyone noticed. If the house stayed asleep then he grabbed what he could and was away. Maddie still remembered interviewing him. There was one question specifically that she'd never forget. She had asked what he had used to break into a particular house.

His reply had been instant: 'A blunt instrument, miss.'

Maddie had been desperate not to meet eyes with Rhiannon; it was all she could do to stop herself bursting into laughter. The term 'blunt instrument' must have been something he had heard on a cop show — no way he talked like that. They pushed him on it and he confirmed what they had already established — it was a loose brick from an extension site a few doors up.

Maddie couldn't resist asking, 'Why didn't you just say it was a brick?'

'That's what you call it, though . . . a blunt instrument, innit?'

Maddie could hardly disagree. Both women had kept their laughter at bay. But an instant nickname was born.

Maddie had a smile for Harry now. 'It was indeed. I didn't go to bed expecting to be burgled by a "blunt instrument"!'

'No . . .' Harry rubbed his chin. Maddie could tell he was trying to find more words.

'I'm hoping that, this time, when they ask him how he gained entry to Vince's place, he explains that he had a whole toolbox with him but he didn't use the sharpest one!' Maddie chuckled to herself.

Harry smiled but it looked awkward.

'Vince's place,' he repeated back.

Maddie turned to him. 'Yeah . . . This wasn't how I wanted people to find out.'

Harry used silence so well. She knew it was for her to continue. 'It wasn't how I wanted you to find out.'

'You're an adult. It's none of my business.'

'But I feel like it is. I was going to talk to you.'

'I've not exactly been around. And it's a step up from picking off men from the outskirts of a major criminal network.'

'Picking off!'

'Poor turn of phrase.'

'So you don't approve.'

'You don't need my approval.'

'Maybe not. I guess I—'

'Actually, I do approve. Vince is a good man. You're a good woman. What's not to approve of?'

Maddie didn't know what to say.

Harry let her off the hook. 'First order of the day then is to get Janet Taylor in.'

'I've sorted that. Vince is heading out there for eight a.m. Well, I said just after. That's when they all start work over there. I thought it would be better for a couple of uniform officers to cause a bit of a stir in the office. Someone built like Vince, someone you can't miss.'

'Vince? And you didn't think to consult with me?' Harry snapped.

'Consult? No, I didn't. It made sense to me and I didn't think about it until late last night. I figured this way we could work on some prep and get uniform to bring her in. That's what they do, after all.'

'Late last night? Because Vince just happened to be lying next to you at the time and we all know he loves an arrest? I assume that was part of the thinking. This is already affecting your judgement, Maddie.'

Harry's angry growl was very much apparent, but there was something different about his manner this time. She was stung. Her first reaction was to bite back . . . but Harry couldn't hold it. His face cracked, his lips curling into a subtle smile. Then he actually laughed.

'You bastard!' she hissed.

'Well. You will put it about, Maddie. You can't just sleep with a colleague because you want something done.' He spun away and made towards the kitchenette. 'You want a coffee, you slut?'

His laugher was as genuine as she had ever heard from him. It felt good to hear it. It felt good to have him back in the office. It felt good to have hope that he was going to be able to function as the old Harry Blaker. She had the feeling that he was feeling good too. That being back to work was agreeing with him entirely. Even if he had just called her a slut.

CHAPTER 23

Janet Taylor had been left to sweat for just over an hour in cell number eleven of Canterbury custody. It was the first of the female cells on the west side of the custody wing. The fact it was labelled a female cell made no difference at all. It was purely a logistical thing based around the walk to the shower. All the cells were the same irrespective of the gender assigned to them: a grey box with a shelf for a bed, a steel toilet and a lack of natural light.

Janet was close to the door when Maddie opened it. The moment she recognized the detective she had lied to the day before, she took a step back and her head dropped.

'We're ready to speak to you.'

'Look, I know—'

'Not right now.' Maddie pointed up above the door, to where a camera was hunched in a corner behind a Perspex cover. 'You're under arrest for conspiracy to murder. That's a very serious offence. This has to be done the official way. On tape.' At this, Maddie reckoned she could see the last of the colour run out of Janet's already pale face.

Harry was waiting in interview room two. It was the smallest of all the interview rooms. They had chosen it for that very reason. The walls were all dull white. The ceiling was the same colour to add to the oppressive feel of the place. Harry guided Janet to the seat he had prepared. It faced theirs. Maddie put three cups of water on the table. She pushed one towards Janet. Then she turned to the recording machine behind her.

'The time is twelve minutes past ten on Tuesday, twenty-sixth of May. I am DS Maddie Ives of Major Crime and my colleague . . .'

'Detective Inspector Harry Blaker, Major Crime and SIO.' He leaned in to aim his growl directly at the woman sitting opposite. Janet's reaction was instant. Her eyes grew wider as they focused on him, and she pushed herself back in her seat a little like she needed the distance.

'Could you give your full name, date of birth and current address, please,' Maddie said.

Janet did as she was asked. She spoke too loudly, her eyes darting around the room as if searching for the microphone to direct her voice towards. Maddie pounced the moment she finished the last line of her address.

'You lied to me yesterday, Janet. That's why you're here. Why did you lie?'

'I . . . I panicked. I saw the news. I saw that Marie . . . I saw it was her. Then you asked me about Adrian and I just panicked. To think that he might have been part of that . . . to think that he might have worked it out while he was spending time with me.'

'Tell me about that.'

'About what?'

'About what he worked out? That suggests to me that you have a theory.'

'A theory?'

'What's Adrian's surname?'

'Hughes.'

'So I know we're talking about the same person. Adrian Hughes killed your mate. Did he meet Marie via you?'

'Meet? No. I wouldn't say it was through me especially.'

'What would you say?'

'He . . . his company were installing a new computer system, so he was round our office a lot. He worked for the company that were doing it. They came round and put something on every computer, some of them they had to swap completely. There were problems with mine . . . he was there a while.'

'And Marie was right next to you the whole time?'

'Yes.'

'Did they speak?'

'Well, yes. But nothing more than work stuff — just about the computers, you know. Not that I saw anyway.'

'But Marie knew about you and Adrian?'

'No! I was . . . embarrassed.'

'Embarrassed? Why?'

'Have you met him? He's a bit . . . well, a complete computer geek. That's what Marie called him, right from the off. She took the mickey out of him. I could hardly say, "actually we're dating", could I?'

'You could have done.'

'Well, I didn't.'

'Did he know? Adrian, I mean. Did he know that Marie was mocking him behind his back?'

'I don't know how he could have done. I never said, and we never talked about it.'

'Did you and Adrian ever talk about Marie?'

'Marie? No. I mean, sometimes I would talk about work in general and she was a part of that. But not specifically, not that I can remember.'

'And did he ask about her? Did you ever get the impression he had an interest in her in any way?'

'No! I've been in that cell, just sitting there thinking about it. We never talked about her . . . All that time, I thought he was well into me. I just keep thinking that he was only with me so he could get close to Marie. Do you think that's right? Do you think that's what he was doing?'

'You tell me. What was he like? As a lover. As a boyfriend. You know when someone's into you, don't you?'

'You're right . . . and he was. I know that. We . . . we got engaged. It was all a bit quick. I don't think he's had many girlfriends before. You know like when you're young, sixteen or seventeen, the first time you get with someone? Love hits you hard, doesn't it? I mean, if love's even what it is at that age. It's like everything all at once. I think he was caught up in that. He was sweet . . .'

'Sweet? That's not how I would describe someone I was in love with.'

'No. I suppose not.'

'Were you in love with him?'

'No.'

'But you got engaged anyway.'

'I was . . . I mean, yeah, but I was seeing how it went. He was really nice to me and he had bought this amazing ring, and when he proposed he told me about a holiday he had booked that sounded amazing . . . that sounds awful, doesn't it? I wasn't with him just for that. I just mean that he treated me like a princess. It was lovely. I was seeing how it went, you know? If I had said no at that stage it could have killed the whole thing dead. So I went along with it, thinking something might develop . . . I mean, "engaged" is just a word, isn't it? There was no way he could have afforded a wedding anyway. I definitely couldn't. He was dreaming, in a bit of a bubble. I didn't want to burst that bubble if something good might have come out of it.'

'You mean like an expensive ring and a trip away?'

'I'm not like that. I didn't care about the ring. I didn't even wear it much. I didn't want people to ask about it. I didn't wear it to work.'

'How did Adrian react to that?'

'He was angry at first. A little hurt. I told him that I didn't want to be the source of any gossip, that it was no one else's business but ours.'

'You fobbed him off, then?'

'No, I meant it. You know what offices are like. You're everyone's favourite gossip subject when something like that happens. I met him at work. I just didn't want people talking about me.'

'It's not like he gave you an STD, is it?' Harry waded in, blunt and brutal as ever.

'A what? Er . . . he didn't, no.'

'An engagement is something to be happy about, right? Something to show off — the ring for definite. It's not like it's a brand-new relationship and you don't want people to know in case it doesn't work out. You're committed.' Harry continued.

'I don't really know the people I work with. It was no one's business but mine.'

'Were you even sleeping with him?'

'We . . . I did. We were together for a while.'

'How long?'

'A few months. Four, maybe.'

'How many times?' Harry kept up the pressure.

'Sorry?'

'How many times did you have sex with Adrian Hughes?'

'I don't really think that's imp—'

'More than twice?'

'Yes. Well, twice is right, I think.'

'You *think*? You can't even remember a number like two? I could understand if it was so often you couldn't remember. That's what I would expect from a newly engaged couple. But your body language when you talk about him . . . you weren't attracted to him at all, were you?'

'I . . . I've been arrested! In connection with a murder. Something to do with my association with Adrian. This huge policeman came to my office and put me in cuffs and that was what he said. He said Adrian had admitted to killing my friend. What do you expect from my body language? I'm appalled with him!' Her voice began to wobble. She sat back again, fearful of another verbal assault from the DI. Maddie took the lead again.

'Conspiracy to murder. That's the offence you were arrested for. Because you lied to us yesterday. You said you didn't know Adrian Hughes when you obviously know him very well. Then you gave me an old address so I couldn't find you easily. I've been asking myself why you'd lie like that. The only reason I can think of is if you were very aware that Adrian had murdered your friend — because you were involved in it.'

'What? That's ridiculous!'

'Maybe you disliked Marie. Maybe the two of you fell out, maybe she did something to you and you manipulated a man who was infatuated with you to kill her for you.'

'No!'

'You might not even have meant for it to happen. It could have just got out of hand or he went too far, maybe he just did a little extra on his own initiative?'

'No! I loved Marie! She was lovely. She had a brutal sense of humour, but there was never any malice behind it. And never to people's faces. She was just taking the mickey, being funny. Like people do.'

'We've got your phone. Your flat's being searched as we speak. We're not going to find any evidence of a falling out? Anything that might give you a reason to wish Marie harm?'

'No! Nothing at all. You can search all you want.'

'We intend to. You've lied to us once already, Janet. And that gets you into a custody cell here for up to twenty-four hours. If we find out you lied to us again, you're a big step closer to spending the rest of your life in one. People who lie to the police are the ones who have something to hide. Like conspiring to have a colleague murdered.'

'I didn't! You have to believe me. I just sat next to her. I had no idea that Adrian was even taking any notice of Marie. It wasn't like he was at my desk much at all. I told him to keep away.'

'Because you were embarrassed by him?' Maddie cut in.

'No . . . it wasn't like that.'

'You were embarrassed by him but you liked the ring. Where did he take you on that holiday?'

'It was going to be Egypt . . . A five-star place. Who knows what could have happened out there? I thought, spend a week with him, that's how you really get to know someone. I could have fallen head over heels in that time.'

'So you haven't been yet?' Maddie said.

'No.'

'When was it booked for?'

'September. He's not so good with the heat. It's in the forties for most of the summer. It's not much less in September. He'd casually mentioned holidays and I picked out the pyramids as somewhere I'd always wanted to go. He booked it based on that. I told him we could change if it was a problem.'

'But he was happy to go wherever you wanted, no matter the discomfort it might cause him.'

'I didn't ask him to. Listen, you have to believe me! You won't find anything at my place. You won't find anything that says I knew anything about this. Adrian's a weirdo — I can see that now. I thought it was just his way. A bit of a geek, that was all. I had no idea that he was capable of anything like this. Do you think I would have agreed to go away on holiday with the man if I'd thought he was capable of murder?'

Maddie stayed silent. Harry didn't speak either. She wondered if this was one of his tactics of making people feel awkward enough to keep talking, to increase the pressure. Or if it was because he had the same feeling about all of this that Maddie herself was getting. Janet Taylor was telling the truth. And the man who had admitted to Marie Foreshaw's murder had a five-star holiday booked later in the year with his new fiancée. He had a whole new life waiting for him. That was hardly the point where he should choose to go off on a tangent of killing strangers and then confessing his evil deeds to the police in full.

Maddie had one last thing to cover, one last question. It wasn't so much what Janet might say in response that interested her; she just needed to see a reaction. She had a folder tucked down beside her chair leg, out of sight. She wanted the contents to be a surprise — even the fact that she had anything to show Janet at all. But she did. It was a high-definition photo of Marie Foreshaw's body. She was sitting upright in the metal chair and the plastic had been removed to show her washed-out face, her dead eyes, her teeth exposed in her last, desperate gasp for breath. The question she'd use to accompany it was one she always used: *one last time — did you have anything to do with this?* She wanted to study Janet closely, looking for just a flicker of something that she could use. She had seen people fake their reactions before — some were very good at it — but the one constant with all liars at this point was a moment's delay. It was barely noticeable. A genuine person would give an instinctive, shocked reaction, while someone who had seen it before, who knew exactly what state they had left their victim in, would show nothing at all in the split-second after the reveal, using that window to work out exactly how they were *expected* to react.

Janet Taylor fell to pieces instantly.

CHAPTER 24

Linda Morris had somehow drifted off to sleep, proving that, no matter what the situation, exhaustion would take over at some point. She woke to the all too familiar feeling of the cold, firm concrete digging into her lower back where she rested against the curved wall. The smell was instantly familiar too: damp and musty with undertones of mud. But the most familiar element was the blackness. This time it seemed blacker still. She moved a hand in front of her face and could easily fool herself it had never happened. She had never known real darkness, not like this, never so complete.

She remembered being brought back here. She had no idea how long ago that was; any sense of time had long since been surrendered to the blackness. There had been light then, enough for her to look around, enough for her to be led to the chains left laid out on the floor from her earlier release, enough that she could see there was no one else in the room.

And now she sat in the darkness. Rubbing her face was the only way she knew she was awake at all. She had never felt desperation like this. She had done all that they had asked. The second task she had completed comprehensively, despite what it might mean, despite what she knew she could be unleashing on that family. They had asked her to choose

— her family or his. She had made her decision. Without her, her daughter had no family left; only Linda's release made them a family. *So why was she still here?*

She heard movement. Noises were amplified in the space; each scuff was more like a shout. They bounced from the walls to bellow in her ear. She was startled. Her chains clinked and scraped as she tried to ascertain the source.

'Is somebody else here?' A man's voice. It was weak but gaining strength with every word. And there was fear in those words.

She heard another scuff, then metal scraping on concrete. Someone else was down here, in chains. Just like before. She looked to her right, despite the totality of the blackness. She remembered from last time that this was where the door was located. She'd seen it flung open the moment someone spoke. There was surely someone waiting there now, ready to lurch in and administer a beating. She knew the rules. She didn't reply immediately. She could feel the desperation turn to a panic that grew in her chest. She had to speak. She had to let him know.

'You need to be quiet,' she said. Her throat felt dry and scratchy, as if layered with tiny thorns trying to claw every word back before its release into the darkness.

'Linda?' The word echoed like it was all around her. For a moment she doubted it had even been said, her mind playing tricks.

'You know me?'

'It's Ian! Ian Hessey! Of course I know you. What the hell is going on?'

'We can't talk. They . . . they beat you if you talk. Or worse.'

'Who? Who the hell are *they*, Linda?' There was anger in his voice now. It mingled with the blackness, bouncing around the walls like a threat surrounding her, itching for a fight. She tried to move away from it. The solid concrete met her to push her back, like a ring of baying spectators, hungry for blood.

'I don't know,' she managed.

'That's not what they told me. They said you brought them to my house. Is that right? Is that why you came over? What did you do, Linda?' His anger was growing; the threat grew with it. She heard the scraping of chains, the walls again reverberated with the sound, amplifying it, the threat increasing. Suddenly she considered there could be more assailants in here, all pointing towards her, all ready to be unleashed.

She shook her head. She sucked in a deep breath of the muddy air. She had been hit hard. She remembered that now. The first blow had knocked her clean off her feet. The next had put her back down to the floor when all her instincts yearned to get her back up. She remembered the straw. She had inhaled it from the floor when she was face down; it had coated her lips and throat and made her hack and retch instantly. That was why her throat was still sore. Everything after that was a blur. She had been moved to another car, the familiar hood pulled over her head. No one had talked. She remembered stumbling, her legs refusing to work and a hold refusing to let them stop. Then the chains waiting for her . . . it was just flashes, glimpses of a journey that had ended here with another blow to the head when she tried to plead with them. It wasn't sleep she had woken from at all. She had been concussed before. Now she recognized her confusion.

'They hit me in the face.' The words tumbled from her sore lips. She worked her mouth. Her jaw cracked and popped in her ears.

'What?'

'My face.' Her head hung so her jaw bumped her own chest as she spoke. She was beaten. Suddenly the anger in the room, the total darkness, the pain in her back and neck, the solid, freezing cold chains . . . none of it mattered. Her memory was coming back. She was putting things in order. She knew what it all meant.

'I got a whack in the head too, Linda! What the hell is going on?'

'Before . . . the first time it was just the body. Bruises on my side, my chest and my hip. Just the body. Then it could all be hidden under my clothes . . .'

'What the hell are you TALKING about!'

The shouted word was like a gunshot. It ricocheted off every surface. Linda didn't even lift her chin from her chest.

'I could still blend in at work, at home. Now I can't. Now I can't do anything more. They're finished with me.'

She heard a low groan, then something like a deep breath.

Ian Hessey's voice came back softer. 'Linda, we need to work out what's going on here, okay? I was dragged into a car just outside of my house. They said you had brought them to my house. Who are they, Linda? What do they want with me? With us?'

The light hit like a mini explosion. Linda dropped to the ground and rolled away from the source onto her right side with her eyes shut tight. It seemed like an age before she could open them enough to see anything. Ian was pushed back against the wall, sitting where the bruised man had been. He squinted as he looked around. The monitor was the source of the light. It changed, dimming enough for Linda to struggle back up to a sitting position. The screen darkened to a grey surround with white movement in the centre — a digital clock: 07:10, 14s. The seconds ticked up. Linda watched, entranced by the movement.

The monitor changed.

'That's my . . . that's my house!' Ian's voice was higher and brittle, as if his next words would surely break.

The footage was of a silent kitchen. Linda recognized it herself from the night before. The kitchen table by the bifold doors was still busy with untidy boxes and the two dressed dolls. The fridge was captured on the left-hand side; the view of the room as a whole suggested the footage was streaming from a camera positioned somewhere high up and angled to take in as much as it could. She could see the fridge was busy with pieces of card and paper. It was too far to see the details, but she knew they were the children's cheery drawings of their new home. Crayon houses. And Linda knew that each window would be filled with its own smiling member of the family.

The screen flickered. The kitchen was snatched away and a different view appeared, one Linda didn't recognize. Again it was from an elevated viewpoint, but this time the downward angle captured an untidy bed. The duvet was half on, half off. The floral pattern at its end was rucked up against two paint pots stacked against the wall. The tone of the whole image was washed out, but even so the colour of the paint was vibrant enough that she could make it out. The tins were predominantly pink. The floor was scattered with teddies. The bed sheet that was now visible had a ruffled texture, as if someone had been dragged from it. And Linda knew they had. She just knew it.

'Oh God . . .' she murmured. Ian was sitting as straight as his chains would allow. So far, he hadn't shown any reaction. He just looked frozen. She wasn't even sure he was breathing.

The footage flickered and changed again. It was a similar scene. More bed linen dragged from a single bed across the room, more spilt soft toys and, this time, a wardrobe door left to hang open.

Then came a bigger room. The bed was a double. This scene was different, more disturbed. The bed had been roughed up but also skewed at an angle across the room, as though it had taken a blow to one of its corners. A bedside table lay on its side, the top drawer leaking its innards. Items littered the carpet by the door as if they'd been thrown at it. The curtain blowing out from the window gave a sense of calm after a storm of violence but also served as a reminder that this footage was live, this was now. The story of what had happened here was missing its beginning.

Linda broke away from the screen to find Ian staring straight at her. The light from the screen mingled with the moisture pooling heavily in his eyes. It leaked out as a single droplet with his first word.

'What did you do?'

* * *

Maddie Ives lifted her phone to her ear. It was the patrol sergeant, the grouchy old man she had called ten minutes earlier to ask for assistance with running Janet Taylor back home. They were done with her. She was being bailed. The moment they confirmed her home address, a team had been sent out to search it. They'd found some love letters linking her with Adrian Hughes — nothing they didn't know already, of course — but it served to support her account somewhat. Maddie had asked for the letters to be seized. She wasn't really sure why. Her mind was already turning away from Janet Taylor as having the answers. Her interview had only served to confirm Adrian's ever-increasing significance in all of this. If he hadn't murdered Marie Foreshaw, he was nevertheless their best chance of finding out who had.

'DS Ives?' Her uniform sergeant colleague was far brighter than he had been on the first call.

She had been looking for someone to take on a twenty-minute round trip to drop Janet home, but the way he had reacted — with a curt 'has she not got money for a bloody taxi then?' — it was as if she'd been asking him to take her to the moon and back. Maddie had assured him that it didn't matter, that she would task one of the detectives currently investigating a murder to break away instead. The sergeant had huffed and puffed in the silence that followed, and then grumbled, 'I'll see what I can do.' Just like he was supposed to. And now he was calling her back.

'Sergeant Smith . . . thank you for getting back to me.'

'Not a problem. As it happens, I have just the man for the job. He's light duties at the moment. Too ugly to be seen outside of the nick! He seems very enthusiastic to take your lady home. Either he's had a sneak peek and she's a cracker, or the man has had enough of these four walls and processing case files. No idea which. Either way, he can meet you at front counter.'

'Perfect. The bail is all on the system. I'll go down to custody now and get her out. Should be ten minutes.'

'I'll let him know.'

Janet was sitting on her bed this time. The heavy door of her cell was opened in slow motion by the custody officer assisting, revealing Janet's pathetic form, slumped under the heavily frosted window and in the weak light it cast. Eventually she looked up.

'Come on,' Maddie said. 'We're getting you out of here.'

Janet followed her up the hall, dragging her feet with every step. Her replies to the custody sergeant were all mumbled, one-word answers. Maddie had very little patience with the pathetic, even less so with someone whose situation was all of her own making. Janet signed some paperwork and collected her property, which was in a see-through bag with a blue clasp wringing its goose neck. It hung limp in her hand to bounce off her leg with every step to the front counter. Her head stayed slumped forwards, her gaze appearing to chase the faded pattern in the carpet.

Maddie stepped ahead to use her pass on the door that led to the front counter — to freedom. Janet froze in the doorway.

'You're good to go!' Maddie said, her voice full of encouragement.

'With him?' Janet gestured at the uniform officer who had stood up from the fixed plastic seat.

'Yeah. Blimey, I see what you mean! What happened there?' Maddie referenced the fact that half of his face seemed to be taken up by bruising.

One of his eyes was only just visible through a bruise that was so shiny as to look moist. The part of the eye that was visible was shot through with red.

'Ah, this?' The officer grinned. 'Let me just say, if my wife asks you to do the washing up, you do the washing up!' He laughed.

Maddie did too. Janet looked a lot less jovial.

'Go get yourself a nice hot shower, Janet, okay?' Maddie said. 'The moment you step out into the sun I'm sure everything will seem a whole lot better.'

'Spot on!' The bruised officer chuckled again. 'Now ... let's get you home.'

CHAPTER 25

'He said no.' Rhiannon's tone matched her face. Maddie nodded her acceptance. Harry was sitting next to her.

'Of course he did,' Maddie huffed. 'He knows he doesn't have to talk to us anymore.'

'Maybe he likes it in prison?' Rhiannon said.

'They must have a good selection of shower gels. Did you speak to them about his correspondence?'

'Of course. They now have all the relevant forms and justification. I went heavy on the *suspicion of corresponding with co-conspirators* angle. They lapped it up. They'll share any letters with us that he sends out. His calls, too.'

'Has he been writing or calling since he's been in there?'

'Not a sausage. He's not made a call, not written a line. Not received a thing either. His mum's been in touch with the prison to organize a visit and he turned that down too.'

'Not in a talking mood, it seems. So then' — Maddie got up to pace the room — 'we need to work without the help of the one man who can reveal all. So, someone tell me why Adrian Hughes would admit to a murder he did not commit? Bearing in mind his sad little life was just starting to take a bit of an upturn. Also include in your explanation why, when he was such a prolific writer of letters and poems back when he was able to speak to his fiancée, he has not felt the need to put pen to paper now that he cannot?'

Harry responded first. 'That relationship was going nowhere. No way were they getting married and doing the happy-ever-after thing.'

'I agree. But I'm not sure Adrian knew that. The search team read out some of the love letters they found at her place. They were recent. It was one of my more bizarre phone calls. From those letters, I'd say Hughes is a man obsessed and infatuated. His mother said their relationship was over but it clearly wasn't. He was talking plans. Long-term plans ... starting a family to complete his life, blah-blah-blah. He couldn't see beyond that. He still can't.'

'Any suggestion Marie was blocking their relationship?' Rhiannon said. 'Or even just making a nuisance of herself. Maybe she was running him down to Janet and he thought she could ruin everything.'

'Okay, good, that's the sort of thing.' Maddie said. 'We have a couple of DCs at the council offices now. Everyone is being spoken to and we're also looking to track down any-one mentioned who works elsewhere but knows any of the three. We're doing social-media trawls on all three again, too. We're also talking to Adrian's recent employer. So that's a theory that can be explored with the information that comes back. Good ... anyone else?'

'What if he was forced into it? Someone got some-thing over him, makes him cough to summin' he didn't do.' Maddie turned to a familiar voice that was new to the room.

'Duress. Thank you, Vince.'

Vince flushed. She didn't think she had seen that before. Maddie made the briefest of eye contact with Harry. He was smiling. That hardly ever happened either. Suddenly she was stumbling over her words.

'So then ... duress ... meaning someone forced Adrian to walk through our doors to give his admission — so who? And how are they keeping this hold on him now he's in prison?'

'His mother?' Rhiannon threw out a guess. She shrugged as if not convinced of it herself.

Maddie wasn't either. 'I didn't get that. Harry?'

'No, I didn't either. If there's any threat to Audrey then she definitely doesn't know about it.'

'She doesn't. And I'm not convinced that she means enough to him anyway. This is a man throwing away the one chance of a life he has. This has to be something big.'

'So not a threat to his own life.'

'That doesn't make sense to me either. He might as well be dead in prison, without Janet. What else does he have to live for now?'

'Say it like it is!' Rhiannon chuckled.

'Being locked up permanently is the only way his life could get any worse,' Maddie said. 'All he has is Janet and the promise that they'll be together again. Janet Taylor is his everything. She is the only thing that could be holding him behind that door in silence.'

'So someone's threatening her?'

'If they are, she doesn't seem to know about it.'

'So he's protecting her,' Harry said.

'Could be.' Maddie wiped her hand over her mouth. 'That could explain the lack of contact, too.'

'Protecting her from what?' Rhiannon breathed.

'And there it is. The million-dollar question. What we are missing — and, again, the answer sits with Adrian Hughes. We find that out and this whole thing unravels.'

'How do we do that?' Rhiannon said.

Maddie was back to rubbing her face. 'The mother . . . you said she tried to see him?'

'She did.'

'Then we go and see her.'

'We only just upset her. What's the thinking?' Harry's tone carried a warning.

'She can't see him if he's refusing to come and meet her but she *can* write him a letter. I just want to be sure she's aware of that option.'

'You're lovely like that.'

'I am.' Maddie swept up her suit jacket from the back of her chair.

'Go on,' Harry said.

'Go on? And . . . are you coming?' she chanced.

'Not until you tell me why you're really going all the way out there.'

'Victim care. She's a victim too, Harry. She should know that she can still make contact with her own son by letter. And if she mentions in that letter that Janet might have moved on, that there's a new fella on the scene, then at least he won't need to be worrying about her, will he?'

'You're going to stoke him up,' Harry said.

'I'm going to take a swipe at the whole reason he's in there. Maybe then he'll talk to us.'

'You could be barking up the wrong tree entirely, DS Ives. This is a guessing game.'

'Isn't it always? Catching bad guys, I mean. We need to get him to talk to us. This will do it. Someone once told me I had good instincts.'

'He might not even read a letter from his mum.'

'He will. He wants contact. He wanted to see his mummy, too, no doubt about that. But something stopped him. He doesn't belong in there. He's not part of that world. I bet he cries for his mum every night.'

'So your solution is to coerce a mother to lie to her recently imprisoned son. Where does that sit on the moral and legal compass?'

Maddie pulled on her jacket and straightened it. 'You're right. I shouldn't even suggest it. So maybe it's best I take Rhiannon.'

Maddie was giving Harry the opportunity to distance himself but she knew him too well; he could very easily stop her dead. She continued her walk away before he did. Vince had slunk back to lean against the wall. He pushed off it now.

'Oh! PC Arnold, a word,' Harry called after them.

When Maddie looked over, Harry was already halfway across the floor.

'Sure thing, boss. I'll catch you up, Mads.'

Harry was closer than Vince realized, right on top of him, close enough to reach out and grab Vince by the wrist. She saw Vince tense. Harry leaned in. His growl was low but she could still pick out the words.

'You hurt her and I'll bust you down to PCSO with one working arm before the sun goes down on that day. You understand me?'

Harry's grip changed to become a handshake and his other arm rested on Vince's shoulder. Then he turned to Maddie.

'I'll come out with you. Sorry, Rhiannon. I have an errand to make anyway.'

CHAPTER 26

Maddie had given up asking questions of Harry. She had tried when he had insisted on a detour that turned out to be a garden centre, tried again when he had emerged with some unidentifiable object — disguised by white mesh, it looked heavy and awkward to hold — and she was damned if she was going to try and be rebuffed again, now that they were standing on Audrey Hughes's doorstep and he was still holding whatever it was he had picked up on the way.

She knocked on the door again but this time with a doorbell accompaniment. She had parked in a different position for this visit. It was deliberate; she had wanted to walk around the side to see if Audrey's curtains were drawn like they had been the day before. Audrey had talked about her migraines, how she had learned to spot the signs and would cover the windows and stay in bed for a day or two to fend them off. With all the excitement and stress of their last visit, Maddie feared that today was destined to be a non-starter. But both the curtains and the doors were pushed open. She was definitely home and apparently fit enough for a visit, if unwilling to let them in.

'Again!' An exasperated Audrey peered out through the smallest of gaps. 'You came into my home, you searched, you took what you needed and I told you everything. There's nothing more for you here!'

Her fury seemed to grow with every word, and she moved to shut the door in their faces. Maddie intended on letting it close then giving Audrey a moment before she tried again. Getting through that door, she reckoned, was going to take time.

But Harry seemed to have a different approach in mind. He brushed past where Maddie was stepping back, leading with his shoulder to meet with the door before it could close. He removed the mesh cover from his purchase to reveal a plant in a large, square pot balanced in his right hand. The lip of the pot bumped against the plastic of the door. He still held the white mesh in his other hand, like a butler who had just revealed the main course beneath a covered platter.

'An English climbing rose. Beautiful. I have one myself. Flowers all year round. It's for you, Audrey.'

Maddie could see only Harry's broad back as he spoke. She lifted herself up on her tiptoes to see the crack in the door widen slightly. Audrey was back to peering out as Harry continued, 'This is a small cage at the top here. The roses climb up it. You can either swap it for a bigger cage now or set the rose at the bottom of a wall or trellis. It climbs straight up, so the pot will be fine as a base. I saw your patio. It's lovely. I bet that's where you sit to drink your coffee — when we're leaving you alone, that is. I've got a similar patch where I like to sit. I hadn't realized a rose like this was the one thing missing from it until I bought one. It's the scent of the blooms. All year round. It's wonderful! I saw a place that I thought would be just right for it on your patio.'

The door widened further. Harry stepped in. Maddie followed. They didn't stop until they were at the open patio door. Grunting from the exertion, Harry moved the solid-looking pot to the far-right corner. He stood back up and dusted his hands.

'That will climb right up there. Quickly too.'

'You bought that for me?' Audrey said.

Harry had moved on to dusting his trousers. 'I know this must be stressful for you. We deal with offenders and victims all day every day. We're good at it. We have plenty of experience, but we can forget that there's more to it than that. We can forget that even the offenders have families . . . mothers. Yesterday would have been a big shock. We left as quickly as we could because you needed time to process that. Today we just want to be sure you're okay.'

'You bring everyone you deal with roses?'

'Far from it.'

'So you'll be wanting more than just to check that I'm okay, rattling around in here. If it's more information you need then I already told you—'

'It isn't. I admit, the plant was just something to get your attention — so you would listen. But not to more questions.'

'Well, it's bought you that much. What am I listening to?'

'Your son is in prison for something he admitted to doing. But we're not convinced. It *might* be that he didn't do what he claims. At the very least, we think he's protecting someone else.'

'I told you th—'

'*Might*. I'm not here to give you false hope — not now, Mrs Hughes. I know you might not appreciate that in the long run.'

'Okay. But what more could you need from me? I don't know anything about his life. I told you that.'

'There's something we'd like to try.'

'Go on.'

'We know you tried to speak with him, to visit him in prison and he didn't want to see you. That's out of character, wouldn't you say?'

'Yes. I called the prison to make an appointment. There was already a note on his file that said he didn't want anyone going up there. Said me specifically. They checked with him again and then they called me right back to say he wasn't interested in a visit from his own mother. And they can't force him. Why wouldn't he see me?' Mrs Hughes had grown tearful. Now she was close to breaking.

Harry stepped closer to her. He squatted down a little so he was on her level. His voice came back lower and softer.

'My bet is that he was desperate to see you. And that he would still love to hear from you. We think someone out there has a hold over him, something that's making him act differently, making him hide himself away. Right now, he's acting as if he thinks this will all blow over. But he has to help himself.'

'This Jan girl . . .' She wiped at her watery eyes. She was angry now; she wouldn't be needing tears.

'Maybe.'

'It will be, I tell you. Right from the start, since he first got together with her, he's been different.'

'So help us. You can still write him a letter. There's nothing he can do to stop that and I bet he reads it.'

'A letter? What good's that going to do?'

'Maybe nothing. You can put the normal stuff you would in a letter but in among those words we want you to mention that you think this Jan has moved on already. Got herself involved with someone else.'

'Moved on . . . someone else? All he ever talked about was getting back together. You want me to break his heart? A desperate man who's locked up and in need of hope?'

'Yes,' Harry said.

Mrs Hughes's lips pursed together. She scowled at first but it dropped away. 'So he doesn't care about her anymore. So he stops doing what she wants, sees her for what she is! Maybe she wants him in prison for killing someone he didn't?'

'Have you ever thought of becoming a detective, Mrs Hughes?' Harry even pulled a laugh out of his box of tricks.

Mrs Hughes joined in. Maddie could barely believe what she was seeing.

'Actually, I'm a big fan of those programmes — the policey ones, you know. I always work out who the killer is long before the end! Adrian always said I would be good at all that.'

'Real-life policing is just like that, too.'

Harry made brief eye contact with Maddie, who was forced to suppress her laughter.

'A letter, then. Okay, I can do that. What should I write though? We want him to believe me . . . Oh, I don't know how I could make him do that.'

Harry was still holding his smile. 'Mrs Hughes, if I may . . . How about a sweet tea under some climbing roses and we'll see what we can come up with together?'

Audrey suddenly beamed. 'Part of the team! Maybe you could tell me what other clues you have around this dead girl. I'm good at all that! I'll put the kettle on then.'

Mrs Hughes almost skipped across the lounge and into the kitchen. Harry stepped back out into the small yard. Maddie followed him.

'English climbing rose . . . Harry Blaker charming a witness to the point that she's eating out of his open palm . . . What the hell did I just see in there?'

'We'll get what we need.'

'Oh, I know that! I just didn't realize you had it in you. And what happened to that "moral and legal compass" you were talking about?'

'It got smashed to pieces. Over the years. By people who seek out and murder others, people who take the lives of their victims and destroy the lives of the families they leave behind. That woman has one kid. What else does she have?'

'You, right now. And I think she's rather fortunate, Harry.' Maddie meant it.

'And I'll be gone when this is all finished.'

'He didn't do it, then? You don't believe Adrian murdered that woman?'

'Not a chance.'

Maddie let out a lungful of air. When she took a breath back in through her nose it was tinged with the smell of roses.

'I've missed you, Harry Blaker,' she murmured.

If he heard her then he didn't reply.

* * *

The screen had changed the moment Ian Hessey had been dragged from his chains. He had fought hard, as hard as Linda had seen anyone fight back at them. Numerous blows rained down on him, but he wouldn't go down. The beating only stopped when they had him under some sort of control. The scuffing of feet, cries of pain and roars of defiance had combined to fill the stone walls like steam building inside a pressure cooker. Linda felt sure that the intensity would blow the walls out.

It hadn't happened. Once it had all ended, the only sounds left were of heavy breathing as Ian had been dragged out exhausted, his heels scraping along the grey floor. He had held Linda's stare all the way.

'What did you do?' were his final words.

Then they dragged him out the door and the silence came rushing back in, like air filling a vacuum.

Linda had gathered herself together to peer back at the screen. This was the moment she realized the picture had changed once more. Any panic or anxiety that might have been dragged away with Ian Hessey now returned in an overwhelming wave. Had she been standing it would have knocked her off her feet. The screen showed another bed-room. It was in her flat. Hope's room.

Hope was gone. Just like the rooms they had been shown in Ian's house, this one had obviously been vacated in a hurry. The duvet had been dragged off the bed and now lay heaped up on the floor; one of the curtains looked to have been roughly pulled back and the mirror Hope used to do her make-up was tipped over. Hope's shoes were still in a neat row under the bedroom window. She only had two pairs; she had trimmed her wardrobe down to the barest of essentials before giving up her own place to go travelling. Both pairs were there. There was a low table to the side of the bed where Hope's phone still sat. It was the one thing she would never leave behind, wherever she went.

The screen changed. From here, it stuck to a rolling pattern, showing her each of the rooms in her home in washed-out colour. They were all empty. There were no other clues as to what might have happened. She could feel the desperation and panic that had so affected Ian build in her with every flicker of the screen.

It was as if they knew. As her rage and panic reached their peak, the darkness returned.

CHAPTER 27

'Rhiannon, how are you getting on?'

'I was just calling to ask you the same thing. You sound pissed off.'

Maddie had spoken with her eyes closed, her finger and thumb tracing the lines of her eyebrows as she tried to massage some life back into her brow. She felt like she had been scowling all day. When she opened her eyes, the sandy-coloured brickwork of the main entrance to HMP Elmley still dominated her view, jutting forwards from the dark grey walls either side to give the impression that it was lurching out towards her. Making a break for it, perhaps. She could understand the desire to run from this place — inmate or not. The facade was a bland, featureless slab of stone, imposing and intimidating in equal measures. Today, it just fuelled her frustration. The staff inside that building had seemed just as impenetrable as its walls.

'I am a little,' Maddie admitted. 'I thought we had a very strong reason to come up here. I thought I'd be able to talk to someone and we could maybe get some work done. The moment I told them who I worked for, I could see their interest wane. No one's listening.'

'Where are you?'

'Sat outside Elmley, waiting for a call. We were waiting inside but I couldn't take it anymore. I'd rather sit in the car.'

'What are you doing up there?'

'Trying to get to speak to Adrian Hughes. Him and his answers are just the other side of the wall I can see from my damned window. I'm convinced he'll want to talk to us this time. But only if we do this right — if we get him while he's angry.'

'Angry?'

'His mum wrote that letter. You should see it — beautiful it is! All the things we needed are in there. It gives him just enough that he might think his girlfriend is in with someone new. Then it suggests talking to us — that we know more.'

'And they won't pass on the letter?'

'They've taken it. The idea was to come up here, hand deliver it and get it to Hughes. I know he'll read it straight away, no matter what he says about visiting. I want to be in front of him the moment he puts the thing down. It's a coincidence, see? We were just in the area on another matter and thought we would check to see if he had any questions.'

'He won't fall for that.'

'He won't if he stops to think about it. We got the envelope stamped at both ends to make it look right, but you're right . . . it won't stand up to any scrutiny. That's why I need to be in front of him around the time he finishes reading it. I don't want him having the time to smell a rat. He's going to want to talk to us. He'll want to know about Janet.'

'But the wardens, they're not playing ball?'

'We're outside of visiting times and we didn't pre-arrange. I'm waiting for someone in charge and with half a brain cell to call me back. I'm concerned I may not get either.'

'I'll get off the phone, then. Just to let you know, there's nothing more to report from social media. The techies had a good look at what they could find on our victim and any links to the happy couple.'

'Okay. I wasn't expecting much from that.'

Rhiannon sighed. 'Adrian Hughes is all we have, isn't he?'

'Yes. And he has been from the start.'

'Do you think he'll help?'

Maddie lifted tired eyes back to the solid grey walls. They seemed higher somehow, even compared with when they had first arrived.

'We have to get to him first. Speaking of which' — she sat up straighter, the tiredness clearing — 'someone's calling the other line.'

She cut the call immediately and scrabbled with her phone to try and answer the incoming line.

'Is that DS Maddie Ives?'

'Yes, here with Detective Inspector Harry Blaker from Major Cr—'

'So I've been told.' Maddie had hoped that Harry's rank might add something to her request. The voice shutting her down sounded already less than impressed.

'I am Daniel Gooding, part of the SLT at Elmley Prison. I've been made aware of your request and of your situation. I am calling you out of courtesy, to let you know that you will not be able to speak with prisoner Hughes today. I know this is not the outcome you wanted, but we have a duty of care to all and a strict schedule is very much part of that.' His voice was nasal. It was perhaps more irritating than his matter-of-fact denial.

'I understand your duty of care, Mr Gooding. I understand your schedule is important but—'

'That decision is mine, and it will not change, DS Ives. I make no apologies. I know you have your urgent priorities out there, but we have ours in here, too. Let me tell you, no matter what you think of our scheduling in here, you cannot understand just how important it is. It is all we have. Incarcerated men and women will fall in line with a system, a schedule, if that schedule is constant. A number of full-scale public order incidents on prison estates have been sparked by something as minor as a late lunch. And I'm not joking. The presence of police officers on the prison estate will *always* have an impact on a prison population. That's true for both the persons you may meet and those that you do not. A prison is a powder-keg and we, as the employees of this estate, are responsible for spotting potential sparks. Let me tell you this . . . you and your colleague are one of the more obvious sparks and you will not be allowed to enter HMP Elmley today. Police officers may come and go between nine a.m. and two p.m. Outside of those hours and our inmates will know instantly that there is a shift. They will be anxious. Anxiety inside a prison estate only grows.'

'It'd be a five-minute conversation. No other prisoners need know what—'

'The answer is no, DS Ives. I'm about to offer you a slot first thing in the morning. The policy is a seven-day notice for visiting police officers, as you know. I can enforce that policy—'

'That will not be necessary,' Harry jumped in. 'This is DI Blaker. We understand what you are saying. The last thing we are looking to do is cause issues for you or your population. Can I ask, with that being the case, would you be able to hold off on delivering the letter to Adrian Hughes until the morning?'

'We had no intention of giving him that letter this evening either, DI Blaker. Post is made available from eight a.m. Most inmates will check as part of their breakfast routine. If Adrian Hughes checks his mail then he will have an opportunity to read it just prior to your visit. I understand this is what you are looking to achieve?'

'It is, yes.'

'And what reaction are you expecting? Is this something we need to be aware of?'

'We're expecting him to discuss it with us, that's all. He might be upset but he will have his opportunity to vent any concerns he may have at us. That's the point of our visit.'

'Nine a.m., then. But I must warn you . . . prisoner Hughes can refuse to speak to you, as I understand he has done so already. If that's the case then your trip will be a wasted one.'

'I understand that. You mentioned the possibility of him checking his mail. Would there be any chance of someone there giving him a little prod? Just making him aware that something has come for him?' Harry's tone was as warm as it ever got.

Maddie heard a huff through the speakers.

'I'll see what I can do. We can't get too involved. Forcing our inmates to do anything they don't want to do is against our policy.'

'That's all we ask,' Harry said. The call ended. 'It's not like he's in prison or anything, is it?' Harry's growl was back.

He gripped the steering wheel so tightly that it squeaked.

'I wanted to get in there tonight.'

'I know. Me too. He's right though, about the bigger picture. This works better anyway.'

'How's that?'

'He said the post is a morning thing. Always. Hughes will have slotted into the daily routine by now. We need to fit in with that. This helps us do that better.'

'He still might see right through it.'

'Even if he does, I reckon he'll still see us.'

'And if he doesn't? Any ideas?'

'No. But I'm tired. You look it too. We need to get some rest. Who knows what ideas I'm capable of when I'm fresh.'

Maddie grinned. 'I really don't know what to expect. Part of me thinks you might bring along some sort of pretty foliage as a bribe!'

'A climbing rose would be ideal in a prison, actually.' Harry peered out at the wall while his right hand turned the key to start up the car. 'Would take a while, mind.'

CHAPTER 28

Time was nothing more than a concept in total silence and total blackness. Linda had found the least uncomfortable position and prayed for a sleep that might be permeated with dreams of colour and smiles. It hadn't come. Instead she had spent the time trying not to shiver, which only served to inflame her bruised side and ribs. When the familiar sound of the door mechanism came, it felt like Ian Hessey had been gone a while.

The screen switched on at the same time. Its dull grey light was hardly bright, but after the total darkness, it still made her squint. Ian stumbled as if he had been pushed. He rubbed at his forearms and wrists. When the door closed again, he was left standing, his chains still unclasped at his feet. She looked up at him, but he didn't so much as glance at her. Instead his attention was fixed on the dull grey square of light. She could just about see to the wall behind him. There was no one else in the room.

The light changed, drawing her attention to the screen. A cursor blinked like on a computer monitor. Words started appearing. She recognized them almost straight away.

A CHIEF CONSTABLE'S COMMENDATION IS
AWARDED TO
PC IAN HESSEY
FOR HIS PROFESSIONALISM AND DEDICATION
TO THE SAFEGUARDING OF VULNERABLE
VICTIMS IN THE COUNTY OF LENNOCKSHIRE.

Replace Ian's name with her own, and it was exactly the same as the commendation she had received at the same ceremony. They had stood together in the lecture theatre at the force training school holding framed versions of these very words, signed by the chief constable, who was also in attendance. The force photographer was there to capture a moment that would later be sent to her internally, framed and presented. It had felt good. She had been commended previously, but that was for playing a small part in something far bigger. And she had felt a bit of a fraud. This time was different: she'd felt that they both truly deserved it, that they had made a difference.

The text continued to the next part of the commendation typed out on the screen.

OPERATION ICICLE IS A MULTI-AGENCY OPERATION THAT COMMENCED IN 2018, WITH THE PROTECTION OF THOSE MOST VULNERABLE MEMBERS OF OUR COMMUNITY AT ITS HEART.

PC IAN HESSEY WAS INSTRUMENTAL IN THE SETTING UP OF OPERATION ICICLE AND, TO DATE, THREE OF THE FAMILIES DEEMED TO BE AT THE HIGHEST RISK HAVE BEEN SAFEGUARDED, THEIR FUTURES SECURED. THIS PILOT WILL NOW BE ROLLED OUT ACROSS OUR COUNTY AND PERHAPS FURTHER TO OTHER FORCES. MANY MORE VULNERABLE FAMILIES WILL BE AFFORDED THE BEST POSSIBLE PROTECTION FROM AN OTHERWISE UNCERTAIN FUTURE.

PC IAN HESSEY IS COMMENDED FOR HIS PROFESSIONALISM AND DEDICATION TO DUTY. THE CHIEF CONSTABLE.

The wording remained on the screen for another minute or more. It dimmed rather than cut away, as if scorched onto the screen. A cursor appeared again in the middle of the screen. Then came a popping sound from above her. Someone was testing a mic. As Linda looked up, the sound changed to a hiss that came through loud then settled at a lower volume. A voice followed. It sounded condensed, through speakers of poor quality, but she recognized the words and the voice immediately.

'Anything! Please . . . I did what you asked . . . I didn't know . . .'

Linda sucked her breath in so hard it forced a whimper. She could remember exactly where she'd been when she had uttered those words. The memory was so vivid she could almost smell the plastic that had forced its way up her nostrils while her view of that barn closed in around her. Her face had been wrapped so tight she couldn't breathe. Then they had brought another chair out, for Hope, if Linda didn't do as she was told. She had been convinced she was going to die. It felt like a lifetime ago.

'There is a police officer . . . Hessey. You know this man. He is your friend.' A man's voice now. It sounded different to how it had on the day. Then it had been delivered right into her ear, close enough to feel the breath carrying the words. Now it was no less intimidating. She knew what was coming. She knew what she had said. Ian still stood over her, untethered. The recording continued.

'Hessey . . . Ian Hessey? Yes, I know him.'

'He lives with his family. You are tasked with finding where this is.'

'His fam . . . Why do you need that? What has he—'

'His family or yours, Linda Morris?'

The speakers made a sound like the microphone scraping, then the voice came again. *'An address on a piece of paper is not enough. You must go there. I want to see where he lives, I want the layout. The front door, the windows . . . the security.'*

'*Okay, I'll do it. I'll find out!*' Linda's terrified voice filled the space again.

'*So . . . his family or yours?*' The male voice persisted.

She heard herself whimper then sniff. She remembered that she'd been sobbing. She knew what she was about to answer. They hadn't given her a choice. Not then. Not now.

'*His family . . .*' It had been barely a whisper at the time but now her words filled the space. There was another sound, this time like someone tapping a microphone. The hiss was gone. The recording was finished.

Linda looked up. Ian still stood over her, stiff and straight, but he was looking at the screen. His hands were by his sides, both of them balled up into fists.

'Ian! Look, it's not how it sounds! You didn't hear the bit where they threatened my daughter. They suffocated me. They sat me on a chair and they wrapped plastic all round my face. They had another chair out for my Hope . . .'

'They said we should be quiet.' Ian's intensity cut her dead. He was still staring at the blinking cursor in the middle of the screen.

'Ian, we need to t—'

The blow caught her by surprise. Ian had moved so quickly. He hadn't turned towards her, just flicked out with his left hand to sting her across her face. Her hair fell over her eyes. She looked out from under it to where he was standing. He looked almost as shocked as she felt. He bent down. His expression of shock didn't last; the anger was quick to return.

'They're six and eight years old, my girls. They answered the door to you. You looked them right in the face.' He stood back up.

The bile in his words felt worse than the slap. Linda stayed silent. The light of the screen changed again. She looked up at it. More words were being typed.

IMAGINE BEING RELEASED FROM PRISON TO FIND YOUR FAMILY HIDDEN . . .

. . .

The door scraped open. Ian turned to walk towards it. He seemed calm, as if this had all been choreographed, as if he knew exactly what he needed to do next. Linda tried to move but her chains held her to the floor. She called out.

'Ian, please! It wasn't like that! You can't leave me here like this! IAN!'

He was gone. The door mechanism made its familiar locking sound. The screen washed itself blank. The cursor was back to blinking in the middle. It started moving again.

YOU HID OUR FAMILIES.

BUT WE ARE BETTER AT IT.

'Please! I did what you asked! I did EVERYTHING!' Her voice bounced round the walls, coming back louder. 'PLEASE!'

There was no response but the wiping of the screen. Then the typing started again.

YOU WILL NEVER BE FOUND.

This text seemed to be the brightest yet. Even when the surround turned black and the monitor was switched off, it didn't disappear. Instead it faded slowly, burned into the screen. Another few seconds and the characters were gone entirely. And all that was left was the total blackness.

CHAPTER 29

Ian Hessey stumbled out into a warm night and lifted his head to a sky spattered with stars. He took a deep breath, inhaling the freshness of the night air. At any other time, it would have been beautiful. But right now, the vista barely penetrated the fug of shock as he continued his walk away from Linda Morris, from the tomb in which he'd left her. That was exactly what it was now. They had been clear on that. He couldn't see past the last image of her trying to reach out to him, straining against chains that had glinted in the weak light. He shook his head. He couldn't be thinking about her. He focused on his own family instead.

The last time he had seen his children, he had put them to bed like he always did. It involved a game where one would climb on his back while he tucked the other in. He would pretend not to notice, moving around the house until he got in front of a reflective surface. Then he'd 'see' them and pretend to be furious — dumping the child back in bed to administer a tickle while the other snuck onto his back for the game to start all over again. He had to have those moments again. He just had to.

The car was waiting for him, already ticking over. It was the same marked police car he had been bundled into to get here — one of the old Skoda estate cars from a few years back. You still saw a few of them buzzing around but only as temporary replacements for the newer cars in the fleet, had they been crashed or sent in for a service. The officer in the driver's seat was the same man who had pulled into his road. He recognized him from work; he was attached to one of the other response sections but had been out most of the time running fast-road training for new starters. He didn't think he had been there long, a transferee from another force he had heard. A Velcro slot on his load vest carried the name, *PC HARVEY*. There were no introductions. The moment Ian closed his door, the car pulled away. He quickly checked the back; there was no one else in the car.

'We just left someone back there. Just left her.'

'We don't talk. Talking is a deviation. You should know the rules by now.' PC Harvey had a deep and determined voice.

'I'm the same as her. I did the same. Now she's going to die. I'm not going to just be able to walk away from this, am I?'

The car braked suddenly enough to throw Ian forwards into the dashboard and he yelped in pain. He hadn't thought to belt up. His left forearm took most of the impact.

'We don't talk. We don't deviate. This is about my kid, too.' PC Harvey kept his eyes forwards. He seemed to grit his teeth; the action was visible through his heavily bruised cheek. When Ian didn't reply he pulled away again.

Ian sat back and nursed his arm. It was still painful but nothing more than a bump. He looked again at the bruising on the driver's face. It was worst around his eye. It looked a few days old at least. He dragged his gaze away to peer out of the window. It was too dark to make much out. The landscape was barren. The ground seemed as black as the night sky but with jagged rocks to break it up rather than twinkling stars. It looked scorched, as if they had emerged after the apocalypse. Ian was relieved when the scenery changed and they found a proper road. Immediately PC Harvey picked up the pace.

This time, of course, Ian knew where they were going. He knew they had maybe forty minutes until they got there. He'd been there before. It was why they needed him.

The building still looked familiar, despite his last visit being carried out under a barrage of rainwater nearly eighteen months earlier. Then they had needed to move fast — too fast, perhaps. Neither little Peter Loxton nor his mother had made any move to get out of the car that night. Ian had had an umbrella in the boot. He remembered Peter watching his battle to get it up in the driving rain, his little hand wiping a porthole in the condensation to see out. Ian had managed the umbrella eventually, but it had hardly been worthwhile. The umbrella turned out to be riddled with holes.

Peter's mother was called Anna. With her help, Ian had been able to coax Peter out of the back seat. She'd made sure Peter was wearing his favourite Spiderman tracksuit bottoms for his big adventure. And, of course, he had his drumsticks. He held them tight in his hands the whole time. Ian had asked him to tap out a quick rhythm on the door rim while he watched in the pissing rain, trying to show as much enthusiasm as he could manage. Drumming was essential for Peter; it seemed to be the only time he could relax. It wasn't like he was beating out his frustration, more that he needed the rhythm to move forwards with his life. All through his police interviews, they had taken breaks to allow him to drum out a beat. Sometimes Ian had played along on the keyboard he had brought in from home. He had forgotten the stand. The only time he had ever heard Pete laugh properly was when he had propped up his keyboard on a rickety old stool that had collapsed almost instantly into Ian's lap. It trapped his thumb and hurt like hell, but it had been a wonderful moment. Maybe it was the only time he had ever seen Peter truly happy.

It was this memory that lingered as he crossed the car park, two steps behind PC Harvey. It was dry this time, the artificial light the only element washing over the building. The lit windows made up a random pattern. He didn't think the light was on in the place he had last left Anna and Pete.

The communal doorway was lit, too. PC Harvey stepped back for Ian to press the buzzer. He made sure he stood right in front of the camera so Anna would see it was him. The buzz-in reply took half a minute. PC Harvey pushed the door open. From here it was three flights up.

Ian had seen a digital clock in the car. It was close to ten p.m. He heard shrill laughter as he passed one of the numerous identical doors that marked out individual flats. Another flat emitted tinny shooting sounds, someone on a video game perhaps? They arrived at Anna's door and PC Harvey gestured at him to knock. Ian hesitated.

'Do it!' Harvey hissed. He looked far more wired now. His eyes ran all over the door, then he stepped back a little to look down the corridor. When he turned back to Ian, his head jerked towards the door. This was Ian's whole purpose. He had offered to just give them the addresses, but they had refused. He had been forced to go along. The people behind each door knew him. They trusted him. And why wouldn't they? He had made them safe.

Ian knocked. His head fell forwards as he waited. This was the biggest step yet, past the point of no return. Before this moment, he could still have walked away, still have gone back for Linda, still have called it in.

The door opened slowly. Anna peered out. She revealed enough of herself for Ian to see hair that looked like it had been dried in a hurry and pulled back into a ponytail — maybe in the time it had taken them to walk up the stairs. Her face was flushed. Disturbed from a hot bath, he reckoned. She was wrapped in a robe and smelled like soap. He couldn't help but recall the first time they had met. She'd had wet hair then, too, but it had been accompanied by an ugly welt on her face from where her husband had forced her head down the toilet, tearing out a chunk of her hair in his huge fist as the police had finally rushed him. There was no bruising now, just a drop of water that started from her temple. There was still fear in her expression but also a smile that dared to cut through.

'Ian!'

'Hey, Anna.'

Her eyes flicked to the uniform standing close behind him. Her expression changed again. Ian could feel Harvey at his shoulder, edging forwards like he might be going to rush her. Ian held his ground, casting an angry glance over his shoulder. He looked back to see Anna's eyes had dropped to the doormat that had scrunched and skidded under their feet.

'It's late. Is everything okay?' Anna said.

'Can we come in? We need to talk to you.' Ian's smile was forced. He hoped that wasn't obvious.

'It's late.' She looked more and more unsure.

'I know that. I wouldn't be here unless we really needed to talk. Listen, Anna, we think . . . we think he might know where you are.'

Her hand found her mouth in an instant. Her chest rose and fell quicker, her breaths were shallower.

'How? How could he know? You told me—'

'We need to move inside.' Harvey's voice was gruff and this time there was no stopping him. He pushed past, something firm on the front of his load vest buffeted Ian's elbow.

Anna stepped back, her face a mask of panic. 'You can't just turn up here and—'

'We need to move! Get dressed. Where's the boy?' Harvey scoured the interior. The kitchen was visible off to the left, the living room to the right. The bedrooms were on the other side. Ian knew they were off a hallway accessed through the lounge.

'Move? I can't just move! Please . . . I've just got him settled. I can't move my son again. You're the police . . . if he knows we are here, if he comes here, you can just arrest him. There is a restraining ord—'

'That ain't worth shit, love!' Harvey said. 'No way we can guarantee your safety. You don't get police sat outside your door twenty-four-seven just because your son's found a view he likes. Leave your stuff here. We'll come back for it later.'

260

'Leave it here? Why can't I take it with me?'

'Because we're not a *fucking* removal service!'

Ian stepped in. He pulled Harvey by his shoulder to get in front of where he was squaring up to the terrified woman. 'We're anxious to get you away, that's all, Anna. We don't want anything to happen to you. Please, listen to what we are saying. We need to get you away from here. We have somewhere else for you to go, somewhere you'll be comfortable.'

'We're comfortable here! You've moved us three times. Two B&Bs . . . both awful. I know you've helped us, Ian, but we're happy now. Please don't make us leave!'

'We don't have a choice. You might be able to come back. If he breaches his order, he'll go back inside . . .' Ian's lie trailed away. He could see she didn't believe him. He knew he wasn't good at lying; it went against the grain for him.

'Where would you have us go? Not another B&B? And not tonight, Ian, please. My son's asleep.'

'We need to go now!' Harvey insisted.

Anna reacted to his tone, she flinched and backed away. The fear in her eyes was genuine.

'Why is he threatening me?' She was still talking to Ian only.

'I haven't even started yet! I'll get the boy then, if you don't want to.' Harvey turned towards the living room. Anna lunged at him, grabbing him around the waist. There was no time for Ian to react, no time to get to her before his colleague brought his elbow down hard on her back. She collapsed to the floor, crying out as she went down. Her arms shot out to grab at Harvey's shins. He stumbled, reaching for the doorframe to the living room. Ian stepped towards him and grabbed his load vest, pulling him backwards into a wall. Anna yelled. Harvey pushed back. He was bigger than Ian and shrugged him off — then he launched himself back at Anna. Ian bounced off the front door to come at Harvey again, throwing himself at his back. It was enough to unbalance Harvey and he fell forwards into Anna. They all ended up on the floor. Anna's scream was loud and shrill enough for the neighbours to hear.

'Okay! OKAY!' Ian shouted. 'STOP! We're not getting anywhere!' He pushed off to stand up. Anna was on her back looking up. She snivelled as Ian reached down to pick Harvey off the floor. He stared up at Ian, his rage clear.

'We are going. Five minutes from now. She either walks out or I drag her out, I don't care. We don't have time for this.' Harvey's words were loaded with intent.

Ian turned back to Anna. 'Look, this does need to happen now. We're only here because this threat is real. We need to go. We can't leave without you. Get yourself dr—' Ian stopped. Over Anna's whimpering, came a familiar drumbeat. It was coming from the living room. Anna heard it too. Her head dropped.

'He's awake . . .' she murmured, 'and he's scared.'

Ian was still frozen to the spot. Harvey took a step towards the living room and Ian's hand shot out to grab him by the scruff of the neck. This time he wasn't going to be shrugged off. 'No! I'll talk to him. You don't talk to Pete.'

'Friend of yours?' Harvey snarled back.

'Five minutes, you said. We'll be out in five minutes. But I get the boy.'

Peter was sitting on the floor of the darkened living room. The window above him glowed a dirty yellow. The scene was so similar to the first time they had met that it stopped Ian in his tracks. He had to wait for a sudden urge to break down to pass. That time Ian had been there to help him. In the year since Ian had seen him — on the occasion of his last follow-up visit — Peter didn't seem to have grown any bigger. His scrawny arms reached out of a vest top. His bottom half was clad only in underpants. He didn't look up, perhaps blocking out the fact that there was anyone in the flat at all. His focus was downwards, his head and eyes following the movement of the drumsticks in his hands. It was the same coping mechanism he had developed as his dad's violence towards his mother had worsened.

His dad, James Loxton, was a man who revelled in his perceived control over his family, who declared himself 'the head of his family' and never once saw an issue with how he asserted himself in that role; a man who had once leaned forwards to leer at Ian, despite the solicitor's hand on his shoulder, and declare, 'If I can't have them, no one can.' Ian had been in no doubt that the threat was real. He and Linda had quoted this line in their report. It became the main justification for Loxton's family to be the first Op Icicle case.

'Pete!' Ian's voice broke a little as he called out. The boy's drumming stopped instantly. He smiled up at his friend.

'Ian!' He was on his feet with his thin arms hanging round Ian's neck before he could speak again. Ian tried to pull away at first but he quickly relented and wrapped Peter up in a hug.

'We have to GO!' Harvey growled from behind him.

Ian turned to where Harvey held Anna's bicep. She wriggled then hissed in pain as he tightened his grip.

'He needs clothes,' Ian said.

'Be quick. We'll be in the car.'

'No! I'm not leav—' Anna was dragged out of view. The front door opened and Ian heard her yell out. He needed to get the boy dressed and down to his mother. He didn't want to leave Anna alone with that man.

Peter didn't drag his heels. He was excited even. His policeman friend was here to take him on a night-time adventure! A few minutes later, Ian dropped into the passenger seat of the patrol car. Peter climbed in the back, but his excitement dissipated the moment he set eyes on his quietly sobbing mother in the seat next to him. He looked forwards with big eyes, looking elsewhere for assurance that everything was going to be okay. Ian turned away from him to face forwards.

'You're going to have to toughen up,' Harvey said. 'Remember the choices here. Remember what's at stake. We've still got two more addresses.'

'Just let me do the talking,' Ian hissed back. 'They'll come with me.'

Two more addresses. Two more families who had learned to trust him, two more families who associated him with getting them to safety. They would come with him; he was confident of that. But they shouldn't.

If they knew the truth, they would slam the door in his face and run.

CHAPTER 30

Wednesday

Adrian Hughes walked in, still clutching the letter in his right hand. He stopped as the guard who had been escorting him closed the door behind him. He looked at Maddie first then lingered on Harry Blaker sitting next to her. Harry got up to extend his hand.

'What is this?' Hughes's voice was just as she remembered, weak and morose.

He folded the paper up untidily to stuff it into the pocket of his shapeless blue jeans. On top, he wore a grey sweatshirt. His hair was brushed but only enough to have swept it out of his eyes. He looked tired, his eyes flushed and heavy, as though it was an effort just to keep them open. His head hung forwards, his tiny frame looking all the smaller for it. He dabbed his nose with the back of his hand and his sniff sounded full of fluid.

'I'm Detective Inspector Harry Blaker. I work in the same department as DS Ives. I'm her boss effectively.'

'So what? You need to speak to me too? I already told her all I know.'

'Sergeant Ives isn't convinced. The way it works is that she comes to me to sign off her jobs. We had a conversation that was supposed to be about me signing off your case, but she wasn't happy that it was time to move on, that she had all the answers she needed. That you should be here in the first place. And neither am I.'

'This again! I told you what I did. Why don't you believe me?'

'Because we know you didn't tell us everything.'

Hughes shrugged. 'I told you everything that mattered.'

'Why didn't you tell us about Janet Taylor?' Maddie took up the questioning.

'What does she have to do with anything?'

'You know what. Janet sat next to the woman you murdered. They were friends. You told us the killing was random, someone you saw on a running app. That never really made sense. You chose her as your victim when you saw her at the council offices. Is that right?'

'Is this an interview?'

'No. It should be. I should be doing this properly, asking if you want legal advice, recording it, reminding you of your rights, telling you that you don't have to answer any of these questions . . . but I wanted to talk to you off the record. I wanted you to know that we can protect you. If there's something more to this, we *can* help.'

Hughes's body language was shut down, closed to them. His bony arms were crossed over his front, his eyes were down, his head slightly to the side and he still hadn't taken the seat opposite them. Maddie needed him to engage, to participate in the conversation at least.

'I tell you what . . . let's do this a different way. How about you sit down and you ask the questions? Of us. That way, you can control what we talk about. How does that sound? You do have questions, Adrian. We all know it. That's why you're here.' Maddie said.

Hughes unfurled his arms and finally made eye contact. Then he broke away to look at the empty seat in front of him.

They were in a square room with long windows along one side. They offered no view of the outside world — only an internal corridor — and there was no natural light. A water jug and a stack of cups were the only items not bolted to the floor. Maddie poured out three cups of water. She pushed one to where Hughes might sit and he finally slumped down in front of it.

'My mum . . . she wrote to me. She tried to come and see me but I said no.'

Maddie bit her tongue, resisting the urge to prompt him.

'She said that Jan's been in touch to ask for the receipt for the engagement ring I bought her. She wants to take it back — says I can have the money an' that. Mum said she's moved on, got with someone else already and feels bad keeping the ring. She said you lot had talked to her — to Jan. I guess it was you specifically?'

'Yes,' Maddie said.

'Did she mention anyone new?'

'You seem surprised.'

'It can't be right. My mum . . . she gets the wrong end of the stick easy. Jan moving on . . . that can't be right.'

'Your mother told us she was your ex anyw—'

'She's NOT!' Hughes raised his voice, shaking off his lethargy in an instant. He even looked like he was sitting up straighter. 'That's just something I told my mum. She was giving me hassle about Jan the whole time. I moved out so—' He stopped himself.

'Even if that were true, Janet's facing a lifetime without you now. And she thinks you're a murderer so—'

'She DOESN'T!' Hughes banged the table with a tight fist. The water jumped and rippled in the cup in front of him. His face contorted, barely concealing an internal battle. 'She knows who I am.' His teeth were gritted. His eyes still on the table.

'But you admitted to Marie Foreshaw's murder. That makes you a murderer. We told her you admitted it. We told her the evidence supports what you said. You killed her friend, Adrian.'

'But she knows why.'

'Why you killed Marie?'

'No!' Hughes's lips moved as if there were more words to come. Except they didn't. He rocked silently back and forth. He clearly didn't know what to do with himself or what to say. He opted for, 'And this is all off the record?'

'Yes.' Maddie's reply was instant.

'I have to stay in here, okay? No matter what I say or what you think. For now.'

'For now?'

'They told me I would be out. Let out. As soon as this all revealed itself. I'm not a murderer, okay? You're right. And Janet knows that. She knows I would never hurt anyone!'

Another silence grew to fill the room. Hughes was stewing right in front of them. He jerked forwards suddenly, as if he had been prodded in the buttocks, pulled out the letter from his back pocket and threw it onto the table. He slid it over to Maddie. 'This can't be right . . . it can't be. Why would my mum make that up?'

Maddie looked down at the paper. She made no movement to open it. She knew what it said anyway. 'I think you need to start from the beginning, Adrian.'

'The beginning . . . ha!' He thrust his hands into his pockets and sat back. Now he looked just like he had in interview. 'I don't even know where that might be.'

'Tell us a story, Adrian. Every story has a beginning, a middle and an end. We know the ending to this one. It's you, rotting in a prison cell, possibly for the rest of your life. I think you're being used, Adrian. I don't know why yet, but if that's the case, you need to tell me that story. Because I don't think you have anyone you can trust right now, not with something as important as your freedom.'

Hughes's hands came back out of his pockets so he could lean forwards on his elbows. 'A queue at a petrol station. There you are — that's as good a place as any.'

'A petrol station?'

'I was there to kill myself . . . okay?'

The last word was so low that Maddie struggled to catch it. She leaned in. She didn't want to miss a word. She didn't want to make Adrian say anything twice, not while he was on a roll.

'I meant it, too. That day was going to be the day I ended it. I'd had a few false alarms but . . . things just weren't getting any better.'

'What made you feel like that, Adrian?' Maddie leaned in further still, forcing his eyes to meet with hers. 'It's okay — to talk to us. Life's hard. We see people struggling with it all the time.'

'I was in a queue. It was a warm day. Last summer — *late* summer. September the nineteenth. My son's birthday . . .'

Maddie shot a glance at Harry. *How did they not know he had a son?*

'Just another day for the rest of the world. But for me it was the final straw. I didn't get to see him. She wouldn't even let me *talk* to him! Who does that?'

'You have a son,' Maddie said.

'I do. Not that anyone would know — me included most of the time. I've barely seen him since he was born. His mother . . . she's a lot younger than me. She was sixteen when we got together — I mean, legal! But I was nearly thirty. Her dad was angry. Called me all sorts. Said I would never see my boy or his mum again. They were everything I had. The only thing I'd ever had. I didn't care what he thought, what he said. All I ever wanted was a family. We all want that, right?' He lifted his sad eyes back to Maddie. 'I woulda been a brilliant dad.'

'I think we all have a right to be happy. That might mean different things to different people. But if a family is what makes you happy then you have every right.'

'I would have been good, too. I would have loved him so hard. That's all you need. I know I don't have much money or a fancy house — any kind of house in fact! But I would have loved him.'

'Would have?'

'I can't. Not now. Her dad moved them away. I don't know where. He said if I ever found them then he would have me arrested, make up some story about me being a wife beater, get me locked up. Or at least get a restraining order. I looked online — it's so easy. You don't even need proof to apply for one. Not really. And then if I even tried to speak to my son, I'd get arrested. I couldn't see a way out. I saw that boy as my one chance for happiness, to have a normal life. And it was gone.'

'I can see why that might make you feel low.'

'I was in a queue for a bottle of water at some petrol station. I had a coat on, a big one. I was sweating in it, but it had deep pockets. I'd stuffed a couple of fistfuls of painkillers in there. My mum has them for her migraines, for when they're really bad. She'd be out of it on just one of them. I knew I had enough on me to never wake up. That coat rattled! I was going straight out of there to walk to a bench on Dover seafront. That's the last place I took my son. I must have been acting weird. I was sweating, I know that much. This bloke behind me . . . he asked if I was okay. I told him I was fine. I tried to ignore him but he kept on at me. He could see I wasn't fine. He said he would buy me a coffee. There was a separate counter for that in this place, a couple of stools too. He said it'd just be a chat and then he would leave me. He said he could see I was upset. I still bought that bottle of water but I did have a coffee with him. I broke down. I'd done the same with Jan an hour earlier.'

'Jan?'

'Yeah. We were friends at that point. I mean, I wanted more but I didn't think she was interested in me in that way at all. I got so low I just wanted to hear a friendly voice. She must have thought, "who's this weirdo calling me out of nowhere?" But she said it was okay, said she didn't mind.'

'Did you tell her what you were planning?'

'I told her about the drugs and where I was going. So yeah, I suppose I did tell her . . . without telling her, if that makes sense. It was pretty obvious. She did try and talk me round . . . told me not to do anything silly. I was hoping she would come and find me. I left it a while, but of course she didn't. Can't blame her. I was nothing to her then.'

'And this man who bought you the coffee, did you tell him what you were there to do?'

'I told him everything. And I got lucky. Turns out he was in a similar situation. He'd even been to prison over it all. His wife had done exactly what they'd threatened me with . . . she'd made up a load of stuff and got him arrested. But it went further than that. And you know what happened then?'

'Tell me,' Maddie said.

'Your lot. By the time he came out of prison, they'd hidden his family! How can you do that?'

'Hidden? What do you mean by hidden?'

'He said they had moved them somewhere. The day he gets out, the police tell him they've moved his family and that he isn't able to see them anymore. He couldn't even know where they'd gone. There was one of them restraining orders against him. He wasn't even allowed to *try* and find them! We talked for hours — about how unfair it was. Then he said that he was part of something . . . a group of blokes in situations just like me and him. He had started it all. He said he had been part of that outfit . . . the ones who put the flag out over the palace' — Hughes clicked his fingers as he tried to recall — 'fathers something?'

'Fathers for Justice,' Harry supplied.

'That's it! He was with them a while but they weren't for him. He said they were all about getting together and moaning but they never wanted to act. He had some big ideas. He told me some of them. He wrapped them up in clever language but I saw through them. I started asking exactly what he meant. Once I'd worked it out, I told him . . . I said I didn't want anything to do with it.'

'So what happened then?'

'Nothing for a while. I walked away. Ditched the pills. He may have had some crazy ideas, but he gave me a bit of hope.

271

Now I knew that there were other blokes suffering like I was and that there were people out there trying to do something about it, trying to make the system fairer. I remember thinking how he had saved my life and how I never thanked him for it.'

'But he came back?' Maddie hazarded.

'Later. Much later. Janet called me back, just to make sure I was still alive. She seemed really concerned. That was kinda the start of something more between us. I thought, maybe she does care about me, you know? Turns out I was right. I asked her out the next day. She said yes straight away. All of a sudden we were dating!'

Hughes sat back, his expression brighter. It was the first time Maddie had seen anything other than angst register on his face. He had stopped talking, as if clutching at the happy memory for as long as he could. Maddie didn't have the time for that.

'So that's the beginning, Adrian. The end is you in this place. So tell me about the middle part.'

Hughes sighed and the smile fell away. 'We were together, had been for a while, and we agreed to meet at the bus station in Canterbury, like we had done a thousand times. I was taking her out for a meal. She never showed. That was a first. When I called, her phone was switched off. I walked to the restaurant just in case. Then I got a call from her. She said she was sorry, that she was running late. She was feeling tired and could we just meet for a coffee at the twenty-four-hour McDonald's in Sturry at eleven p.m. She said she would explain everything. I went there . . .' Hughes looked upset now, close to breaking, even. 'I was grabbed . . . bundled into a car with something over my head and chained up somewhere dark. There was a video . . . I was shown a video . . .'

Hughes's face was a mask of shock and fear. Whatever he was recalling, Maddie was in little doubt that it was real to him. He took a swig of his water. She let him gather his thoughts.

'That was the first time I saw what they did to Marie. It was on a screen but it was just like being there. I saw her from the back. She was alive at first . . . fighting, too . . . but then . . . then they wrapped her head up and she didn't fight much longer. I never got to see the girl up close. I didn't even recognize her at the time — I thought it was my Janet! I've never felt so desperate . . . so helpless. The picture changed. When it changed, it was Janet's building. Someone was walking up to it, through the door and right up to her flat. Then everything just went black. I was dragged out of that place, punched in the stomach until I was sick and then told that I had to carry out a task — or else Janet would be the next woman they tied to a chair somewhere, her face wrapped in plastic. *Dead.* I had no choice!'

'And your task was to walk into the police station and admit to Marie's murder?'

'That was part of it. They gave me a backstory. A few details about how I did it, how I got there, what I touched. I had to touch an axe that had been used to force the door and I had to . . . I had to touch her, too. This woman! I touched her neck like I was feeling for a pulse. She was so cold. I saw her eyes too . . . Jesus! Who can do that to another person?' This time when he swigged at his water his hands were trembling so badly that liquid spilled out of the sides to dribble down his chin.

'It's okay, Adrian.'

'None of this is official — you said that, right?'

Maddie held her palms up. She knew things had gone well beyond an 'off-the-record chat', but this didn't seem like the time to break the news.

'There was a police officer, okay? He was there at the end. He was the one who told me that, when this was all over, I would just walk out of here. So if you go back and tell your people what I've said in here, he'll find out! What then? My Janet! They said it would be her next!'

'You let us worry about Janet. What police officer?'

'I don't know his name. I don't know any names.'

'The guy you met in the queue. What about him?'

Hughes shook his head emphatically. 'I'd been drinking that day. I'd had a few. I don't drink often. He was a bit older than me . . . early forties. A white man with stubble — dark stubble. Big build, too — looked solid. That's all I remember. It was a long time ago and I didn't think I would need to remember his face.'

'And the police officer . . . what did he look like?'

'Same description, really. Middle-aged, white, clean-shaven — but then police almost always are, aren't they?'

'And he told you he was a police officer?'

'He didn't have to. The uniform and the police car he got out of were a bit of a giveaway!'

'When was this?'

'A week before I came into the police station. That was when I came out of that dark place, when they told me what I had to do and cut me loose. There was a police car waiting. He drove me back to find my car. It was staged like that, so he could be telling me how I would be out in less than a month. But he also reminded me that if I spoke to the police, if I said anything I wasn't supposed to, then he'd know. He'd pass that back up the line and Janet would end up dead. They'd already killed someone — I knew that!'

'Marie Foreshaw.'

'I didn't know it was her. I was just happy it wasn't Janet in that chair, okay? It *looked* like her on that screen. She was the first person I tried to call when I got away. I hadn't heard from her for a while. I couldn't get hold of her. I thought she was dead!' A tear spurted down his cheek, seemingly from nowhere — just as Maddie was beginning to think he had fought them off completely. 'But it wasn't her . . . it was Marie. I didn't even recognize her when I went to take her photo. They look so different, don't they? Dead people. I never really took much notice of her when I was in the council office. Janet didn't like her — she told me to stay away anyway. She didn't want anyone gossiping about what we had.'

'She didn't get on with Marie?'

'She was a right bitch apparently. Up herself. She didn't deserve . . . *that* though . . .'

'Why Marie?'

'I don't know. I turned up and there she was, just sitting there. I didn't care either. All that matters to me is my Janet . . . I have to get out of here. I need to see her again. That letter . . . it's bollocks. No way would she go off with someone else. No way she thinks I'm a murderer. She should know the full story by now. They said they were going to tell her. They said she would know the sacrifices I made so she would be waiting for me when I got free. I did this for her!'

'You said "when this is all over" . . . What does that mean, Adrian?' Harry's voice seemed to break a spell. Hughes's previous comment had been plaintive, almost like he was thinking out loud. But now he turned fiercely to Harry.

'It's something big. Something bad. The hooded men, they were talking about hidden families — more than one. They said they were going to find them and then . . . then they were going to show you lot that you can't just play with people's lives. They told me that when it was all over, the whole situation would change back in our favour. That I would be able to see my son again. They seemed to think they were about to change the whole system. It was the same sort of thing that guy talked about when he stopped me taking those pills. That's how I knew it was the same people.'

'What were they planning?'

'I don't know any more than that! One of them, he talked about Marie, about how her suffocation had been slow and how he wanted to do something similar again. He wanted people to watch while they were helpless. They were excited about that. I've never been so scared!' Hughes wept now. His face crumpled and his tears shook free like they were falling from a rain-covered branch in the wind. 'He talked about how they were all going to die.'

'Who, Adrian?'

'I don't know! Just not Janet. I begged them. They said as long as I did what they said, she wouldn't be hurt.'

'Who was doing the talking?'

'All of them. They all had something over their faces. I didn't get a proper look at any of them. There were a lot of voices. I don't even know how many. And they were all so excited.'

'They're using you, Adrian. Janet might be, too. She didn't say anything to us about being under threat.'

'Of course she didn't! She's out there! This place might be a lot of things, but them people can't get to me. Not in here! You just need to promise me that you won't go shooting your mouth off. You need to promise me that you'll look after my Janet. That's the only reason I'm telling you any of this. Can you get a message to her? Can you make sure that she knows enough of what's going on? Enough that she knows I'm only doing this for her? So she's waiting for me when I step outside of those gates? They said they would tell her, but I'm not so sure anymore . . .'

'We need to regroup,' Harry said to Maddie.

She knew what he meant. 'We do. Adrian, we need to get back and start working with what you've told us. Not just for Janet. We need to keep everyone safe. The next time I ask to come and see you or I call for you I want you to pick up the phone. Is that clear?'

'Are you going to keep Janet safe?'

'We're the police. We're here to keep everyone safe.'

'That letter . . . they must be threatening her. That's what my mum means. She must have seen her with a man, a chaperone maybe. Maybe just while I'm in here, to make sure I do what I'm supposed to. Keep her safe!' He sucked in a panicked breath; there was a new intensity to his stare as he locked onto Maddie.

'I told you we will. Thank you, Adrian. Remember what I said . . . if I call, you need to pick up.'

'I know. I will. I'm sorry, okay? I didn't want this, not any of it.'

'I finally think you're telling me the truth,' Maddie said.

* * *

Their pace through the inner sanctums of Elmley prison was a jog, where possible.

'I knew there was a lot more to this,' Maddie said, the moment they were free of the prison's imposing entrance. The car was in sight across the small car park.

'We still don't have the whole story.'

'"Hidden families," he said. There was a pilot for the most at risk. Who was the copper that ran that? Got a commendation for it? Always cheerful. I can't think of his name.'

'Op Icicle,' Harry said.

'That's it. It was a big thing. They came into our team meeting to promote it. Hessey! Ian Hessey.'

Maddie was already fiddling with her phone. They were back at the car. She brought up the function where you could search for shift patterns on the force intranet. The phone was laggy and the signal not great. 'Ian Hessey' came up finally.

'He's eight-till-four for today and tomorrow, but there's a cell note here. Says he's on a residential driving course. They do them all over the place now. His work mobile is on here . . . let's just hope he can be disturbed . . .' She waited for the phone to confirm it was connected to their car before she dialled. Harry was already pulling away.

'Hello, you're through to the voicemail of PC Ian H—'

'Dammit!' Maddie hung up. She punched in more numbers and the car speakers blared out another dialling tone.

'Good morning, Force HR.'

'Good morning, HR.' Maddie tried to use brightness to mask the urgency of her request. 'I need a favour, please. I need a personal mobile number for a PC Ian Hessey as part of a Major Crime investigation.'

'We don't give out personal numbers over the phone, I'm afraid. We'll need written authorization from an inspector or above with just—'

'This is DI Harry Blaker, Force Number 9009. I authorize this request. There is no time for the paperwork, unfortunately. I will make sure it is completed retrospectively.' Harry was gruff and impatient.

The only reply was the dull hiss of a connected call. Maddie watched the timer ticking up, one second passed, two seconds, three—

'Okay. Justification?' The reply was curt.

'We're investigating a murder. We have reasonable belief that PC Hessey has knowledge of other persons at risk.'

'Oh!' The voice suddenly seemed more interested. 'Standby please, sir.'

The dull hiss returned. Maddie drummed her fingers. She couldn't stand it. It was just a few more seconds but it felt like a lifetime. The voice came back with a number. Maddie noted it down.

'Thank you.' Maddie was reaching out to end the call when the woman cut back in.

'He's off sick at the moment. Not sure if that makes any difference? Reason code is migraine. It was called in yesterday. He might have switched his phone off.'

'Let's hope not.' Maddie pressed to end it there. She had already typed the number into her phone.

'The phone you are calling is switch—'

'Dammit!'

'HR for his home address?'

'It doesn't have to be Hessey. We just need someone who knows Op Icicle. I'll call his sergeant. He might have access to his daybook or something.'

'What about calling the office? Rhiannon has a talent for getting what's needed.'

'She does. Op Icicle was all run very separately, though. Very much on a need-to-know basis. We might need rank to get access.'

'Sergeant Randall.' A pleasant female voice answered quicker than Maddie was expecting. She almost sang her name.

'Sergeant, this is DS Maddie Ives, Major Crime. We have an investigation that appears to overlap with something Ian Hessey was working on. Op Icicle. Does that ring any bells?'

'Ah, the *commendation man*! Sorry, that's just what we call him in here. He'll never live that one down. I know the operation, of course, but only from the briefing we were given and the information on the force site. Hessey's back to his day job now. We released him to that op for a good year or more. We got him back seven weeks ago.'

'Any chance you could tell us the cases he worked with under that op?'

'No. I don't think that's general knowledge either. Ian talked about it a bit when he came back. Interesting stuff, actually. He might be the only one who knows the full details of the families that came under that op. I think he met them all from what he was saying. It was his baby. I think he's a little sad it's all over if I'm honest with you.'

'Is his daybook there? Any way you could get those details?'

'No. It was kept on a separate system. All very secure. Some of the work he was doing was very sensitive. He was rehoming beaten women and children. The whole point was that it was very much a secret thing. I'd say phone him direct but he's off sick at the moment. Due on a course he's been badgering me about for years and he rings in! It must be a leg hanging off or something. Definitely the first time I've known him to call in sick. He didn't sound right. I don't mind it so much when you get a genuinely apologetic one.'

'I see. Anyone else there that he worked with? Anyone else who might have access to the same information?'

'No one here. We're a response team. He was seconded to CID for that whole op. This is urgent, is it?'

It must have been leaking from Maddie's voice.

'It could be.'

'Okay. Well, I'm not sure how much more help I can be. I can try and get hold of Ian's personal mobile for you? I've noted your number from my scr—'

'Tried that. Thank you, though. I'll think of something else. Thanks for your help.'

'There was someone else. He talked about her lot. Works CPS. She was commended, too . . .' Randall's words trailed away. Maddie could hear she was thinking.

'Do you remember her name?'

'Hang on. They were pictured together in *Policing Now*. Someone cut it out to stick around the office with a copy of his certificate. Some of the words have been changed, of course. Bunch of kids down here! Here we are . . . *PC Ian Hessey and Senior Prosecutor for the Eastern Region Linda Morris*. She's based here — Canterbury nick. A few floors up, I think?'

'She is. I know her.'

Maddie cut the call to get back to the screen with numbers listed. The system lagged again as they dropped out of range of the signal. They were gathering pace. Maddie lifted her eyes to where the Sheppey Crossing lifted up on stilts and swept away to the right in the distance. When she looked back at her phone *CPS Linda MORRIS* appeared, with a desk number only. She called it.

'Hello, Helen Newman, CPS.'

'Helen, hi. This is DS Maddie Ives, Major Crime. I need to speak to Linda Morris, please.'

'Ah . . . I've picked up her phone. I'm afraid she's off sick at the moment. She was last in Monday but she wasn't at all herself.'

'Sick?' Harry glanced over to meet Maddie's eye.

'Yeah. Not sure what her issue is exactly. She said she'd be working from home and would be contactable but we had a query in here earlier and her phone was switched off. Must be really under the weather. No one in here can remember her having a single day off before — poor love!'

'Can I take that number?'

'Sure . . .' It followed almost instantly, as though Helen kept it stuck to her screen on a Post-It note.

'Thanks.' Maddie decided to try her luck. 'She was working on something sensitive . . . Op Icicle—'

'Yes, she's the lead for the region. It's just a pilot for now.'

'Do you have access to the cases that have been worked under Op Icicle?'

'Unfortunately not. That information is locked down. We get involved when we're asked, but Linda hasn't asked! She's a bit independent like that. Likes to take on what she can.'

'I see . . . this is rather important. Do you have access to her daybook or any other file where that information might be? Sorry to put you out, but it's rather urgent.'

'I'm in her office right now!' Helen laughed like it was obvious.

Maddie smothered her growing irritation.

'Her drawers here are all locked up,' Helen went on. 'I came in here the other day and she had the Op Icicle folder up on her screen. I got the impression she was working on it again. She printed something then shredded it straight away. All very odd. I mean, I don't like to pry, you know . . . people's business is their own business. You said you were from Major Crime? Has something happened?'

'Not that we're aware of, Helen.'

'This is Detective Inspector Harry Blaker. Who is next up the line from Linda Morris? Her boss.'

'Inspector! Sorry sir, I didn't realize you were listening in.' Helen sounded suddenly delighted. 'Linda isn't someone I've ever considered as having a boss! I'm really not sure . . . I can find—'

'Don't worry. Thanks for your help.' Maddie cut the call, her patience finally run out.

'Good morning, Force HR.' The same voice as a few calls back, the same casual disinterest.

281

'Ah, yes. I called you a minute or so ago about Ian Hessey. No luck unfortunately. I spoke to his sergeant too, and they're a little concerned about him. I said we'd swing past his home address to check he's all okay. Any chance you could provide that?' Maddie waited for her bluff to be called.

'Is the inspector with you?'

'Yes. Section 17 PACE — to preserve life or limb, if you still need justification.' Harry's growl was growing impatient.

'Okay then . . . Yes. I'll just bring that up.'

'Can you text it through, please? I have some urgent calls to make.'

'I have your number — just give me a moment.'

Rhiannon was Maddie's next call.

'Maddie.'

'Rhiannon, I need your help. Something's not right here. We spoke with Hughes. He said this whole thing started when he met a random man at a petrol station. This man was upset about the authorities taking away or restricting his access to his children. He gave Hughes some story about us hiding his kids. I know there are a lot of measures where kids are removed from parents, *et cetera*, but that's normally Social Services leading the way. He didn't even mention them. It was all about us. Police hiding kids. The only thing I can think of—'

'Op Icicle?' Rhiannon said.

'Exactly. I thought it was a shot in the dark at first, but I've tried calling the copper and the CPS prosecutor who were leading the pilot and they've both called in sick.'

'That's quite a coincidence.'

'And you know what I think about those . . . Neither has taken a sick day ever — and that's all I have up to this point. There's a lot we need to know. The most important thing is to find who the families are that have come under that operation. Find that and I feel sure we'll find all the answers we need. Can you start the digging from your end? We're going to Ian Hessey's home address. I'll call you when I can.'

'Understood.'

Maddie already had a message waiting on her phone. It was from HR.

'Head for Lympne, Harry, just off Stone Street. Message says Hessey's only just updated HR with a house move. I'll bring maps up and guide you in.'

Harry didn't react. Even from the side she could see he was scowling, the way he did when he was anxious about something. Maddie was feeling it too. The struts of Sheppey Bridge were now passing at a far faster blur.

CHAPTER 31

Lympne was a village tucked into leafy hills that overlooked West Hythe, Dymchurch and parts of the Romney Marsh. Ian Hessey's road seemed typical of the area: family-sized homes, neat front lawns, mid-range cars and well-spaced trees lining the pavements. It was a cul-de-sac too, with houses turned to face them in the distance.

'There!' Maddie spotted the number *19* next to a white UPVC door with patterned glass. It was beyond an estate agent's board that boldly stated *SOLD*. The garden gate met her at hip-height and squealed as she bundled through. She hammered the door. Harry hung back, his eyes lifted to scan the first floor. The curtains were drawn at every window. She saw Harry move forwards to push up against the largest window on the ground floor. His hands lifted either side of his face to give him a better chance of seeing in — of seeing anything. He shook his head as he made his way around the side of the house. Maddie hammered the door again. She rang the bell and glanced round for anyone who might be of help. They had passed an elderly woman who had been out digging up a section of her front garden, but that was several doors back.

Harry reappeared. He was still shaking his head.

'Back door's locked, curtains drawn everywhere, no response to knocking.'

Maddie snatched at her ringing phone. 'Rhiannon.'

'Maddie, where are you?'

'Outside Ian Hessey's house. No answer. What have you got?'

Maddie held the phone away from her ear and pressed a button to put it on speaker. Harry moved closer to it as she turned the volume down. They both leaned in further to the point of almost touching heads on PC Hessey's front path.

'Okay, so I called HR about Ian Hessey and Linda Morris. Both called in sick at around the same time yesterday morning, just before eight. Neither of them has had a day off in—'

'We know that. What else?'

'Sorry. HR also had a separate call from Linda. This was Monday — mid-afternoon. She called them for Ian Hessey's personal number. She said she had something important she needed to discuss with him and it couldn't wait until he was back on shift. They gave it to her. They shouldn't have, but she pulled rank. She's pretty senior and they caved. She said it was "life and death".'

'Life and death! So on Monday they spoke off duty, and the next day they both call in sick for the first time in anyone's memory? And no one around them seems to know anything about it.'

'That's odd, isn't it?'

'It is.'

'I put an urgent request in for some technical help and got Rob Ford almost straight away. He's done some work on Linda's PC. There are software-tracking keystrokes on force computers. It takes some high-level authority for the data to be reviewed, but I spoke to the DCI and bigged it up a little. A lot actually. He called a superintendent to give the green light. You'll need to speak to him when you're back to clarify the parts I couldn't.'

'Okay, fine.'

'Okay, so Op Icicle is a folder on a secure part of the network. Linda used her password on Monday to access this folder, which means I have it. We also know that she printed documents for each of the Op Icicle cases at the same time. Prior to yesterday, the last time she accessed this folder was five weeks ago. The documents in there are all marked *secret*.'

'So you can't print them,' Maddie said.

'You *shouldn't* print them. And if you do you have to fill out some separate paperwork as to why and then again when it is destroyed.'

'And Linda didn't do that?'

'There's a handwritten log by the office shredder. She's not put anything in it.'

'What information was included in the stuff she printed?'

'Everything. She ran off a summary of each of the cases. So, details of all the people involved: names of victims, witnesses, locations and the offenders.'

'How many cases?'

'Three accepted. A lot more rejected. But it was the three that she printed.'

'Sticking to them, what do we know about the offenders?'

'We have a Malcolm Grant, aged fifty-one, lives in the Medway area. We have a James Loxton, aged forty-two, lives in the Canterbury area but out in the sticks. And we have a William Watson. You might have bumped into him, actually.'

'Bumped into him? What do you mean?'

'Current home address shows as HMP Elmley! As of five weeks ago. He got himself banged up for three months for a handling stolen goods offence in the Maidstone area. Though this is his first foray into stolen property that we know of, he's got a lot of form for violence. He's not very good at fencing either, from the case review. Put a load of stolen stuff up on his own social media, then went guilty. Hence he's now at Her Majesty's pleasure.'

'History of violence, you said?'

'Previously, yes. Attempted murder is the standout charge. He's been nicked for that twice, convicted once. The conviction was for an assault on a male victim back in the early nineties. The latest attempted murder was his partner and their two kids. Hence his family being moved under Op Icicle. It never looked like it was going to stick — the victims wouldn't support. They remanded him and then the family were moved when it became obvious he was going to be released.'

'Moved . . . hidden, you mean!' Maddie breathed.

'Elmley . . . it's a remand prison,' Harry cut in. 'All our remands go there.'

Maddie stared at him. 'I know.'

'So do they — the offenders, I mean. Rhiannon, can you bring up the court papers for William Watson? Are there any terms attached to the guilty plea?'

'Hang on . . .'

Maddie made out clicking noises and the murmur of Rhiannon talking to herself as she trawled through their computer system. She looked over at Harry. He had his head down. It only took Rhiannon a couple of seconds to find what she was looking for.

She read from the court papers: '*Guilty plea. Request for the court to take into account an early guilty plea from William Watson. A request is made for any time served to be at the HMP Elmley facility due to proximity to family with mobility issues.* Is that what you were after?'

'He *requested* Elmley,' Harry said.

'Because he knew what was coming?' Maddie said.

'Or who was coming,' Harry growled back.

'What's that, boss?' Rhiannon's voice was raised; it cut through Maddie's thoughts, as she was trying to make sense of it all.

It was Maddie who answered. 'Have we got the addresses for where they were moved yet? We're going to need welfare checks done on those families — right away.'

'No. These files just show the emergency accommodation. They're all B&Bs and the last family was moved on eight months ago. Normally they're good for a couple of weeks at most, then they're moved somewhere more permanent. The permanent addresses aren't on there. Social Services would have arranged that through their housing team. I've already put the request in.'

'Okay, fine. I need to make a call. Stay in touch. Good work and keep digging. I'll need a summary of the offenders and their respective families. Get the whole office on this.'

Maddie worked her phone again, going back through the received calls until she was sure she had the number she needed. She lifted her phone to her ear and watched as Harry walked back along the drive to step out of sight. He was only gone a short time. But it was long enough for everything to change. It must have been written all over her face when he returned.

'What's the matter?' He was holding a shovel, just like the one she had seen propped against the wall of a house a few doors down.

'The prison. They couldn't put me through to Daniel Gooding. He's dealing with an "incident".'

'Incident?'

'An inmate's been assaulted. Stabbed. The attacker hurt himself too. I asked them outright if it was Adrian Hughes. They wouldn't confirm the name, just that it was a serious and ongoing incident . . . but it was in their voice . . .'

'William Watson.'

'What the hell is going on here, Harry?'

Harry lifted the shovel towards Maddie. She stepped out of the way as he lurched forwards. The metal dug into the lip around the door. He grunted as he pushed. The end of the shovel popped out with a bang and a scrape. A neighbour's door flew open.

'OI!'

Maddie waved her warrant card at him. 'Police! It's okay. We're just doing a welfare check.'

'With a shovel?' The man was well dressed, a pressed shirt tucked into smart trousers and a silk tie hanging from an unbuttoned collar. He walked to where his garden met with Ian's. He was chewing and held a bitten cracker in his hand. Maddie moved towards him. Behind her, the sounds of metal slamming into plastic continued. She had to concentrate, to focus on the neighbour and not the whirl of ideas in her mind.

'Have you seen him? Your neighbour?'

'Ian. He said he was one of your lot. A police officer.'

'That's right.'

'I see . . . Well, I haven't seen him, but her from over at number thirty-three made a point of telling me he was out early yesterday morning. You can't do anything down here without someone seeing, even at five in the morning!'

'She saw Ian yesterday morning?'

'Yes. At least, she thought it was him. She came over claiming to want to talk to me about the village hall, some fundraiser or other, but she was desperate to ask about my new neighbour.'

'Ask you what?'

'She had some conspiracy theory. Telling me how he's wanted by the police. She didn't know he was a police officer himself. She seemed almost disappointed in the end!'

'Disappointed?'

'Yeah, I guess. When I told her that, the police car picking him up first thing in the morning suddenly made a lot more sense! I think she had a more exciting idea about him being a convict rather than a passenger! She had this theory that he—'

'The police were here?'

The man took another bite of his cracker. His reply was peppered with crumbs. 'Well, yes. That's what she said at least. She was woken up by a car ticking over. She's the nosey neighbour you always read about. It was a police car. Ian was talking to them. She said she was pretty sure it was him anyway. I think he was the other side of it from where she was standing. Then, when it turned around to drive away, he was gone.'

'So, she didn't see him get in the car?' Maddie winced as Harry made the loudest *thud!* yet.

'I didn't ask that question specifically. But now you're breaking into his house? What the hell is going on?'

The noises had stopped. She turned to see Harry taking a breather, reassessing his methods perhaps. He still held the shovel tightly in both hands.

'Get on the radio!' he gasped. 'We need entry forced. Whoever's closest with an enforcer.'

'We sure we want this out over the radio?'

Harry shrugged. 'Give as little detail as you can, but we don't have any choice. I know what was said, but we need answers quickly.'

Maddie put out the call. She didn't mention that it was an officer's house, just that entry was required. Three patrols called up to assist, all fighting over who was closer, eager for the chance to smash a door in. She called back, cancelling the two who were furthest away to limit the number of officers who would have knowledge. Then she fidgeted with her phone. Rhiannon picked up instantly.

'Mad—'

'Rhiannon. There was a marked car up here first thing on Tuesday — we are on Octavian Drive, Lympne. Run a search on STORM for any calls up here between midnight and seven a.m. I want to know which officers attended. Don't make contact with them, just call me back with details.'

Rhiannon just had time to say 'got it' before Maddie cut the call. She lifted her head at the sound of an approaching siren. It cut out with two parps of a horn. Maddie stepped out onto the road to greet the new arrivals, her hand extended. Fifty metres back towards the junction and on the other side of the road, she saw a front door open. A woman stepped out, wrapping a shawl around her shoulders. She stopped halfway up her garden path. Maddie could see her door number written large and bold on her black bin: 33.

Ian's door caved in on the second strike, snapping and wobbling to reveal the hallway beyond. Maddie was first in. The first sweep through was for people. She held her breath

290

as she entered the children's rooms and puffed her cheeks when she found them empty. She met Harry on the landing.

'There's no one here,' she said.

'I found two mobile phones. One I reckon to be the wife's from the screensaver. It's still on charge beside her bed. No missed calls, no messages.' Harry's reply was quick.

'The bedrooms are a mess. Everywhere else seems all in order — to say they only just moved here, of course.'

'You're right about the bedrooms. Like someone left in a hurry.'

'Left in a hurry and against their will.' Maddie gripped her nose, trying to think fast.

'Have you seen the master bedroom?'

'Yes. Looks like a general disturbance — a fight maybe.'

'We need to get a welfare check done at Linda Morris's address.'

Maddie already had her phone in her hand. 'I'm on it.'

CHAPTER 32

'Vince, what have you got?' Maddie barked into her phone then quickly moved it away from her face so she could once again activate the speaker. She laid it down on Ian Hessey's kitchen table for both her and Harry to hover over, glad to have something to focus on that wasn't the colourful children's drawings stuck on the fridge door.

'We got in, no problem. This Linda bird's got a nice place here, but one of the bedrooms is a bit messed up.'

'Messed up?'

'Bedding's been dragged off the bed. We're either looking at a fight or one hell of a night!'

'Not really the time or place, Vince. Anything else of interest?'

'Funny you should mention that. Seems you're not the only one who's good at this investigating lark!'

'What have you got?'

'A mobile phone. On the bedside table in the messed-up room, which I assume belongs to the daughter.'

'The daughter's phone?'

'Screensaver shows a young woman, early twenties, sat on an elephant. Has to be hers! Only I can't see the elephant too well. There's a message pinged through covering a lot of it over.'

'What message?'

'Seems she's playing a game of chess with someone, user-name *L.M.0.7.7.1.5*. Which, if you were detective minded, you could say looks like *L. Morris*, couldn't you?'

'Jesus, Vince. Spit it out or I'll come over there and personally beat it out of you.'

'Okay, okay! It's some chess app. It shows the first few words of a message . . . *electrode . . . compliant . . . choirs.*'

'What the hell does that mean, Vince?'

'You don't know? With the full stops in the middle?'

'Vince!'

'Okay, okay, sorry! What Three Words. It's a mapping app. Clever, too. Basically they've divvied the whole world up into three-metre squares and every one of those squares has three words assigned to it. They're all totally unique. So I could direct you to a three-metre square anywhere in the world just by telling you three words. Make sense? Everyone on response has it. And this is the format. Three random-looking words but with full stops between them. Anyway, I put these into my app and it took me to a place in Bladbean.'

'What sort of a place?'

'Looks like the middle of a field to me. But it's not far from here — it just has to be a code for that app. What else could it mean?'

'When was that message sent? Does it say anything else?'

'Ah. I can't tell you that, unfortunately. The phone's locked and there's no time on the notification. I've sent this kind of message before, just three words to direct someone. It's well known.'

'What Three Words?' Maddie repeated for confirmation. 'I'll download it. Are you there on your own?'

'No, I'm crewed up with—'

'Leave your crewmate there and head to the location in Bladbean. We'll meet you there.'

Maddie shut off the call. Harry was already down the hall and approaching the front door. She shouted a quick instruction to the officers who had broken down the door, telling them to stay and hold the scene until it could be properly searched.

'Bladbean?' Harry said.

Maddie pulled the passenger door shut.

'Yeah. Give me two seconds and I should be able to tell you exactly where in Bladbean.' The app finished downloading to open as a map. Once Maddie had entered the three words, it shifted to a zoomed-out picture with Canterbury visible in the middle. When it zoomed back in, it had moved to the outskirts, replacing the city's muddle of roads and lines with flat squares of green and brown. A red pin dropped into the middle of a field, just as Vince had described. The map showed a white line heading in the general direction of the pin, but it ran out long before it reached its destination. Maddie was rocked forwards by an urgent change of gear as Harry pressed on towards the location. She moved the map around on the screen, trying to pick out landmarks. She could see the outline of buildings nearby — a farm perhaps — but they were just drawn lines, offering no real clues as to where they were headed.

'I'll call Rhiannon. She can run any addresses nearby, see what we know,' Maddie said.

'She could do . . . We're only seven minutes out, though. I think we're just going to have to tip up and see what we've got. Rhiannon won't be able to tell us much before we get there.'

Harry was right. Rhiannon hadn't called back by the time the red pin reappeared on Maddie's phone screen, hovering beyond the end of the farm track that was now visible through the window. Harry needed to slow considerably. The terrain shook the car and picking out anything in the distance was difficult. Ahead, the track sloped away to the left. The fields either side were made up of clumpy mud, no doubt churned up with the assistance of the winter rains and now scorched into solid clods.

'This is where the track runs out on the map,' Maddie said. 'There's an outbuilding here somewhere out on its own and then a few more buildings grouped together further on.'

'Surely the track ran out a while ago.' Harry spoke through gritted teeth. The car still lurched and rolled but he pressed on.

'There it is!' she pointed.

The car slowed to an almost stop as Harry took a break from wrestling the wheel to look out over the terrain. An open-sided barn came into view. The track now ran down-hill. The barn was on their right, around fifty metres ahead. The open side was facing them and the sun shone from the left to force an angled shadow across its front, punctured by a blossom tree that stood out on its own. Maddie could make out dark shapes inside the building's shell. Harry pushed on. As his pace quickened, the ride worsened and Maddie had to hold the phone with both hands for it to be steady enough to make out the details. The map had zoomed right in now that they were close, close enough to see the gridlines of the three-metre squares breaking up the screen.

'The square we want, the one Linda typed . . . it's right in the middle of that barn.'

Harry pulled up outside. It was a small building — more a shelter for farm machinery than a barn — but it was plenty large enough to drive a car in. As Maddie stepped out, a pleasant breeze blew through the ruined walls carrying some of the tree's bright white blossom. It looked to be bursting with more, despite the ground showing a decent smattering of its petals. Inside the barn seemed equally serene. To the left of the opening was a small, vintage-looking tractor. It had a steel seat patterned with drilled holes and a spindly steering wheel that reached up from a slim nose. It was parked tight against a wall and didn't look to have been driven for some time. On the opposite side was a stack of squared bales of straw, placed to avoid cutting the light from the only win-dow. Straight ahead, a tennis ball hung from the steel raft-ers to swing gently in the breeze. It was towards the back.

Maddie walked up to it and Harry answered her questioning look.

'I've seen them in tight garages, so you don't hit the wall. You stop when it rests against the windscreen.'

Maddie looked to the back wall. 'Hardly a tight space, though.'

The breeze suddenly became a high-pitched wail as it pushed through a gap in the window on the right. It drew her attention. From there, her eyes dropped to take in a chair. It was pushed up against the leftmost column of hay, resting with its back to it. 'Harry!'

He was back by the entrance door, looking out across the area perhaps. He turned on his heel, his feet kicking up dried straw from the mottled concrete as he hurried back over. Maddie pointed at the seat and at the loop of slim rope that hung from its metal frame. She pulled the chair out; the sound of its four legs scraping the floor was so loud it was almost violent. She spun the back towards them both and pointed at an identical-looking loop on the other side.

'Restraints?' Harry said.

'What else could they be for?' Maddie stepped around the chair to find there was a gap between the stacked hay and the wall. In the gap she could see a second chair. She pulled this one into view too. It was identical. They reminded her of old dining-room or canteen chairs with their metal frames and faux-leather pads for the seat and back. They looked out of place in this barn.

'Anything else behind there?'

There was just enough room to step between the bales and the wall. Maddie walked the length of it, her hand in front of her to cut through the dusty webs that yawned across the gap. She tried not to think about the spiders that had put them there.

'Just those two seats . . . and this . . .' She emerged from the other end, her hand raised to show Harry the long strip of clear plastic she had found on the floor. It was the size of three mouse mats lined up next to one another but heavy due to its thickness. Harry took it off her to study it. He scowled as if confused then laid it out flat on the floor. He flipped it over.

'What's the matter?'

'It's two layers. Look here, there's tape holding on a thinner layer.'

Maddie could see what he meant. Harry had laid it out so the thicker layer of plastic was face down. On the back of this, two rows of tape along the top and bottom secured a second layer of very thin plastic — clingfilm, perhaps. It wasn't pulled tight. There was some give and it had rucked up in the middle.

'And these slits either end' — Harry gestured at them — 'they're handles. Do you see what this is?'

'You're thinking Marie Foreshaw? This is the same type of plastic that killed her?'

'I'd bet on that. But this is a torture device.'

'Torture?' Maddie looked back at it. She had seen torture devices before. They were normally more obvious in their application.

'It's the right size to wrap round someone's face if you were standing behind them. Use these handles to get it tight enough over the face and the thinner plastic would be forced into your mouth. You couldn't breathe.'

'Just like Marie Foreshaw . . .'

'Yes. But she was wrapped. This, you can take away and apply again. Like I said, a torture device.'

'For information?'

Harry shrugged. 'That's what torture is usually for.'

'Linda Morris. What did she know that someone might need?'

'Op Icicle!' They both spoke together.

Maddie scrabbled in her pocket for her phone.

Again Rhiannon was quick to answer. 'Hey.'

'Op Icicle . . . where are we with welfare checks at the families' new addresses?'

'It's a non-starter so far. Social Services are not giving them up easy. The request is now sitting with the senior management team here to progress.'

'Social Services!' Maddie turned to the sunny scene outside of the barn. Her mind was a whirl as the breeze picked up and there was a rush of blossom.

'What's the matter?' Rhiannon said.

'Marie Foreshaw. Where did she work?' Maddie breathed.

'She was a social worker.'

'She was. And she's dead. And who sat next to her . . . ?'

Maddie looked up at the sound of a car engine. A marked police car was moving up the track, approaching from the opposite direction to the one they had come by. Vince must have overshot, gone right past and headed for the building further down the track.

Maddie barked back into her phone. 'We're going to need some DCs out here. Uniform support too. There are other buildings on this land — maybe a farmhouse. Anyone here needs to answer our questions or they're coming in.'

'Okay, do you want me to head out?'

'Not for the moment. Look, I've got to go. Vince is here. I'll get him to hold this location.'

'Is he?' Rhiannon sounded confused. 'He literally just called me for directions. His signal dropped out and he got a bit lost. He said he was fifteen minutes away. He must have been a lot closer than he thought!'

The police car was closer now. Harry broke the cover of the barn to stride towards it. It looked older than Maddie had been expecting, a Skoda estate. They hadn't used them as response cars for five years or more. *It wasn't Vince.* She broke into a jog, the call now discarded.

'Harry! The car!'

There was a clear reaction from the driver. The front wheels scrabbled for grip, clumps of mud and stones spewing out from under the vehicle as the engine surged. Harry stopped, his hands lifted against the sudden dust cloud that swept towards them. Maddie did the same. They both stood still, frozen to the spot. Maddie met eyes with a shocked Harry. It lasted just a moment. Then he broke away to sprint for their car.

CHAPTER 33

Now there was no time to pick a route through the rutted ground and Harry met the first ridge straight on and at pace. Maddie felt the jolt through her buttocks but the whole car seemed to shudder, followed by a grinding sound that had her doubting whether the car would hold together long enough to reach the road. Her whole world tilted and rocked as her head was thrown back and forth, and she scrabbled for the grab handle attached to the roof to try and steady herself. She managed to look ahead but all she could see was a cloud of dust lifting up from the loose surface.

As the ground changed to tarmac under their wheels, the improvement in the ride and visibility was instant. But the bandit car was now a lot less conspicuous without its billowing tail of dust; they needed to get closer to their quarry. Harry worked the car hard, holding each gear until the engine screamed as they flashed along a country lane barely wide enough for two vehicles to pass. The marked police car was some way ahead, the back of it just a glint of white in the distance. It dipped over a brow where the road leaned left and then vanished from sight altogether. Harry moved their car out as far to the right as he could to try and keep the Skoda in view. He didn't slow. Maddie found herself mumbling words of prayer for nothing to come the other way. She looked away from the chase to work her radio.

'Yankee One to Control . . . we are at Bladbean, Canterbury rural. We have a vehicle making off. Request assistance from other units. General direction is towards Barham . . . I—' She let the button go on her radio, trying to make out a landmark in the blurred scenery of greens and browns. A road sign appeared with three white arrows pointing in different directions. Harry flashed across the junction so quick that it made the whole car lift — like they might leave the road entirely — and Maddie couldn't make out a word of the signage. Other patrols were calling to make their way to the area. A booming voice came over the radio that she recognized as Vince. There was urgency in it.

'Control, we are in the area but it's a bit of a warren. Can you track DS Ives via her radio, please, and get us a better location?'

Harry cussed. It came out as hiss through his gritted jaw. The roads closed in tighter still as they raced up a gradient with steep, solid-looking banks either side that pushed out into the road. There was just time for Maddie to glimpse a thick root overhanging the bank; its spindly fingers flashed close to her window like they were making a grab for her and she ducked instinctively.

'Slow it down, Harry!' she couldn't help but cry.

'That's not how you catch someone,' he growled back.

'Nor is upside down in a ditch.'

'Save your I-told-you-so's.'

Maddie was back to gripping the handle, her eyes fixed forwards as the gradient peaked on a brow that instantly gave way to a sharp right. Harry stepped hard on the brakes to slow for the corner — too hard. She felt the skid through her seat before she heard it. Harry's hands made a thumping sound as he fought the steering wheel and, for a moment, their forwards momentum was all through Maddie's window and towards a high bank. Maddie closed her eyes when the impact seemed inevitable. It never came. She dared to open them again when she heard the sound of the engine revving hard. They'd almost ground to a halt. Harry stomped back on the accelerator. The front wheels crunched and slid, then threw them forwards into a clearing where the sun was suddenly bright and the dust was thick enough to hang in a cloud.

'They made a mistake — same place!' Harry said. 'They hit something here.' He gestured to where the bank's innards now littered the sun-drenched tarmac in chunks beneath a fresh-looking wound. Ahead was another sharp bend in the road; this time it was a left-hander over a steep hill. When they came around it, the back of the police car rushed at them.

Harry worked the brakes hard again. They were far enough away for him to bring them to a stop a few car lengths apart. Harry expelled air after holding his breath. The police car was moving away now — but slowly, as if only the gradient of the hill was providing momentum. Then it shuddered; its rear end kicked up in a bounce. Maddie could see a scrape down the left side as it moved around the bend.

'It's stalled,' Harry said. 'This is our chance. Seatbelt!'

'What?'

'Is your seatbelt on?'

'What are you going to do?'

'We have to take it out. We need to hit it hard to snap the axle.'

'Snap the axle? Are you crazy! There are other patrols coming. They might be ahead of it.'

'They might not.' She felt the car surge again. Harry gripped the wheel with both hands, his face locked in a grimace. The distance between them and the car in front halved in a second.

Maddie had lifted the radio to rest against her ear and pick out updates. *Surely Vince couldn't be far?* Now the radio fell from her grip, her fingertips suddenly unable to function. A face at the rear window of the car in front had her frozen in horror.

'HARRY!'

She forced the scream but Harry was already reacting. The car slewed right to miss by inches. They took the impact of a high bank around the offside wheel. It was low speed but still the force of it was enough to wring a groan from Maddie. She watched as the rear of the marked car bounced and jerked again — this time accompanied by the sound of an overrevved engine.

'There's kids in there!' Maddie breathed.

'I saw them,' Harry growled.

As Harry spoke, a tiny palm pressed the back window. Two pairs of frightened eyes turned to stare at them. The little hand now moved to cling to the headrest as the Skoda sprang to life again. Maddie couldn't tell their age exactly, but they were primary schoolchildren — she was certain of that. The Skoda kicked up gravel and stones that bounced and pinged off the front of their car, then it moved away again at pace.

Harry was hard on the throttle himself, tearing a chunk of earth out of the bank to get back onto the road. She felt the rear wheel ride up over it as they set off, quickly making up enough ground to get the marked car back in view.

'*DS Ives, are you receiving? DS Ives? Maddie . . . welfare check!*'

Vince's voice on the radio cut through the atmosphere. The car ahead took a left turn into a road that looked more like a track. Tufts of grass and loose rocks gathered in the middle of tarmac stained with dried mud and straw. It was hardly suitable for cars. A rock popped under the wheel to thump into the underside of the car. Harry's reaction seemed to be to accelerate harder. The car in front was in trouble again. There was an explosion of white from the nearside wing mirror, as if someone had pelted it with a bag of flour. Maddie peered left as they whipped along. A lump of chalk had been dug into the bank, its side now a smooth, crisp white.

'We need to fall back,' Maddie yelled over the continuous noise of debris under the wheels. 'There're kids on board!'

Harry didn't reply.

302

Maddie snatched the radio to her mouth. This time she managed to speak.

'Yankee One to Control. We are in pursuit of a marked police vehicle. It is a Skoda estate. No registration at this time.' Maddie narrowed her eyes at the car in front as it bucked and twisted, following the contours of the road. The terrified faces of the two children were gone. The back window was clear. All she could see was a jerking of heads in unison from the occupants of the two front seats. Harry was closing the gap.

'There are children on board. At least two. Ages unknown at this time but . . . *young*. Have you got me on GPS?'

'*Yes, yes, Yankee One. We are tracking your location. Zulu Echo Three are a short distance behind you and were requesting talk-through. Confirm you are in pursuit in company with a marked vehicle?*'

Zulu Echo Three: Vince's callsign.

'No, no. We are *pursuing* a marked vehicle. A marked Skoda, approximately six years old, full police livery.'

This prompted a pause. Maddie was glad of it — she could see the bend that was now rushing towards them. She took the opportunity to drop the radio into her lap and brace herself. She was certain they were going too fast. The car clung on at first but the corner got sharper and their grip ran out.

Maddie felt the slide first, then the solid strike that seemed to start from her right thigh. Then everything was thrown right. She heard the sound of glass popping and spreading, a solid bang and then nothing but colours in blurred blocks of movement. The scenery through her window flashed with the bright sky for an instant, then her head was forced right and she could see nothing but darkness. Harry shouted out. She might have done so, too. The next bang emanated from beneath her, accompanied by a judder in her seat as if it were coming loose. She tried to orientate herself by the view through the window. It took her a moment to make sense of it. She could see the road, but from an angle, like she was looking down at it. For a moment she concluded they were upside down, but this was not the case. The engine had stalled. The only sound was birdsong drifting through Harry's popped window. She tried to blink away her confusion. She looked down at her chest to see what was banging against it and was quick to realize it was her own heartbeat. Her head turned slowly to the jingling of metal. Harry was handling the car keys. The engine made an unhealthy sound, like it was in pain too. Harry cussed as silence returned. The engine whirred again. He was trying to start it. He slapped the steering wheel hard.

'Harry,' Maddie managed.

The car coughed, then fired. She turned her gaze back out of her window as they bumped down from Harry's side of the road. The car spluttered like it might cut out again. Then came a noise like something being dragged behind them as they moved off. Harry had to nurse the engine back up to speed, but the tone got back to normal quickly. Something was caught in the wheel to make a whirring sound that stopped suddenly as the scenery started to blur once more.

'*Maddie! DS Ives, DI Blaker, can you respond please!*'

The voice was earnest, close to panic. It was Vince again. He was after another welfare check. Maddie had been aware of tinny voices emanating from the footwell, from where her radio must have been thrown. She felt her heartbeat behind her eyes this time when she bent to retrieve it.

'Yankee One. I think we came off the road. We are okay. We are back in pursuit.'

Her voice sounded different, like she was listening to it through a thick ear. They emerged at the start of a long straight road. No sign of the car they were pursuing but nowhere to turn off either; they had to have come this way. Harry must have had the same thought; his pace was quicker than ever.

'Harry — please! We need to slow down.' Maddie was still trying to shake the fog from her mind.

'They have kids. There were kids in that car.' He kept staring forwards.

'Exactly why we need to back off. What if we force a mistake and they crash?'

'So we just let them go?' he snapped.

His face turned to her for just a moment — long enough for her to see a trail of slick blood down the right side of his face.

'You're hurt.'

'It's a nick. I'm fine.'

'I am too by the way. Thanks for checking back there.'

'They went this way,' Harry said simply. 'They had to have done.'

Maddie was about to argue but her words caught in her throat as more harsh braking lurched her forwards. Her seat-belt caught her, gripping hard at her shoulder, which stung like hell.

'*Maddie. Where are you?*' Vince barked out of the radio. '*Do you still have sight of the marked car?*'

'No, no. We're heading in the direction it was last seen. There are no deviations off this road yet, but I think we lost it.'

The car was still accelerating. Harry seemed to take her update as a challenge. The next reply was the monotone voice of the radio operator.

'*Yankee One. The FCR Inspector has reviewed this CAD and you are to immediately terminate any pursuit. You are in an unmarked, unsuitable vehicle and children have been sighted. Please confirm this is received and you are standing down?*'

Maddie glanced across towards Harry. Their progress was no slower down the slim road. He was still picking up pace where he could. He was still fixed forwards.

'Harry?' she prompted. He didn't react.

'That is all received.' Maddie spoke back into her radio.

'*Confirm you are terminating your pursuit? I have other patrols now showing close-by to assist with an area search.*'

'Harry? You need to slow down. We're not to be chasing anyone. You heard them.'

'We can't just let th—'

He broke off. Maddie was thrown forwards; the skid was instant and her head snapped up to look out front. The car they had been chasing was now pulled sideways across the road in front of them. She screwed her eyes up tight and lifted her hands instinctively. They were going to hit. Hard.

CHAPTER 34

Ian Hessey fought with the door as the camper van pulled away. The acceleration, the bouncing front tyres, the floor he skidded across and the impact on his lower back and hip — it was all rough. He shouted out for the driver to slow down but he was ignored. He'd expected no less. From the moment they had seen those detectives at the barn, the man's driving, the calls for a pickup, the plan to lose their pursuers, the dragging of people out of the police car and into the van — it had all been panicked . . . desperate. The first time anything had seemed rushed or unexpected from the moment this whole nightmare had started. It was instantly obvious that those detectives back there were closer than expected. Close enough for him to hear the sickening impact of metal on metal as they came around the bend and into the car they had just left. It had sounded serious. Ian had been glad to keep his focus on forcing the kids into the waiting van, and then sliding the door shut behind them. He had been thrown to the floor when they pulled away — away from the windows, away from the sight of his colleagues colliding with the car they had just left pulled across a blind bend.

It was part of a spur-of-the-moment decision from the driver — as was shouting at the kids in the back when they'd lost control and he was struggling to get the engine started. PC Harvey had shouted at them to stand up, to make themselves seen by the car behind.

Ian had asked him what the hell he was doing — this would surely count as a deviation, like he was trying to send a message as to who they had on board. But it hadn't been about that at all. Harvey had stared over at Ian, his eyes wide, his whole persona that of someone wired on adrenalin. 'Now they either back off or they come at us faster. I've sorted a change of cars just ahead. We'll leave them an obstruction. I know these roads!'

The detectives behind hadn't backed off. They'd come up behind them faster than they would otherwise have done, fuelled by a new determination. Ian knew exactly what it was like to drive a police car with that sort of desperation running through your veins. You made mistakes — threw caution to the wind. Ian didn't want to think about the result of that. Not now.

He had taken advantage of the chaos to throw Harvey's phone into the rear footwell. After his hurried phone call for their lift, he had ditched it in a cubby hole. Ian had done his best to push it under the driver's seat while Harvey's attention was on their pursuers, hoping he didn't notice, hoping the police would find it . . . praying it might be relevant if they did.

He turned his attention back to the family clinging to whatever they could find as the van rattled and rolled round the bends in the road. It looked to Ian like a normal-sized van that had been converted into a camper. There was a sink and hob down the left side and the boys faced him from the other side of a table that ran down the middle. A curtain slid open and shut against the side door, depending on their momentum. Most of the rattles seemed to come from inside the cupboards. This was the last family they needed to transport. The plan had been to use the police car during daylight hours to move them from the farmhouse to where they were needed today. Harvey had keys for the house. It was at the end of a long track. It seemed like a familiar place to him.

They had kept all three families there. Ian had been forced to chain them up for the night. It was part of his task that he be the one to tell them the real reason he had come to their houses in the dead of night and bundled them into a police car. This last family, the three sharing the back of the van with him now, had been the worst experience, even worse than telling little Peter. Adene Laskall sat to the left of him. Her two young boys sat opposite, their eyes cast down at their laps. He remembered how hard he'd needed to work to gain Adene's trust when he had first met her. Almost a year had passed since then. She had been a shell of a woman back then and it had broken his heart to see a young mother in such a way. The only flicker of hope in her life had been from her two boys, Zachary and Jonathan. He had worked on her, used that spark to light a fire inside her. He had told her he could make her boys safe but she would need to help him. He had given his word — she just needed to trust him with her story.

When it came, her tale might have been the worst of them all. He could still remember the claustrophobia of the interview room at Canterbury Police Station as she had detailed the misery inflicted on them by her partner, a vile human being by the name of Malcolm Grant. It had felt like the walls were closing in . . . the longer she spoke, the more emotional and physical horrors she revealed at the hands of that man. Ian had to call a break at one point. He'd needed to step out of the police station and into the darkness of the early hours . . . The DC leading the interview had followed to check that he was okay. Ian couldn't help it; he couldn't help but suck up some of the emotion, the sadness, the desperation when he heard it. You needed a thick skin to be a police officer but not so thick that you didn't let it affect you, that it didn't make you angry. He didn't know if he had the balance right.

The memory of that account — the first time she had really opened up to him, *trusted* him — was so clear it felt like it was just last night. But it wasn't. Last night was when he had lied to her, tricked her out of her house and into his car. Then, when he was chaining her to a post in a farm outbuilding, he had been forced to tell her why. There had been no swirl of emotion, no denial, rage or panic. And no slap to his face like Peter's mum had delivered — despite him begging her to lash out at him. Instead there was simply an instant return to the emptiness that had impacted him so much a year before. She hadn't looked at him since. He knew why. He had given his word that he would keep her safe, that he would keep her and her sons away from the man who had sworn to murder them all.

And now Malcolm Grant was here with them again, driving the van.

Ian turned to him now. He only had a view of the man's profile from the side. The exchange of vehicles had been rushed, panicked. There hadn't been time to take in who was picking them up. It wouldn't have changed anything anyway. He had realized when one of the boys had reacted. The younger one had clammed up, become a dead weight the very moment he had needed to run. The other boy had seen Grant a moment later and taken hold of his little brother's hand. They had both backed away, eyes like saucers. Ian had needed to pick them both up together, one over each shoulder, shouting at Malcolm to 'just go away' while he made for the side of the van.

Ian had met Malcolm Grant only once before. He had handed himself in at the police station on his solicitor's advice. Ian had arrested him, then sat in on the interview. Malcolm had spent the whole time hunched over in his seat, studying his own lap in the same way his boys were doing now, barely moving. He gave no visible reaction at all while his wife's seven-page statement was put to him bit by bit, question by question — blow by blow. It was the testimony of a woman tortured for eight years, mentally and physically.

The DC had thrown questions that should have hit the man like punches: *What sort of a man treats his wife like that? Did it make you feel good, powerful maybe? Do you feel good now, knowing that your own sons are terrified of you? That your eldest still wets the bed aged eight, that the other still doesn't speak at five years old? Post-traumatic stress disorder . . . two young boys, both suffering, both because of what they have seen done to their mother . . . because of what you have done to their mother and forced them to watch. What does that make you?*

Malcolm Grant may not have flinched the whole time, but Ian had. He had thought of his own two children — the comparison was too stark for him not to have — and he had made a promise to himself there and then that he would make the Grant boys safe under Op Icicle. He had even muttered it under his breath, just to know he'd uttered it out loud and in Malcolm Grant's presence. He would change that family's fortune; he would keep them safe.

And now Malcolm Grant was driving the van and in charge of all of their fates.

CHAPTER 35

The impact this time was through the front and from directly ahead. The last thing Maddie saw was the flash of the Skoda's police livery where it caught the sun. The skid didn't seem to slow them much at all.

The seatbelt yanked Maddie back tightly; the pain flashing through her shoulder was excruciating. The impact sounded like explosion and her vision still flashed bright white, no matter how tightly she closed her eyes against it. Then there were only sensations: the taste of metal, the smell of talcum powder and the noise resounding all around her. She was totally helpless. All she could do was wait for it to stop. When it did, she was left with ringing ears and a sharp pain in her neck when she tried to move. She opened her eyes and looked down her body to find all of her limbs were seized up tight, her hands locked in fists, one still wrapped around her police radio. She could move nothing but her eyes. The windscreen was frosted in a spider-web-like pattern. Beyond it, the sprung bonnet blocked most of the light. She sucked in a breath that burned inside her tight chest. She had to focus to loosen her limbs enough to move. Pain stabbed at her neck again as she turned to the door, her left arm reaching out to it. It was all instinct now — she had to get out. The door pushed open. Her shoulder flared — her seat belt was still attached and holding her tight. She had to twist in her seat to unclip it. Her neck ached when it wasn't shooting with pain, it was noticeable when she reached for the door rim to pull herself out. She got to her feet. Her throat burned with something. She coughed it out. She heard a banging sound and stooped back towards it, feeling a sharp pain in her right ankle as she shifted her weight. The noise was Harry. He had both his legs lifted, kicking out at the driver's door.

Maddie looked forwards to the obstruction that had stopped their progress so suddenly. It had shifted in the impact but was still positioned across the road. They'd never stood a chance. The damage to the side of the car was clear: the letters *O*, *L* and *I* of *POLICE* were mangled inwards; the pillar separating the doors was bowed in the same way. The windows had popped out, spilling shattered glass all over the interior.

'The kids!' Maddie's awareness returned all at once. She moved forwards, able to ignore the stiffness in her neck and ankle in her panic. She got to the back door and pulled on the handle. It was stuck firm. She looked in — *empty*. 'Thank God!'

Harry stumbled around the front of the car, leaving the driver's door flapping open behind him. He took one glance at the police car and continued past it, down the hill in a clumsy jog. Behind her came a siren, distant but approaching quickly. Maddie still had her radio gripped tightly in her hand. She snatched it to her mouth. There were voices on it. She pressed her emergency button to shout over them all. The siren was already much closer, the sound now strong enough to fill the slim lane.

'Vince! We're round that bend! SLOW DOWN!'

There was a split-second delay then the sound of skidding wheels. The sound led, then another marked car came into view — this one with flashing headlights and flickering roof bar — its wheels locked in a skid.

She heard the inevitable impact. Maddie's car bucked and bounced towards her. She flinched at the sight but it stopped just short of her. She looked through it to where Vince was sitting behind the steering wheel of his own car. He looked scrunched up and utterly shocked. She heard two blasts of the horn to kill the siren.

Harry marched back up to brush past her, snatching the radio as he went.

'Yankee One, we are stop, stop. The marked vehicle was left as a road block. There are tracks from a second vehicle used to continue from this point. Is there anyone else in position at the end of the road we are shown on?'

The scene fell suddenly silent. Maddie felt like she had seized up again. She watched as Vince stepped out of his car and jogged over to her. He had his hands out and took her by the shoulder to assess her.

'Mads — you okay?'

'*Negative, Yankee One. Patrols are in the area but unable to get ahead. That lane re-joins a major road after the next bend and there are numerous deviations from there. We are trying to co-ord . . .*'

The transmission continued but Maddie didn't catch the rest. Her radio slid off the cracked tarmac to meet with the bank on the far side with Harry screaming after it.

'DAMMIT!' His voice caught under the canopy of the trees.

Maddie stepped away from Vince, her limbs now fuelled with rage. She strode over to the inspector.

'What the HELL was that? You trying to get me killed? Not once either, that wasn't enough, you thought you'd have another go? What the hell is wrong with you?' Her voice sounded shrill as it broke. She was shaking — her whole body. It was sudden and involuntary. Shock.

'Stand down, DS Ives.' Harry stopped his pacing to growl back.

'I won't stand down. That was stupid and it was reckless. What the hell is the matter with you?'

'Mads . . .' Vince attempted to grab her arm. She batted him away.

'Well? Tell me just what the hell you were thinking!'

'They had kids in that car! That's what this is all about, isn't it? They wanted to find those kids. And then what?'

'I don't know. But we won't find them if we're dead!'

'We're not dead, though, are we? But those kids, they might be by now.'

'We don't—'

'Don't even start with what we don't know! We can't find the addresses for the Icicle kids but they did. Marie Foreshaw died giving them up — or maybe she died because she wouldn't. But they have Ian Hessey and he has a wife, two kids — all missing. He would have given those addresses up in a heartbeat if it meant keeping them safe.'

'We don't know that. We don't know wh—'

Harry rounded on her. His pacing had started back up but now he was in her face, close enough for phlegm to settle on her as he hissed, 'I DO know! He'll give them whatever they want if it means protecting his children, because I would have done the same. Had he given me that choice. If he had given me ANY chance whatsoever, I would have taken it in a heartbeat. And TO HELL with anyone else. So don't tell me what I don't know!'

Maddie was aware of Vince's bulk. His arm pushed between them, then she was nudged away to stand behind him as he fronted up to the inspector.

'This isn't helping.' Vince's tone was softer, appealing for calm. 'We need to think straight. We have options. We just need to work it out. We can't do that by yelling at each other.'

Maddie turned away. She was still shaking but now she was going to vomit. She rushed over to the bank on the far side. Vince left Harry to follow her.

'I'm okay. Just leave me alone a moment,' she snapped as he came too close. He backed away, shamefaced. She watched him all the way back to his patrol car. He came back with a bottle of water. Another officer jogged past Vince's car; he had a phone to his ear. Other patrols were arriving all the time. He called over to Maddie who spat out swilled water.

'DS Ives?' he said. 'A DC Davis is trying to raise you on the radio.'

'Rhiannon?' Maddie stood straighter. 'What does she want?'

'She says she has something important. She's tried calling your phone.' Maddie checked her pocket. She had three missed calls. All Rhiannon. She took a longer swig of the water while she waited for her to pick up.

'Maddie! Are you all okay? The radio got very exciting. It's on in the office.'

'I think we're all okay, yeah.' She eyed Harry who turned away, his face a scowl. 'Look, I'll call you back. I want to see if there's anything on the radio, see if anyone's picked anything up. You never know . . .'

'It's now an area search. No one has visual and no one knows what they're even looking for. They're lost, but I might have a better option anyway.'

'Better option?'

'When I heard the commotion, I opened STORM. They were tracking your radio and you said you were following a police car. I ran a general search for other radios in the area.'

'Okay . . .'

'Dean Harvey's radio was tracking in the car ahead — the car you were chasing.'

'Dean Harvey? Who's that?'

'A transferee. Recent — in the last year or so, from Devon and Cornwall. I can't tell you much else at the moment. But — this is interesting — his radio came on shortly after you reported the start of the chase and then switched off a few minutes ago — right where you're tracking now.'

'He was listening. To the pursuit.'

'You would, wouldn't you?'

'And he knows we can track him by his radio.'

'He does. So he switched it off.'

'We need to know more. Everything you can find out about him. And please tell me he hasn't reported his radio missing.'

'He hasn't. He isn't supposed to be on duty today either, according to what I can see. His radio should be secure in his locker.'

'And it isn't.'

'And it isn't. The radio trick . . . he's done it before.'

'Radio trick?'

'Officers come on duty, they turn their radios on at the start of their shift and off at the end. Dean Harvey seems to like turning his radio off *during*. He seems to favour a specific car, too. He always turns the car radio off at the same time. It's an old response vehicle that's now just a pool car. Uniform officers use it for going to and from courses or for road-traffic training. Harvey has been running some fast-road training recently. He's had the use of that car. And right now the keys are not here where they should be.'

'It's a Skoda. Tell me it's a Skoda.'

'Skoda Octavia. An estate. Six years old.'

'Can you see where he's been turning off his radio?'

'When he leaves the police station. He doesn't turn it back on until he gets back.'

'Dammit! Can you see how long for at least? That might give us some sort of idea of how far he's going.'

'I could give you that . . .' Rhiannon's voice had a sparkle to it.

'Or . . . ? Don't hold out on me, Rhiannon.' Maddie looked over to where Harry was sitting on a bit of raised bank opposite. He had pulled his trouser leg up to inspect his shin. 'If you have something, let me know.'

'Radios you can turn off and that kills the GPS tracking. The patrol cars and their black boxes, however . . .'

Maddie almost leaped to her feet. Her attention was on the crash-damaged Skoda directly in front of her. 'His car will tell us exactly where he's been going.'

'It will. It has to be relevant.'

'He turned his radio off because he didn't want us to know. Of course it's relevant.'

'I checked with Fleet. You can't do anything remotely. You physically need the car. They need to plug something into it. They can do it at a couple of places around the county. Or they can come out with a laptop.'

'From where?'

'There's a vehicle technician at Canterbury who can do it. Otherwise it's a tow to Coldharbour.'

Maddie was on the undamaged side of the Skoda now. The driver's door came open. There were no keys.

'Does he need me to get it started?'

'Nope. Just needs access.'

'I need them to come here then! Now!'

'He's already on his way. I made a call. They're flashing him to your location. Should be with you any minute.'

Maddie stepped away from the car. Her face must have shown the energy that Rhiannon had injected into her. Harry got back to his feet to stare over, a bottle of water hanging limply in his grip. Vince was next to him. They both looked expectant.

'Good work,' Maddie said. Emotion, shock and just a little hope flushed through her to make her voice break as she said it.

CHAPTER 36

Malcolm Grant pulled the van in tight behind Dover's dilapidated and abandoned sports centre and the feeling of dread, for Ian at least, was at its strongest yet. He leaned to take in the view out of the side window. Progress and a regeneration of Dover's seafront had condemned this building to the demolition mob while a new facility on the outskirts of town now housed all its life, laughter and colour. This one had the impression of a building that had suffered a slow death. Its faded exterior gave way to musty insides with stained ceiling tiles, hanging wires and cracked flooring.

Entry was via a door that had once served as a fire exit. Even the vibrant green running man on the exit sign was now covered in a layer of dust to dim its effect. The main entrance doors were visible over to the left. The whole of the lower half of the building was a mishmash of wooden boards nailed shut and metal fencing made up of a fine mesh, covered in a sheet of plastic and with raised barbs on top to deter would-be climbers. Ian wouldn't need to be climbing. He knew how to get in by now. This was the third family he had walked through its miserable interior. They got behind the fencing around the back of the centre, close to where Grant had parked the van. Here, the mesh had been snipped. Then they could walk all the way around, effectively screened by the plastic, until they got to the forced fire exit. Once inside, they turned right to walk down a short corridor that opened up into the main sports hall where the families were being held. This was the part Ian had been dreading the most — walking out into that hall, a row of faces there to meet him, a roomful of people lined up with their hands bound, their voices constrained by gags — after he had promised to keep them safe.

PC Harvey opened the door and gestured for Ian to lead the way. Ian had hold of the boys' mother. Maybe the thinking was that the boys would follow on. He led Adene with a loose grip. It was all that was needed. She'd slipped back into her old mode of behaviour: accepting, non-questioning — a terrified victim.

He needed to push the doors to the hall wider. The right one stuck on the floor each time and the sound resonated through the empty space. The scraping sound came as expected. What he hadn't expected were the empty restraints laid out where the families had been trussed together when he had last been here. The dust was disturbed in circular patterns among the faded court markings where a set of footprints had circled them. He didn't know who had made them. He hadn't seen anyone else here. Grant had been out at the farmhouse, instructed to pick up the camper. They'd been planning on ditching the police car anyway. Grant was always supposed to follow along. The switch had just been forced on them sooner.

Grant appeared now. He had hold of the two boys; he must have taken them from Harvey.

'What's going on?' Ian said.

'We need to wait here.'

'For what?'

'For the safety of your family,' Grant growled back.

Then he smiled. The bastard was enjoying his position on the other side of the table — now it had turned on the man who was once his arresting officer. Ian knew he wasn't going to get anything out of Grant. He watched as Grant led his boys to the middle of the paced circle and picked up the rope that had been left behind. The boys sat when pushed to the ground. Adene stepped instantly towards her ex when beckoned. This was a family used to doing exactly as Grant told them. As he trussed them together, they used it as an opportunity to link hands tightly. None of them looked up at Grant and he didn't speak — not a word. Ian's sense of dread was worsening with every passing moment. Malcolm Grant wasn't here to talk.

He tied them tight. Tight enough that one of the boys couldn't catch a whimper in time. He looked terrified the moment it escaped his lips to echo around the interior. They all seemed to tense, as if such a whimper had been enough to trigger their father's temper before. But Grant didn't react. When they were secure, he walked to a large wooden door that was flush with the wall. It folded open to reveal a store-room. From here he lifted out a canteen-style chair and sat it against the wall. He went back for a bag that contained a metal flask. The lid squeaked off. The chair creaked when he lowered himself into it. He poured a measure of hot liquid out into the lid and took a sip. The steam did nothing to hide his dead eyes as he peered back over towards his family. When he swallowed, he bared his teeth.

He was side-on to Ian. Ian could still see into the store-room beyond him, specifically, a metal-framed five-a-side goal leaning against the far wall. It was broken, the rear stanchion rusted through to the point where it was hanging off. It could be a decent weapon. Grant was a big man with a history of violence, but a solid metal bar would surely give Ian the advantage he needed. But what then? Say he rushed this man, took him out, let his family go . . . what happened to his own family then? He still had no idea where they were, who was with them . . . even, if he was honest with himself, whether they were still alive. He shook the idea from his head. *They were still alive.* He had to believe that. He just needed to bide his time.

His family or yours? Ian's mind flicked back to that dark place, to that tinny conversation played out above their heads on invisible speakers. *His* . . . Linda Morris's reply had been without hesitation. She was going to die for that choice so that her daughter wouldn't. That feeling of dread that had followed him around this condemned building was growing all the time. But now there was clarity with it, and determination. He knew what part he had played in Op Icicle, in the lives of men like Malcolm Grant. It had been identical to the part Linda Morris had played. He had accepted that he was likely to get the same choice — whether or not to put his family first and maybe to die in their stead. And he was ready to do so.

CHAPTER 37

'How's it going, Nigel?' Maddie avoided eye contact with Harry. The last time she had asked that question, Harry had stared at her, a stark warning poorly concealed within. He was right; she should stop asking. Nigel stopped working to answer questions. His head was in the passenger footwell where he was trying to manipulate a lead into a socket that came out under the glove compartment of the old Skoda. This time he came right out to stand to his full height. They had already had his life story: he had spent most of his career as a traffic copper and, at the point where he could have left the force to enjoy retirement at home with his wife, he had returned immediately as a civilian member of staff, fitting out and maintaining the fleet of police cars. That had been ten years ago. Since then, he had gained a pot belly round his middle and a shock of white hair on top.

'It's going as quick as it goes. The plugs have changed recently. God knows why they do that. The adaptor I've got ain't tight, but it seems to have recognized it okay. I don't always carry one, so it's lucky really . . . Looks good enough for the transfer.' He lifted his hands to his hips and glanced down at the open laptop in the passenger seat. Its screen was largely black with a rectangle in the middle showing a blue bar that was filling slowly.

'How long does this bit take normally?' Maddie couldn't help herself.

Nigel took a moment to consider, his eyes darting over the debris on the country road. The background of birdsong and the gentle shushing sound provided by the tree canopy belied the urgency of the job at hand.

'You're Major Crime you said, right? You lot have always been the same. In my thirty years, the people with the least patience w—'

'How long?' Maddie cut across him. 'I'm really sorry, Nigel. There's just no time for war stories. Those kids were taken somewhere. This car is now our only lead. You are our only lead . . .'

Nigel sniffed. He looked to the laptop then back to Maddie. 'Anything between five and fifteen minutes for this bit. But what you get then is a file that looks like gobbledy-gook. So you gotta use a programme from the force intranet to make it out. You have to email the file to yourself, then open it on this programme and hopefully it comes up in a way you can make sense of it all. I can't do that bit here. We'll have to head back t—'

'Can we email it from here?'

'Email? Well, no. I mean, the laptop needs to be plugged into the internet for that.'

'I can make a hotspot from my phone.' Maddie pulled it from her pocket to inspect it. 'The signal should be good enough to get an email away at least. Then we can send it to my colleague back at the office and you can talk her through it — how to use it, I mean.'

'Talk her through it?' Nigel forced laughter. Maddie wanted to punch him square in the face. 'They sent me away for a week's course to learn that. Intensive, it was. Some of the reports and things I can tell you about a car using the SONOS programme will make your hair c—'

'Where it's been. That's all I need. Might a layperson — with your expert guidance over the phone — download that programme and tell us where this car has been?' Maddie stepped closer. She reached out with her hand to rest it on his shoulder and capture his eye. 'Please, Nigel. With your help we can find these kids. Without it, with any more delay, we might never see them again. You were a copper for three decades. You must have done some incredible things in that time. I need one more from you.'

Maddie couldn't big it up any more than that, but she got the response she wanted. Nigel's chest seemed to expand, it pushed his scrawny shoulders back and even his belly seemed to shrink a little. He folded himself back into the car.

'Your colleague needs to download SONOS from the list of force apps on the intranet. It can take a while.'

'I'll get her to start now.'

Rhiannon was breathless as she picked up her phone. 'Maddie! I was just calling you.'

'I need you to do something right now.'

'Okay.'

'Force intranet . . . are you at your desk?'

'Yes. The intranet . . . what do you need?'

'Go to the apps menu. You need to download something called SONOS.'

'Okay . . .'

Maddie had to bite her tongue while she listened to Rhiannon reading out a list of apps as her eye moved down them.

'SONOS! Okay, here it is. I selected *download*. It's doing something . . . Yep, it's moved to the desktop and it's doing its thing. What is it?'

'Tracking app. We're going to send you a file. You need to open it using this SONOS programme. I have a man here who's going to help you work out what we need from it.'

'What's in the file?'

'It's the download from the Skoda's black box. The technician you sent out to us is going to send it back to you. I need to know where this car has been, places that stand out. There has to be something in there that helps us find where he's taken them.'

'Okay. I've mapped Dean Harvey's radio location for the last four weeks. He turns it off and on fairly regularly. My plan is to run the car's use against his radio GPS. That should tell me that he's in it for a start, but it should also map where he goes when his radio's turned off.'

'That's it! That's exactly what we need.'

Nigel climbed out of the car. 'Give me the email address and this hotspot you talked about so I can get it ready to go. It's halfway done.'

Maddie barked back into her phone. 'Keep your email open. I'll call you back in a second.'

'Wait! Maddie, I said I was going to call you.'

'You did. Sorry. I just need to get this set up here . . .'

'It's important. Dean Harvey . . .'

'What about him?'

'I've done some digging. He transferred from Devon and Cornwall right enough. It was under a cloud. His ex-part-ner made some accusations of domestic violence — serious accusations. She wouldn't support though, so they couldn't convict him . . . or sack him.'

'So they moved him?'

'*He* moved himself. He put in for a transfer. It seems he played the game, made sure he kept his job. His HR record shows that he offered to move to another force to put some distance between him and his ex. He was even served the non-molestation order at work by appointment *and* he paid the deposit for his family to move to a new place that he agreed wouldn't be known to him. I guess they thought sacking him wasn't really an option as the ex wasn't supporting and he was moving himself two hundred miles aw—'

'I get it, Rhiannon! That doesn't change much though.'

326

'Except it does. Devon and Cornwall Social Services spoke with their counterparts in this area. They had to because Dean Harvey requested supervised contact with his son — who is Dillon, seven years old. There was an agreement that a grandparent would bring Dillon up once a month to start with. But the fact that the contact was to happen in this county meant that Social Services here owned the risk, so *they* had to approve it.'

'And they didn't,' Maddie said.

'They didn't. And because Social Services don't exactly work fast at times, his transfer had all gone through — the house move . . . everything. And *then* the contact with his son was blocked. A senior social worker looked at the case. I've got the summary report in front of me. They took advice from a panel that included the CPS DV lead for the area and a copper specialising in the area of domestic violence and social care — and, between them, they all agreed that Dean Harvey had not done enough to clarify his intentions towards his family. His ex-partner had alleged that he had threatened to kill them all, Dillon included, and in his interview, he had replied "no comment" to all questions. So his request was blocked on the grounds that he hasn't ever answered that allegation — formally or informally. "No comment" means he never denied it.'

'What about the disciplinary process?'

'He wasn't obligated to speak about criminal allegations at an employee tribunal.'

'And so he didn't.'

'He did not. But, Maddie . . . the panel that was consulted was the same one set up for Op Icicle. So the senior social worker who took it there to be discussed was Marie Foreshaw. The CPS lead for the area? Linda Morris. The police officer sitting on this panel—'

'Ian Hessey!'

'Yes. And Marie Foreshaw is the only one who would have known all of those names and their involvements. HR's notes only state that CPS and police in this area were consulted. No names. But this report I have in front of me is the one that Marie wrote. It names both Linda and Ian as being consulted. It wasn't exactly easy for me to get hold of this, either — even in these circumstances.'

'So Harvey needed Marie to give him the names of the others involved in the decision-making.'

'And not just that. It seems he also wanted the address for where his own family had moved to . . .'

'What's the matter, Rhiannon?'

'Devon and Cornwall attended his ex-partner's new address at our request. They're still there now. It's a murder scene, Maddie. They found two bodies.'

'Dillon?'

'No. His ex and an adult male that might be her new lover. They were sitting opposite each other, knee to knee. Both wrapped in plastic. No sign of the son.'

'Shit!' Maddie was pacing now, aware of Harry stepping closer and closer. He would be desperate for the update. She tried desperately to clear her mind. She needed to think . . .

'We'll get this file sent over to you. It could still be the key we need. We found a phone, too. It was in the rear footwell of the crashed police car. It's a cheap burner that's locked with a code. I'll have Vince run me back in — the techies should be able to access it easy enough. Harry can stay here and get the file sent. There isn't time for me to be standing about here by the roadside.'

'Okay.'

'And, Rhiannon . . . any luck with the new addresses for the Icicle families yet?'

'Still getting brick walls there. We put in another urgent request with Social Services but now they've got wind of a threat linked with a police officer. That's probably my fault. I've had to make a lot of calls to Social Services. One of our bosses is about to walk into the building in person to pick up what we need. It was the only way they would release it.'

'The offenders?'

'Halfway house for one. NFA for another. And the one we know about in prison. We haven't been able to physically locate any of them.'

'We need urgent welfare checks on those families the moment we have somewhere to look.'

'What do you think we will find, Maddie?' Rhiannon's voice was suddenly different — tentative. As if she had already worked out her own answer.

'Honestly? I don't know.' Maddie tried to make sense of all the information swirling around her head. 'The Hessey family . . . what do we know about his kids?'

'It's here somewhere . . . hang on.'

'Boys or girls?'

'Oh . . . two girls.'

'And Linda? Her daughter's all grown up, isn't she?'

'Twenty-two. Just out of uni.'

'I saw two boys in the back of that car today, I'm sure of it. Two boys, Rhiannon. Those Op Icicle address checks . . . we're not going to find the children there.' Maddie hung up the phone.

Nigel stood with his hands on his hips as if he'd been waiting to talk to her. 'Five more minutes, give or take.'

'I don't have five minutes.'

Harry looked at her expectantly. She summarized the call as best she could, directing him to stay with the file and for Vince to flash her back with the phone they'd found in the footwell. Harry didn't argue, either because it was the logical thing to do or because she didn't give him the chance. Either way, it didn't matter.

Maddie had to go. Now.

CHAPTER 38

Maddie swung her right leg out of the car and placed it gingerly on the ground, careful how she put weight on her injured ankle. Vince had blue-lighted through meandering traffic to get back to Canterbury Police Station and the constant tension of the journey had caused her stiffness in every part of her body. It must have showed.

'You alright, Mads?'

She was struggling to keep up. 'Yeah. Leg took a bump in the accident, that's all. Just need to loosen it up.'

Rob Ford was perhaps the most competent of the techies employed to interrogate electronic devices and Maddie was relieved to see him ready and waiting at her desk, poring over a laptop that he had simply laid on top of her other stuff.

'Rhiannon, any luck?'

Rhiannon was on her feet, a desk phone pinned to her ear. Maddie had called out on the way to her desk.

She put her hand over the mouthpiece to reply. 'The file's still downloading. Nigel just keeps telling me, "another minute, give or take". I'm on the line with Harry, coaching him on all things hotspot. He should be heading back any minute.'

'DS Ives!' Rob Ford was smug at the best of times. She certainly wouldn't tell him how competent she considered him to be. Maddie instantly handed him the phone. 'Ah yes, just as described. The Hastings phone, preferred device of your esteemed drug dealer.'

'Hastings?' Maddie snapped.

'An Alcatel 10.66. Cheap shit.'

'And easy to open?'

'I don't need to open it. The software doesn't care about a code lock. It'll just bypass that to show us what's on there. Very easy . . .'

'But?'

'Deleted data is not retrievable. Memory in phones is an expensive commodity. There's no room for part memory on a burner phone, which is where your del—'

'Rob!' Maddie gestured at the phone that he still held in his hand.

'Right . . . sorry!' He woke the laptop. A lead already trailed from it. He plugged the Alcatel in the other end. 'Basically, what I'm saying is that, with these phones, stuff is either on there or lost forever.'

Maddie rubbed at her face. 'Right this moment it's all we have, Rob. Tell me there's something . . . please . . .'

'Well, okay then . . . there is something!' Rob clicked his mouse and dropped into Maddie's chair to get a better angle. 'Not much, though. Some outbound calls today, the last one just over an hour ago . . .' He paused to write down a phone number and handed it to Maddie. 'And one text message left in the drafts folder.'

'Drafts folder?'

'Yeah, if you type out a message on one of these and then abandon it, it gets saved in there. We've found some good stuff in drafts folders in our time. Anyone who doesn't know what they're doing, they empty the inbox and the outbox, and never think about the drafts folder. Ah . . . looking at the message, I don't think it's going to help you.'

'What is it?' Maddie snapped again.

'Just three words: *elections driver vegetable*, written out like a list. What is that? Some sort of code?'

'Yes! Vince?'

Vince was already fiddling with his phone. 'Hang on, I'm in there now . . . Yep, it's a location. Fifteen minutes out.'

'Or less with your driving.' She was already halfway to the door, her aching ankle all but forgotten. She was aware that she was attracting attention from the rest of the office.

'Someone do what they can with that phone number!' she called out to her captive audience while pointing back at Rob. The phone number would lead nowhere; she was already certain of that. She glanced over at Rhiannon, a picture of frustration, still on her feet, still scowling into a phone handset. The three words on that phone were just about her only lead. They had to give her something.

* * *

Grant stood up and stretched. Then he dragged his chair back into the storeroom, his movements slow and deliberate. It was maddening. Finally he looked over to where Ian had found a seat on the solid floor with his back against the wall.

'Time to move.'

'Where are we going?'

'*We* are going to another part of the building. *You* are staying here.'

Grant dug around in his bag again. Last time, he'd taken his flask from it. Now he pulled out something else. He slid it firmly towards Ian, who looked down to see a set of police-issue handcuffs bounce off his foot.

'What are these for?'

'Take an educated guess. Find something solid to attach yourself to.'

'Why? What the hell is going on?'

'It's for your own good. You lot are all the same when it comes to it, some hero shit that runs through you. This ain't the time for that.'

'What are you going to do?' Ian's voice started to shake.

'Something you don't want to be part of. You want your family back, right?'

'Yes, b—'

'Then find something solid. I'll be back for you.'

* * *

Vince pulled the car to a stop. Even at low speed, the wheels slid on the loose ground. Maddie got out and frowned. The What Three Words app was open on her phone and telling her she was just a few paces away from the three-metre grid labelled *elections.driver.vegetable*. But her eyes told her there was nothing to see here — only levelled ground covered with black shale and grit. She could see a Portakabin in the distance and a wooden outhouse a little closer that throbbed like an engine. Vince was already making for it. Pulling the door open amplified the sound. Maddie got a glimpse of a small generator before he quickly shut the door again. He stooped to take hold of an orange wire at the foot of the door.

'Has to be powering something,' he muttered.

He lifted the cable to lead him in the right direction and Maddie followed, eyes ahead to where it arched up from the ground — until it suddenly vanished, like it had been swallowed up by the ground. They got closer. The ground dipped away. A path had been worn into the black banks, leading downwards. It was well camouflaged. Maddie followed it down to a half-buried structure of some sort.

'Like a Hobbit hole!' Maddie said.

'Only if the Hobbit was a miner.'

Vince referenced their location. They were on the outskirts of Snowdown Colliery, near Canterbury. The site had been closed since 1987 but before that it had been a busy, working pit. In the distance there were still some brick and steel carcasses of old buildings, monuments left to rot and decay but defiant with it, as strong and unrelenting as the men who had once earned their living here.

Now they were surrounded by slag heaps. The wire continued under a flattened piece of black plastic that butted up against a sturdy metal door. The wall that spread out either side was of the same material and quickly swallowed by the compressed shale. The door was mottled green, heavy with rust and had a wheel jutting from its centre that wouldn't have looked out of place on a submarine. Vince gripped it tightly, his neck and face showing the strain. It did turn. It did come open.

A few paces behind it was another door. This one was wooden with thick strips of black rubber nailed all around its edges in a kind of seal. This door looked like a recent addition to a structure that had been standing for decades. The opening mechanism was far simpler too: a tarnished brass handle that Maddie leaned on. The door pulled towards her, skipping and dragging as it did. The daylight bent round her to flood the interior of a black room with rounded edges. Directly in front of her, a screen flared bright white. She flinched at the sound of a human voice.

'Please!' The voice was rasping, dry, weak and desperate. It was coming from the floor, from a darkened heap of limbs — one of which reached out towards where Maddie stood. 'I'll do anything! Just let her go!'

Linda Morris.

Maddie bundled in and bent down to her. Thick chains were wrapped around her middle. Her eyes were squeezed tightly shut. She took hold of Maddie by the wrist as Maddie pulled lightly on the chains to try and work out where they went. They were pinned to the ground either side of her by thick metal loops.

'Please don't hurt her! *Please!*'

'It's okay, Linda. It's the police. You're okay, you're safe.' Maddie squeezed her hand.

'Hope! Please! You have to help her!' Linda's eyes were still scrunched up tight. She was filthy, her face dusted in black.

'Where is she, Linda? Tell me where she is and we can go and get her.'

'The screen! They want me to watch!'

Maddie's eyes jerked up to the screen. It was bright white in the dark interior, but she still struggled to make out what it was showing. Vince stood over her. There was movement on the screen. It was an angled view, wide, distant and in differing tones of grey. She got a little closer, narrowing her eyes. A square trench perhaps? No, it was too neat. A square pit, like the sort car mechanics worked in, maybe, but bigger — much wider and with crumbling surroundings. Maybe a dry dock for a boat?

The screen changed: another fixed angle, this one closer and in full colour. There was no mistaking what it showed: four women arranged in a row, chained across their chests and under their arms. It looked like they were pinned to a tiled slope. Their eyes bulged above wide strips of tape across their mouths. Even in a moment like this, Maddie recognized the stuff. *Bright blue, the type hikers use to tape their socks up.* That was how Adrian Hughes had described the tape they found on Marie Foreshaw's lifeless body. Now more women had been left to scream into it, fighting against their restraints. Something terrible was happening. Maddie could also see a torrent of white froth passing between and over them, as if someone were spraying them from above with a fire extinguisher.

It changed again: back to the first view, like the cameras were programmed into a cycle. Now she was able to make more sense of it all; the lack of colour had made it difficult without context. It wasn't a pit or a trench she was looking at — it was a swimming pool. At the far left of the screen, two thick pipes were angled down towards the middle of the pool, a white moving shadow spread out from them, merging to rush for the deep end, a deep end shown as a far darker shadow that had a subtle movement. As she squinted, Maddie realized that the women's heads were near the top of the slope that descended to the deep end and their legs were already part submerged.

'He's drowning them!' Maddie shouted. 'We need to get her out of here. We need to move!'

Her focus was back on Linda but Vince grabbed her by the shoulder.

'Mads!' His thick finger pointed out more shadows on the screen as the distant view looped back around. Maddie leaned in closer. There was another row over to the side of the women. Their heads were slightly higher up the slope. They were distinctly smaller.

'Jesus, Vince! The kids!'

They were wriggling, fighting to move away from the same rising shadow, a shadow that was covering the feet of the tallest child. There were three of them in total. There was no sound, but Maddie didn't need any to reinforce the terror in that room. They didn't have long.

'Linda, where is this?' she barked. 'Is it somewhere near here?'

'Not here. I was just told to do a task, I was told I would get Hope back. But she's there. They're going to drown her! I saw the film of them walking in. It's a sports place, changing rooms . . . She's so terrified! Oh God! Do SOMETHING!' Linda's voice became a sob. She was out of control.

Maddie met eyes with Vince. 'There are some bolt croppers in the car. Standard kit.'

He spun away. Maddie did too. She needed the phone reception outside. Rhiannon was quick to answer as ever.

'Rhiannon . . . a disused swimming pool! Tell me the car has given up the location of a disused swimming pool and you know exactly where it is!'

'A . . . no . . . we're having trouble. This programme is all over the place. I thought it would just overlay onto a map but it just gives—'

'Is Harry with you?'

'Yes, he's b—'

'Put him on.' Rhiannon didn't argue.

Harry's was the next voice Maddie heard. 'DS Ives.'

'Harry, he's drowning them. All of them. Right now. We found Linda Morris. She's been left in a bunker of some sort and given the means to watch them drown her daughter. It looks like a disused swimming pool. Have we got one?'

'Got one?'

'Do we know of one, in the area? Let's hope to fuck it's in the area, Harry . . . I can only see the inside. The water's rising.'

'I don't know of anywhere like it.'

'Let's think, Harry! What have we got in the area?'

'I really don't know.'

'Has Rhiannon got anything out of that car's black box?'

'We have a few locations. One out in Aylesham that looks like a field . . . a couple in Dover — one we think is a beauty spot near the coastguard building and one at the foot of the cliffs where it looks like he's been numerous times — more than any other. It could just be where he's parked for the port. There's another two in Canterbury . . . one in Maidstone—'

'Dover!' Maddie cut in. 'There's a brand-new leisure centre in Dover. Out near Tesco. Barry's a member — he was talking about it. Put him on.'

'Maddie, you okay?' Barry took nearly thirty seconds to come on the line and his voice was far too casual.

'You were talking about a new leisure centre in Dover?'

'Whitfield, actually. They moved it out of town.'

'From where? Where was it before?'

'The old one's on the seafront. Well past its sell-by-date, too. The old place was falling down.'

'Under the cliffs?'

'Well, yeah, I suppose it is. Bottom of Castle Hill.'

'Is it still there?'

Barry was chewing something. It delayed his answer. If he'd been in front of her, she might have lashed out.

'It was still there the last time I drove past. It's going as part of the—'

'*Everyone* needs to go there, Barry! Everyone who can — not Rhiannon . . . she needs to stay on what she's doing.

Have Harry call me on the way. We'll meet you all there. And bring bolt croppers!'

Maddie ended the call. She dipped her head back into the darkness. The monitor was still scrolling its loop. It was on the distant view. The shadow was getting darker, lifting upwards, now lapping at the women's thighs. The screen changed — back to the close up of the four women's faces. From Linda's reaction, Maddie knew that one of them was her daughter. The women all had long hair that was being pushed around by the water that still rushed against them from behind. One of the women spat droplets of water into the air in panicked gasps, she was having to lift her head away from the torrent just to draw breath.

'We need to go!' Maddie barked at Vince. He was kneeling over Linda, working the bolt croppers. Something snapped and he stumbled backwards.

'Just about there,' he said.

The screen changed back to the wider view. The shadow of death already seemed bigger. And it was unrelenting.

* * *

'Look, there's no need for this. I know what I have to do. Trust me — I just want my family back. I'll do what's necessary.'

Ian Hessey was still cuffed tightly behind his back as he walked a musty corridor, dodging hanging wires and an empty vending machine. Malcolm Grant didn't reply.

Ian was led into the old reception area. Above him, a plastic sign announcing *CHANGING ROOMS* hung at an angle, secured at one end only. The changing rooms themselves had the worst smell yet. Most of the benches had been stripped out; the flooring tiles that had been disturbed as a result presented a trip hazard to a man with no free hands to break a fall. One wall of lockers still remained. Ian could see where the others had been. T-shaped strips of bare concrete jutting out from the wall were all that was left of them now.

They continued through, past empty showers and a toilet that had been pulled from its fixtures to lean against the wall, into a short corridor with coloured tiles depicting a waving cartoon crab. It led out to the pool area.

It was the sound that grabbed Ian's attention first — water, being sprayed hard. It was louder than the two big, throbbing water pumps over to their right. Both had thick, black pipes jutting out of their middles that were angled down into a large pool. Four more pipes lifted out of a discarded drain cover to connect into the back, two into each pump. The combined noise was almost overwhelming. The pumps seemed to work in distinct surges and the pipes shivered in time with each one.

Grant led Ian up the left side. The moment he was close enough to see the tops of heads, Grant grabbed his arm, hard enough to cause him pain, and dragged him forwards. Harvey stood at the far end. He had stripped down to a black T-shirt and trousers. Ian looked down to take in the people laid out on the tiles of the pool. Despite the frothing water and wet, plastered hair, it took him only a moment to recognize among them his two children, his wife and Pete, whose hands were free enough for him to be tapping out a rhythm on the steel chain across his chest.

Ian opened his mouth to shout, but at that moment he felt a firm shove. He stumbled to the right until the floor ran out and then fell over the edge. With no hands to cushion the blow, his right knee and then his head took the full force of the solid tiles. An old injury exacerbated the damage to his knee. It gave out instantly, his leg bending in an unnatural angle at the bottom of the pool. Ian's yelp of pain was stolen by the freezing cold water that rushed past, his breath too. It drummed against his pounding head and aching back, filling his ears to add to his confusion. The flow got stronger — enough to roll him over so that he was looking back at the source, getting glimpses of someone now holding one of the pipes up close to him. He was pushed to roll over again; the pool had a gentle slope and the water was washing him towards where it fell away suddenly into the deep end. He scrabbled for a foothold but it was no good. He could only use his left foot and there was no grip on the slick tiles. He was on his side, looking down the slope into a filthy mass of dark grey water that gurgled and spun as it grew ever deeper. He lost his battle; the force of the water behind him was too much. It sent him down the slope, his tied hands powerless to stop it. He tried to get his left foot planted, anything to push him up. But the torrent of water turned him and his right knee shot with pain; it wouldn't take any weight.

Ian Hessey was drowning.

He thrashed against it, fighting with everything he had to get a foothold, to push himself back to the surface. He needed a breath; his chest felt like it was going to burst. His knee flared in agony. His wrists pulled hopelessly against the solid metal of the cuffs. He could feel the cascading water just above him — he was so close to the surface.

Then he felt a thump on his back: someone was trying to get hold of him. He stopped thrashing to let them get a fistful of his shirt and he was pulled out from under the water. He spluttered for breath. He had taken in some of the filthy water and now he gagged as it all came out at once. When his vision cleared, he saw Grant's face leering down at him.

'Not just yet, PC Hessey,' he grinned.

He hooked Ian under his arms and pulled him back up the slope. Ian cast a look to his right and, for a brief moment, he locked eyes with his wife. She looked like she was shouting at him but the sound was smothered by the thick blue tape over her mouth. He was thrown back to the floor and rolled onto his front. His cuffs were released and then he got a dig in the back to distract him while his hands were brought round to his front and secured again. He was pushed into a kneeling position. The impact through his right knee was pure agony. He could see his cuffs now. They were partly concealed by the swirling water pummelling into him from behind, but he could still make out the thick steel chain that ran over the top of them. The chain was pulled tight from behind. It ran through his legs and pulled the cuffs forwards. He had no choice but to follow in a sort of bow. The cuffs rested against his groin while he was still on his knees. The water hit him hard on the soles of his feet and the back of his thighs. It arced around him and his wife, who was laid out on her back directly in front and straining to look back over her forehead. To her right he could see his little girls. Their heads were higher up, level with the top of the slope. He could just see Pete, too, furthest away in the row. His smaller frame meant his head was positioned lower.

'You're going to die, Ian!' Harvey's voice boomed above the din of the gushing water. 'You'll be under the waterline eventually. But you'll be last. You get to watch your family die. That way, you'll have plenty of time to think about what you did. This is all your doing, Ian.'

Grant walked over to stand next to Harvey, his white shirt soaked to the point of being see-through.

'Please! I did what I was asked! You said my family would be safe!' Ian bellowed back. His chest burned with the exertion.

'I lied, Ian. Just like my wife did. You believed her, no problem at all. You just took her story on trust — no need for corroboration. You decided that I was just as she described. So I thought, well, if that's the kind of guy Ian Hessey is then this should be very easy. Seems I was right.' Harvey's lips finished in a grin.

'What lies? What are you talking about?'

'My name is Dean Harvey. My wife is Heidi Harvey. We lived together in Torquay. We were happy, too — or so I thought. I had my dream life down there . . . me and my boy by the beach. I'd just got a new camper van. You should have seen his face! We always said we would do it up together, go on adventures.'

'Torquay?' Ian was confused. The cold water, the pain in his knee, the anguish of his family still fighting against the rising water, he couldn't *think*. But Torquay . . . there was something he remembered about the place.

'That's right. But then *she* wanted to take all that away. So I agreed. I put in to move forces, to come here. I agreed to play by all of their rules — all so I would at least get to see my boy once a month. I wanted a lot more than that, but "play by the rules," they said. "Show you can be a good dad and we'll review it . . . see if you can't get more time."' Harvey muttered something to Grant, who then walked away.

Harvey dropped to sit at the edge of the pool, his legs trailing down directly over Ian's girls. The noise of the pumps was abruptly silenced, the water that had been hammering down gradually became a trickle. Harvey was buying himself time. He leaned forwards, his eyes holding Ian's.

'We can't be a family now. Not anymore. Never like it used to be. You took that away from me.'

Ian stammered. 'I . . . I—'

'I've been coming to this place, back and forth, for a few weeks now . . . an hour here . . . an hour there. These things take an age to fill up! But I don't need it full. Not from here. From here it's twelve minutes to put them all under. There's enough water in the holding tank to get us there, too. I've run this a couple of times. But we don't want this all to be over too soon, now, do we? At least not until you've had your chance to give your side. That's something I never got to do, see. Maybe you'll tell me that I'm wrong. That you weren't the copper that Social Services in this shit-stained county talked to . . . that you didn't give your opinion that I should be blocked from seeing my son? You and your CPS bitch? In which case it will be apologies all round — no hard feelings!' He grinned. He actually grinned. This was all part of the game. Grant still hadn't reappeared.

'Dillon,' Ian said. Then he scanned the faces of the children laid out in front of him, mouthing and fighting against the thick blue tape over their mouths.

'Oh, he ain't here! I don't treat my own family like this. Nor does Malc.' Harvey gestured up and away to his right.

Ian looked up into the viewing gallery that once hosted proud parents for decades of swimming galas. Now it held two young boys sitting together, their hands tightly gripping each other. Grant's two sons.

'But Anna, here, and little Pete . . . Well, the head of that family was quite insistent about what he wanted done. A little too insistent for me, but I guess it takes all sorts and that's what happens when the authorities think they can send you to prison just to steal your family.'

'Steal families? You're talking about Icicle? We didn't steal anyone. People like Pete's dad . . . they don't deserve a family!'

'And there you are! Humble PC Ian Hessey . . . the man who gets to decide who deserves what. The man who takes it on himself to decide if I can see my son. You don't know me. You don't know Malcolm or Bill Watson or James Loxton . . . But I know you.'

'I was protect—'

'MY JOB!' Harvey leaped to his feet to thump his fist against his chest. 'MY JOB, MY FUCKING JOB! Don't you *dare* say you were protecting my boy! That is *my* job. No one in the world will ever do that better. My Dillon is my *everything*!'

'I do remember Dillon,' Ian said. 'They didn't tell me any of the specifics but someone let that name slip when we were talking about it. I knew it was a case from Torquay . . .' Ian shook his head. Water ran down his back as he did. 'You didn't give me any choice.'

'Choice! You want to talk about choice? My wife lied, PC Hessey! You got sucked in by her lies — everyone did. Then she retracted it all. She said there was *no* abuse, *no* beatings, *no* threats. And, most important of all, there was *no* evidence. I knew that, because the police told me when they dropped the case. I believed in that, too. This is a system I've been part of for eighteen years. I'm a police officer. We put people away when we have evidence that they've done wrong. Then I fall the wrong side of the law, the wrong side of the interview table and guess what? Evidence don't mean shit! She lied. She had a new lover, PC Hessey. We've all heard this story before, right? She didn't want to go through the hassle of admitting she was unfaithful — a cheat — so she called the police. Told them some story about abuse, hoping that the cops would come along and free her of the burden of a husband she no longer wanted. So she could be free to take the parts of her old life she still wanted — half the house and a son — and just move in with somebody else. And me? Tossed away, into another county. Needing to start again, seeing my son once a month — with the empty promise of more for good behaviour. Do you think that was what I deserved?'

'You never denied it!' Ian shouted. 'Even now, you're not denying it. The abuse, the beatings, the threats . . . You said she retracted. You've never said you didn't hurt her. You can project this on me all you want — on my family. It won't change a damned thing about what you did. You did beat her, didn't you? You did threaten her. Her sister didn't retract her statement. Was she lying, too — about the bruises? About everything else? I remember your case. It was the only decision we could have made. You can't blame me or the operation for your own failings. Neither can those other men.'

Ian's shivers were becoming more and more uncontrollable, to the point where there was almost no gap between each one and he was struggling to speak. The water was freezing cold. He could see that his two girls were shivering too. Their hair was spread out in a mess that stuck to the tiles of the pool floor. They were looking over at him, their eyes sore, their faces red as if they had been crying so long it had scalded the skin. The shadow of filthy water covered their midriffs.

'Please . . . you don't have to do this. This isn't you! You're not thinking straight.'

'I am. For the first time in a long time. I had everything I ever wanted. You took that away from me.' Harvey nodded then opened his fists to dust his hands.

An engine started up. Another followed within a second. The water started as a surge against the soles of his feet, but soon it was back to buffeting the whole of his bottom half. He pulled upwards on his cuffs. There was no give, not a thing. The solid metal dug painfully into his wrists.

The water seemed to come back more quickly. He looked back at his wife. Peter's mother was next to her, Adene the next one over and then — oh God — it was Linda's daughter! She had shown him a picture, told him she was away on her travels.

They were women and children he had sworn to protect. He'd convinced them to put their trust in him, and he had failed every one of them. The water was up to the women's chests now, their breathing noticeably more panicked. Ian saw movement in the shimmering water where Clare reached out to the woman next to her to grab her hand under the water. Soon they all had hold of each other's hands.

He looked beyond them to his daughters. The water was now covering the chains that held them in place.

'I'm sorry,' he said. 'So, so sorry . . .'

CHAPTER 39

The barrier was down across the car park but it was just a kerb that marked out the perimeter. Vince aimed for it without really slowing down and Maddie felt the impact through her seat and winced as her foot rolled enough to agitate her sore ankle. There was another marked police car here already but it had stopped outside of the barrier with a door cracked open. Maddie heard the door slam shut and the engine fire as she stepped out. Then came the scraping sound of the second patrol car bundling over the raised kerb to pull up beside her. She looked in to see the vehicle was single-crewed, with just one officer sitting behind the wheel. She barked instructions at him the moment his door opened.

'We have someone on board. You need to keep her out here. Put her in your car. She doesn't leave — no matter what!'

The officer nodded. He looked young, his glasses poorly fitting on his nose. He opened the back door and started shifting kit around to make room.

Maddie jogged over to speak to Linda. 'You have to stay here! Do you understand? This is how you help your daughter.'

Linda stared back, her mouth flapped open and shut as if she was trying to find the words.

'There's no time for a conversation about it. Just stay here, okay?' She slammed the door and called over to the young PC. 'Don't worry about your kit. Just sit in here with her! And watch for anyone coming out of that building!' He nodded back.

Vince was making his way across the car park with the steel enforcer. Maddie had been holding the bolt croppers since they had left Snowdown. They were heavier than they looked and awkward when she tried to break into a run.

The car park was at the rear of the building. There was a tall metal fence running parallel to the brick sides — too high to climb. On the other side, she could see windows but they were opaque — the washed-out white of an eye gone bad. She reckoned the swimming pool would be behind those windows. Vince was already moving towards the pavement that led around to the main entrance at the front but Maddie hung back to think. The road was busy beyond that pavement, she could see cars flashing past either side and it got busier still when it met with the main thoroughfare into Dover's shipping port. It was constant traffic and hissing hydraulics from the lumbering HGVs. She didn't think you would walk hostages around there — too many sets of eyes.

'VINCE!'

He was already disappearing into the distance. She jogged across the car park to the left side. Here she was hidden from view on three sides. This was where it made sense to breach the fence. Its starting point was up a grassy bank that was too steep to walk up until it met with the stone wall of a crumbling church. The steel fence was made up of panels joined together. Maddie counted six altogether. Then there was a break before the next six started, with a chain between the two runs of six. It was wrapped tight but she couldn't see a lock anywhere. She started to unwrap it; it kept coming until it fell away. Vince was back to her in time to help her heave the panels apart. They stepped through, dragging their clumsy equipment with them. Now they were the right side of the fence, they could see a walkway that was a metre or so

347

wide — room enough to run along. The opaque windows reached down to ground level at certain points, but they were covered over by thick wooden boards. Maddie was glad — she wasn't sure the glass would be opaque on the other side and didn't want to be on show — not that there was time to worry about that.

The walkway created by the fence line had them hugging the building all the way around to a short flight of stairs. Maddie's shoulders and thighs burned as she ran to the top to find the doors were just like the windows — a wooden barrier nailed from top to bottom. Vince rattled it; there was no give at all. He put the enforcer down to jog further around. Maddie stepped back. Vince had run in the direction of a set of metal steps. They doubled back on themselves to meet with another boarded door on the first floor.

'Dammit!' Maddie exclaimed.

Vince reappeared from under the steps. 'Mads!'

She ran at him. He held a door open that was labelled as a fire exit. She followed him in. Immediately the smell of the shut-up building hit her: dust, moisture and decay all at the same time. Vince froze in the face of various corridors and stairs leading off from their entry point, but Maddie spun instantly left, her bolt croppers bouncing clumsily off a set of double doors. She was certain that the swimming pool was back the way they had come. The doors led to a reception area. Changing rooms were signposted to their right. She took the door with her shoulder. Vince was right behind her. On the other side, she skidded into a brightly coloured montage of a crab on the wall.

Now she could hear it. The room opened up and the sound of gushing water mingled with pulsing engines. The pool was straight ahead. She stepped out.

The blow came from her left. She reeled away from it, losing her footing, and heard the shrill clang where the bolt croppers fell from her hand and skidded over the solid floor. Her sight was blurred from the blow, but she heard Vince roar. Then came sounds of scuffing, of grunts and fists being thrown behind her. She shook her head clear. When she looked up, she was staring straight over at the source of the engine noise. She could see thick pipes pushing out of two large engine blocks. They were angled into the pool on wooden splints. Water pumps. She made for them, pushing off the floor like a sprinter. The bolt croppers scraped as she gathered them up.

'Mads!'

Vince's breathless shout came from behind her but there wasn't time to turn back. She skidded into the nearest pump, almost knocking it over. There was a raised yellow button. She pushed out towards it with her palm. She never made it. A stinging blow knocked her sideways and stole her focus. She could just see the outline of a man in a white shirt. He moved towards her and she lashed out instinctively. He was quick to duck away — a swing and a miss. Beyond him she could still hear sounds of a fight, even over the chugging engine, then another shout of 'Mads!'

The white-shirted man closed in quicker this time and the blow to the side of her face was harder. It twisted her head and made her drop to her knees, leaving her peering out over the smooth floor of the pool. Frothy water raced across the tiles.

Maddie turned back towards her attacker, her eyes down. His feet moved first and it gave her the split-second she needed to react. She sprang towards him, keeping low. The blow still came but it wasn't clean, the connection not as good as it might have been on the top of her head. She pushed up, forcing herself to stand, hoping she'd be too close to take a hit. The man was quick; he had already stepped back and she was instantly reeling from another blow. She couldn't get a clear shot in herself. She couldn't focus enough to see him. Her mind flashed a message: *Do not go down! Whatever happens, do not go down!*

He grabbed her by the hair and she folded forwards with the pain. A sweaty forearm slid under her chin and she felt a hip press against hers — a pivot to turn her towards the pool.

Her head was dipped, she could see her feet on the edge, the rushing water below. *Do not go down!*

She heard heavy breathing in her ear. Then a voice cried out in pain. The man pushed her off — towards the pool. She shifted her weight, throwing her arms back to teeter on the edge for a sickening moment. Then she was able to rock back onto her heels and spin away — to where Vince was now wrestling the man in white.

The two men broke apart. Vince's top was ripped and hanging ragged round his neck. He threw a punch that landed; the man in white roared and threw himself forwards in a rugby-style tackle. Vince was braced for him, but his opponent's weight and momentum were too much. Vince was forced to the brink where they both paused. The man scrabbled with his feet. Vince had run out of floor. He suddenly accepted that he was going in and reached out to grab a big handful of the man's clothing, making sure he took him with him.

They both went into the pool with a thud. White water spilled instantly around them. Vince seemed dazed, as if the back of his head might have taken a smack as he landed on the pool floor. The white-shirted man had been thrown off him as they landed but he was first up. Vince lolled onto his side; his movements were still those of a man not quite with it. His attacker pushed him onto his front, put his weight through his knees onto Vince's back and lashed out to punch him in the back of the head. The man then pushed Vince's head under the rushing water, pressing down with all his weight. Vince freed his arms from under himself to try and push out of the hold, but the man on his back was almost as big as he was and wasn't to be moved. Vince's face emerged to one side, retching and gasping for breath. The white-shirted man still had the positional advantage and he used it, striking Vince again then grabbing his head firmly to straighten it up, holding his mouth and nose against the tiles — under the running water.

'VINCE!'

Maddie glanced around desperately for someone or something to help — anything. The bolt croppers were a couple of paces away. She scooped them up and jumped into the pool. Her ankle shot with pain. Combined with the freezing water splashing up her side, it stripped the breath from her. She steadied herself, gripping the bolt croppers in both hands. They were heavy to lift and dripped water in her face as she raised them above her head. She used their weight, letting the momentum build as she brought them down hard through the air. She didn't take her eyes off the target in front of her — the man in white.

Time stood still. The croppers connected with the man's skull. The thud was sickening, but then nothing happened. The shock of the blow ran up her forearms and into her hands and fingers. It was enough to force her to let go and the croppers clanged onto the grubby tiles. The man in white froze. His position hadn't changed and, for a moment, Maddie wondered if he had felt anything at all. Then Vince was able to push out and roll onto his side, his face out of the water. The white-shirted man slipped sideways off his back; his arms hung by his sides to offer no assistance in breaking his fall. The water flowed around his head and was stained instantly red.

Vince sat up. He took a moment, spat water and wiped his face.

'HELP! HELP THEM!'

A panicked voice broke through Maddie's shocked relief. A man was bent forwards like he was bowing. He did his best to look back at them against the torrents of water pushing against him.

'WHERE ARE THEY?' Vince was scrabbling on the floor to pull the bolt croppers clear of the flowing water. Maddie turned back to the water pump but was snatched away by another shout.

'OVER HERE!' the bowing man bellowed back.

Vince made for the deep end. Maddie followed. She saw them almost immediately.

They looked almost peaceful: women, lying on their backs where the fast-moving water gave way to a deeper stretch that was almost still, still enough to make out faces laid out in a row under the water, their mouths covered in thick strips of vivid blue like some bizarre burial ritual. Shock had Maddie frozen above them for just a moment. Then, a step to her right, a child broke the surface to take a gasped breath through her nose and make her jump. She fixed on the children: two girls, their hair floating out from their pale faces, a little boy with stick-thin arms lying the other side of them. The water now pushed out onto the floor where she stood; the shallower part had been breached. Maddie threw herself forwards to catch the head of the little girl, who looked in danger of slipping back below the surface.

'THERE'S ONE CHAIN THAT HOLDS THEM ALL!' the bowing man yelled. 'CUT IT!' He was staring straight over at Maddie. Vince threw himself to the floor with the bolt croppers. The biting end found a chain that stretched across the pool. It was fed through loops to pin each of them down and was fastened off at the end.

'NOW, VINCE!' Maddie screamed. 'IT HAS TO BE NOW!'

The little girl was slipping back under. Then Maddie was aware of a splash to her left. She turned to face it, knowing that there was no way they could see off another attack. It was Harry Blaker. He had jumped into the pool to run through the standing water. Beyond him, more officers ran along the poolside. The pumps had been silenced.

'PULL IT!' Vince discarded the croppers and tugged the end where the children were. His biceps bulged with veins but nothing happened. 'BOSS! THE OTHER END! FROM THE OTHER END!'

Harry broke off to make for where Vince was pointing. Maddie was still holding up the girl. She tried lifting her gently by her shoulders. She didn't budge. Then the chain snaked over her, catching in the light like the scales of a fish as Harry tugged it away. Now Maddie could sit her up.

Again, air rushed out of the child's nose. Maddie ripped the blue tape from her mouth. Next to her, a uniform officer tugged one of the women above the surface. There was no sign of life. She turned to Vince who pulled the other girl out onto the floor where she retched and vomited water. He couldn't reach the smallest boy; he slipped down the slope, disappearing under the filthy water.

'MORE!' Maddie yelled. 'I NEED MORE IN HERE!'

There were splashes all around her as officers piled in to pull at the bodies, lifting them up the slope and out of the water. Another of the women coughed instantly — she was alive! They weren't all so responsive. Vince had scrabbled to get the little boy back above the surface, but he looked desperate as he assessed him for signs of life. The man who had been chained up at the edge of the deep end was now free to take the two girls. He wrapped them up in a tight hug. One of the women who had been laid under the surface crawled to them too. They all embraced. The man's wrists were encircled by angry red wounds. They all wept and Maddie knew she was watching Ian Hessey get his family back.

She looked back at Vince. He was facing away, his wide back turned towards her. She could just see the tiny feet of the little boy. His body jerked up and down where Vince had started doing compressions.

'Oh no!' Maddie whimpered. There was a shout to her left. Two more officers had a woman laid out on her back. They had started the same process. This time, they were facing Maddie and she could see their anguish. There was no direction left where someone wasn't fighting for their life.

Maddie stepped away in a daze. She lifted her eyes to the spectators' stand, her gaze drawn by movement near a set of stone steps littered with broken plastic seat tops. Two boys stood holding hands, their faces frozen in shock as they looked down on the scene below. Even from here she recognized them as the same terrified faces she'd seen peeking out from the back of the police car earlier in the day. She suddenly felt unsteady. The chaos was everywhere. Her vision was starting to close in. She stumbled. It shook a tear down her cheek. She was going to vomit again.

A strong arm wrapped around her side. 'Maddie . . . steady, okay . . . It's over. Let's get you out into the air.' Harry had her.

'Dean Harvey!' Maddie inhaled sharply the moment the name was out. Shock and the fact that she was cold and soaking wet conspired to shake her violently 'It isn't over. He was here . . . he was fighting Vince!'

Everything had been a blur for so long, but now she was finally starting to remember, her senses sharpening by the second. She noticed the pain in her mouth and tasted her own blood. Her head, shoulder and ankle were all tender and aching, and she was tired, so tired. She just wanted it all to stop.

'He can't have gone back through the building,' Harry said. 'We came that way.'

'There was a lad outside.' As Maddie turned to Harry, she followed his stare to the opaque windows they had passed on their recce round the building. Now she could see that part of them was not a window at all. It was a door that was swinging open. Sunshine leaked in to paint a vivid square on the floor. She glanced back to survey the chaos around the pool. All the officers were focused on something, those that weren't tending to the casualties were comforting the survivors. Two more were reaching up to the brothers in the stand, trying to coax them down. Someone had pulled the white-shirted man from the pool too. Maddie had left him lying face down. Now he was on his side, facing away and unmoving, the back of his shirt washed red with blood.

'Harvey's gone! He must have slipped away when we were fighting.' Maddie gasped.

'Then we have to go after him. Let's go. There's enough resources here.'

'I'm so tired!' Maddie felt like sobbing.

'I know. Me too. I'll tell you what . . . you stay here. But where would Harvey go? What can you tell me to help me find him?'

'I don't know!' She felt the tears building and her lip quivered. She wasn't going to be able to hold it back. 'We were too late. Look what happened . . .'

Her watery gaze settled on Vince and the little boy. Ian Hessey had taken over the compressions. He lifted his head to shout at the officers to get his own daughters away. A saturated woman was screaming at him — no words, just hysteria. His little girls looked on, still weeping. On the other side of the pool, two officers were still taking it in turns to pump the chest of a young woman. Maddie didn't know who she was. Just past her, the two boys had finally agreed to come down from the viewing gallery. She didn't know who they were either. She hadn't known much the whole time — certainly not enough.

'This isn't the time for that. Not now.' Harry cut through her misery. He took her by the shoulder, spinning her to face him. Barry Carter appeared next to them. Some other DCs filed in through the sunlit door.

'There was a copper outside,' Barry said. 'He said that someone came running out of that door and made off across the car park. He didn't go after him. He said he thought the bloke was with you, that he looked like a copper . . .'

'Harvey,' Harry said. 'Where's he going, Maddie?'

'I . . .'

'Think, Maddie! What do we know?'

Maddie couldn't think. Not there at the poolside. She made for the block of sunlight. She'd taken just a few paces towards it when she suddenly doubled back to make for Ian Hessey. Her presence seemed to silence the hysterical woman for just a moment.

'Ian! Where's Harvey? Where is he going now?'

Ian was still pushing down on the chest of the small boy. He was breathing hard, a breath forced out with every compression. He didn't reply, just shook his head.

'He needs to swap with someone,' Maddie barked at Vince who shrugged.

'I've offered.'

'Ian, you need a rest. You're knackered.'

'No . . .' Ian breathed. 'I promised him I would look after him . . . I told him I'd keep him safe . . . Please . . .'

'You're not helping him, not anymore. You're too tired. Swap out. You can come back when you're rested. You know it's what you need.'

'NO!' Ian snapped back.

She was aware of Harry moving past her. He grabbed Ian in a solid bear hug, lifting him off the ground to throw him into the side wall. Vince had bent in to replace him with compressions before he hit the ground. Harry leaned over Ian, his words delivered like kicks to the ribs.

'Dean Harvey has gone. You were here before any of us. Did he talk? Where is his son? Where is he going?'

'Dean . . . his son? I don't know about his son. I never saw him.'

'How did he get you here?'

'We changed cars! It was you . . . you're okay!' Ian's face cracked a smile that flickered and died all in the same moment.

'What car, Ian? What car did you change to?'

'A camper van. A VW . . . T5. Green with a white roof.'

'Maddie, we need to go.' Harry turned away and Maddie was already following.

'When you find him . . .' Ian called after them. Harry didn't stop to listen; Maddie only half turned. 'You make sure you kill him for me.'

CHAPTER 40

'Yankee One to Control!' Maddie spoke breathlessly into the radio. It wasn't hers. She didn't know where hers had gone. She had snatched one from a uniform on her way out. She had to press it to her ear as an ambulance pulled up as close as it could get to the sports centre, its siren still blaring. She was crossing the car park at a half-jog.

'*Yankee One, go ahead.*'

'Control, requesting air support and all available patrols to conduct an area search for a green-and-white Volkswagen camper van — that is, one with a green lower half and a white roof. Believed to have left the area at the bottom of Castle Hill, Dover in the last five to ten minutes.'

'*All received. Do we have a VRN?*'

'No, no. It's a T5 model, which may mean something to some officers. But all vans matching that description to be stopped and searched for a uniformed police officer and potentially a young boy.'

'*All received.*'

'Request for air support, too, please. Any chance?'

'*Negative. Air support are offline today.*'

'Of course they are,' Maddie huffed, away from her radio. 'Understood. Just everything you have left then, please.'

'*Zulu Echo Three on the last.*' Vince was calling up, the strain clear in his voice. '*DS Ives, I am going mobile now. Where do you want me?*'

She had made it to the car. It was a Major Crime pool vehicle. Harry obviously hadn't had time to get a good one. It was already ticking over, it had all been such a rush. But now Maddie realized they had no place to go. Vince wanted direction but she didn't even know where to start. Sitting next to her, Harry must have been thinking the same thing. They both looked out at the busy road ahead. It was more snarled up than before, the occupant of every car now slowing up to gawp at the pretty blue flashing lights outside the derelict sports centre.

'We have to start looking,' Maddie said. 'We have to head somewhere. Left is Jubilee Way. Takes us back towards Canterbury. Right is towards the M20 — that way he can get to anywhere in the country . . . He'll go that way, won't he? Let's get moving!'

'And if he hasn't, we lose time going in completely the wrong direction,' Harry warned.

'We can't just sit here!'

'What do we *know*? Think, Maddie. There's a clue we've missed somewhere.'

Maddie rubbed her palm down over her face.

'I'm clueless, Harry.' Her mind swirled with all that had happened. But then it settled on Adrian, on their prison visit, on what had been said. 'Adrian!' she snapped. 'He said that Janet knew what was going on, that they were in contact with her.' She snatched at her phone, careful to block her caller ID before she dialled out. She was aware that Vince was calling up again on the radio. She ignored him.

'Hello . . .'

'Janet . . . DS Maddie Ives — don't you dare hang up.'

'What's happened? What's the matter?' Janet Taylor sounded instantly panicked. Maddie's tone must have conveyed her desperation. She just hoped she could keep Janet on the phone for long enough.

'Dean Harvey . . .' Maddie forced herself to pause. She let her eyes fall shut, her breath catch in her throat. *Please let her know something.* The phone was silent, too silent. *Had she hung up?*

'Oh God!' Janet's desperation sounded just as clear as Maddie's. 'What did he do?'

'Exactly what he told you he'd do, Janet.' Maddie pushed her luck with a guess.

'His son! Oh God! I never thought he would. I just thought he was blowing off steam. He was so angry.'

'What did he say, Janet? Listen to me . . . this is very important.'

'What now? Over the phone?'

'Dean Harvey ran. We got here too late. He tried to kill them all, but he still has his son. What did he say he was going to do next?'

Janet wept. The sound seemed amplified over the phone. Maddie had to grit her teeth to refrain from snapping at her. But it was neither the time for threats nor for telling her exactly what she thought of her.

'His son . . . he lost him . . . it was all so unfair.'

Unfair! Maddie wished Janet was there with her so she could give her a tour of the swimming pool.

She managed to come back measured. 'And we think he found him, Janet. But this is important now . . . this is where every second counts. What has he done with him?'

'I don't know! I haven't spoken to him today. I haven't really since . . . since you started sniffing around, okay?'

'Where would he take his son, Janet? They can't go home.'

'Home, no, no, no! He doesn't have a home anymore. He said that.'

'What was his plan, Janet?'

'His plan . . . I didn't think he was serious, okay? I would have told you if I'd thought he was serious . . .' Janet sniffed as if she was in tears again.

Maddie felt like she was going to explode. 'Tell me now.'

'They have a game they play, Dean and his boy. They always have. It's a card game. When the mother got Dean kicked out of the house — when the court stuff was going on — Dillon used to sneak out to meet his dad so they could still play together. He got a camper van. It's their thing, his pride and joy. He only got it so he could take Dillon camping. They would sit in the back of it and play for hours when his mother thought he was asleep.'

'Okay . . . but there's more, Janet. There's something else that'll help us find them?'

'That was it! That was his plan. He talked about picking Dillon up and taking him away from his mother for a game of cards in the back of his camper and he said . . . he said they would just slip away together.' Janet's weeping was more prominent now.

'Slip away . . . What does that mean, Janet?'

'I didn't think much of it at first. But then he said how he had researched it all, how it was actually really peaceful . . . He said Dillon wouldn't even realize it was happening and then they could be together. He said he had messed up this life, that it could never be repaired and this was the only way. He called it a second chance. He made it sound so easy, just a pipe in the window . . . I didn't think he was serious!'

'Where! Did he have somewhere in mind? Where did they play?'

'Torquay. When he lived down there. Even when he was living here, he was still secretly in touch. He would still drive there, be up all night by the time he got home. Sometimes he would go straight to work. Dillon told him where to find him and then he would sneak out. I don't know where exactly. He said they went somewhere on the cliffs down there. Dillon liked to look out at the sea. Are you in Torquay now?'

'Listen to me, Janet . . . You need to get yourself into a police station, you hear me? If you make me come looking for you, I *swear* I'll make you pay. Do you understand?' Maddie's voice was now a growl. She couldn't contain her rage any longer.

'Me? What have I—'

Maddie cut the call. When she looked up, Vince was by her side, parked up in a patrol car with his window down. She dropped her own window to shout across. 'He's gone up to a beauty spot on a cliff somewhere. He'll be with his son.'

'You know that for sure?'

'I think I do.'

'There's no good reason for that, is there? Him taking his boy up there . . .' Vince said.

'No,' Maddie said.

'Well, there's Samphire Hoe or the Western Heights that way, or he could've gone up Castle Hill and towards Deal in the other direction.'

'Okay,' Harry said. 'We'll take Castle Hill.'

Vince didn't wait for any more confirmation. He pulled away, his roof bar already flickering blue. Harry didn't ask anything more either. He spun the car roughly towards the foot of Castle Hill, so-called because it passed up the side of Dover's medieval castle. It was steep. Harry had been accelerating hard but he slowed for a coach park halfway up. He peered across Maddie to scan it.

Maddie sighed. 'Nowhere like this. It's too open. He'll be somewhere tucked away . . .'

'Somewhere he's been before!' Harry exclaimed, braking hard at the same time. There was a tight turn on his right, but he was too late to take it. Someone honked their horn behind him as he pushed into reverse.

'Move, move, MOVE!' Harry leaned on his own horn now. The car behind must have reacted to get out of the way. Harry made the turn, immediately picking up the pace when they straightened up. 'The black box . . . one of the locations he'd been to was along here — near the coastguard building!'

'A recce?' Maddie said.

'It has to have been.'

Maddie clung on as Harry was back to taking bends on the limit. Her ankle complained as it rolled a little underneath her, the first time she had felt it in all the excitement.

The road was tight and twisty, even more so than their earlier pursuit. She was thankful when he was forced to slow for the first beauty spot. It came up on Harry's side. A white metal bar hung down over the entrance, stopping anything of height going in. The wheels of the pool car fought for traction as they met with the gravel of the car park. It was laid out as a square, a fenced-in tree in the middle that Harry spun around. It was a small area, enough for a dozen parking spaces facing out towards an obstructed view of the sea. They were all empty.

'Dammit!' Harry snarled.

Back out on the road they picked up the pace again. The road still bucked and twisted. The right side was woodland with glimpses of the sea beyond, the left side now fields. They came around a bend and onto the start of a longish straight. Maddie could see where the woodland ran out on the right, but there was one more beauty spot before it did. It was sign-posted but with a sign of the tiny, blink-and-you'll-miss-it variety. Harry missed it.

'Harry!' Maddie shouted, 'it's here!'

He braked hard. The turning seemed to unmerge itself from the treeline. Maddie leaned over to try and see into the thick woodland plot.

'There's something green! I think I saw a flash of something green!'

Harry crunched into reverse in his haste. The car whirred backwards to the point of screaming. He drove in slower, lingering in the entrance in case he needed to block it off. Maddie *had* seen something green. It was a camper on the left side as they entered. It had a white roof with one side lifted to form a triangle on top. A black pipe trailed from the exhaust. Harry gave the engine a dose of revs, skidding the pool car to a stop to block the camper in. Maddie blurted their location into the radio then threw it down, reaching out to grab her asp instead.

She ran at the van shouting Harvey's name. Now she was out, she could hear that the camper's engine was roaring, despite being stationary. Harry made for the back of the van, where he tugged on the pipe. It was taped in. Harry was pulling so hard the van was rocking. It didn't look like it was coming away. She grabbed the handle to the side door. It didn't budge. She peered in. Harvey himself was the first thing she saw. He sat side-on at a table directly opposite her, his head back, his eyes closed, his hands resting on the table with cards arranged neatly in front of him. Opposite him was a young boy. He looked over to her, his head wobbling like he was struggling to hold it up. Maddie tried the door again. The handle hurt her hand. She released her grip and it slapped back with a *thump*. She stepped back and swung her asp at the large window. It took two hits to put it through, the glass shattering inwards to cover the table. The boy barely reacted. She leaned in. The door unlocked from the inside. She could just reach the catch. The door slid back. It was the starting gun Dean Harvey had been waiting for.

His eyes shot open and he rolled to his right, shifting his weight onto his hands. They slapped down onto the ground. Using the floor as a springboard, he prepared to throw himself at her. Maddie was ready. She was already swinging her asp. Instinctively she closed her eyes, but then she felt the asp strike something solid. She heard a shout and she opened her eyes to see Harvey stumbling past her, his hands reaching out to cushion his fall to the ground. He bounced straight back to his feet, kicking up a clump of mud as he turned. Maddie levelled her asp to swing again. He hopped back. He had a leering smile and fresh welts on his face from his earlier meeting with Vince. He lunged at her and she swung out instinctively. Her timing was perfect — the blow caught him on the side of the head and he shied away from her. His hand lifted to where a stream of red now covered his left ear and he dropped to a sitting position. When he looked up at her, the smile was gone. Maddie stepped forwards to press home her advantage. This time his raised arm took most of the impact. He struggled to his feet and turned to stumble away. Maddie ran after him. His steps took him through a thin layer of greenery and he jumped awkwardly over a low wooden fence. Here he had to stop suddenly as he emerged onto a chalky shelf — after which point the land ran out. The sea suddenly dominated the horizon as a seething mass of sparkling blue. It was a long way beneath them. Dean Harvey straightened up and looked out over it, then turned back to where Maddie was stepping over the fence. She still had her asp raised. He backed away from her, his feet as close to the edge as they could get.

'Don't come any closer!' He spoke into a gust of wind. He was still bleeding freely from the side of his head and a new split had opened above his eye.

'Children!' Maddie spat. 'You're killing children!' It was all she could manage, to sum up the horrors she had seen.

'Don't come any closer! I'll jump! Get a negotiator up here! I want to see my boy before I jump . . .'

Maddie stepped towards him. She leaned in as close as she dared, close enough to be sure she was holding his gaze as she freed the handcuffs from their holder and threw them at his feet.

'I assume you know how they work. Put them on, just as soon as you realize you don't have the bollocks.'

'I know how this works. Get a negotiator up here! Or I'll jump.'

'Put the cuffs on or jump. Either way you don't get to see that boy again. Not ever. You have my word on that.'

'I'll jump!' Harvey looked past her now, to where Maddie could hear sticks snapping under heavy footsteps. He was talking to Harry, appealing for a different answer. Harry's growl drifted past where she stayed fixed on him.

'You heard what my colleague said. You have your options.'

Harvey's eyes flickered between the two of them. He looked like he had something more to say but he suddenly drooped, like all the fight had left him in an instant. He took a last glance over his shoulder, at the crisp blue of the ocean then dropped to his knees. His hands reached down for the cuffs. He snapped them over his right wrist first then secured the other. He looked up at Maddie who was already backing away.

'Walk over here!' Maddie demanded.

He did as he was told. Maddie stood in front of him, her asp still levelled, her mind still swirling with everything she had seen. She gritted her teeth. Her grip on the asp was tight as she fought the urge to smash it through his skull.

'Please,' Harvey whispered, 'just let me say goodbye to my boy . . . please.'

He looked pathetic now. His shoulders slumped forwards, his hands in cuffs, blood from his cut mixing with his tears. She relaxed her grip a little.

'Harry,' Maddie said, 'go and get Dillon, will you?' Harvey looked up at her, fresh hope in his eyes. 'And make sure he's well out of this man's sight. I just gave him my word.'

Harry turned away. Dean started to cry out in complaint but he was silenced by a swift asp strike to the groin. Maddie knelt down beside him where he writhed in the foetal position.

'There's still a cliff there,' she spat. 'You can still do everyone a favour.'

CHAPTER 41

Maddie got to the part of the corridor where the rubber ran out. Now the floor was just concrete for her exhibit to scrape loudly against. She didn't have the strength to pick it up off the floor. She paused at the door, avoiding Harry's gaze, knowing that he had protested that they should go and get cleaned up first — at the very least, he'd advised coffee and maybe a bandage for her ankle. But she needed to do this now.

She was clumsy opening it. The exhibit bounced and smacked off the surround and then she dragged it across the floor. She kept her head down, ignoring those already seated. Even so, she was aware that someone in a black suit had started to get up the moment she entered. She threw the exhibit down. Harry bundled in after her. The machine was all set up. Maddie pressed to start the recording before she even sat down. When she did, she fixed Janet Taylor firmly in the eye, ignoring the grunting and huffing from her solicitor, a woman in her mid-twenties in a charcoal-grey skirt and jacket, occupying the seat next to her client. Janet's mask of shock was well and truly back. She was now seeing an image of Maddie that Maddie herself had only glimpsed in the car's window, the image Harry had insisted they clean up. But

Maddie had wanted Janet to see her swollen face — her left cheek specifically. She had a split bottom lip and her teeth were coated in dried blood. There was a lot more on the side of her head, the combined effect of a cut somewhere and the bleeding from her ear. It was enough to make her hair crunchy. She also had blood up her arms and on the backs of her hands. Her right hand was worse; it had a fresh-looking wound, despite it being nearly two hours since she had put her hand through the camper-van window. She was sure to lean on her elbows, to bring her hands up to her chin so that Janet would see the worst of it. She looked filthy in general. Battered, bruised but not beaten yet.

Janet glanced away to look at Harry. He was dirty, too, and had that dishevelled look that came with wearing a full set of clothes that had dried from soaking wet.

Maddie decided she had waited long enough to speak. She certainly had the room's attention. 'I want you to explain to me, Janet, *why* I just suffered the worst afternoon of my entire career . . . my entire *life*.'

She let this hang in the air, wiping the phlegm from her lips, adding to the atmosphere of fear and uncertainty. She waited until Janet's mouth formed a reply and then cut back in just as she was about to start. 'I want you to tell me *why* I just watched a seven-year-old boy drown. Seven years old, Janet. His name was Peter. He loved the drums and football. He supported Liverpool and one day he dreamed of going to a game. But he was undernourished, small for his age. Too small and too weak to keep his head above the water. So he died.' Janet tried again to speak but Maddie hadn't finished. 'Hope Morris . . . twenty-two years old, recently finished university and just back from travelling. Her whole life ahead of her, Janet. I watched her drown too. She's dead. And I'm just getting started. But you tell me now. You tell me what just happened.'

'I . . . I don't—'

'My client has prepared a statement,' the solicitor said. 'Unfortunately I was given no disclosure and as such I am not able to effectively defend my client's interests, or comment on these . . . extreme accusations. As a result, my client would like to offer the following . . .' The solicitor cleared her throat and raised a handwritten piece of paper from the desk.

'Is this what you want?' Maddie directed her question towards Janet. She hadn't looked away from her. She wasn't going to either. The solicitor huffed at the interruption. Then she continued with her reading.

'This is the statement of Janet Elisa Taylor. Earlier today I was arrested for the second time for the offence of conspiracy to murder after I took a phone call from DS Maddie Ives and answered a question about a previous intimate partner. This was a brief relationship and I have no recent knowledge of him, or his activities. I have no knowledge of any offences and I have never conspired to murder anyone. As I am upset, confused and unaware of the full reason for my arrest at this time, I will not be answering any further questions.'

The piece of paper fell to the table. It was the first time Maddie had broken eye contact with Janet. She lashed out at the paper, catching the edge as it settled and spun it to the floor. She then stood up to retrieve the exhibit she had thrown down on entering. She deposited it on the table, making sure the clawed end rested right under Janet's nose. The inside of the plain bag was smeared red.

'This is a set of bolt croppers. Standard issue in any police car. This morning it was just a piece of kit. Now, it is the weapon I used to split open a man's skull. He died, Janet. I *killed* someone today.' Maddie was still on her feet. Her hands slapped down on the tabletop to accompany the word *killed*. She fought to control her tears. Saying it out loud added to the enormity of it all and it was threatening to overwhelm her. She moved on quickly.

'Little Peter Loxton, seven years old . . . dead. Hope Morris, twenty-two years old . . . snatched from her bed, chained to the bottom of a derelict swimming pool to be drowned in a row of strangers. She might never even have known why, Janet!'

Janet lifted heavy-looking eyes from where they had been fixed on Malcolm Grant's blood.

'I . . .'

Her solicitor was quick to speak. 'You will remember my advice, Janet. This is all very intimidating — oppressive, even — and you can request a break at any time. But my advice remains: *no comment*. You're confused and tired and you cannot answer for the actions of others.'

Maddie ignored her and continued. 'And then a man you know well drives his own son up onto the cliffs to poison him slowly to death, to poison them *both*, hiding his intention behind a game of cards — and I know you knew that part . . . So, again, what's the story here, Janet? Why all this suffering? Why all these lives ruined? And your smug solicitor here might even be able to get this whole interview scrubbed off as being oppressive or intimidating, like she said. But I don't care because I just wish I could show you their faces, Janet. Their faces under that water. The panic, the fear . . . Children, Janet! Can you *imagine*?'

Janet looked like she was trying to. Her eyes were downcast and flickered from side to side. Her mouth hung open in shock.

Maddie kept up her onslaught. 'Dean Harvey is here. He's in one of these cells and he will answer for what he did. But you *knew*, didn't you? You knew what he was doing, what he was planning, what he was *capable* of. And you did nothing. Twice you stood in front of me. Twice you said nothing. That murdered boy, seven years old, that murdered woman, twenty-two years old . . . that's on you, Janet. You might as well have been the one strapping them to the bottom of that pool while the waters rose.'

Janet gripped her nose and sat back. The assault on her was taking its toll. She rocked forwards as if to speak but changed her mind. Her eyes dropped back to the blood-stained bolt croppers.

'I didn't know. Not all of it, okay?'

'What did you know? Because I'll tell you what we have . . . we have a mess out there. Bits of a story that we know started off as one big plan that I think you were part of. We will put it all together — all of it. *I* will. And when I do, I'll be coming for you hard. Help me now. Tell me what that plan looked like before it was dropped on those people. Before it killed those people.'

'I don't even know how it got this far . . .'

'Janet, again I will remind you that we have not—'

'I can chuck her out if you like.' Maddie jabbed her thumb towards the solicitor. 'You see, another thing we've learned in all this is that there were people involved who did terrible things, but under terrible duress. They did them because they were terrified that if they didn't, then someone they loved would be hurt. But that's not the case with you, is it? You've only been protecting yourself this whole time. And a solicitor like that . . . she's here to protect your interests, too. That's her job. She doesn't care about this seven-year-old boy any more than you do. She's here to protect you and for a pay cheque at the end of the m—'

'Now hold on just a minute there, officer! Janet is protected by law and I am a p—'

'Well, maybe she SHOULDN'T BE!' Maddie still fixed on Janet. She took a breath to stop her voice breaking. She could feel herself quaking with rage. 'Maybe it's time you waived some of that right to save your own neck. Maybe it's time you looked at the bigger picture. Maybe it's time you did one thing that isn't about you, that isn't to *save* yourself. If you have one shred of decency in there, maybe it's time to show it.'

Janet turned to her solicitor, to look at her for the first time. Maddie took the opportunity to do the same. She wasn't one of the usual faces. She was younger, maybe new to the custody block. She was pretty. Her blonde hair was scraped back over her ears and tied off as if maybe she had been winding down in joggers at home before getting the call to turn back out into the early evening — her first murder case, perhaps. She had laid a card on the table at some point that had *Jasmine Ellis* imprinted in a delicate font. Ms Ellis looked more than a little intimidated, but Maddie didn't care. She knew that solicitors had a part to play in this game. She was normally respectful of it, but not today. Today she had left her respect for anyone who stood in her way at the bottom of that derelict pool.

'It's okay,' Janet said. Jasmine Ellis had given her advice; now she gestured her frustration and threw herself back in her chair. 'So what do you want from me?' It was the question Maddie had been waiting to hear.

'Dean Harvey. Tell me about him. Your statement says you were intimate partners. I assume you do mean Dean. Tell me everything you haven't up to this point.'

'Okay . . . so, yeah, he was my boyfriend. But it wasn't like a normal relationship. I know that now. He used me, too, okay? It was all a lie.'

'What was?'

'He came in one day. To the office. Maybe as long as a year ago. He was asking lots of random questions about social care and kids. He was mainly asking Marie to start with, which made sense because she was the supervisor in there. Marie was dismissive — she can come across as rude. She's never really liked the police. He gave up and went away. Then I was on my break. There's a canteen that's kinda part open to the public on the ground floor. I went in there for a coffee and he was behind me in the queue — Dean, I mean. He bought my coffee so I sat with him. I apologised for Marie and we talked a bit about what he needed to know.'

'And what was that?'

'It was all generic stuff about parental contact. I didn't think much of it at the time. It's not unusual for the police to talk to us about situations they see out and about. Social care and policing are closely linked. But then we swapped numbers . . . he was a good-looking fella but I honestly thought . . . he seemed to really care. I thought he had a good heart.

You know how rare that is in a guy these days? Now I know why . . .'

'Why what?'

'Why he cared so much. It was his own situation he was asking about. He was from another county — Devon. He'd been living there with his family and it had all gone to pot. His ex was causing him issues. He told me about it all a bit later on, when we had been seeing each other for a while. She made up a pack of lies to tell the police and from that moment he had been stopped from seeing his son. From seeing Dillon. It didn't seem fair to me. I told him that. Coming here was supposed to mean that he could see him again. He had an agreement with someone — his old bosses, I think. Anyway, he got here and it was all blocked. He was angry — and I mean *so* angry. I guess he hid it at the start but it didn't take long for me to see that side of him. I've never seen anyone like that. It was like he was obsessed.'

'So what did he plan to do about it?'

'He asked me to help.' Janet sniffed. She bit down hard on her lip, back to fighting her own emotions. She scrunched her eyes shut and when she opened them a tear leaked out. 'I did, okay? I got him some names he needed — but he told me he just wanted to speak to them! He said that if he could just get to speak to them then maybe he could make them see reason! And I believed him!'

'Who did you give him?'

'Marie he already knew about. She was the one who was talking to Devon Social Services about his case, but she wasn't the one making the decisions. I mean, it might have looked like it came from her, but she just followed the process we use. I told him that. I told him that she ran it past a CPS contact we have who then discussed it with the police at a monthly meeting. It was part of a pilot. Op Icicle. This meeting was where his access to Dillon was blocked. I told Dean who the CPS contact was . . . And the police officer we used . . . Dean really got fixed on him.'

'On who?'

'Ian Hessey. He works closely with us. I've always really liked him but Dean . . . he *hated* him and it was instant. How can you hate someone like that when you've never met them? The way he saw it, Ian was personally keeping him away from his son. He would say how Ian was no different, how he had chosen to sit on his high horse and judge others and believe his ex's lies. He was obsessed with Ian. He talked a lot about getting even.'

'What did he mean by "even"?'

'I didn't know, not at first.'

'At first?'

'He changed. His behaviour towards me. I started to think that maybe his wife wasn't lying about him at all. He would get so angry and he was so . . . controlling. Then he told me that he needed to *act*. That was what he said. He moaned a lot that no one actually ever did anything. He joined this justice group — it was made up of other dads in a similar situation, but he fell out with them straight away. I think his ideas were too extreme. He wasn't welcome. Then he met Malc.'

'Malc?'

'I guess Malcolm, but I only ever knew him as "Malc". He said he met him at this justice group but I think he found him by using the police systems. He was in a similar position. He wasn't allowed to see his kids and Dean needed allies. But he was . . . different.'

'Different?'

'Yeah . . . he didn't talk about his family like he was missing them, he just wanted them to suffer — the kids, too. It was like if someone steals your property, you know? And you don't want it back, you just want the person who stole it to suffer. He always looked like he wanted to hurt someone. I stayed away from him.'

'So what was Dean going to do? To act?'

'Adrian Hughes. You know all about him. He got talking to me at work. He was a pain in the arse. The rest of the office was making fun of me. He had some sort of obsession

373

with me from day one. Marie was the worst. I think she was just put out because there was a man who was actually paying someone else some attention. It wasn't like I wanted it. He was another one moaning about not being able to see his kid. Like I cared. I told Dean about him and he was interested straight away. He wanted me to find out as much as I could about Adrian, to befriend him. I didn't realize then, but he was exactly the sort of person Dean was looking for.'

'A fall guy?'

'I guess that's it. I took a call from Adrian. It was a cry for attention. He said he was going to kill himself. I was with Dean at the time and he sent Malc out to sort of bump into him. That was when it all changed. Dean forced me into a relationship with him . . . Adrian made me sick — just being near him — but I had to. Dean, Malc . . . At first, they said it was for their cause, but when I said that I didn't want anything to do with it they threatened me — said I would end up getting hurt. I was still going to walk away but then they showed me a video . . . It was Marie! They snatched her when she was out on her run . . .' Janet was breaking down again. Maddie let her have a few moments. 'They killed her. I saw it. They took her somewhere. A big place that looked like it was falling down around them. There was a camera set up. They walked her across the floor . . . It was from a distance but I could see everything that was happening — all of it! I even saw Malc laugh at her when she kicked out at him . . . That was when I knew I just had to do what they told me. When I knew how much danger I was in.'

'And what did they have you do?'

'I was chained up in, like, a bunker. It was part of the old pit at Aylesham. It was filthy and so scary. Dean was there too — chained up. This other guy — Jim — was helping. Dean got this Jim to knock him around a bit first, then Jim dragged us out of there at different times. Malc was there too. It was all designed to make sure the woman from the CPS did as she was told. I knew they were after her daughter. I heard them talking about that, but they couldn't get hold of her in time. They were worried that Linda would go to the police, even when they showed her Marie on a video. They said they were watching her, too. They needed to keep her quiet until they could get hold of her daughter.'

'What woman?' Maddie knew the answer, of course.

'Linda Morris. That's the name I gave Dean. It must have been her. She spoke to me in that place and said her name was Linda. I'd only ever swapped emails with her before. CPS don't really like phone calls or meetings. They always want everything in writing . . .' Janet suddenly stopped like she had been stung. 'Linda *Morris* . . . You said someone died who was called *Morris*! Is that . . .'

'Her daughter. They killed her.'

'Oh Jesus! That poor woman!' Janet's hand slapped over her mouth.

'What did they need Linda to do?'

'Dean needed information about Ian Hessey. They had an address for him but found out that he had just moved. I heard them talking about that — Dean was so angry! I don't know what else they wanted. I was just in there to be dragged out, to make it look good and then I had to tell her that she needed to do whatever they asked or I would pay for it. I just did what I was told.'

'What else were you *told* to do? Where did they get the addresses from? For the families?'

Janet's head lolled from side to side. She was fighting back tears. 'I did get those. Marie . . . they said Marie refused. That was part of why they showed me what happened to her — so I would know what would happen to me!'

'Why did he want those addresses?'

'You know why!'

'I want you to say it. I want you to say what you knew.'

'He did have a plan — Dean, I mean. He talked about it, but never in detail. I knew he was building up to something big. I knew people were going to get hurt, alright? I did know that. With Dean, Malc and Jim . . . it was never going to end any other way.'

'Tell me about Jim. You've mentioned him a couple of times now.'

'I never knew someone like Malc existed. He was so awful. But he was nothing on Jim. Jim was pure evil! Dean didn't like either of them. They both just wanted to find their families so they could punish them. Dean saw himself as different.'

'But he wasn't?'

'I didn't think so. Not once I'd seen what he was capable of. I'd never say it, though. He'd talk about Jim and Malc, about how they both wanted to murder their wives — and, for Jim, his kid too. He was just using them. He needed them. Most of the time they were falling out . . . You gave me over to him. That was when he told me about Jim . . .'

'What do you mean?'

'When you arrested me before. We spoke just like this, then you said you were getting me a lift home and handed me over to Dean. He was delighted. He was showing off, showing me how he could always get access. He asked for every detail of what we talked about. I just said I told you nothing.'

'And what did he tell you about Jim?'

'His bruising . . . it had all come out. I commented on it and Dean changed. He was furious at Jim. Jim had been supposed to give him a dig when he was chained up, make it look realistic. But they'd been arguing. Jim wanted to just go to the addresses and kill the families outright. But Dean had a different idea. I thought it was resolved, but then Jim used one of them knuckle things to hit him with. Damned near knocked him unconscious. Dean and Malc had a theory that that was exactly what he was trying to do. Maybe he was even thinking of leaving Dean in there and going about it all his own way. Dean was planning on getting Jim back when this was all over.'

'But now you mention it, why didn't they just turn up at the addresses? Why get all the families together?'

Janet started shaking her head. The motion shook more tears free. 'You don't get it. He wanted them to suffer. But he also wanted to make a statement. This whole thing was about giving the system a black eye. He wanted a big enquiry. He wanted to start a conversation about access to kids from the father's point of view. He wanted repercussions for women who lied. But he also wanted reputations dragged through the mud. He found out that Ian Hessey had been given some commendation for Icicle. And Linda too. There was a copy of his commendation in the room where they all worked at the police station, along with a picture of them at some glitzy awards night. He got to see it every day, and I've never seen a man so furious. He wanted to see it all to come crashing down.'

'And then he planned to kill his son?'

'His wife, his son . . . and himself. I thought that was his plan, yes.' Janet was almost whispering now.

'And you did nothing?'

'I wanted to. Both times we spoke, I knew I should be saying something but . . . I knew what they were capable of . . .'

'Marie Foreshaw. Your friend.'

'She wasn't my friend. I know I said she was, but I was lying. Truth is she was a bully. I hated her!' Janet checked herself, realizing how loud she'd become. 'I didn't want to see her hurt, though. That's not what I'm saying. She didn't deserve that. She used to take the mickey out of me a lot. She wasn't a nice person. She was smart and beautiful. One of those cool people that everyone wanted to be around. But she knew it, too. She used to mock people like me.'

'So you weren't sad when she was killed?'

'I was terrified. They didn't show me that video for me to be sad — that wasn't the message. They were making sure I knew what would happen to me. But I *am* sad. I didn't want her to die — of course I didn't. And certainly not like that. But once Dean knew who she was, the part she had played . . . she was always going to be on the kill list. So was Linda. So was Ian. In his mind, they all needed to die.'

'And Adrian?'

'What do you mean?'

'He was a risk. He could have talked at any time and ruined the whole thing.'

'He didn't know much.'

'He knew he didn't kill Marie.'

'He wouldn't have said anything. He was never going to talk.'

'Because of you.'

'Yes, because of me. I'm not proud of that, okay? I know what I did to him . . . I know the part I played in all this. He's a sweet guy, really. It's not his fault that he is what he is . . .'

'He's dead, Janet. He was killed in prison.'

Janet's eyes flared wide. She flopped back in her chair for her mouth to loll open. 'Oh God!'

'Did Dean ever mention William Watson?'

She buried her head in her hands. 'There was a *Bill*. They talked about him. He was in prison. He was supposed to make sure Adrian stayed in line in exchange for Dean murdering his ex. Dean didn't have any intention of doing that. He said it wouldn't matter, said that Bill would never find him. They used Bill too, just to keep an eye on Adrian. I said that wasn't necessary — he wouldn't talk to anyone.'

'He did. He talked to me. I think he had an inkling that this was about something bigger than just him. But he spoke to me because he thought he needed to protect you. He sacrificed everything for you. His freedom and then his life.'

'Oh God!' Janet buried her head. 'It's all such a mess.'

Harry spoke to her for the first time. 'You talked about Dean, when he took you home. He said he was planning on getting *Jim* back when this was all over. Did he expand on this?'

'He said Jim wouldn't be a problem anymore — said he was out of control and just wanted to hurt his son. Dean couldn't understand that.'

'What did you take that to mean — Jim not being a problem anymore?'

'He was going to kill him. I had no doubt. I know what Dean's capable of. He didn't say that, but he didn't have to.'

'We found a James Loxton beaten to death in a squash court, another part of the same building where his seven-year-old son was drowned. The boy's mother survived. Seems *Jim* got his wish regarding his son.'

This time Janet lifted both her hands to cover her face completely. A sob escaped from behind them.

Maddie turned to Harry and sighed, her heaviest sigh of the day. Janet's sobbing quickly became louder as she fell to pieces on the other side of the table. Maddie felt like doing the same.

It was over. She had her answers. She stood up. She picked up the bloody bolt croppers. They had made their impact.

When she opened the door there were two cups of black coffee on the floor outside. The custody sergeant had taken one look at them on the way in and announced that she knew just what they needed. It was close enough. Maddie downed hers in one. Harry managed a tired smile as she balked at the fact that it was lukewarm and bitter.

'Let's go get a proper one, shall we?' he said.

The door fell shut behind them. It took the sound of Janet's weeping with it.

CHAPTER 42

'Up there? What the hell did you say we were doing up here again?' Maddie looked up. It was a short flight of stairs, slimmer than those in the rest of the building, and it finished at an emergency exit. Harry stood in the doorway, jamming it open. She looked over her shoulder to where Vince and Rhiannon were following close behind.

'I didn't, DS Ives. I thought perhaps you should have at least one surprise left in your life.'

Maddie didn't want a surprise. Right now all she wanted was to go home, shut her door and pour a glass of wine large enough that she might be able to forget, or at least large enough to help her get some sleep. But Harry had been insistent. She had been packing up to go home when he had rung and said it would be the most important thing they would do that day. Then he had given directions that had led her through largely unused parts of Canterbury Police Station.

Now they stepped out onto the flat roof of the custody block. Maddie didn't have the first clue why. She had been about to turn back when she had seen Harry's face appear at the top of the steps to encourage them up.

'Well, this is a surprise, alright. I can't say I've ever been out here before.'

Maddie lifted her tired eyes to where the sun was setting over the City of Canterbury. She could see the road at the front of the station and down into the vehicle yard at the end of the long roof. It was close to half past eight in the evening so the traffic was calmer and the air was still warm. She could feel extra warmth coming up from the black rubber roofing material, which had spent the day absorbing some of the sun's energy. The roof itself was a mash-up of flat solar panels grouped in the middle and pigeon droppings everywhere else. Harry walked along its length, towards the vehicle yard. He stopped around halfway to wait for the others to catch up. He had his hands thrust in his trouser pockets. He was still wearing the same filthy white shirt, the sleeves rolled up above his elbows.

'When I was first in Major Crime — and yes, a long time ago, before you and your smart mouth jump in, Vince' — Vince feigned a hurt look — 'I was based in Chatham and we had something of a tradition. Major Crime is all about shit days. Let's face it, by the time an investigation gets to us, someone has already had a shit day. That's the whole point of this team — the whole point of us. But, just sometimes, in amongst all the shit, there are little victories. But that's not what we remember.' Harry turned to walk a little further along the roof.

Maddie exchanged glances with Vince and Rhiannon, then followed on. When Harry stopped, he was standing in the middle of a rectangle that looked to be freshly drawn in white chalk. Maddie could see the offending piece of chalk near Harry's feet.

'This is an outline of Dean Harvey's cell. It's spot on for size and I've paced it out right — so he's directly below us. Right now. And we put him there — all of us here. People died today. We all saw things we don't ever want to see again. But I want you to know that the souls of those dead are in this tight little box, right now. They are downstairs tormenting Dean Harvey. Because all he has now are these four walls, a door slammed shut, and his memories of what happened today. Nothing torments a man like the souls of the dead. Not when you've nothing else to do but sit and listen to them.' Harry paused to take in his audience. There was no response but a light breeze and the sound of a car door shutting in the yard below. 'So tonight,' he continued, 'we leave the dead and their memory in this little box with Dean Harvey. He deserves them. For tonight only, we forget them, we forget what happened to them, we find the nearest bar and we drink to our victory. We drink and we drink together.'

'Drink?' Maddie called out. 'You mean, like alcohol? Who is this drinking, swearing detective inspector I see before me and what did you do with Harry Blaker?'

Harry smiled. 'As you get older, you take for granted that you'll get wiser. Bad days when I was a young lad . . . I shook them off. I went out with the team — the people who had seen the same things I had seen, who were feeling the same as I was — and we all met it head on. Together. Getting older, I've been doing that less and less. Now when I have a bad day, I go home and the souls of the dead come with me. And I don't deserve them — *he* does.' He thrust a pointed finger at the floor. For a moment Maddie thought he might break. 'None of us does . . .' he growled. 'Now . . .' Harry raised his head again. 'This traditional drink-up has to start somewhere and it always used to start here. On the custody roof. Chatham had a flat roof too, see. And you should know, before you judge, that it was a very different time. It was the brainchild of the inspector I was working for at the time. He's a DCI now. Anyway, at this point we would all take it in turns to hit a golf ball from the very centre of the cell of our captured criminal . . .' Harry looked down then screwed his toe into the black rubber to make a mark. 'So, about here. The idea is to hit it outwards, out there over the yard. Then the rule was simple . . . if you were able to go down and find your ball within sixty seconds of reaching the ground floor then you didn't have to buy a drink all night!' Harry looked back from the yard to take in each of their faces in turn. 'Of course, at Chatham we were hitting towards a shopping centre so there were plenty of idiot officers sprinting across a busy road to find their drink ticket. Like I said ... a different time.'

'Not the sort of thing you would be able to get away with these days, boss,' Vince observed, laughing. 'The fun police closed that sort of thing down a long time ago.'

'And what happened if everyone found their ball within the time?' Rhiannon was laughing too. 'Did you all have to go home thirsty?'

'Nope.' This was a new voice. Maddie and the rest turned to where DCI Julian Lowe had stepped out onto the roof. He was holding a golf club in one hand and a small bucket in the other. 'If that happened, the DCI stupid enough to come up with the idea had to buy the drinks all night!' He pushed past to drop a white golf ball onto the thick rubber. He nudged it with his foot so it sat over Harry's mark. Rhiannon was closest to him. He offered her the club. 'Someone always has to be first.'

Rhiannon took it. She met eyes with Maddie then with Harry and finally settled on the DCI. 'Sir . . . is this a wind-up? A test maybe?'

'Hit the ball, Rhiannon. Out across the yard, and for goodness sake not into the road!'

'But I might hit a police car!'

'If you do, try and keep your eye on where the ball goes afterwards. That's the trick, see. Then someone else buys your beer.' The DCI stood back. Harry was yard side and moved out of the way, too. Rhiannon still looked unsure but lined up anyway. Vince clapped his hands.

Rhiannon was good. Maddie could see this wasn't the first time she had swung a club. It hit with a satisfying *ting* and the ball arced off the roof. She was able to follow its bright white path, even in the failing light. Right until it smashed through the window of a marked police van that was parked side-on. Rhiannon's hand shot to her mouth.

'The Tactical Team van!' Maddie squealed her delight. 'Rhiannon, did you do that on purpose?'

'No! I swear! I'm so sorry!' She dropped the club. Now both her hands were covering her mouth. The DCI reached down for it. Next he handed it to Vince. He could barely hold it out for laughing. Suddenly Rhiannon had permission to laugh, too. Suddenly they all did.

'That's a good swing you have there, Rhiannon. And now you know exactly where your ball is! So that's the idea, see. Go on, Vince. Take note.'

Harry stepped over. He led Maddie a few steps away as if he wanted to talk. They both kept a humoured watch on a posturing Vince.

'You need to keep this sort of thing up when it's your department.'

'Mine? They would have to scrape some barrels, Harry.'

'The ball's in motion. The DCI will support you. You'll be temporary inspector from your next working day. There's a board in six months or so. You just need to keep doing what you're doing and you'll fly through that and come back as substantive. You are Major Crime, Maddie. It needs you.'

Maddie ducked away from Vince's second attempt to hit the ball. 'Inspector? But we already have one of those.'

'I've got under two years left. And I can't do it here. My decision-making . . . my ability to step away and think rationally . . . my driving! I could have killed us today. You were right.'

'Look, I know this was raw for you. But you'll—'

'I can't, Maddie. I've had a whole career of horrible. Enough is enough. That drowned child today will be the last thing I will ever see and have to accept as part of my job. The training-school gig is still open to me. I can see it out there.'

'And after that?'

'My garden. Maybe a nice climbing rose.'

'But I can't do this, not without you . . . I froze today. In that building, when we needed to get moving.'

'And I didn't. What does that make me? And when you stop freezing surrounded by something like that, maybe it will be time for you to step away, too. Just make sure you do what I did . . . get good people around you. You led this whole job, Maddie.' Harry pointed back at his chalk outline. 'He's in there because of you. The people that did survive . . . that was because of you, too. Promise me you'll focus on that.'

'You can't just walk off into the sunset, Harry.'

'Funny you should say.' Harry gestured behind her. She turned to where the last rays of a dying sun reached out over the City of Canterbury. Then she was drawn to the ironic cheer as Vince finally hit his golf ball.

'Fair point!' she said, turning back to where there was now just an empty doorway.

'Harry!' she called out.

'Fooled you!' He had stepped away in the opposite direction. Now he was back by her side. 'How corny would that have been! And besides, we have a lot of drinking to do.'

THE END

AUTHOR'S NOTE

I am inspired by what I do and see in my day job as a front-line police detective, though my books are entirely fictional. I am aware that the police officers in my novels are not always shown positively. They are human and they make mistakes. This is sometimes the case in real life too, but the vast majority of officers are honest and do a good job in trying circumstances. From what I see on a daily basis, the men and women who wear the uniform are among the very finest, and I am proud to be part of one of the best police forces in the world.

Charlie Gallagher

FREE KINDLE BOOKS

Please join our mailing list for free Kindle books and new releases, including crime thrillers, mysteries, romance and more, as well as news on the next book by Joy Ellis! www.joffebooks.com

DO YOU LOVE FREE AND BARGAIN BOOKS?

Thank you for reading this book. If you enjoyed it please leave feedback on Amazon, and if there is anything we missed or you have a question about then please get in touch. The author and publishing team appreciate your feedback and time reading this book.

Follow us on Facebook, Twitter and Instagram @joffebooks

We hate typos too but sometimes they slip through. Please send any errors you find to corrections@joffebooks. com. We'll get them fixed ASAP. We're very grateful to eagle-eyed readers who take the time to contact us.

FROM CHARLIE GALLAGHER

Sign up at www.writercharliegallagher.com to be the first to find out about future releases and special offers.

And if you get a chance, please spend a few moments to leave your review on Amazon.

I'd also love to hear from you on social media:
Twitter — @Gloriouscharlie
Facebook — www.facebook.com/writercharliegallagher

Thanks so much for reading,
Charlie.

Made in United States
North Haven, CT
22 May 2023

36843950R00236